Hiding in Plain Sight

Hiding in Plain Sight

Essays in Criticism and Autobiography

EDITED AND WITH AN INTRODUCTION
BY WENDY LESSER

MERCURY HOUSE
San Francisco

Published in the United States by
Mercury House
San Francisco, California

United States Constitution, First Amendment: Congress shall make no law respecting an establishment of religion, or prohibiting the free exercise thereof; or abridging the freedom of speech, or of the press; or the right of the people peaceably to assemble, and to petition the Government, for a redress of grievances.

Text designed and typeset by Star Type
Printed on acid-free paper
Manufactured in the United States of America

Library of Congress Cataloging-in-Publication Data

Hiding in plain sight : essays in criticism and autobiography /
edited and with an introduction by Wendy Lesser.
    p. cm.
  ISBN 1–56279–037–4
   1. Art criticism—History—20th century. 2. Arts,
Modern—20th century. I. Lesser, Wendy.
NX640.H54   1993
700'.1—dc20
                                        92–42345
                                          CIP

5   4   3   2   1

Contents

WENDY LESSER / *Hiding in Plain Sight*   VII

MUSING

◆

STEPHEN GREENBLATT / *Storytelling*   3

LOUISE GLÜCK / *The Idea of Courage*   7

DIANE JOHNSON / *The Importance of Plot*   11

ROBERT PINSKY / *Poetry and Pleasure*   23

READING

◆

THOM GUNN / *Christopher Isherwood: Getting Things Right*   39

ROBERT HASS / *Wallace Stevens*   57

ELIZABETH HARDWICK / *Gertrude Stein*   66

HAROLD BRODKEY / *Jane Austen vs. Henry James*   76

CHRISTOPHER HITCHENS / *In Defense of Daniel Deronda*   93

AUGUST KLEINZAHLER / *Elevated Shtick: S. J. Perelman*   107

ARTHUR LUBOW / *Unbridled Restraint: J. R. Ackerley*   114

PHILLIP LOPATE /
The Dead Father: A Remembrance of Donald Barthelme   121

LOOKING AND LISTENING

•

CHRISTOPHER RICKS / *Bob Dylan*   145

DANIEL WOLFF / *As News Spreads: Danny Lyon's Photographs*   159

W. S. DI PIERO / *On Modern Art & Artists*   164

HARRIET SHAPIRO / *The Artist's Model*   176

MINDY ALOFF / *Rilke Dancing*   180

SUSAN SONTAG / *A Note on Bunraku*   188

STEVE VINEBERG /
Home and the World: Reflections on Satyajit Ray   191

LEONARD MICHAELS / *The Zipper*   201

GREIL MARCUS /
The Last American Dream: The Manchurian Candidate   208

REMEMBERING

•

GAYLE PEMBERTON / *Do He Have Your Number, Mr. Jeffrey?*   221

IRENE OPPENHEIM / *On Waitressing*   230

LARS EIGHNER / *On Dumpster Diving*   237

GORE VIDAL / *Glorious Reflections upon the
Five of Hearts and Other Wild Cards in the National Deck*   247

THOMAS LAQUEUR / *Clio among the Old Folks*   265

AMY TAN / *Mother Tongue*   274

SIGRID NUNEZ / *Chang*   280

JOHN BERGER / *Her Secrets*   295

NATALIE KUSZ / *Vital Signs*   300

ABOUT THE CONTRIBUTORS   321

PERMISSIONS   326

ACKNOWLEDGMENTS   329

Hiding in Plain Sight

PEOPLE SOMETIMES ASK ME HOW I get the essays that are published in *The Threepenny Review*. Do I commission them? Do they come unbidden in the mail? What, exactly, is the mechanism?

I always have a hard time answering. "Neither," I say, unhelpfully, when faced with the solicited-versus-unsolicited choice. A magazine which, for most of its history, has had payment rates in the high two figures can hardly *commission* work from the likes of Elizabeth Hardwick, Susan Sontag, and Gore Vidal. On the other hand, it would be misleading to suggest that one can pluck gems like John Berger's "Her Secrets" or Thom Gunn's "Christopher Isherwood" or Irene Oppenheim's "On Waitressing" out of the flood of mailed-in manuscripts that drift through the office each week.

The essays in *The Threepenny Review* come to me through a series of delicate and unpredictable negotiations. I hear that Susan Sontag has written the program notes to a Bunraku performance: might I print the piece in *Threepenny?* I attend a conference at which Amy Tan delivers "Mother Tongue" as a talk, and persuade her to let me have it as an article. (Sometimes I cheat in this respect, organizing a lecture series precisely so that I can afterwards print the talks.) I know that Thom Gunn has a longstanding interest in Isherwood's work, so I drop hints and make suggestions and wait (years, in this case) for the flowering of an essay whose seeds had been planted decades before I even started the magazine.

Once I find the writers, my hope is that they will come back on their own, bringing me new work of theirs to publish. Do they write a new essay specifically for the magazine? Generally not. Is there any other place equally suitable for its publication? Often, no. In this respect I have benefited greatly from the tragic decline of American journalism. Only other periodicals as small as *The Threepenny Review* (and with equally small payment rates) are willing to publish the kind of idiosyncratic, timeless, personal essays in which I take so much delight. The big-circulation glossies, the magazines which could afford to buy away *Threepenny*'s best pieces, foolishly don't want them; they only want something topical and to the point. But an essayist rarely does her best work when she is writing on assignment, topically and pointedly. She usually does her best work for herself.

The writers who are writing for themselves become my regulars. Some of them—Irene Oppenheim, Thom Gunn—have published in the magazine since its first issue. Others, like John Berger or Leonard Michaels or Steve Vineberg or Daniel Wolff, have long since carved out a niche for themselves, regularly or irregularly addressing a particular set of topics in a particular voice. Together, these writers define *The Threepenny Review;* if they disappeared from the magazine's pages, it would cease to be itself.

And with the regulars come their friends, their students, their colleagues. Leonard Michaels found Natalie Kusz and Sigrid Nunez; Thom Gunn drew in August Kleinzahler; Robert Hass introduced me to Louise Glück and Mindy Aloff; Arthur Lubow brought in Harriet Shapiro. Often I get credit for "discovering" new people, and though I'm happy to reap the benefit, the credit should go to the writers. They are each other's best discoverers.

Which is not to say that I've never discovered anybody. Sometimes wonderful work *does* come out of the "slush pile," that dishearteningly huge and always increasing stack of unsolicited manuscripts. I distinctly remember, for instance, the moment when I opened the large, taped, proverbially dog-eared envelope that contained a hundred pages of Lars Eighner's writing. It had been sent to me by someone I didn't know—a friend of Eighner's named Steven Saylor—who said in his cover letter: "I think you will find the enclosed to be an extraordinary document." I am in the habit of ignoring cover letters like that; they usually come from megalomaniacs speaking about their own work. But this time it was accurate. I read the first few sentences of Eighner's manuscript: "This is not a tract on the horrors of homelessness. An account of the life of the homeless would be a valuable document, but I have not attempted to write it for a number of good reasons. My experience with homelessness seems to me atypical…" Then I picked up the phone and called Saylor at his San Francisco number (I had to call Saylor because Eighner, being homeless, had no phone) and said, "Don't send this to anyone else. I've only read the beginning, but I know I'll want part of it." It was one of those moments editors live for, one of those leaps of certainty.

What drew me to Lars Eighner's work was not just the subject matter, though that was fascinating; it was the voice. There on the page, hiding in plain sight, was a real essayist, someone who could simultaneously reveal and conceal himself, who could use language as a transparent but nonetheless effective cloak. I knew nothing about this author (I still, after publishing him for several years, have never met him), but I knew he belonged in *The Three-penny Review*.

It's hard to define what makes a *Threepenny* writer. The magazine has always published poetry and fiction as well as essays, and the categories are not meant to be radically distinct. But over the years I've noticed the gradual emergence of a particular sort of writing that I think of as "a *Threepenny* essay"—a piece of nonfiction prose that, while talking about something in the world at large, discusses and reveals the author's own personality as well. It does so with the rhythmic precision of a poem, with the delicate evasiveness of a story. And it does so whether the essay is autobiographical or critical, whether it's explicitly about the author or explicitly about a work of art. For the best essays, in or out of *The Threepenny Review*, are those which exist on the borderline between criticism and autobiography.

• • •

Randall Jarrell, in "The Age of Criticism," had a good explanation for why this borderline might be such fertile ground. "Criticism demands of the critic a terrible nakedness: a real critic has no one but himself to depend on," Jarrell said. "He can never forget that all he has to go by, finally, is his own response, the self that makes and is made up of such responses—and yet he must regard that self as no more than the instrument through which the work of art is seen, so that the work of art will seem everything to him and his own self nothing."

The threat of nakedness and exposure has long been inherent in the essay. One of the originators of the form, Montaigne, wrote in his introductory note to his readers, "Here, drawn from life, you will read of my defects and my native form so far as respect for social convention allows: for had I found myself among those peoples who are said still to live under the sweet liberty of Nature's primal laws, I can assure you that I would most willingly have portrayed myself whole, and wholly naked." He tells us that he is, for pro-priety's sake alone, keeping his verbal clothes on. And yet in the very next sentence he announces, "And therefore, Reader, I myself am the subject of my book: it is not reasonable that you should employ your leisure on a topic so frivolous and so vain. Therefore, Farewell..." This at the *beginning* of the book. Montaigne is indeed clothed—in artifice of the most purposefully self-revealing sort. He dons the Emperor's famous suit, not in self-deluded con-viction, not in ignorance of its actual transparency (as the original wearer did), but with full awareness that the outfit itself is pure convention, pure illusion. He assures us that he will not mortify us with his nakedness, and meanwhile he lets us see everything.

No, not everything: only what he chooses to let us see. The crucial art of the essay lies in its perpetrator's masterful control over his own self-exposure. We may at times be embarrassed *by* him, but we should never feel embarrassed *for* him. He must be the ringmaster of his self-display. He may choose to bare more than he can bear (that is where the terror comes in), but *he* must do the choosing, and we must feel that he is doing it.

There is a moment in every love affair when the participants risk everything by revealing themselves to each other—a moment of decisive self-revelation, when one person, yielding up her weakest point, exposes her jugular (as wolves do, in surrender), and the other meets the challenge by accepting the offered knowledge and perhaps giving up something in return. All great autobiographical essays contain such moments, moments at which we are made the recipients of information so threatening to the author's integrity, so revealing of her own sense of her weaknesses, that we could destroy her if we misused it. She depends on our love (or, if that is insufficient, then on our distance) to protect her.

Jarrell's point is that this happens in criticism as well as autobiography, when it is written by "a real critic." It is salutary to be reminded, in these days when professional literary criticism has so come to doubt the existence of the self that the academy has renamed it "the subject" and then proceeded to deny its existence—it is salutary, under such circumstances, to be reminded that real criticism can only be written by real selves. Good criticism, much like good autobiography, depends on the struggle between the exposure and the evasion of that determining self. To convey herself clearly, the autobiographer must plunge deep into her personality and also rise above it. To tell us about a work of art, a critic must do something similar: he must minutely examine his own responses, and then he must get out of the way so that we can see the thing itself. But he cannot do this sequentially, or alternately, as my grammar implies. The trick lies in doing both at once, in revealing himself to us as the rendering medium and simultaneously making that medium transparent.

This is what I assume George Orwell meant in his much-abused statement, "Good prose is like a window pane." Most people have taken this remark to refer to the necessary disappearance of the author; and some have argued that Orwell, in conveying through his essays so much of his personality, did not follow his own instructions. But this remark comes near the end of an essay in which Orwell also says about the writer that "before he ever begins to write he will have acquired an emotional attitude from which he will never completely escape. It is his job, no doubt, to discipline his temperament and avoid getting stuck at some immature stage, or in some perverse mood: but if he escapes from his early influences altogether, he will have killed his impulse to write." Windowpanes are transparent in both directions. One can look out through them, at the world, and one can also look back inside, at the artist viewing the world. The perfect essay allows one to do both.

In this, essays are not entirely different from all other kinds of writing. Their

"I" may more explicitly point to itself than that of a poem. Their sentences may present themselves as more actively conversational than those of a novel. But the essay shares with both these forms (and others) a combination of honesty and artifice, of truth revealed and truth selectively concealed. With all the books we read and love, we seem to get something of the author's personality and to hope for more than we get; the essay simply raises those hopes to expectations.

In his essay on Shakespeare, Henry James gets at the nature of our curiosity about the author—that person behind the art, that private individual who produces the great works. This was a concern that colored much of James's own fiction, from *The Aspern Papers* (which set the claims of biographical research against those of privacy) to "The Private Life" (in which the author figure was actually composed of two separate selves, one who went out in society and the other, his shadowy twin, who sat in a darkened room and wrote). In his fiction James always questioned that sort of curiosity about the person, made it seem unworthy of, or inappropriate to, the transcendent value of the art. But in his Shakespeare essay he admits to sharing the curiosity—admits, moreover, that it may be central to our interest in the art.

"The secret that baffles us being the secret of the Man," he says at the end of the essay, "we know, as I have granted, that we shall never touch the Man *directly* in the Artist. We stake our hopes thus on indirectness, which may contain possibilities.... The figured tapestry, the long arras that hides him, is always there, with its immensity of surface and its proportionate underside. May it not then be but a question, for the fulness of time, of the finer weapon, the sharper point, the stronger arm, the more extended lunge?" It is James, throughout the essay, who has played the sharp critic, the murderous Hamlet trying to unravel the playwright's mysteries. But now he turns the weapon against himself. For the person hiding behind the arras is not only Shakespeare, in the form of his creature Polonius, but also James himself, whose story "The Figure in the Carpet" looms forth in that unnecessarily "figured tapestry." The master of indirection is showing us here precisely how pointed and powerful an instrument it can be.

If the person hiding under James's immense piece of cloth is the shivering, trembling, naked author, he is also the critic, whose weapons for piercing and revealing become agents of his own exposure. Polonius is the ultimate critic: the list-maker, the categorizer, the judge of literary quality. "The best actors in the world," he says of the players-within-the-play, "either for tragedy, comedy, history, pastoral, pastoral-comical, historical-pastoral, tragical-historical, tragical-comical-historical-pastoral..." To be a critic is to be both a figure of fun and a tragic meddler. To be a critic is to throw oneself bodily into the argument. Like the autobiographer, the critic gives away more than he can afford. When you hide behind the arras to peek at a work of art—to moderate the encounter between that work and its other viewers—you are tremendously vulnerable. You become a wretched, rash, intruding fool.

♦ ♦ ♦

Farewell.

The editor too is a kind of essayist, hiding behind the Emperor's Clothing of her writers, appearing only to introduce them and then depart, offering nothing of herself directly, leaving only "indirectness, which may contain possibilities."

When I began *The Threepenny Review* in 1980, it was with the intention of finding and publishing writers that I loved—loved even as much as the good, old, dead writers like Jarrell and Montaigne and Orwell and Henry James. You will judge better than I whether the writers I offer you here have achieved anything near that standard, and time will judge better than either of us. But I do love these writers.

I have wanted to do a collection of these essays for a long time, but future prospects kept tempting me to postpone. "Oh, if I just wait three more months I can include *this* beautiful piece as well," or "Let's hold off for that one particular essay I've been promised." So I delayed. But the fiftieth issue of the magazine seemed an arbitrary and therefore useful stopping point. Fifty quarterly issues meant over twelve years of continuous publication, over three hundred essays ushered into the world. It was hard to choose among them. In the end, I chose not just by intrinsic merit, but also by how nicely the essays would work together, how well they would show the blurring of categories practiced in *The Threepenny Review*. I wanted you to see how, in the capable hands of the *Threepenny* essayists, literature blends into performance, performance into visual art, visual art into politics, politics into memoir, historical-pastoral, tragical-historical, tragical-comical-historical-pastoral...

I retreat behind the arras, and leave you to the writers.

WENDY LESSER
August 1992

Musing

Storytelling

by Stephen Greenblatt

MY EARLIEST RECOLLECTIONS OF "having an identity" or "being a self" are bound up with storytelling—narrating my own life or having it narrated for me by my mother. I suppose that I usually used the personal pronoun "I" in telling my own stories and that my mother used my name, but the heart of the initial experience of selfhood lay in the stories, not in the unequivocal, unmediated possession of an identity. Indeed the stories need not have been directly about me for me to experience them as an expression of my identity: my mother was generously fond of telling me long stories I found irresistible about someone named Terrible Stanley, a child whom I superficially resembled but who made a series of disastrous life decisions—running into traffic, playing with matches, climbing out onto the window ledge, or trying to squeeze through the bars on the cast-iron railing that enclosed the back porch where my mother would hang the washing. We lived in Roxbury then—in those days one of Boston's main Jewish neighborhoods—and Terrible Stanley's worst, and most delicious, misadventures involved the nearby Franklin Park Zoo.

I am presumably one of the few Americans who woke regularly as a child to the sound of lions roaring in the distance. I can still remember pacing back and forth on the porch and imagining that I was a caged lion. My mother has a picture of me holding on to the bars and with my mouth open wide. I suppose I was roaring. Contrary to *his* mother's explicit warnings and his own solemn promises, Terrible Stanley would sneak away from Maple Court (where we also happened to live), walk down Wayne Street past the Garrison Public School (where my brother was caned in the early 1950s for refusing to recite the catechism), cross Blue Hill Avenue, and go to the zoo. On innumerable occasions, he narrowly escaped being eaten by the lions or crushed in the terrible embrace of the pythons. The zoo was hard to resist.

As I grew slightly older, the sense of identity as intertwined with narratives of the self and its doubles was confirmed by my father, who also had a penchant for storytelling—stories not so gratifyingly focused on my small being as my mother's were, but compelling and wonderfully well-told stories of himself and of a cousin, a few years younger than he, by whom he was virtually obsessed. My father and his cousin came from almost identical backgrounds: first-generation Americans born in Boston to poor Jewish immigrants from Lithuania. Like my father, the cousin had become a lawyer, and here began the story. My father was named Harry J. Greenblatt; his cousin, Joseph H. Greenblatt. But when the latter became a lawyer, he moved into the same building in which my father had his office, and he began to call himself J. Harry Greenblatt. He managed, or so my father thought, to siphon off some clients from my father's already established practice. By itself this would have been enough to cause considerable tension, but over the years J. Harry compounded the offense by apparently becoming considerably richer than my father, Harry J.—wealth, as far as I can tell, being measured principally by the amount of money donated annually to local charities, the contributions printed annually in a small but well-perused booklet. There were, as I grew up, endless stories about J. Harry—chance encounters in the street, confusions of identity that always seemed to work to my father's disadvantage, tearful reconciliations that would quickly give way to renewed rancor, great potlatches of charitable contributions. This went on for decades and would, I suppose, have become intolerably boring had my father not possessed considerable comic gifts, along with a vast repertory of other stories.

But a few years before my father's death at eighty-six, the rivalry and doubling took a strange twist: J. Harry Greenblatt was indicted on charges of embezzlement; the charges were prominently reported in the newspapers; and the newspapers mistakenly printed the name of the culprit—convicted and sentenced to prison—as Harry J. Greenblatt. Busybodies phoned our house to offer their commiserations to my mother. The confusion was awkward, but it had at least one benefit: it enabled my father to tell a whole new set of stories about himself and his double. When you are in your eighties, new stories can be a precious commodity.

My father's narrative impulse, I can see from this distance, was a strategic way of turning disappointment, anger, rivalry, and a sense of menace into comic pleasure, a way of reestablishing the self on the site of its threatened loss. But there was an underside to this strategy that I have hinted at by calling his stories obsessive. For the stories in some sense *were* the loss of identity which they were meant to ward off—there was something compulsive about them, as if someone were standing outside of my father and insisting that he endlessly recite his tales. Near the end of his life, he would sometimes abandon the pretense of having a conversation, interrupt what was being said, and simply begin to tell one of his stories.

This sense of compulsiveness in the telling of stories is not simply a function of garrulous old age; it is, I think, a quality that attaches to narrative itself, a quality thematized in *The Arabian Nights* and *The Ancient Mariner*. In response to the compulsiveness, there have arisen numerous social and aesthetic regulations—not only the rules that govern civil conversation, but the rules that govern the production and reception of narrative in books, on screen, on the stage. And there have arisen, too, less evident but powerful psychic regulations that govern how much narrative you are meant to experience, as it were, within your identity.

One of the worst times I have ever been through in my life was a period—I cannot recall if it was a matter of days or weeks—when I could not rid my mind of the impulse to narrate my being. I was a student at Cambridge, trying to decide whether to return to America and go to law school or graduate school in English. "He's sitting at his desk, trying to decide what to do with his life," a voice—my voice, I suppose, but also not my voice—spoke within my head. "Now he's putting his head on his hand; now he is furrowing his brow; and now he is getting up to open the window." And on and on, with a slight tone of derision through it all. I was split off from myself, J. Harry to my Harry J. (or Terrible Stanley to my Stephen), in an unhappy reprise of my early sense of self as story. It was unhappy, I suppose, because by my early twenties my identity had been fashioned as a single being exactly corresponding to the personal pronoun "I," and the unpleasantly ironic "he" sounding inside my head felt like an internal violation of my internal space, an invasion of my privacy, an objectification of what I least wished to objectify. I experienced the compulsive and detached narrativizing voice as something that had seized me, that I could not throw off, for even my attempts to do so were immediately turned into narrative. It occurred to me that I might be going mad. When the voice left me, it did so suddenly, inexplicably, with the sound of something snapping.

If the experience I have just described intensified my interest in narrative, it made me quite literally wish to get the narratives outside myself. Hence the critical distance that I attempt to inscribe in and with the stories I tell, for the narrative impulse in my writing is yoked to the service of literary and cultural criticism; it pulls out and away from myself. Hence too, perhaps, my fascination with figures of estrangement: I could not endure the compulsive estrangement of my life, as if it belonged to someone else, but I could perhaps understand the uncanny otherness of my own voice, make it comprehensible, and bring it under rational control by trying to understand the way in which all voices come to be woven out of strands of alien experience. I am committed to making strange what has become familiar, to demonstrating that what seems an untroubling and untroubled part of ourselves (for example, Shakespeare) is actually part of something else, something different.

•••

We spent last spring in Boston, and I wanted to take my wife to the apartment house in Roxbury. My mother and everyone else in my family told us that we shouldn't go back to the old neighborhood. I had lived in California too long, they said, and didn't know what it was like. There are murders every night, said my cousin Sherman; whites aren't welcome, said my cousin Ann; there is nothing to see, said my cousin Eldon; the animals in the zoo have been killed off one by one, with BB guns and poison, said my brother, and the park is a nightmare, even in broad daylight. Of course, we went anyway. That is, after all, the lesson of the Terrible Stanley stories.

There were lots of animals in the zoo—I don't know if the cages had been restocked or if the story of the killings was merely a grim joke that had eventually, in the tense and racist atmosphere of Boston, been received as truth. The park, designed by Olmstead, looked beautiful, easily the loveliest green space in the entire city. But my family was right that the neighborhood looked awful: the streets empty, shops boarded up, trash piled on the sidewalks, windows broken everywhere, graffiti spray-painted on walls. No landlord or bank had put any money into the buildings for years, probably for decades. We found the great old synagogue, Mishkan Tefilah, whose vast neoclassical bulk still dominates the area: it was torched, I don't know when, and stands in massive, burned-out desolation. About half the windows of the apartment house on Maple Court were boarded up, but there were people living there, and I could see washing hanging from the porch where I used to practice my roaring. On the driveway below the porch, a young woman was waxing her car. She heard me say to my wife that that was the apartment we used to live in, and she beckoned to us. "Stand here for a few minutes and let people see that you're talking to me." She spoke in the tone of quiet urgency with which my mother used to enjoin me not to go to the zoo, not to wander off from the haven of the apartment. "Then get out quickly," she added. "It's not safe for you to be here."

The Idea of Courage

by Louise Glück

OCCASIONALLY, DISCREETLY, A NEW ENCOMIUM introduces itself into the critical vocabulary. Not a new theory, which makes, necessarily, a more splendid debut, being, like all comprehensive visions, explicitly corrective, fueled by the ancient human impulse to reform. The process I mean to discuss is more covert: if not covert, unconscious, and the particular term under scrutiny one much more likely to be used (in my experience) by the poets themselves than by critics.

Poets have something to gain by giving currency to the idea of courage. In a solipsistic culture, no criterion of objectivity checks the need driving such analysis: when the world mirrors the self, recognition is experienced as a claim. Repeated use, moreover, lends to any terminology certain totemic properties: around a single word, brotherhoods and sisterhoods are created, the word itself coming to stand for all jointly held ambition and affirmed belief.

That courage animates a body of work seems, as an idea, immensely attractive. It dignifies the materials, infusing them with qualities of urgency and danger. In the ensuing confrontation, the poet becomes Perseus slaying the Medusa. Equally appealing is unconscious, helpless courage: Cassandra who cannot help but see. This alternative carries the additional benefit of suggesting that truth and vision are costly, their purchase secured by sacrifice or loss. The glamour of these, and related, images stimulates the aspiring visionary, who need simply reproduce the outward sign to invoke the spiritual condition: in this instance, need simply arrange to have paid.

Obviously, my focus here is narrow: courage takes on a more pointed meaning in more oppressive societies, societies in which it is literally not safe to speak. As is often noted, art benefits in such regimes (though artists do not) in that it acquires immense prestige, a prestige American poets may quite reasonably envy. But reasonable envy does not excuse muddled thought, nor

7

can assertion of another, more amorphous species of courage convincingly argue the issue of peril.

In its local use, the term "courage" responds to poetic materials felt to be personal: in so doing, it concentrates attention on the poet's relation to his materials and to his audience, rather than on the political result of speech. Its obligation as analysis is to suggest analogues for exile and death: to name what is at risk.

Courage, in this usage, alludes to a capacity for facing down the dark forces. (Lust for generalization ignores the fact that not all people fear the same things.) From time to time, some permutation of the term acknowledges a range of essentially combative tones, tones one hears, say, in Lawrence (who uses them brilliantly): picking fights with the reader seems weirdly daring (and, by inference, courageous) in its apparent disdain for poetry's single reward, namely, approval. In an extension of this reasoning, courage is also accorded the writer who makes some radical change of style and so courts disfavor. Present use of the term cannot be restricted to that poetry which arises out of genuine acts of physical or moral courage, perhaps because examples of such courage are so rare, perhaps because most examples seem corrupted by any first-person account, perhaps because the occasions themselves seem suspect, tainted by an air of contrivance. Ultimately, however, the point is that this sort of definition will not extend the uses of the term, and it is exactly this extension most poets desire. The need for incentive runs deep: the free society, the society that neither restricts speech nor values it, enervates by presenting too few obstacles.

Desire notwithstanding, these assertions misunderstand the act of writing and, as well, the nature of courage.

No matter what the materials, the act of composition remains, for the poet, an act, or condition, of ecstatic detachment. The poem's declared subject has no impact on this state; however assessment is subsequently revised, the poet engaged in the act of writing feels giddy exhilaration; no occasion in the life calls less for courage than does this.

What seems at issue is the discrepancy between the impression of exposure and the fact of distance. The poet, writing, is simultaneously soaked in his materials and unconstrained by them: personal circumstance may prompt art, but the actual making of art is a revenge on circumstance. For a brief period, the natural arrangement is reversed: the artist no longer acted upon but acting; the last word, for the moment, seized back from fate or chance. Control of the past: as though the dead martyrs were to stand up in the arena and say, "Suppose, on the other hand..." No process I can name so completely defeats the authority of event.

Such defeat naturally imbues the poem with an aura of triumph. And it may be that this encourages misreading: the exhilaration of victory—over confusion, blankness, inertia, as well as over the past—resembles in appearance the victory of courage over dark matter, or the victory of passionate spirit over the impediments of civilization.

In this misreading, the material, or civilization, stands for the adversary, whose identity, whether human, animal, or inanimate, physical courage must always specify. Courage implies jeopardy, and jeopardy to the body depicts itself in correspondingly concrete terms. Whereas spiritual jeopardy, being invisible, lends itself to more speculative discourse, conception of the adversary growing very easily abstract.

But questions persist. If courage informs a poem of personal revelation, what, or who, is the adversary? What is at risk?

And the ready answer is: the possibility of shame. But it seems to me that no presumed confession, no subtle or explicit exposure, no ferocity of tone, no brazen (or compelled) shift in style can, through the mediation of the reader, transform the poem into an occasion which truly risks shame.

The empowering distance of the poet from his materials repeats itself in another equally useful distance: that of the poem from its reader. That the poem, that art, makes a bridge between one being and another—this commonplace perception—says as much: no bridge is necessary in the absence of distance. Inherently, the dynamic of shame depends on response: but response, for the poet, to the poem, occurs later, in an elsewhere distant in time from the time of composition; for the duration of active composition, the poet remains insulated from the future as from the past. Insulated, consequently, from any real exposure, from any present source of censure or mockery. True, the act of writing posits a listener, that one-who-will-understand. But an idealized listener differs from any actual listener in that the actual listener cannot be controlled: only the latter is a legitimate threat.

At such remove, the artist seems enviably shameless (or courageous). This perception is not so much false as skewed: indeed, the artist is shameless, protected from all humiliation, all real source of shame—as shameless, as easy in the performance of nakedness, as a naked dancer, whom the stage similarly protects. This is not to say that the motive of speech is exhibitionism. But the fact remains: for the artist, no *contact* occurs. And there is no confession, no possibility of shame, in the absence of contact.

A case can be made that publication reinstates vulnerability, collapsing the distance between both poet and materials and poet and reader. This overlooks the artist's most stubborn dilemma, itself a corollary of distance: specifically, the impossibility of connecting the self one is in the present with the self that wrote. The gap is both absolute and immediate: toward a finished work, only the most tormented sense of relationship remains, not a sense of authorship at all. The work stands as a reprimand or reproach, a marker permanently fixing an unbearable distance, the distance between the remote artist self, miraculously fluent, accidentally, fleetingly perceptive, and the clumsy, lost self in the world. Critical assault of a finished work is painful in that it affirms present self-contempt. What it cannot do, either for good or ill, is wholly fuse, for the poet, the work and the self; the vulnerability of the poet to critical reception remains complicated by that fact. And the sting the poet may suffer differs from the risks of more immediate exposure: the ostensibly exposed self, the author, is, by the time of publication, out of range, out of existence, in fact.

As to the argument that courage informs certain radical shifts in style: the need to write is, after all, the wish to be caught up in an idea; for the writer, thinking and writing (like thinking and feeling) are synonyms. Style changes when one has got to the end, willingly or not, of a train of thought. The choice, then, is between another train of thought and the spiritual equivalent of lipsync. In any case, to deal in the written word is to deal, at the conscious level, in the future. The reader lives there, and the artist of unusually powerful or unusually fragile ego will favor the long future over the immediate, in part because an accumulated audience offers greater possibility of response, in part as protection or insurance against the potential coldness of present readers (the hunger for revenge against circumstance translating easily to this set of conditions). Toward his critics, the artist harbors a defensive ace: knowledge that the future will erase the present. Not all writers possess in equal measure these preoccupations: that they are available at all, psychically, to diminish the force of critical judgment, separates the judgment of published work from the more annihilating judgments which can occur in actual contact.

Our claim on this particular fortifying virtue cannot be made regarding the act of writing. For poets, speech and fluency seem less an act of courage than a state of grace. The intervals of silence, however, require a stoicism very like courage; of these, no reader is aware.

The Importance of Plot

by Diane Johnson

THOSE OF US WHO ARE SERIOUS readers or writers are apt to share a certain guilty feeling about reading an engrossing novel, if indeed we can find one. There are certainly people who feel no such guilt. One sees them on trains and planes, raptly absorbed in something by Sidney Sheldon or Stephen King, oblivious to the social and intellectual condescension they have invited by this shameless reading. It's irrelevant whether we would strike up a conversation with someone reading Sidney Sheldon—the question is, would they want to break off their clearly great enjoyment of a good read to talk to us. No. We, tensely clutching our Nadine Gordimer, our collected letters of Flaubert, leaf fitfully through our books, eyes restively darting up, hoping the movie will come on, looking for the drinks cart.

Writers are told not to consider the reader. Think of art or money. Yet surely every writer asks herself, himself, what the secret is of engrossing the reader. I know as a writer I ask myself that. However much we may construe the purpose of writing as being to express, or to comment, or to create a formal whole, it is inevitably also to be read and, somehow, liked. Oh dear yes, as Forster said: the novel tells a story, but Forster was almost the last person to say so, and one hears his tone of apologetic regret, while educated readers regularly complain that novels aren't as wonderful, or something—they hardly know what—as they used to be. Someone told me, of my recent novel *Persian Nights*, that he had admired it, adding "and it's also good!" I was complimented, of course, but also sympathetic, for as a reader I'm happy to find something good, or, as I suppose as he meant, readable. It tells a story. It's true that the more we read, the more sophisticated we are as readers, the more we are unable to enjoy certain clumsy or obvious airplane novels. It takes more to please us—more intelligence from the writer, basically—but that doesn't stop us from wanting to be pleased. Walter Benjamin has pointed out that "the greater

11

the decrease in the social significance of an art form, the sharper the distinction between criticism and enjoyment by the public." As a novelist, you know what he means, and you'd like to find a way of being enjoyed, and with enjoyment there might be some hope of restoring the novel to its influence.

I think the novel's loss of influence has to do with the loss of plot. How is it that the idea of story, and particularly of plot, has become so discredited that a respectable novelist denies having one? Here's an excerpt from a recent interview with Wright Morris:

> INTERVIEWER (OLGA CARLISLE): To this day your fiction is considered experimental. Critics have never had an easy time fitting you into any particular group or movement. How do you see yourself? Do you consider yourself a story teller?
>
> MORRIS: I can tell a story and often do, but it has never occurred to me to "plot" one. If I'd taken writing courses, as is done today, someone would surely have instructed me in plotting, but I doubt that the advice would have been taken. In practice I had discovered that a narrative could be sustained without plotting, and I have held to that practice.
>
> INTERVIEWER: Since you don't plot, what is it that carries you forward in the narrative?

And Morris goes on to explain how he arrived at the story—we might say plot—of Bundy and his dog. It is the word "plot" which he has learned to abhor. "There is a narrative line, but no plot," he insists. "I accept what happens—what occurs to me—and imagine an appropriate resolution."

Is there some way that the serious writer can acknowledge and go back to plot; and the serious reader can find, again, enjoyable books in the sense that the books of childhood were enjoyable, in the days when one found oneself wrapped up, heart nearly stopped, in the excitement and suspense of a wonderful story? To try to answer this, I found myself turning to—reading engrossedly—some readable popular nineteenth-century novels, hoping to get at the mystery of plot, to ask what it is, and why it has fallen into disrepute, and whether or not it might be a more essential component of fiction than we have been thinking. I'm going to suggest—but am by no means able to prove—that plotting is *the* essential artistic activity in fiction, and an important, innate ingredient—a dynamic property generated, as it were, in the spaces between the words, invisible but powerful, and something that happens to the reader. Without plot, fiction is collapsing into smaller and smaller units—it's starving to death. Each generation of little story gets smaller and smaller, like plants grown in poor soil, or fleas left in the carpet.

E. M. Forster, in his influential *Aspects of the Novel*—still one of the few books about writing that is written from what one might term the writer's point of view—made a well-known and I think misleading distinction between plot and story: story is sequential and plot emphasizes causation. In the process,

Forster perpetuates attitudes which are implicit in the two words "plot" and "story." A story is an innocent tale, such as those we began to hear at our mother's knee (and only incidentally a little lie), and goes "and then, and then, and then," while plot smacks of the illicit, over-complicated, unnaturally contrived. To tell the story of what happened implies historical truth, while to tell the plot is to separate out the elements of gratuitous ingenuity from the character interest, beautiful language, or whatever else. I wish to contend that the activity of plotting, the ingenuity of the writer, is as essential an artistic activity as the selection of the *mot juste* or the supplying of, say, motivation to the character, and may be more important. In this connection, I am going to talk about, among others, Wilkie Collins, the nineteenth-century detective story writer, and his use of plot in the disapproved sense of a story with whatever elements of gratuitous ingenuity the writer can devise. Collins, talking of his own work, made another distinction that may be helpful in trying to get at, first of all, what plot is. Most novels, he said, were studies of the effect of events on character. His sort of novel—he didn't call it a novel of plot, but others did, or called them "sensational novels"—was interested in the effect of character on events. Upon examination, this probably flippant inversion does serve to describe something more about the novel of plot. Collins is alluding to a debate that raged among the Victorians themselves, and among the French dramatists, and indeed has raged since Aristotle, between the sensationalists, so called, and the antisensationalists. Aristotle, of course, was a sensationalist. He believed foremost in plot—"action," as he called it.

The classical novel of character, antisensational—we'll think of *Emma*—describes the effect of events, of misunderstandings and embarrassments, on the character of an immature, rather bossy young woman. To be sure, she has herself caused some of the events: the relation of character and event is inevitably circular. But the direction of the action is toward Emma's change in character. She learns to be better. The novels of Collins (he is right) and the novels of Trollope, Charles Reade, Sheridan LeFanu, some of Dickens, and of other nineteenth-century novelists we classify as readable, plotted, and probably, except for Dickens, minor, have the opposite propensity. A character, evil or stubborn or honorable or fiercely independent, because of this trait, sets in motion a series of events. Think of the rigid Jeanie Dean's religious scruples, in *The Heart of Midlothian*, which do not permit her to stretch the truth to save her condemned sister's life. Or, to take less familiar examples, I'll be talking about Wilkie Collins's novels *The Dead Secret*, a bad novel, and *No Name*, quite a good one. (*The Moonstone* would be a familiar example; but I wish to begin with the bad novel of plot, these bad relations that have given the good novel of plot a bad name.) The novel of plot seems more apt than the novel of character (if I may persist with this old-fashioned distinction) to go awry, and the point is that while good characters cannot rescue a book that has a ridiculous plot, the reverse is not true: a good plot can carry a book where the characters are pale or conventional.

In *The Dead Secret,* Sarah, a maidservant with prematurely white hair, is entrusted with a secret at the deathbed of her mistress, who compels her to promise, under the threat of being haunted forever, to deliver a letter to her husband, after her death, which will reveal a dreadful secret. The maidservant, for reasons we do not know (but soon can, alas, imagine all too easily), is unwilling to disclose the secret, and she finds a reason, in the wording of the promise to her dead mistress, to hide the document rather than deliver it by hand. She hides it in some floorboards of the house, hides the key, and vanishes. Collins would have us believe that events are set in motion by the defects in Sarah's intelligence and understanding:

> The oath which had been proposed by Mrs. Treverton under no more serious influence than the last caprice of her disordered faculties, had been accepted by Sarah Leeson as the most sacred and inviolable engagement to which she could bind herself. The threat of enforcing obedience to her last commands from beyond the grave, which the mistress had uttered in mocking experiment on the superstitious fears of the maid, now hung darkly over the weak mind of Sarah, as a judgment which might descend on her, visibly and inexorably, at any moment of her future life.

Riddled with superstitious fears and later by other scruples—"under no circumstances could she have expected to remain in her situation, now that the connection between herself and her mistress had been severed by death... could she accept protection and kindness at the hand of the master whom she had been accessory to deceiving still?"—Sarah disappears. Time passes. Rosamund, the little daughter of Captain and Mrs. Treverton, is now eighteen and has just married her childhood sweetheart, Leonard Frankland, despite his having been recently blinded. His family has bought the house where Rosamund grew up, and where the secret letter is still hidden. A mysterious nurse appears, her head always covered with a veil or scarf. She tries to warn the young couple away from the house, naturally strengthening their resolve to go back....

Collins's contemporaries complained that the mystery is not mysterious: "The book has sufficient interest to make you read it, but not sufficient to make you regret the revelation of the secret when it comes at last." "He makes his secret as if it were a pancake, and keeps tossing it about from one pan to the other, and hiding it, and seeking it, and missing it, and getting nearer to it, and farther from it again, till at last the poor thing is scrabbled over with incident and description, as if it had been raked with a small-toothed comb, and still we do not know what it is, and when we do know, we feel inclined to say 'Oh, is that all?'"

The Dead Secret is an unsuccessful novel because the plot, to the modern reader at least, is absurd. You have guessed that Rosamund turns out to be the daughter not of the dead Mrs. Treverton, but of the servant Sarah, the babies having been exchanged at birth. Rosamund is thus not the heiress her husband took her for—though this makes no difference, as it proves, and the secret, when revealed to a reader obtuse enough not to have guessed it from the clumsy clues throughout, is anticlimactic.

The plot has let us down. Other plots may let us down in several ways; plots can be boring—insufficient conflict—or implausible: coincidence, unexpected good fortune, acts of God, unbelievable motivations. Plots can for one reason or another be too distressing to continue with. If, as I imagine, Victorians were more like us than it would appear from their literature—one sometimes glimpses reality through the cracks of their melodramas—it is a question how their toleration grew for reading about events, situations, and denouements which had so little to do with reality, which were simply expressive of moral destiny, like the convention by which the unwed mother or fallen woman must die in the course of the fiction, situations as stylized as the Noh drama or the Chinese opera. Perhaps this is only a matter of literary fashion, but it may be that the actual circumstances of Victorian life were bound by the melodrama which issues from the conflict of law or custom with impulse. Hans Sachs, the analyst and critic, has told us "the basic subject matter of fiction is the struggle between impulse and inhibition."

♦♦♦

Certainly the circumstances of Wilkie Collins's own life were such as to make him believe in melodrama. We have the rough outlines of the story: when he was walking one night with his brother and the painter Millais, they were accosted by a frightened young woman in white who pleaded with them for protection. She was fleeing from a man who had been holding her prisoner. Collins took this lady under his protection, as the phrase went, and lived with her, and her daughter, a number of years. When, finally, at her ultimatum, he refused to marry her, she married the plumber. But she returned, mysteriously, to Collins when her venture into married life did not work out; he in the meantime had taken up with a second lady who bore him three children....These irregularities were secret, of course, to everyone but Collins's most intimate friends, Dickens and a few others.

We complain about the looseness of ties, the anomie of modern life. In the nineteenth century, you really had an uncle who might leave you out of his will. Your cousin was at hand to hate you. What you did or didn't do had effects, like the effects of a pebble in a pond; the literary character had the hard instrumentality, therefore, of a thrown pebble. People were sustained by their plots—while modern life is plotless, and has rendered us suspicious of the will, the secret, the shadowed birth.

Above all, the conflicting social classes of Victorian England ordained plots now unavailable to us. All conflict engenders plot, but consider how many of the most elaborate Victorian novels concern mysteries of social class or origins—everywhere in Collins and Dickens—the mystery of Estella's birth, or of Rosamund's in *The Dead Secret:* will the husband, Lenny, still love Rosamund when it is known that she is not the child of the Trevertons but of the servant? And above all, now that she does not inherit?

There was a law in England that the subsequent marriage of the parents of illegitimate children did not make them legitimate, a law Collins, of course, had reason to condemn on behalf of his three children. His novel *No Name,* then, is the story of Magdalen Vanstone, a beautiful young woman who, angry at finding that her illegitimacy deprives her of her father's estate, determines to cheat the heir out of it by marrying him under an assumed name. The heir, a selfish, foolish invalid, is protected by a sinister housekeeper, and the point of the story, as one reviewer described it, is "the contest between these two deceitful, wicked, obstinate women."

We can imagine, from this, that the rise of the plot in Victorian times has something to do with the fall of God. Without a divine sense of direction, each person must act on her own, and this may make a girl like Magdalen watchful, secretive, in competition with others. The secret is, above all, the salient feature of the Victorian plot—and, I would hold, of all plots, a matter I'll return to.

On the other hand we can see how the fall of the plot since then is connected to the rise of Freud. It is easy to find the origins of plot in the Gothic novel of the late eighteenth century. The mainstream eighteenth-century novel was with some exceptions a realistic, picaresque, burlesque affair—a novel of quest. But our Victorian novelists also read, in their youths, *The Castle of Otranto,* or *The Mysteries of Udolpho,* finding in them the rusty keys, the lost will, the prisoner in the attic; and taking these creaking but symbolic articles out of the castle into the daily lives of people living at Barchester or Richmond Park was their great achievement. *Wuthering Heights,* published in 1849, is a beautiful example of a Siamese twin of a novel concerned to fuse the Gothic with the everyday world. In the novels of Anthony Trollope, it is not a desperate monk but a friendly cleric who secretly hides the fatal letter. The idea of a secret, so essential to Freud's view of character, gives some clue to why the plot gave way in respectability to character. That is, after Freud the emphasis shifts from what the person does to protect his secret to why he has got the secret in the first place: did he get it from his unhappy childhood, or the sordid conditions of his society? Forster manifests the post-Freudian preference, perfectly orthodox for a novelist of his day: "We believe that happiness and misery exist in the secret life, which each of us leads privately and to which (in his characters) the novelist [and, he might have added, the analyst] has access." It is not to be revealed by action at all, not so much as by a speech or a sigh. It is tempting to say that it is with this pronouncement, when the secret was denied expression in action, that things begin to go wrong with the modern novel.

Did not many of us feel that our Victorian grandparents had something hidden in the attic? At any rate, the secret accompanied by action was a feature in Victorian life. People didn't confess, they concealed. We might think of Matthew Arnold burning biographical evidence—probably in particular the evidence of his French affair—or Dickens's trips "oystering and roystering" to Paris. The secret was as tangible a possession for the Victorian as a locket containing the strand of hair. And the secret is a metaphor for the mysteries of life—the particular inner thing each of us holds away from others, as Forster saw, but also the secret which destiny refuses to reveal, the secret of our fate. So productive of anxiety in real life, fictional secrets can be unwound, revealed; life can unroll before the characters like a safe road. And this, I think, is the satisfaction of the plot which consists of a mysterious secret: it can be solved.

So to tell a great story requires an understanding of secrets as well as an unusual degree of candor. To return to *No Name,* the Victorians were consternated by the character—in the old-fashioned sense—by the bad character of Magdalen. They were disgusted, particularly, in a day when heroines should be passive, at her instinct for self-preservation. "A career of vulgar and aimless trickery and wickedness, for which it is impossible to have a shadow of sympathy, but from all the pollutions of which he intends us to believe she emerges, at the cheap cost of a fever, as pure, as high-minded, and as spotless as the most dazzling white of heroines," writes Mrs. Oliphant. "Hard and coarse elements which deprive her of our sympathy," writes *The Atheneum.* It's a measure of Collins's boldness and his modernity that he rewards his bad heroine with a change of heart and a rich, good husband at the end of the tale, even if he did have to resort to the feeble device of having her fall into a fever, from which she recovers reformed.

◆ ◆ ◆

The novels of Collins brought up a critical discussion on the whole subject of the plotted novel versus the novel of character, and, as I've said, "character" was universally preferred as somehow more moral, reflecting the romantic interest in individuality—a shift in Freud's direction even before Freud. In general, the disparagement of plot was so widespread that it alerts us to the fact that Collins was on to something close to the heart of literature, to the way novels work. Character is safe, but plot is dynamite. The influential *Westminster Review* deplores the fact that "Mr. Wilkie Collins's productions

sell by thousands of copies, *Romola* with difficulty reaches a second edition."
(Which would you rather read, *Romola* or *The Moonstone?*) The *London
Review* goes so far as to say that plot causes crime: "the tendency of the multi-
plication of these tales is to create a class of such criminals [as Collins's char-
acters] if they do not already exist. Writers...scatter impressions calculated
to shake that mutual confidence by which societies, and above all families are
held together, to abate our love of simple, unpretentious virtue." Only one
reviewer, in the *Saturday Review*, feels that

> all that criticism has to say against this reduction of fiction to a rule and a con-
> test of low artifices is too obvious and has been said too often...it is more
> important to notice the merits of this sort of book. Criticism says that Mr.
> Wilkie Collins invents a puzzling plot and does nothing more. This is true; but
> then it is so very difficult to invent a puzzling plot. Anyone who has ever tried
> to sketch a story will remember that there were many things that came at once
> ...the descriptions of scenery, the moral reflections, the colour of the heroine's
> eyes...all these welled up spontaneously in the breast of the fertile dreamer.
> But between him and an embodied dream there was the great barrier of an
> unimagined plot. Who was the heroine to be, and why was she to be unhappy;
> and who was to bring in the philosophy; and how on earth was it to come in
> naturally? A good plot—a plot that interests, excites, and properly balances
> bewilderment and explanation—is a very considerable effort of the mind and
> one which demands great practice, patience and inventiveness...but if art
> means something which requires labour and foresight, and a subordination of
> parts to the whole, then we can understand how it is that Mr. Collins...boldly
> claims to be an artist.

And anyone who has ever tried to write a novel (I read somewhere that ninety
percent of college-educated women try it sometime or other) can attest that
it is very hard and slow.

The reviewer who said that plot was an attack on simplicity has simple-
mindedly struck at the heart of one objection to plot: plot as a very metaphor
for complication produces anxiety, moral fear; the reader takes pleasure
when complications are resolved in the plot the way they rarely are in life. By
the experience of fear or suspense and reassurance, we can be reassured that
life's situations, however complicated, can also work out—and this is why
we read fiction. A third Victorian reviewer senses this unconscious operation
the way Freud might have described it later: "the tale is very powerful; the
poison is distilled so subtly that the evil is wrought almost before suspicion
is awakened; the art with which the whole is managed is so complete, that
the mind unconsciously drifts on into an acquiescence in a state of things
which, were it free from the glamour which the author throws over the mental vision, it would at once condemn."

This concern for the moral poison of plot came up in the case of *No Name*.

Reviewers attacked the ending because it didn't conform to poetic justice. The bad girl should have been punished, but was allowed to reform and marry: "after all her endless deceptions and horrible marriage it seems quite right to the author that she should be restored to society, have a good husband and a happy home," Mrs. Oliphant objects.

The novelist of plot, then, by the third quarter of the nineteenth century, was facing suspicion and critical disapproval. The novel was reverting to a mode which we saw in the eighteenth century, the novel of quest. It seems to me that plots, when looked at closely, resolve themselves into not forty-nine basic ones, or even seven, but two: there are the quest and the secret, or puzzle, or mystery—different words are used. Tom Jones's was a quest for his birthright. Ernest's quest in the next century—in a novel, *The Way of All Flesh,* whose modernity has struck us all—is for maturity, but now the concern is his inner life. He has to "adjust." We do not experience quest novels as being highly plotted; they are stories, in Forster's sense. The novel of elaborate plot combines the quest and the secret. *Emma,* as we've noticed, is partly a quest, Emma's for maturity, but there are also secrets galore—Harriet's paternity, Jane Fairfax's piano, and so on. In fact, the novels of the seemingly so natural Jane Austen are models of plotty complication.

As the "serious" novelist began to eschew secrets, other forms sprang up which specifically require them, above all, the detective story. Here a character, the detective, quests for an answer to a secret. The detective story is also, in Wilkie Collins's sense, a novel of the effect of a character upon events—the resolute character of the detective and the defective character of the criminal. These are the opposite of novels of character in that the personages of the narrative are by definition capable of doing anything, so that we cannot be sure which of them has committed the crime. It's only the detective—resolute, judgmental, equivocal, or compromised—who generates the denouement. It's no surprise that Collins in his masterpiece, *The Moonstone,* should in effect invent this form.

◆ ◆ ◆

Any novelist is conscious of having in her workbasket two sorts of disparate materials, let us say yarn and paint. The yarn will knit up into the plot, the paint is for painting the portraits. But what form can you arrive at with yarn and paint but a strange sort of messy construction like the gods-eyes the Greeks wind up out of yarn and paint, or like kachina dolls? One of the qualities we respond to in any work of art is a sense of making, of craft, of pain and ingenuity on the part of the artist; we like to see the wrapping and tying, and this is as true in fiction as in woodcarving. Style is one kind of painstaking, up to a point compelling the same admiration, but better lavished on a short form, a poem or story. The novelist must lavish pains on structure and plot, which contain within them a dynamic of conflict and solution which we find eternally pleasing. We will look briefly at other reasons why this might be so.

Simon O. Lesser, in his notable *Fiction and the Unconscious,* published in the fifties, has suggested that "fiction provides us with images of our emotional problems expressed in an idiom of characters and events." We have always found this easy to see in the case of characters; events are less easy to discuss because, simply, they are more powerful. It is they that make us anxious or reassured or cautioned. It wouldn't matter what the inner lives of Emma Bovary or Anna Karenina were if they had not taken poison or thrown themselves under trains. Lesser goes on to add that fiction "provides a forum in which the positions of the id, the ego, and the superego all receive a hearing—compromise formations whereby repressed and repressing forces obtain expression in the same work. For this reason the latent and manifest content are often contradictory." A work which seems to say you must respect your elders, say, can also argue powerfully for the ascendancy of self. Plot is the place where the narrative expresses these ambivalent messages: a woman yearns for love and freedom, and rebels against the strictures of marriage. These things are covertly permitted by the vitality of the art at the same time that the cautionary endings would seem to warn against them.

If you've ever taken a book off that small shelf of books about how to write fiction, you will have noticed that few discuss plotting, though many discuss the plots of novels after the fact. The activity is mysterious. The effort, the considerable effort of the mind, is akin to a very hard acrostic, or algebra, as anyone knows who has tried it. A novel must have an action, and it must be rendered in some order. A body of complex information must be presented; the reader must know some things before he can know others. Most of us have learned from childhood the principles of rudimentary narration—the "and then, and then" of Forster's "story." But this seldom suffices to render a universe freighted with thematic and moral significance, psychological nuance, suspense, sadness, comedy, whichever of these things the writer is striving for (one always hopes to get them all). These chaotic and often contradictory impulses must be gathered and ordered, we must resort to a plan, and that's a plot. So the greatest novels are really deeply plotted. The writer turns to her chart, her list, her calendar. The serial writer, like Dickens or Trollope or Collins, had also to fit the work into the format of the monthly installment. Sometimes writers look at the plots of other works. Someone once pointed out to me that *Gatsby* has the plot of *Wuthering Heights.*

It has always seemed curious to me that Anthony Trollope, another innate storyteller and good spinner of plots, should have denied that he did anything of the kind. Indeed, he said, no author, impatient to get on with the story, could be expected to spend much time on such an exhausting aspect of composition: "The plot is the most insignificant part of a tale." Yet, in *Orley*

Farm, Lady Mason forges a will. In *Barchester,* Mr. Slope schemes for episcopal power. In *He Knew He Was Right,* Emily and Louis Trevelyan and Colonel Osborne are locked into a drama occasioned by their respective characters. Louis Trevelyan is from the outset a jealous, overbearing husband: "he liked to have his own way." When he cannot domineer over his wife Emily in the matter of whether or not she should allow the old family friend, Colonel Osborne, to the house ("Emily also liked to have her own way," Trollope tells us), Louis Trevelyan will not apologize for his unjust suspicions, and so it must end in madness and death. The characters do not change; the imperatives of their natures sweep them into cataclysms of misery. It's a riveting plot.

◆◆◆

However many pains he may or may not expend on the plot, evidently the great storyteller cannot help himself from making things interesting. In the face of whatever current fashion for plotless narrative, his view of the world is as a series of events connected by strange quirks, coincidences, the desires of people and their consequences. Trollope was a great storyteller. It was Dorothy Sayers, herself a great storyteller, who said that the gift is innate and compulsive: "it is mightiest in the mighty," she said, "and by itself it can produce the minor immortality of a *Sherlock Holmes* or a *Three Musketeers.* In the hands of a great poet it produces the major immortality of an *Odyssey,* a *Paradise Lost,* or a *Divine Comedy.*" And another great storyteller, Somerset Maugham, believed this too. He defended the plot more forthrightly than anyone in this century: "the novel of incident...has as much right to exist as any other. The plot is a lifeline thrown to the reader, to help him through the tale." What Maugham calls a lifeline, Forster called a tapeworm: "the lowest and simplest of literary organisms," but also the "highest factor common to all the very common literary organisms known as novels."

Sayers's mention of Dumas is endearing. The writers of these essays were asked to speak of their own literary responses, so this is the place to confess my early and abiding love for the works of Alexandre Dumas (*père*). At any rate we must add Dumas to our list of nineteenth-century readable novelists. *The Count of Monte Cristo* is a perfect example of an enduring, beloved, eternally pleasing tale in which the plot is the most important thing. The means by which the implacable count gets revenge on those who blighted the life of the young Edmond Dantes forever gratifies our sense of justice and tells us, contrary to what we know of the world, that wrongs are righted, that the wicked are punished, that a person may be reborn into more favorable circumstances as a fabulously wealthy nobleman, say, and that one's enemies may yet be brought to tremble. But, lest we dismiss this as mere wish-fulfillment, too easily gratifying to be "serious," we learn also that what is past is past: Mercedes is grown old, alas, and has slept with another man; the dead are dead (Edmond's old father cannot be brought back); wealth does not bring happiness. Many and serious are the lessons of *The Count of Monte Cristo*. It is not a trivial but a perfect work, whose fascination arises from action, from what happens, not from character or form. There is a curious sense in which the happening in a novel is free of the words, exists in a third dimension, is an invisible dynamic generated by words but *not* them, where character descriptions or brilliant dialogue lie upon the page in one dimension. To say, as people frequently do, that such and such springs to life off the page is to express just this sense of insubstantial reality, a third or invisible dimension where the action lives, different from the words which are used for it. And in this dimension is the essence of plot, and it needs to be returned to its rightful dominion.

Poetry and Pleasure

by Robert Pinsky

IN MY TEENS, I MEMORIZED the following poem, without trying to memorize it, and without much thought for its meaning:

ON BEING ASKED FOR A WAR POEM

I think it better that in times like these
A poet's voice be silent, for in truth
We have no gift to set a statesman right;
He has had enough of meddling who can please
A young girl in the indolence of her youth
Or an old man upon a winter's night.

I think that what I liked about the poem was physical. That is, it had to do with what I could feel the consonants and vowels doing inside my mouth and in my ears.

About five years after I first read the poem, a teacher—a great teacher—upset me by criticizing the poem for its sentimental and anti-intellectual view of the nature of poetry. My teacher said that while one could not object to Yeats's refusing to write a poem to order on war or on any set subject, the reason Yeats gives is feeble, assigning poetry a trivial status:

> [to] please
> A young girl in the indolence of her youth
> Or an old man upon a winter's night.

This criticism, powerful and perhaps irrefutable though it is, ignores the historical attitude toward World War I of an Irish poet, who a few years later would write "Easter 1916." It also ignores a loyalty I have never been able to shake off, toward the idea of pleasing and being pleased in works of art. Is my desire to make something capable of giving surprise, or giving a sensation of elegance, or a feeling of attraction—my desire to make something *pleasing*—simply a petty or irresponsible aspect of my strivings to make a work of art?

Before you decide that the question itself is contemptible, let me say two things: first, the passion to give the gift of pleasure and interest, the desire to make this gift available (in theory) even to someone distracted by their body's sexual restlessness, or their body's need for comfort in cold weather, is an impersonal desire; Yeats's old man and young woman are not at a poetry reading, they are not book reviewers, he is not talking about their *response,* their compliments or their fan letters. He is talking about the idea of pleasing and interesting them, against odds, and without his even knowing it at the time. Though the poem may be subject to copyright law, and printed in a book that costs money, and though the concert and the museum too may cost money, there is another sense in which a work of art is a gift, a gift of pleasure which some of us aspire to give. (I borrow this idea from Lewis Hyde.)

Secondly, I want to say—as humbly as I can—that despite all the complexities of literary theory, for all the ingenuities of ambition or expectation, the trouble with most poems that fail—one's own poems, or poems written in workshops, or submitted to magazines, or published in books—may be described simply: they are not interesting enough to impart conviction. Most of them fail to be surprising or musical or revealing enough to arouse much interest; to read them, one must be a professional (and certainly not an indolent or drowsy professional). It sounds silly to say so, but some explicit sex, or a few jokes, or a bizarre personal confession, might make these poems more interesting; it is true that such ingredients would not make them good poems. From this we can conclude how difficult it is to make a good poem.

What we mean by "interest," I think, is the free acceptance of the gift of pleasure. Without this component, however important the material in a work of art may be, or sophisticated its technique, we are responding with mere piety, or mere astonishment.

Is it possible to talk about how to be interesting, without sounding foolish? We'll see. I'll start with a rough enumeration of the kinds of interest I find in poems I love, and then try to cite examples.

Poems, after all, are not the only compositions in words. Although poems are the most interesting kind of such compositions to me, I can think of at least three others that please and interest most people, each having something in common with poems: songs, jokes, and personal letters, which embody for me the qualities of physical grace, lively social texture, and inward revelation. (Since good poems often embody all three of these qualities, the examples I choose will be essentially arbitrary; in fact, I choose them partly to underscore the arbitrariness.)

◆ ◆ ◆

In the sixteenth and seventeenth centuries, poets wrote poems that have, to
an amazingly pure degree, the interest of physical grace, the counterpoint of
their music and their sentences. The physical transformation of words, simply by their arrangement, into something that approaches actual song, often
gives an unexpected life, dignity, and penetration to unpromising, formulaic
subjects. Here is Ben Jonson singing the mating song of an older lover, making his embarrassment about himself, and his exaggerated appreciation of
the person he loves, into something that pleases me and cheers me up every
time I read it:

> Let it not your wonder move,
> Less your laughter, that I love.
> Though I now write fifty years
> I have had, and have my peers;
> Poets, though divine, are men:
> Some have loved as old again.
> And it is not always Face,
> Clothes, or fortune gives the grace;
> Or the feature, or the youth:
> But the Language, and the Truth,
> With the Ardor and the Passion,
> Gives the Lover weight, and fashion.
> If you then will read the Storie,
> First, prepare you to be Sorie
> That you never knew till now
> Either whom to love, or how:
> But be glad, as soon with me,
> When you know that this is she
> Of whose beauty it was sung
> She shall make the old man young,
> Keep the middle age at stay,
> And let nothing high decay
> Till she be the reason why
> All the world for love may die.

In a way, my point is that all good art defeats the predictable; Jonson defeats
it with and through music: *with* music, for instance, in the way the most sing-
song of all English meters is made fluent and personal and various by such
means as his placement of the pause-within-the-line—now late in the line,
now early:

> Let it not your wonder move,
> Less your laughter # that I love.
> Though I now write fifty years,
> I have had # and have my peers...

> If you then will read the Storie,
> First # prepare you to be Sorie
> That you never knew till now
> Either whom to love # or how.

But Jonson also defeats the predictable *through* music, because the elements that delight us appear to grow out of the swelling sense that he will sing, even though expectation and age threaten to hold him back. This resolve to sing keeps getting fuller and stronger: from the wry opening lines about faces, clothes, fortunes, then to the rhapsody about language, truth, ardor, passion, and finally on to the apotheosis of the beauty, and the appearance of the verb "to sing" itself—

> Of whose beauty it was sung
> She shall make the old man young—

that follows; it is an elevated, victorious version of the opening lines in which the old lover protests that really, he is young. But who could predict:

> Keep the middle age at stay

Or, even more fresh and venturesome:

> And let nothing high decay
> Till she be the reason why
> All the world for love may die.

That is, the traditional Petrarchan love-language of dying for the personification of Beauty, seemingly immortal, is taken over for the old lover's own purpose: both dying for love and being kept fresh by it are epitomized by him.

Jonson's poem, then, pleases and interests because it is inventively beautiful in sound, and because its beauty dramatizes the poem's proposition that art can make fresh and heartening what would otherwise be drab and discouraging. Though form has been looked on sometimes as the most public, least personal part of poetry, here form is the feeling's physical expression of impatience with the clumsy boundary of what is expected.

As a physical expression, in other words, the attractive form of Jonson's poem is personal, the way one's way of dancing or gesturing or walking is personal. Insofar as this is true, Jonson's achievement of a personal expressive rhythm, within a confining but distinctly forceful meter, is horribly enviable for anyone who has tried to put sensuous life and individual force into unmetered lines.

Part of the effect is not simply metrical, but springs from the freshness and naturalness of idiom: "though I now write fifty years"; "poets, though divine, are men"; "it is not always Face, Clothes, or Fortune"; "you never knew till now"; "be glad"; "this is she." These phrases are Jonson's plain English, as fresh in their historical context as the plain American of Williams, and when they coincide with the measure there is the thrill of sensing that the rhythmic demands of song and the nature of actual speech have been made to coincide, as when a song's pattern and song lyrics seem made for one another.

Finally, it's worth observing that the particular pattern of Jonson's poem seems especially well suited to the theme that skill can elevate and transform an old, inert, provincial, or discouraged body. The pattern is "beheaded" tetrameter, which by dropping the first, unstressed syllable that begins a normal tetrameter line emphasizes the separation of the lines, most of them beginning, as well as ordinarily ending, with a stressed syllable. Then, with a feeling of exuberant transformation, the poet glides things back together by flowing the grammar over that separation; Jonson's last lines might have inspired Yeats in "Under Ben Bulben":

> Irish poets, learn your trade,
> Sing whatever is well made,
> Scorn the sort now growing up
> All out of shape from toe to top.

The note of exultation and scorn—in Jonson's lines, scorn for those who put the body above the arts that animate it, in Yeats's lines, scorn for those who fail to master those arts—in both poems resolves itself into a note of triumph. The sense of victory, of overcoming the shapelessness or fatigue of the body, is near the center of the pleasure of song. By fitting the grunts and vocalizations of language into elegant, expressive patterns, poetry conveys a similar pleasure in the human body as it apparently excels itself.

◆◆◆

As to jokes, it is not their funniness that interests me in relation to poetry, nor is it their structure, which is the aspect of jokes most often taken up when speaking of poetry (as when a Shakespeare sonnet is said to rely too much upon the weak punch line of its couplet). To make it clear that I am not talking about jokelike, funny elements in poems, I will try to pick a fairly solemn poem, with no particular punchline structure, for an example of the principles I do have in mind. These principles concern the alert social texture of successful jokes, and in relation to that texture their sense of context and power to generate context.

I think that the idea of "good jokes" and "bad" ones reflects a misconception; the timing and social placement of the joke, and the textural pleasures of its telling, matter far more than the mechanical burning of a narrative fuse toward the little explosion of a punch line. The joke about the one-armed piccolo player might be right for a certain moment after a picnic, but not for the car ride home. Or the badness or bad taste of one joke might sometimes be more successful than the seeming excellence of another. People naive about jokes fail to see this enormously social, contextual limitation to the form, and are bewildered when the Jewish parrot joke that caused tears in one setting evokes only polite smiles in a slightly different one; moreover, such a teller exaggerates the importance of "how" it was told, while underestimating the original teller's sense of precisely when to time the joke. Also, charm of texture probably matters more, compared to punch lines, than rhetorically naive conceptions of the joke assume: the way the woman who told the parrot joke hunched her shoulders and used head, rather than arm, gestures to suggest the parrot pointing out the *tallis* it would like the tailor to copy for it in miniature; the way the woman pronounces or mispronounces *tallis;* the way the tailor is presented as mixing the teller's idiom ludicrously with the ethnic idiom—touches like these, as they establish context and conviction, make up the living body of a tiny work of art, for which the punch line is merely the graceful closure. These touches are the expressive social gestures which in a poem we sometimes call "taste" or "timing" or "tact" or "wit."

I am afraid that I'll seem to be diddling with superficial matters that insult the serious and vital art of poetry; but I am trying to edge toward the very altar of the mystery, by analogy—and the fleeting, social conviction and alertness that come to life when one person contrives a funny story for others resembles one aspect of the more enduring, freestanding conviction of the successful gift that is a poem. Moreover, this aspect of poems seems to me to be the one that criticism sees least clearly, and is most likely to mangle or bungle inadvertently.

If music conveys physical grace, this contextual alertness conveys a feeling of actual life at its best, of social liveliness. In the joke this liveliness is ephemeral and contingent. In the poem, it is the enduring generosity and subtlety of a human presence:

PIANO

Softly, in the dusk, a woman is singing to me;
Taking me back down the vista of years, till I see
A child sitting under the piano, in the boom of the tingling strings
And pressing the small, poised feet of a mother who smiles as she sings.

In spite of myself, the insidious mastery of song
Betrays me back, till the heart of me weeps to belong
To the old Sunday evenings at home, with winter outside
And hymns in the cozy parlor, the tinkling piano our guide.

So now it is vain for the singer to burst into clamor
With the great black piano appassionato. The glamour
Of childish days is upon me, my manhood is cast
Down in the flood of remembrance, I weep like a child for the past.

D. H. Lawrence modulates the presence of the human voice telling this poem, whose subject—boy versus man, nostalgia versus passion, music versus thought, "manhood" versus "softness," remembrance versus the present, the human voice versus its accompanying "great black piano" of feeling—is a stock source for poems, as mothers-in-law or airplanes with ethnically various passengers are stock sources for jokes. The modulation of the personal presence in the poem is the source of its formal invention, its ability to pierce us with something fresh, and not stock.

At the very beginning, the conventional "softly, in the dusk" and "taking me back" tell us where we are, in the way that in the joke form "a man goes to a doctor" or "a guy goes into a bar and says" tell us where we are. The quasi-social convention tells us that "child" denotes the same person as the adult who is being sung to, and the vivid, nonconventional language—

> A child sitting under the piano, in the boom of the tingling strings,
> And pressing the small, poised feet of a mother who smiles as she sings

—tells us that the energy is going to be in the past: the softness of the dusk in the present, and the "boom of the tingling strings" in the past. And though the "insidious mastery of song" is in the present, it "betrays [him] back" to the past. The words "insidious" and "betrays" put a steely spring into the social component of the poem, the amazing spring of Lawrence's combative, moralistic side.

In relation to the social component of the poem, I want to return to the idea of tact, or social judgment. There are two large ways in which the poem seems related to society: sexually, there is a feeling made out of the Oedipal situation of the child, the infantilizing impact this has on the man, and the suggestion of male impotence; politically, the "cozy parlor" and the Sunday evening hymns place the memory in a certain religious, cultural, and social strand of English life. But how pathetically wooden and imprecise my summarizing language is for the actual, pleasingly deft accuracy with which Lawrence's poem indicates these parts of what he has to say, including the contrast between the Baptist family home of the child and the elegant situation of the grown man. My lament at the clumsiness of my own definition, here, is a standard critical maneuver; but I think that criticism, despite such outward laments, tends to neglect the way that such matters of nuance and degree are not merely difficulties presented to the professional reader, and not even mere beauties of technique that make the work of art more to be prized; rather, the ability to introduce feelings and meanings to precise degrees, with compact, rapid accuracy, is at the core of the work of art. Such calibrations embody the way a work of art struggles for a claim on our attention. I think that this power is in a way a social grace or art—like the ability to time and present a funny story. (Needless to say, the sexual or sociopolitical matters at stake here may be considerably more demanding than the contexts I have adduced as examples for the joke.)

But as poets (rather than readers) our concerns are different. One problem we may have in writing a poem is how to arrange and dispose a feeling—how to put something first, something else second, and so forth. The silliest joke, too, must solve this problem. Lawrence solves the problem in terms of a kind of narrative combat, I have suggested, between resistance and nostalgia, present and past, soft language and hard. In a joke, the comparable elements might be the ordinary and the preposterous, as in the countless stories in which a man goes into a bar with a polar bear, or a horse, or an invisible dwarf, or a mermaid. The skill (or art, if we choose) of presenting the joke is in presenting the dance or tension of the two elements, ordinary and bizarre. In Lawrence's poem, the dance or struggle I have indicated is dramatized by the rhyming, personal voice telling what happens, as it includes the opposed meanings of "cozy" and "insidious," the opposed roots and social contexts of those words, and the opposed social analogues of the rhetorical "great black piano appassionato" and the bare, plain "weep like a child":

> In spite of myself, the insidious mastery of song
> Betrays me back, till the heart of me weeps to belong
> To the old Sunday evenings at home, with winter outside
> And hymns in the cozy parlor, the tinkling piano our guide.
>
> So now it is vain for the singer to burst into clamor
> With the great black piano appassionato. The glamour
> Of childish days is upon me, my manhood is cast
> Down in the flood of remembrance, I weep like a child for the past.

There is something like wit—not mere wittiness, but social wit, an alert brilliance about tone, that calls up our own delight in nuance, our delight in not being stupid or bored—in the "glamour of childish days," the singer in clamor and the great black piano appassionato, piano and singer impotent to compete with the tear-flooded past they have called up. That language has literary and sexual implications—"glamour" and "childish" and "manhood cast down"—touched on so surely and unheavyhandedly that we are flattered, or anyway invited along pleasingly. The same can be said of the way "the old Sunday evenings at home" and "the heart of me weeps to belong" evoke, without mocking, a lower-middle-class elegance of speech.

If the poem's structure has anything like a punch line or final revelation, it is syntactical: after sentences and parts of sentences all beginning with modifiers, the last sentence links three strong substantive subjects that begin its three clauses—"glamour," "manhood," "I":

>   The glamour
> Of childish days is upon me, my manhood is cast
> Down in the flood of remembrance, I weep like a child for the past.

We are given this by the teller to appreciate, like a sudden colloquialism or gesture by one telling a joke, and I think we appreciate it partly for the way he has created a social context for us and exploited that context. In other words, the three strong substantives please the reader not just formally, but as the capstone of a plot, involving the sexual and socioeconomic matters I have (a bit ponderously) outlined. We respond to this social grace and penetration, or rather to this artistic imitation of social grace and penetration, with the pleasure of being taken out of ourselves, and yet also further into ourselves.

Finally, putting Lawrence's poem aside, I want to say again that I am not talking about the narrative element in jokes and poems, but about something communal in the art of presentation. Since I can't show you someone telling a joke, cast your mind to the Gable character and the Colbert character in *It Happened One Night,* when early in their flirtation, in order to fool some detectives, they improvise an argument in which they pretend to be a rather stupid married couple screaming at one another. It is a little work of art the two characters have made, and given to one another, and it is based on social understanding and imagination; and it functions—far more importantly than fooling detectives—to advance their sexual trust and respect. When Lawrence invites us to hear conventional and fresh language, coziness and insidiousness, when he has the child "press" rather than, say, "touch" the mother's feet—he is inviting us to take a pleasure like that of the two characters, based on a similar part of our intelligence, a similar wish to appreciate other people and their sense of themselves in their words.

◆ ◆ ◆

If music's grace is the most basic aspect of a poem's appeal, and lively contextual sense is a poem's necessary social component, perhaps the most profound pleasure by which a poem engages our interest is by revealing to us the inward motion of another mind and soul. I associate this power with letters because I have found it impossible to write a good personal letter without going at least a little further into myself than I might in conversation; the element of planning or composition seems to strip away barriers, props, and disguises, rather than to create them. I think we all find this true in letters from friends—even the brief, hurried note seems to have concentrated some distillate of a person's inner nature. And to read an old letter of one's own is, sometimes, to be amazed at how revelatory the mix of news, musing, inquiry turns out to be. And as surely as the abstract yet physical course of music pleases us, or the skillful weave of telling in a social context pleases us, the revelation of an inward self pleases us.

One poet above all others has trusted this principle, has ruthlessly followed the assumption that what is in him, if he can only follow its tides and creatures as faithfully as a naturalist, will be beautiful and interesting. In this, I find Whitman to be just as he says he is, however calculating and programmatic he may be in other ways. His amazing poem "Spontaneous Me," for instance, presents a kind of deliberate sexual manifesto, with details far more pointed than what the poem calls "the negligent list of one after another as I happen to call them to me or think of them"; but on the other hand this alleged "negligence" is an accurate reflection of the poem's charm and force, which come from opening a kind of door into Walt. The idea of linking sexual energy and poetry, carried to absurd or self-important extremes, takes on the integrity that belongs to any actual single personality:

> The real poems (what we call poems being merely pictures,)
> The poems of the privacy of night, and of men like me,
> This poem drooping shy and unseen that I always carry, and that all men carry.

The self-consciousness of the letter-writer, who is naked in the sense that he is stripped of the cloaking effects supplied by physical presence, social presence, often leads the writer to comment, as Whitman does here, on what he is writing.

But this self-reflection is perhaps more external, less revealing, than the series of set pieces or rhetorical ebulliences that succeed it. And most revealing of all is the movement from one rhetorical flourish to the next. The letter-writer types in apparently random order a series of paragraphs, news, inquiry, anecdotes, asides, complaints, boasts, apologies; and as a whole, the plot created by the paragraphs reflects the characteristic energy by which the writer's personality moves. And as "Spontaneous Me" moves from the hilariously pornographic encounter between "the hairy wild bee" and the "full-grown lady flower" whom he grips with "amorous firm legs" as he "hankers up and down" and "takes his will of her," on to the wet woods, then to the two sleepers "one with an arm slanting down across and below the waist of the other," then hastily to the "smell of apples" and sage, and so forth, leaping with a slightly nervous, elated grin from the erotic to the innocent, the generalized to the personal—the balletic jumps come to seem even more important and heartfelt than the places they touch.

Of course, these inventive loops and plunges and changes of manner are partly a technical feat, alert to what the reader will demand once the title "Spontaneous Me" has been linked to the sexual material. The poem surprises by going on, and then on, and varying catalogue against tender description, alternating shouted lists and whispered descriptions. But leaving technical considerations aside, consider the beautiful passage on masturbation, and the sequence that follows it:

> The limpid liquid within the young man,
> The vex'd corrosion so pensive and so painful,
> The torment, the irritable tide that will not be at rest,

The like of the same I feel, the like of the same in others,
The young man that flushes and flushes, and the young woman that flushes and
     flushes,
The young man that wakes deep at night, the hot hand seeking to repress what
     would master him,
The mystic amorous night, the strange half-welcome pangs, visions, sweats,
The pulse pounding through palms and trembling encircling fingers, the young
     man all color'd, red, ashamed, angry;
The souse upon me of my lover the sea, as I lie willing and naked,
The merriment of twin babes that crawl over the grass in the sun, the mother
     never turning her vigilant eyes from them,
The walnut trunk, the walnut husks, and the ripening or ripn'd long-round
     walnuts,
The continence of vegetables, birds, animals,
The consequent meanness of me should I skulk or find myself indecent, while
     birds and animals never once skulk or find themselves indecent.

The last five lines embody what I mean by the revelation of self through movement from one thing to the next. On the one hand, on the surface, they present a Whitmanian doctrine about the innocence of sexuality, with the line
where he lies willing and naked under the souse of his lover the sea at the ful-
crum. (That line is the most daringly explicit in one way, and draws a seemly
veil of "the natural" over things, in another way.) On the other hand, the
working out in texture of the "red, ashamed, angry" youth, to the souse of
the sea, to the twin babes is full of freshness, invention, and peculiarity; we can
feel his affected, excessive, unerring brain stretching for inspired examples
and finding them. This seems particularly true of the mother "never turning
her vigilant eyes" from the twin babes—a Victorian contrivance of sweetness
that is also the maternal poet (or reader) refusing to avert watchful eyes from
what two people may like to do together. And then walnuts, of all things, and
of all the attributes of birds, animals, and vegetables(!), their *"continence."*
The odd little association of sound between that word and "consequence" is
part of the persuasive psychological fabric. It helps make the poem seem the
easy going-into oneself of

> Beautiful dripping fragments, the negligent list of one after another as happen
>   to call them to me or think of them,

while the sequence of examples for innocence and passion, anxious to persuade and calm the reader, reminds us of how planned and determined the
poem is. This dual sense of a freed, wandering mind in the writer and his
extreme consciousness of the reader, the combination of nakedness and a
rather specific awareness of audience, gives Whitman's structure its energy,
more than selfhood or doctrine could do alone. The subtlety of this movement, more free than conversation and yet more contrived, less formal than
discursive prose and yet more concentrated, resembles the best kind of letter.

What impresses me about the Whitman poem—about all of the poems I have discussed—is the fact that its essential appeal cannot be attributed to the way it fulfills certain (undeniably valuable) standards that pervade creative writing or literary criticism, as they approach poetry. Vivid phrases; striking images; sharp physical details; beautiful, quotable language; important ideas (philosophical, political, psychological): no one could deny that these elements are important, and that they contribute to our desire to read Whitman's poem, Lawrence's, Jonson's, our pleasurable assent to *be* reading them. But if gorgeous, impressive language and profound, crucial ideas were all that poetry offered to engage us, would it seem—as it does to many of us—as necessary as food? Would eloquence and truth, by themselves, be enough to compete with (say) the movies, for our attention?

As I reread the passage in "Spontaneous Me" about masturbation, shame, innocence, exuberance, pleasure, freedom, identity, and search in it for the three qualities I have tried to consider as essential, I find them at the center of the charm and passionate engagement of the passage. In the sounds of a line (the rapid beginning and slow ending of the phrase "merriment of twin babes," the consonants in "merriment" and "twin"; the consonants and vowels in "grass," "crawl," "mother," "never," "vigilant"), there is something comparable to the tune you hear and want to hum, and hum again. In the teasing alternation of preacherly and pornographic phrases, there is something comparable to the bright, socially observant talker's sense of audience and social context, evoking, mocking, and confessing to the prudery and lasciviousness of his time and place. And in the way the structure, avowedly random and ostensibly determined by its political and psychological ideas, conveys the moral drama of Whitman's mind as it moves through its examples and assertions, there is something comparable to the pleasure given by a letter taken out to be read again, because it embodies a considerable soul in action.

This movement—physical in the sounds of a poem, moral in its relation to the society implied by language, and the person who utters the poem—is near the heart of poetry's mysterious appeal, for me. Such movement cannot be affected or faked. It comes from conviction: confidence in the power of rhythm; trust in the social generosity between artist and audience; belief in the movement of one's own thoughts and feelings. Convincing movement is what commands interest. (Boredom appears to be a response to tunelessness, timidity, or weak faith in the work of art, a sense that the soul is standing still.)

I'd like to close with a poem that seems to me to present such movement in a rather naked form, Czeslaw Milosz's "Incantation." It is also a very encouraging poem on the subject of poetry. Rather than apologize for the fact that it is a translation, I'll suggest that it all the more presents the essential movement or conviction I'm trying to get at, and all the more may risk violating standards of poetry we may take from the terms of creative writing or book reviews. With those terms uppermost in our mind, would we have the boldness to write the first line of the poem? Its first three lines, or its first six?

INCANTATION

Human reason is beautiful and invincible.
No bars, no barbed wire, no pulping of books,
No sentence of banishment can prevail against it.
It establishes the universal ideas in language,
And guides our hand so we write Truth and Justice
With capital letters, lie and oppression with small.
It puts what should be above things as they are,
Is an enemy of despair and a friend of hope.
It does not know Jew from Greek or slave from master,
Giving us the estate of the world to manage.
It saves austere and transparent phrases
From the filthy discord of tortured words.
It says that everything is new under the sun,
Opens the congealed fist of the past.
Beautiful and very young are Philo-Sophia
And Poetry, her ally in the service of the good.
As late as yesterday Nature celebrated their birth,
The news was brought to the mountains by a unicorn and an echo.
Their friendship will be glorious, their time has no limit.
Their enemies have delivered themselves to destruction.

It is good to read a poem that suggests that poems are supremely important, and that many good poems remain to be written. The art, says Milosz, is young; and it is the friend of truth. That is, it promises surprises far beyond the clichés of fine writing or self-regard, with the appeal neither of an easy cosmetic rhetoric nor of a secret code that ignores the reader and the world; it promises vital, unsuppressible knowledge. The creation of interest through the most pleasurable ways of knowing: that is what poetry—the fascinating, more physically graceful friend of Philo-Sophia—is. Or anyway, by entertaining such a definition of poetry, as the creation of an interest in truth through pleasure, Yeats's poem about the ambition to please may be a little redeemed.

Reading

Christopher Isherwood: Getting Things Right

by *Thom Gunn*

I.

WHEN I FIRST MET CHRISTOPHER ISHERWOOD he was fifty and I was twenty-five, but I never for a moment felt that he was twice my age. We immediately started speaking together like long-time friends who hadn't met in years. He was tanned and youthful-looking, the famous bright eyes alert and observant; he perfectly adapted himself to his listener; his conversation was enthusiastic, lively, funny; and I said to myself, *this* is the way I want to age.

Gore Vidal has recorded lunching with him at MGM during the filming of *Diane*, a movie nobody ever saw, and this was the same summer, 1955. After we had talked for a while, Isherwood took me on the set, where I was eventually introduced to two of the leads, Roger Moore and Marisa Pavan, the King and Queen of France. I was not introduced to Lana Turner, who played Diane de Poitiers and, when visible at all, was kept at a star's distance, hedged in by attendants. Isherwood had warned me that he would have to leave me from time to time, but I was engrossed in watching the repeated takes of a short scene. It took place during an elaborate court banquet on a table forming three sides of a square, at the head of which the King, standing gallantly behind Diane, had to lean over and spear a strawberry with a fork to pop into her mouth. It went wrong again and again—now he missed the strawberry, now he dropped it, and each time before the scene was shot, even though Lana Turner had not been touched, her makeup man reappeared, fussing over her as if she had been in a pillow fight. It was all fascinating, and just what I had hoped for. She submitted her face to him, like the actress in *Prater Violet*, "as impersonally as one extends a shoe to the bootblack." Isherwood joined me for a moment, and left me again. I noticed then, among the others watching, a boy of about my own age who looked as if he had gone to school on a beach. I assumed he must work here. He apparently assumed the same about me, because he came over and quietly asked me what I was doing. I let

39

it be known, with perhaps a degree too much casualness, that I was a friend
of the scriptwriter. He had climbed over the studio walls, he said, and slipped
onto the set in search of a job in movies, and could I help him?—anything
would do. I promised I would introduce him to my friend, and did, but Isherwood, though warm as ever, told him at once that he had no influence of that
sort. He was amazed at the boy's exploit. On the way to lunch he told me
how difficult it was for an outsider to penetrate a set like this: the walls were
high and the lot was crawling with guards. But though he was sorry not to be
of help, it all crowned the morning, for this was the way life was supposed to
be in a movie studio. It was like an incident from a Hollywood movie about
Hollywood—or like Lana Turner herself being spotted by a talent scout, so
many years ago, an unknown girl sitting at the soda fountain in Schwab's;
and Isherwood was full of glee that he had provided the opportunity for it
all. In the commissary I recognized a satisfactory number of famous faces,
and we went on talking.

I felt free to bring up anything. This was the end of the McCarthy era, and
I asked him if he had ever had any difficulties because of his own past politics.
Not really, he said; at one time he had been visited by two FBI agents, who
had behaved with circumspection. "And I told them everything about myself.
But I did point out to them that the Left had flirted with Communism just as
the Right had flirted with Fascism." Such a remark was unanswerable, of
course, because true, and was a just commentary on the politics of the thirties.
He was not questioned any farther on the matter. It must have been conven-
ient for him as well that the narrators of his books had been almost as guarded
about politics as they were about sex. They *flirted* indeed.

It was perhaps at this time that I asked him which he considered his best
book. He didn't seem to think my question stupid but said at once, "The
journals I kept throughout the forties, but they are safe in the Library of Congress and no one can get at them till after my death." (Later he withdrew
them for use in the writing of *Down There on a Visit* and his autobiography.)
I was surprised, but then, I hadn't read the journals, and figured that perhaps
he was like Sickert, who valued the spontaneity of his sketches more than his
canvases.

A friend asked him, on a later occasion, "What happened to Sally Bowles?"
I thought my friend's question rather crude—hadn't he heard of *artistic creation?*— but Isherwood was delighted to tell him about what Jean Ross, the
original of Sally, had gone on to do ("and now she's worried because her
daughter is running wild!"). He was entirely without pretension or literary
snobbery. For him there was no opposition between the art of the novel and
that of the memoir. It was a question, I think, of the spirit in which the writer
undertook his work: both arts shared the same end, which was of getting
things right, and if the novelist invented and rearranged, it was with the object

of making the shape of the record clearer and finally truer to the essentials of the original experience.

Though he lived in Los Angeles and I was to settle in San Francisco, I was to meet Isherwood many times during the next thirty years, usually with his lover, Don, and mine, Mike, and sometimes with the famous people he had asked to dinner. His novels had meant a lot to me before we met, but knowing him I was especially impressed by the at the time uncommon ease, casualness, and openness with which he carried his homosexuality. And of course he, like I, was an Englishman who lived in California, in love with his new home, and in a state of ambivalence toward his old. I had an irrational terror that on some visit back to England I might fall fatally ill, get *stuck* there, and die there without being able to return to America first. It was absurdly romantic, since my health was sturdy—yet it was a real fear, nevertheless, as though I would by dying there get wedged forever inside a purgatory of dissatisfied adolescence. I asked Isherwood once if he ever himself felt a similar fear. "Oh yes!" he said. "Then my mother would have won!" But he said it with such a cheerfully melodramatic tone, as if guying a past self, that I couldn't tell how to take it.

In his company I remember myself as several times giving way to a pertness, amounting to rudeness, especially when speaking about people I had met at his house. I remember it with mortification. I was no teenager, after all. Was I trying, by this means, to show that I was a free spirit unbound by the conventions, to establish my comparative youthfulness (and so attractiveness, perhaps), and restore the difference between generations he had so completely and generously disregarded on our first meeting? That's the only way I can explain it. He, however, was forbearing with me, though remarks I let drop—about Cecil Beaton, whom I later came to like a lot, and about William Inge—clearly annoyed him, and rightly so, for their sheer discourtesy.

But for a while, until it was clear that I had rather outworn my original charm, I did naively feel that I must be one of Isherwood's best friends, he seemed so pleased to see me and he gave me so much pleasure by *his* company. I wasn't, of course; in fact there were hundreds of people who knew him as well as I, and many who were far closer—I was really on the peripheral rim of his acquaintance; but one night, in the booth of a restaurant-bar in Santa Monica, about 1972, I was able to understand why I had felt so. There were several of us present, and I found myself at one point watching him talk with the wife of a sound-man for a BBC documentary he had just completed. I noticed the way he devoted himself *wholly* to his interlocutor. The rest of us do not, we divide our attention, however politely, our eyes straying to the distractions of the background, but that undivided concentration of attentiveness that Isherwood turned on you ("Yes! Yes!" he would say eagerly) was without equal in my experience. He met you as you were seldom met by others.

Late in the 1970s he made a good many public appearances, on TV or in front of live audiences. I was present at one in 1979, when he spoke before an enormous, largely gay crowd, and I was interested that the passages he read by way of a preface were two that I most admired, one from the "Berlin Diary" sections of *Goodbye to Berlin,* and the other from the concluding pages of *A Single Man.* They did not take up much time, however, and for the most part of the program he answered a variety of questions from the audience, doing so at length, with spontaneity and untiring courtesy. I couldn't help noticing how he had at last aged—he was seventy-six then, after all—a stockiness of bearing having replaced the earlier wiry vigor. He now had the thickened neck and the stiff deportment I associated with the retired English military officer. (Poor man, he probably had a touch of arthritis.)

When I next met him I asked him if he were ever self-conscious doing this kind of thing. "No," he said brightly, "I seem to get the opposite to stage fright." He was *on* in public, in the same way that he could be in private, the public and private manner being on occasion identical—enthusiastic yet confiding, frank yet with a touch of the formal suggested perhaps by the very degree of articulateness. Indeed, he reminds us several times in his writings that he is a "play actor" by nature; and when later, in my last meetings with him, I thought he seemed somewhat out of it, drifting a little, lacking the old intensity to the point of vagueness, it did cross my mind that perhaps he was playing the part of "old man" for the sheer comedy of it. He was not in fact, he had cancer, and was subject to memory lapses by now, I learned from Don after his death; but even in this condition he could be disconcertingly aware that he was unaware, and in an interview with Armistead Maupin remarked of himself, "Yes, the whole of the East Wing has gone dark, I'm afraid," a wonderfully Mortmere joke to make about his own failing powers.

If he was both a performer and someone capable of giving you that supreme spontaneous attentiveness, all it means is that he was not a simple man, as you might already have guessed from his books. The attentiveness, after all, was not something he was born with; rather, it was a habit that he had perfected, much as an actor perfects the habit of his art. But it was not only a discipline that overflowed from the training of the novelist. It was also a form of spiritual courtesy, and courtesy is something that always has to be learned, since we start off as mere selfish babies.

Standing on that platform in San Francisco he had spoken as naturally and unforcedly as if he were speaking to me still in the MGM commissary. He did not leap to distinguish between public and private topics. Once, in my pert aspect, I had made some derogatory remark about the looks of Auden, whom I had met only as an elderly man, his face a map of lighter and deeper cross-hatchings. Oh, but he was so attractive as a young man, Isherwood hastened to tell me. "!?" I responded. "Oh yes, for years we fucked like rabbits every chance we got," he said, and that was a surprise to me, because I had always thought of their friendship as being strictly *literary*. (It came also as a surprise to their friend John Lehmann, as he has recorded.)

Isherwood was not indiscriminate, however: there was still a line between public and private when it was necessary. He did not like it when Allen Ginsberg's entourage started taping his private conversation once without his knowledge or permission, but that of course involved a betrayal of trust also. ("Somebody was saying 'Did you ever *sleep* with Gore Vidal?' and I suddenly became conscious of this little *thing,* this *machine,* whirring amongst them on the floor by the radiator...") He gave of himself widely, it was part of his great charm that he should do so, but he was not going to let himself be exploited. It was sometimes necessary to defend one's privacy, as it was also necessary to keep one's work hours free. "I make it easy for people to visit me," he said, "—the first time." Putting in the work was important, and he wasn't going to become a Truman Capote wasting his days in gossip and literary chitchat instead of writing. As he got older he seemed to become more and more aware that he had little time left to complete what he had projected. The third volume of his autobiography would have dealt, I believe, with the secular side of his early years in Los Angeles, and they would have made absorbing reading. "You actually knew Garbo?" I once exclaimed. "Oh yes," he said, "I knew her probably as well as anyone in the world did—which wasn't much." And he used to go to a gym at which the young, unknown Ryan O'Neal worked out with his even handsomer brother. (It was the brother they all expected to become a star.) I should have asked him about such things in more detail, I should have taken notes—he would have told me, as he would have told anyone; I should have asked him about meeting Chaplin, for example, and Brecht, in those early years—what were those duplicitous and difficult geniuses really like?

Well, presumably the last volume was never written, but there are the collected journals to look forward to. I hear that they have found their ideal editor, so we may expect them to start appearing in print a few years from now. Meanwhile we may reread.

2.

In the middle of writing this essay, I am sent a new book, *Where Joy Resides,* described as "a Christopher Isherwood Reader" and edited by Don Bachardy and James P. White. I am normally suspicious of "readers"—think of *The Marianne Moore Reader,* available in secondhand bookstores everywhere! They are usually nothing more than handsome gift-books, full of snippets and incompletions, easy-reading "samplers" (another word to be wary of) for the real thing. But this, though admittedly handsomely produced, is in effect a Selected Works, and a good one at that. Isherwood gives himself especially well to selection, since most of his fiction takes the form of novellas, of which it is possible to fit quite a few into a large book like this. It contains—from *Goodbye to Berlin*—the first "Berlin Diary" and "Sally Bowles" (originally published on its own), and all of *Prater Violet*, "Mr. Lancaster" (the best part of *Down There on a Visit*), and *A Single Man*. It also includes six reviews and essays and some tastes from *Kathleen and Frank, Lions and Shadows,* and *My Guru and His Disciple*. Isherwood is hardly an inaccessible writer, but this collection would make as balanced an introduction to his work as you could imagine, and I only demur at the presence of the reviews (he was a competent reviewer, but in no way special). There is also a fine introduction by Gore Vidal, which reproduces and summarizes material from his longer essay of 1976, but makes some additions, among which is a sparkling deathbed anecdote.

In looking through the collection I am forcibly reminded about the primacy of memoir for Isherwood. He could say like Tolstoy that hardly a character or event in his fiction was completely fabricated. Not only did Sally Bowles have her original, but minor characters like poor Ruthie in *Down There on a Visit* (Cyril Connolly's first wife) or Grant Lefanu, the physics professor in *A Single Man* (the late poet Henri Coulette). He consciously and continually interpenetrated his fiction with his own literal experiences. I started this essay (as Vidal started his) with a personal memoir, because I consider that the qualities he worked for in his behavior were exactly those he worked for in his writings. In those, from early on, intensity of attention is married to a comparatively relaxed tone of voice. Thus in *Lions and Shadows* (1938), he describes the operating theater in a hospital:

> [It] was like an unnaturally clean kitchen. And the nurses and dressers were like cooks, in their white caps, galoshes and sexless overalls, chatting in groups, or scrubbing their hands at the sink, or busy at the gleaming silver oven doors of the sterilizers. The air was steamy. The atmosphere was expectant, yet somehow horribly domestic.

The first three sentences, one long one carefully placed between two short, would not be out of place in *The Sentimental Education,* with their spare selection of crisp physical detail, their telling use of a sustained analogy, and their economy of summation. But the fourth sentence breaks up the implied formality, for "horribly," unlike every other word here, is recklessly imprecise. Isherwood is fond of similar adverbs like "absurdly" and "terribly," and always they are there for the sake of the tone, which as a result becomes gossipy and offhand, making the whole scene more accessible, putting the reader at ease. Vidal has noted the similar effect Isherwood gets from the strategic introduction of the second person: it brings the reader in.

But for all the informality, for all the ease and lightness, for all the air of having words to waste, Isherwood's prose is written with an unremitting control. His analogies are never decorative, but on the contrary severely functional—how often they belittle grandeur, domesticate the exotic, or make violence appear ordinary (the lesson he learned from Forster). "At the end of [the street], like a tall, dangerously sharp, red instrument, stood a church," he tells us in *Goodbye to Berlin*. Berlin is full of everyday knives that can be put to murderous use. Such a short sentence dramatizes the full complexity of a time and place, the ominous sense of a bad future latent in a troubled present, and the wariness and suspiciousness of the narrator. His prose is a lucid medium for the transmission of situation, character, state of mind, and idea, and for all its succinctness shows how they intersect, criss-cross, connect, or get in each other's way. Simple though it appears on first reading, we come to realize that it does not simplify.

A colloquial directness of style has been around since the early eighteenth century, but Isherwood's particular development of it is admirable because it is so varied in the uses to which it may be put: it can handle the most banal of experiences and it is also capable of eloquence, as I shall show. It is in the nature of a bequest to us—like the plain-style of the Elizabethan poets, it is useful for any subject matter, flexible and all-purpose as it is. And it is a real bequest, for though like most styles it is easy to imitate, like few others it is not a web of mannerisms. You write like Joyce or Proust or James at your peril, but nobody is likely to notice if you write like Isherwood, because you are directing the reader straight to the subject matter, as if style were no intermediary.

Transparency of style is not universally admired, I find. There is no need to pay attention to the view that writing so easy cannot be good, since that is merely the snobbery of the half-educated. But Isherwood's prose has not been much valued by the reigning critics of either his generation or mine. The New Critics, at whom we sneer nowadays (as if everything had changed!), were interested, rather, in "ambiguity," "irony," and "paradox"—that is, in the strategies of indirection and elaboration by which, it was implied, only a complicated style could transmit a complicated subject. The prestigious critics of today are interested in "indeterminacy" and writing that subverts itself: nor is solipsistic confusion frowned upon. Portentousness, jargon, imprecision, and mannerism are widely accepted and imitated in literary criticism now—and Isherwood's kind of transparency, since it clearly springs from a rigorous authorial control, is therefore to be considered authoritarian, thus reactionary, thus fascist. Yet it must have its admirers. It is so obviously practical in getting the job done, in creating meanings at the same moment that it conveys them, that the inheritance is not after all going to waste even though it comes in for so little official recognition. I detect its use in the writing of, for example, the fine first pages of Alan Hollinghurst's *The Swimming Pool Library*, which—without looking derivative for a moment—combines the power of objective perception with that of a subjective ease, very much as in Isherwood.

For such a style is built on the assumption that objectivity is a desirable pursuit. Too much has been made of his phrase "I am a camera," as Isherwood himself knew, but nevertheless—given the fact that humans are creatures of almost uncontrollable bias—a camera is not a bad thing to emulate. Even the practice of analogy is not completely un-camera-like: cameras often record that one thing resembles another, a church is like a knife, for instance, or foam on a brown stream like stout. The attempt to represent with clarity is always worth making, however impossible it is to achieve in absolute terms. (We may call the attempt "fairness.") There is no danger of the writer's ever turning into a real camera, but the imitation of a camera may be good training. And its faithfulness of attention to physical imagery is valuable because through it we may learn about the appearance of the world outside of us, or in other words about things we didn't know before. Doing so helps us to escape from the singleness of our own minds, which, if lived in exclusively, become prisons.

I remember the publication of John Rechy's *City of Night* in the early 1960s, which had a considerable *succès de scandale* and is indeed still available. It was an account of what it is like to be a male prostitute who frequents a number of gay bars. It was an extraordinary chance to explore completely new ground, the subject matter of a stylized but subtly variegated society that, because of censorship problems, had been barely touched in print. It might have been as revealing as *Moll Flanders* or Mayhew's *London,* detailing the social customs, the manners and rituals, the traditions and absurdities and bravados and braveries, of an unfamiliar subculture in the heterosexual midst, one crowded with adaptive humans doing as well as they could, mostly, among rather odd circumstances. Alas, Rechy threw the chance away, concentrating on the reactions of his representative, the self-regarding hustler, instead of the things he was reacting to. Never were Isherwood's virtues more needed and never were they less in evidence.

Such an objective picture as he might have drawn, but of the very different bars of Berlin in about 1930, is one of the ingredients Isherwood would have liked to include in what became the Berlin books, but, because homosexuality was a taboo subject then, the nature of the subculture had to be disguised and encoded. In any case, there was a great deal else from his life in Berlin that Isherwood wished to include.

He had already published one mature novel, *The Memorial,* which is somehow a difficult book to like. It certainly convinces, as a chronicle of the English gentry during the 1920s, and is in addition lively, dramatic, and readable. But, while it is full of rather unfriendly irony, it lacks that essential touch of the ridiculous which characterizes Isherwood's best work and seems to be connected with the presence of a first-person narrator (he is able to make fun of himself: for Isherwood the ridiculous begins at home). This novel, lacking such a personal viewpoint, takes its own sense of the representative a shade too seriously; it is almost schematic.

Isherwood has often told how he had planned to use all the Berlin material in an immense, elaborately structured novel to be called *The Lost*. (In *Christopher and His Kind*, he even offers a scenario he considered using.) Reading *The Memorial*, you can well imagine how it would have turned out: the portrait not of a family this time, but of a doomed society, heavy with drama, clotted with significance, and obedient to the multiple dictates of its ambitious title. But luckily the plot became too congested for him to handle, the characters "couldn't move without getting in each other's way"; so he first of all detached the Mr. Norris material for one short novel, and then at the urging of John Lehmann (the editor of *New Writing*, who was also the instigator of Orwell's career as an essayist) turned the best of the remainder into a series of loosely linked and even shorter narratives. By his inability to do the conventional thing he created his real abilities. It was not that the form of *Goodbye to Berlin*, as the second book ended by becoming, was in itself that new (in a way it is rather similar to Mrs. Gaskell's *Cranford*, or even late-picaresque novels like *Pickwick*, likewise conceived around a society or a group of acquaintances), but that its widespread subject matter is concentrated by the pressure of history. More of that in a minute; but equally important, at the center of it all, is a distinctive narrator: for here in the Berlin stories, in Gore Vidal's phrase, "Isherwood invented Isherwood."

The narrator of these early books is interesting almost to the extent that he is difficult to describe. (I can't help thinking of somebody in a dark bar who, in John Lennon's words, has "got to be good-looking 'cause he's so hard to see.") The literary device of his reticence or, as Isherwood later called it, his "evasiveness," becomes an aspect of character. As earlier noted, he flirts with communism as he does with what his author likes to call his queerness, not committing himself. He is the precise opposite of Rechy's narrator who, the object of desire, positively desires himself. Isherwood's narrator is self-effacing, as if he feels incomplete, but he is fascinated by others. He is one of those people who needs the presence of others to complete him—and they do, giving him so much substance that on occasion he is able to criticize his weaknesses without mercy and make fun of himself. The result is that, quite as much as the Berlin of the title, it is he who tactfully and modestly holds the book together, all the more because a good deal of his specificity is implied rather than given.

The other characters in the book are just the reverse. They are at once sharply individual and casually representative of a time and place. The book is inventive and unpredictable *in continual relation to* the historical record already known to the reader. (When it was first published, Hitler had been in power for six years.) Free agents, they think, but their actions take place in a kind of dance with history, sometimes evading it, sometimes forcibly led by it. A peculiar poignancy and strength is given to the writing by this aspect, then. Isherwood takes on not only the journalistic and fictional tasks of conveying what it is like to be in a particular place at a particular time, but the wider one as well, seeing it from a certain distance, and in its supreme manifestations the writing would be difficult to equal. Its scope may be seen from the start of the last section, entitled like the first "A Berlin Diary":

> To-night, for the first time this winter, it is very cold. The dead cold grips the town in utter silence, like the silence of intense midday summer heat. In the cold the town seems actually to contract, to dwindle to a small black dot, scarcely larger than hundreds of other dots, isolated and hard to find, on the enormous European map. Outside, in the night, beyond the last new-built blocks of concrete flats, where the streets end in frozen allotment gardens, are the Prussian plains. You can feel them all round you, to-night, creeping in upon the city, like an immense waste of unhomely ocean—sprinkled with leafless copses and ice-lakes and tiny villages which are remembered only as the outlandish names of battlefields in half-forgotten wars. Berlin is a skeleton which aches in the cold: it is my own skeleton aching. I feel in my bones the sharp ache of the frost in the girders of the overhead railway, in the ironwork of balconies, in bridges, tramlines, lamp-standards, latrines. The iron throbs and shrinks, the stone and the bricks ache dully, the plaster is numb.

Cold is felt here as a physical and immediate presence, overpowering the innumerable things named—the passage is crowded with *things*. The sensory force of the writing is such as to chill the reader in sympathy. It diminishes our small reserves of warmth, and thus takes from our humanness. The contraction of the cold is to an abstraction, to a *small* dot on the map which seems by reaction to have grown suddenly *enormous*. The fact that the image of the map of Europe, the vast aerial survey, is a favorite one of the 1930s, and particularly of Isherwood's friend Auden, does not take from its effectiveness for a moment. The surveying agent, let us call it a movie camera now, comes in closer, to the plains, an ocean in which you could never make a home, dotted with forgotten battlefields—we are as helpless before the forces of history as we are before those of geography and of the seasons. The agent zooms in to even closer detail. Berlin is a skeleton—and the whole paragraph pivots on a colon, in which we swing round from the metallic skeleton of the city cold with winter to "my" skeleton cold with discouragement, dispiritedness, despair.

There is magnificence in the identification, its claim justified both by the cunning of the apparently plain writing and also by its context in the book as a whole. For the narrator has throughout been at the same time separated from his surroundings and identified with them. His degree of separation and his degree of identification have been the great secret subject of the Berlin stories. Here the Englishman realizes just how far he has become part of Berlin shortly before he leaves it, virtually for good.

In the next paragraph he goes on to speak about the two official centers of Berlin: and then in a third paragraph he changes the word "center" to its apparent synonym "heart"—the heart within a freezing skeleton:

> But the real heart of Berlin is a small damp black wood—the Tiergarten. At this time of the year, the cold begins to drive the peasant boys out of their tiny un-protected villages into the city, to look for food, and work. But the city, which glowed so brightly and invitingly in the night sky above the plains, is cold and cruel and dead. Its warmth is an illusion, a mirage of the winter desert. It will not receive these boys. It has nothing to give. The cold drives them out of its streets, into the wood which is its cruel heart. And there they cower on benches, to starve and freeze, and dream of their faraway cottage stoves.

This metaphor does not diminish or domesticate; rather, it does the opposite. The skeleton is a kind of zombie—it is dead, cold in both senses, and where its heart would be is a cruel absence. The boys freezing on their benches dream of cozy Grimms' fairytale cottages, but they are at the mercy of the "unhomely." This paragraph enacts no sentimental gesture, but takes its place firmly in the action of the book; for these are the boys who will now go on to the bars of the Alexanderplatz and from there to the S.A.—compelled to be other than themselves because outside forces have driven them.

This is surely as good prose as has been written in our time. For all its plain-ness, it has its own defined and various rhythms, rhythms difficult to separate from the sense. The interlocking complexities of situation, from that of a continent to that of an individual, are not subsumed by its clarity but con-veyed by it. A steady attentiveness has brought Isherwood here: he in effect summarizes, but in his summary nothing is lost. Through the transparent medium, each thing, each person presented, is granted its own dignity.

3.

Isherwood's fame is still based largely on the Berlin stories, and probably will continue to be so. That is as it should be: the best known is "Sally Bowles," which it seems can run through as many variations as the story of Antigone, and still be the same in essentials. No matter that in one version the narrator becomes heterosexual and in another bisexual, no matter that Sally, origi-nally described as singing "badly, without expression," is played by Liza Minelli of the robust vocal delivery. Sally has grown greater than her book, joining other mythological characters like Cyrano and Mrs. Gamp and Falstaff, who also have floated free of their original contexts. A myth leads its own life.

50 • THOM GUNN

Goodbye to Berlin was published in 1939, the year Isherwood emigrated
to the United States. Once there, he changed. On the dust jacket of his next
novel, *Prater Violet* (1945), his publishers, Random House, summarized—
and dramatized—the change.

> Christopher Isherwood went into virtual literary retirement after [the Berlin]
> books were issued and...devoted himself to mystical studies while living mo-
> nastically in Hollywood. He became a disciple of the Vedanta Society, a cult
> whose philosophy derives from the ancient Indian scriptures, the *Vedas*. As co-
> translator of *Bhagavad-Gita, The Song of God,* Christopher Isherwood has
> made a genuine contribution to the understanding of religious teachings consi-
> dered by many as almost too occult for the Western mind.

Glibly as it may read, the account errs only in making the conversion sound
perfected. Almost too occult though they may have been for our pitiful Western
understandings, Isherwood's religious concerns were nevertheless to domi-
nate his writing for the next forty years, either directly in the commissioned
life of Ramakrishna and the essays (one of which he himself admitted read
"like the parish magazine"), or indirectly, as in a fiction like *A Single Man*,
which seems at first to be as unreligious as *Alice in Wonderland*.

His last book, *My Guru and His Disciple* (1980), is a sufficient corrective
to the smugness of the *Prater Violet* blurb, being the record of his dealings
with Vedanta, of his religious needs, of his attempts to lead a good life, and
of all the hesitations, reversions, and inconsistencies that accompanied them.
It reads rather like casual conversation, and is so laconic in tone that I didn't
recognize it for the achievement it is until I came to read it a second time. It
seems artless, but Isherwood was never artless. Rather, he had become a master of self-concealing artfulness.

The book is the more unified by its being the story of a love affair, a spiritual one, between Isherwood and the Swami Prabhavananda. The character
of the Swami, in all its credible complexity and attractiveness, is an accom-
plishment that ranks with that of Sally Bowles, though it is doubtful that a
musical will ever be made about him. He is a saint, as Auden grudgingly
admitted, an unexpected and understated one, his religion defined not in
abstract terms but as if inadvertently through his actions and words. To speak
of him so, however, is also to speak of the book's method, which is, precisely,
that of presenting beliefs exemplified and embodied as if inadvertently. Of
course, what the Swami appears so casually may be part of a deep plan. Is it
part of the plan that he seems to improvise, or is it part of the improvisation
that he seems to plan? The same question, which is unanswerable, may be
asked about the design and carrying-out of the book. It may be, further, that
words like seeming and appearing are truly irrelevant when improvisation
and overall design accord with one another so exactly that there is never any

inconsistency between them. In such a context, belief is so lived-in that art-lessness and art become the same.

My account may make the book sound inhuman, even priggish perhaps, and that would be a pity, because it is anything but. There is a sly love of fool-ery shared by both Swami and disciple. They *both* have something of the "play-actor" to them, and enjoy instructing by means of joke and surprise. And like that of actors on a stage, their calculation of effect does not there-fore mean that they are any the less honest.

There is a short passage which may be said to indirectly propose the "poet-ics" of the narrative. The Swami says, after meeting a notoriously promiscuous friend of the author, "What a good man!" Isherwood is at first surprised, but then explains: "When Swami called [him] 'good,' the word had to be under-stood in relation to his statement: 'Purity is telling the truth.'"

The great consistency of the book, then, comes from the fact that in it truth-telling and honesty-with-oneself are not only literary values but religious ones as well. Isherwood was always good—no one has been better—at baring his own or his narrator's pretensions, for example those of vanity, cuteness, smugness, coyness. He had started doing so, searchingly and habitually, in the books of the 1930s, prompted it would seem by a predisposition that pre-ceded his religious interests. (I think of the narrator's scathing self-analysis after his quarrel with Sally over the magazine article.) There are many exam-ples to be found in this last book, of which one of the finest is from a diary excerpt about a visit to his friend Charles Laughton, who is dying of cancer in hospital. Laughton dozes off and Isherwood prays for him that he may have an easy death:

> All mixed up with the praying, which moved me and caused me to shed tears, were the caperings of the ego, whispering, "Look, look, look at me. I'm praying for Charles Laughton!" And then the ego said, "How wonderful if he would die, quite peacefully, right now at this moment!"
>
> It is most important not to make these confessions about the ego as if they were horrifying. They are not—and it is mere vanity to pretend that the ego doesn't come along with you every step of the way; it is there like your sinus, and its intrusions are no more shocking than sneezing.
>
> The really important question is: Why should I pray for Charles? Shouldn't I let him do it? Wasn't I like an agent, trying to muscle in on a deal?

He never reposes in his own correctness, even in the correctness of telling the truth about his vanity. It is still necessary to ask additional questions to pre-serve alertness and to fend off complacency. Much of the virtue of this book emerges from such demonstrations that a ceaseless self-exposure is a religious as well as a stylistic necessity. Art and religion are not, here, separate from the main business of life. There is no clear-cut division suggested between the religious and the nonreligious, and the writer's art must be to work out ways of speaking about them that combine the utmost truth-telling with the skill of persuasion.

In spite of the importance of memoir, Isherwood was a novelist, and referred to himself as such. What does it mean, to be a novelist, when the bulk of your imaginative work consists of memoir in the form of novellas? I just said, harking back to an earlier sense of rhetoric, that he combines truth-telling with effectiveness of persuasion, but that is too general. Clearly, like any writer, Isherwood selected and emphasized in his writing so that irrelevances did not get in the way of what he saw as the historical truth (and we might remember that the young Isherwood was trained as a historian). Of *Mr. Norris Changes Trains,* for example, he tells us in his autobiography that one of the reasons the narrator is not presented as gay is that he as novelist "wanted to keep the reader's attention concentrated on Norris; therefore the Narrator had to be as unobtrusive as possible." All writers, nonfictional as well, have to do this kind of thing. The minutiae of our lives crowd in about us so thickly that we must calculate our ways of presenting what happens, or our account will stifle on its own detail. To that extent, we are all manipulators, but we may at least try to manipulate in good faith. In the event, as we have seen, the narrator of the Berlin stories ends up by becoming a fictional character, someone other than the author. For a novelist, then, the very act of selection may amount to invention. (The historian, on the other hand, cannot allow it to do that, and so in the sentence quoted above from *Christopher and His Kind* Isherwood has to explain why he made himself unobtrusive.)

There are certain specific problems for the novelist with religion on his mind, which may be described in general terms as having to do with the expression of the inexpressible. Isherwood wrote two articles on the subject, both collected in the posthumous volume *The Wishing Tree.* In the more interesting of them, "The Problem of the Religious Novel," he proposes a fiction about the life of a saint, the greater part of which would deal with the progress toward sainthood.

> True, the path of the spiritual aspirant is hard. The mortification of the ego is tedious and painful. But I see no reason for the author to sentimentalize his hero's sufferings or to allow him to indulge in self-pity. Sportswriters find no pathos in the hardships of a boxer's training.

A true novel, then, may be based on the specific incidents of the aspirant's struggles, but the portrait of the perfected saint at the end would be pretty well impossible to do. "The mystical experience itself can never be described." Of course, a traditional method of handling it in poetry has been to treat the union with God through sexual metaphor (Crashaw, St. John of the Cross), but that will hardly work in the kind of realistic novel Isherwood is describing.

The closest he ever came to it was in *A Meeting by the River,* but there he stopped well short of the sainthood itself.

Nevertheless his beliefs were bound to affect his fiction, and I should be more specific about the problems he was up against. The central one here has to do with the fact that the very stuff of novels is that life of attachments which the religious person must ultimately view as bondage. It is that life—the life of the greedy individualistic identity (Sally, Fabrice, Maisie, Emma Woodhouse)— which prevents it from perceiving the *Atman* (the divine nature in other humans), which perception may in turn lead it to the *Brahman* (godhead). In transcendence, even in the promise of it, the novelist risks rejecting all the wonderful specifics of the narrative in which value must, in fictional terms, find its source and make its home.

Isherwood was the ideal writer to present with such a problem, given his relentless honesty and his divided allegiances. In *My Guru and His Disciple,* Gerald Heard says to him with a certain distaste, "What a *grip* on life you've got!"; and yet the book is a record of his attempts to loosen that very grip. The four novellas in which he deals in some way or other with his Vedantist beliefs are, in chronological order, *Prater Violet,* "Paul" from *Down There on a Visit, A Single Man,* and *A Meeting by the River.*

The blurb I quoted, from the 1945 edition of *Prater Violet,* claims that, for all the author's intriguing transformation, "in his new novel…there is no trace of mysticism." This statement must have reassured the potential reader's alarm lest his light reading be violated by an idea, but in fact the concluding pages of the book, in which we come to the night-walk with Bergmann, describe a perception of the divine presence in fully Vedantist terms. It is a great piece of writing, never far from narrative and at the same time never far from exposition. This is the way it starts to combine the two:

> The King's Road was wet-black, and deserted as the moon…. The little houses had shut their doors against all strangers and were still, waiting for dawn, bad news and the milk. There was nobody about. Not even a policeman. Not even a cat.
> It was that hour of the night at which man's ego almost sleeps.

The last statement springs from the locale, describing the ego on the point of joining the other absences: inhabitants, policemen, cats. It initiates a process of mind toward which the whole book has led, too long to quote here, which ends five pages later with "He was my father, I was his son." Out of context, no doubt, the eight words look like mere sentimental assertion, but they have been so carefully worked into, step by step, that they are deeply convincing. Identity is in fact transcended, and what he recognizes in Bergmann, what Bergmann recognizes in him, is the *Atman.* Yet the process is presented without the use of the word, and it is an integral part of the story.

Vedanta and the social life of colony and monastery are directly described in "Paul" and *A Meeting by the River,* yet I do not find either work a complete success. The attempt in both cases is admirable, yet my assent is not granted in fictional terms. In the former I simply don't find myself convinced by the character of Paul, the highest-paid male whore in the world, who loses interest in the things of the world: either too much or too little is attempted with him. Does he briefly achieve spiritual insight? Who can tell? He has a blank at the center, which might be everything or might be nothing. Blanks have no place in novels.... And the resolution of *A Meeting by the River* is achieved through a vision, or a dream, by which Ollie and his brother are brought close. Whereas the closeness between Bergmann and the narrator in *Prater Violet* was effected by a series of closely linked realizations, this one comes from what amounts to an authorial intervention, a *Swami ex machina.*

But *A Single Man* is another matter altogether. The project of the book is similar to that of *Ulysses,* though its total length cannot amount to that of a single chapter in Joyce's book: to take us through a man's day, omitting nothing in it, not even defecation or masturbation. This man was born in England but lives in Southern California, like Isherwood himself, and teaches at a college much like Los Angeles State, where Isherwood had recently taught. At times resembling "a withered boy," he is fifty-eight, about the author's age when he wrote it, and is obsessed with the signs of aging and of approaching death. Not because he is gay (though he is), but because he lives alone, his lover being dead. He literally embodies that legal term, "a single man."

On the first page, we are aware of an odd authorial tone. The mechanics of waking are described with quasi-scientific detachment. The body is presented as a mechanism ("meanwhile the cortex, that grim disciplinarian, has taken its place at the central controls"), but at the same time in a voice of wondering if knowing detachment: how curious and how interesting this specimen is, it seems to say, and though one may know all about the way it works, how unexpected its reactions sometimes are. Finally the processes of waking are completed, and the voice is less that of scientific enquirer than of science-fiction writer: "It knows its name. It is called George."

This absorbed but disinterested observer now gives way for most of the book to an account of George's consciousness, which it records impartially as it follows him through his day. The economy of the book is such that each scene is essential to our picture of George. The concluding sequence of chapters, which he spends in the company of a young and attractive student, Kenny, is done with especial energy and delicacy. The writing has never been cleaner or more eloquent. The day ends with George in drunken sleep, alone, as he has started it, with no male Molly Bloom beside him.

It is at this point that Isherwood calls on his old talent for analogy. Some rock pools on the coast are described: "each pool is separate and different, and you can, if you are fanciful, give them names, such as George, Charlotte, Kenny, Mrs. Strunk." If you are fanciful: he makes the comparison and at the same time evades responsibility for it. Nevertheless, it has been made. The pool and the human identity are each a temporary organization, which by being sequestered for a while resembles a permanent structure of essential attributes. But then the tide comes in:

> Over George and the others in sleep come the waters of that other ocean—that consciousness which is no one in particular but which contains everyone and everything, past, present and future, and extends unbroken beyond the uttermost stars.

(By such words people describe God.)

> We may surely suppose that, in the darkness of the full flood, some of these creatures are lifted from their pools to drift far out over the deep waters.... Can they tell us, in any manner, about their journey? Is there, indeed, anything for them to tell—except that the waters of the ocean are not really other than the waters of the pool?

It is the achievement of the authorial voice in this book that it can accommodate without inconsistency the tones of the reflecting essayist, the scientific observer, and the omniscient narrator as unashamedly Thackerayan puppet-master. In the last of these he goes on to present a hypothesis: "Just let us suppose, however..." What if George dies in his sleep? Again he disclaims responsibility; we are free to "suppose" that George does or George doesn't, but since the hypothesis (like the analogy earlier) has been suggested, it is *there,* on the page, and brings home to us with all the more force that if *it be not now, yet it will come.*

The death is described in the original scientific tone:

> Throttled out of its oxygen, the heart clenches and stops. The lungs go dead, their power line cut. All over the body, the arterials contract.

Bit by bit we watch the body close down.

> And if some part of the nonentity we called George has indeed been absent at this moment of terminal shock, away out there on the deep waters, then it will return to find itself homeless. For it can associate no longer with what lies here, unsnoring, on the bed. This is now cousin to the garbage in the container on the back porch. Both will have to be carted away and disposed of, before too long.

These are the last words of the book, fierce, factual, and yet speculative. What I have to stress yet again is the sheer tact with which the authorial voice has insinuated its analogy and its hypothesis. "Unsnoring" is a word that tells us physically what might be there by its very negation; "associate" quietly and accurately suggests a connection far looser than we regularly assume for the elements of human identity. The effect of it all is double: we are both less and greater than we thought. We are less because we are, after all, mere mechanisms, and because we are just like rock pools, separate collections of loosely *associated* characteristics; but we are greater because the very looseness of the association makes us the more readily part of the infinite consciousness of God. Identity is transcended, as it was in *Prater Violet,* but here far more thoroughly and less comfortingly. The last sentence consists of a firm statement barely softened by the minuscule modification, rhythmical and syntactical, of the final three words—it is bleak indeed. The whole of the book's ending is all the more of a rhetorical triumph in that Isherwood has been enabled by his analogy to make his point about the relation between the individual and God in an entirely unreligious context, and without faltering in the consistency of his fictional terms. No *deus ex machina* here. George has returned to the great ocean, as Isherwood the man has by now. It is a Vedantist emphasis, the main emphasis of the whole book too, made with an exquisite delicacy and in no way that alters the narrative conventions already established.

Everything that Isherwood wrote is worth reading, but *Goodbye to Berlin* and *A Single Man* are the two works which will clearly endure, all the more because they tied into the detail of their own eras. It is surely of permanent interest that reading them we may imagine exactly what it was like to live in the Berlin of the early 1930s or the Los Angeles of the early 1960s. The books are perhaps alike in all their unlikeness through the two principal characters, assemblages of consciousness not completely at home in their respective locations—expatriates who are of an environment and yet at the same time interestingly separated from it. They take nothing for granted: because they are not where they were born and raised, though they have made it their home, they observe it with a fiercer poignancy, they are all the more sharply aware that we are not the same as our attachments.

Wallace Stevens

by Robert Hass

MY NINETEENTH BIRTHDAY WAS ALSO the birthday of one of my college friends. I went to an early class in logic that morning. I think we were reading Aristotle's *Posterior Analytics,* because when I got back to my room a group of my friends was there with several bottles of champagne and I remember that in the ensuing hilarity there was much speculation about the comic possibilities in the title of that treatise. My friend Tom had been to a class (it was a Catholic men's college, St. Mary's) which somehow involved the Latin names for various illicit sexual positions—*coitus reservatus, coitus interruptus, coitus inter femores,* and so on—and this was also the source of a lot of buffoonery that blent nicely into the subject of posterior analytics, and at some point in the proceedings one of the more advanced of us got out the volume of Wallace Stevens's *Collected Poems* in its handsome soft blue dust jacket and read "The Emperor of Ice Cream." I had never heard the poem before and it seemed to me supremely pleasing. It was March in California, high spring, the hills still green, with grazing cattle in them, plum trees in blossom, the olive trees around the campus whitening whenever a breeze shook them, and at some point a group of us were marching through the field full of mustard flowers and wild radish in the back of the dormitory, banging on pans with spoons and strumming tennis rackets and chanting out the poem, or at least the first stanza of it which I find now is what I still have in memory:

> Call the roller of big cigars,
> The muscular one, and bid him whip
> In kitchen cups concupiscent curds.
> Let the wenches dawdle in such dress
> As they are used to wear, and let the boys
> Bring flowers in last month's newspapers.
> Let be be the finale of seem.
> The only emperor is the emperor of ice cream.

57

It is probably significant that I don't have the second stanza by heart. I don't know if I took in the fact that the poem was a proposition about behavior at a funeral. If I did, it could only have seemed to me that morning and afternoon immensely droll. I was a sophomore. I read it as a sophomore poem. The year before in my freshman year—I make this confession publicly—I had taped above my desk along with other immortal lines a little poem by Edna St. Vincent Millay that went something like this:

My candle burns at both its ends.
It will not last the night.
But ah my foes and oh my friends,
It gives a proper light.

I had by the following year understood that it was deeply uncool to have lines of Millay adorning one's room, and had replaced them with something appropriately gloomy by Jean-Paul Sartre, but at that time I took the Stevens line in more or less the same spirit as Millay's, as permission to have fun, to live in the spirit of comedy. I see now that they were in fact probably written out of the same anti-Victorian spirit in the 1920s; they may even have been written in the same year. And Stevens's poem is more or less permanently associated for me with that bibulous and raucous first experience of it. I don't remember for sure what if anything I knew about Wallace Stevens except that he was a modern poet.

I want to come back to "The Emperor of Ice Cream," but let me say a word about coming across a couple of other Stevens poems which complicated my understanding of it. In the fall after the spring I have been describing, a group of us—eight, I think, quadruple-dating—were on our way to dinner and a movie and couldn't decide where we wanted to go or what we wanted to see, and the driver, in a moment of inspiration, said, "Oh, the hell with it, let's go to Carmel and run on the beach." It was a three-hour drive then from Berkeley to Carmel. We stopped for sandwiches and wine; we had very little money, so there was no question of staying in a motel, which meant sleeping on the beach if we didn't drive back in the middle of the night; people had people to notify if they were going to stay out all night. One woman who had a father whom we all hated—an amazingly unpleasant man who actually made his living by running a lab that tested for venereal disease and who insisted on testing his daughters regularly—was quite worried, which made the rest of us feel appealingly reckless. I don't remember exactly who was there. The driver was a year ahead of me in school, famously smart, a philosophy major who at the end of his senior year read a French novel about Dien Bien Phu and, quoting Nietzsche on the true aristocrat, enlisted in a branch of the service I'd never heard of called Special Forces, where he claimed he would learn to parachute, ski cross-country, and fight barehanded in jungles in places like

Annam and Cochin China, which was now called Vietnam. His girlfriend was
Philippine, extremely beautiful, the daughter of some kind of politician, we
understood, and a French major. It was she who produced the white Vintage
paperback volume of Wallace Stevens at some point in the drive and suggested
that we take turns reading the stanzas of "Sea Surface Full of Clouds."

I was stunned by the poem. I am still stunned by the poem. After we had
read around and gotten over the shock and novelty of the way the adjectives
play over and transform the surface of the poem, and had read a few others,
and other books were produced and other poems read, the conversation
moved on, but I got my hands on Marie's Stevens, and after we had arrived
in Carmel and got some more wine and watched the sun set over Carmel Bay
in a light rain, I suggested we read the poem again, which we did—to humor
me, I think, while the last light smoldered on the horizon. Then we tried to
build a fire on the beach, but the rain turned into a lashing Pacific storm and
we spent the night, quite wet, eight of us crammed into the car in the parking
lot, laughing a lot—it was very sexy, as I remember—and making jokes about
cars and autoeroticism. I will start to feel like Kinebote, the lunatic annotator
of other people's poems with incidents from his own life in Nabokov's *Pale
Fire,* if I tell you the story of the lives of each of the people in the car: Marie
who returned to the Philippines and who I know had two children and whose
spine was badly injured when she was struck by a car, Killpack who did go to
Vietnam and then Army Intelligence toward the end of the war and after that
seemed to disappear from sight, another friend who was a classics major and
later managed a café and wrote poems and died of cancer a couple of years
ago. But I will resist, except to say that the poem stays with me in the way
that songs you fall in love to stay with you as a kind of figure for that time
and those people, and their different lives will always feel to me as if they are
playing out in time the way the adjectives of experience play over the adamant
nouns in Stevens's poem: rosy chocolate and chophouse chocolate and musky
chocolate, perplexed and tense and tranced machine.

And there was the incident of "The Snow Man." It was at a wedding at
the end of my sophomore year, of a woman we all liked, large, placid, Irish, a
drama major, and the daughter of the man who conducted the last big band
in the last seedy, once glamorous dance hall in San Francisco in the 1950s,
when dancing to Maury Monohan's orchestra was a city-wide trope for
absurdly retro behavior. She was marrying a guy we only grudgingly liked—
perhaps we were jealous—but we all showed up for the wedding. And at the
reception in one of the rooms of a house that sat over a steep hillside cliff,
one of my classmates announced that he was going to kill himself. I came
onto this drama late and it's still not clear to me how it began, but when I
came into the room, there was a small knot of people standing around one of
my friends—his name was Zack and he was an acting student—who was

standing by an open window. He looked wild-eyed and he was talking to his friend Tony, with whom I knew he had been in the Navy. They were inseparable friends and they cultivated a certain cool bleakness that was stylish then, so that someone of our group had called them the Laurel and Hardy of tragedy. At that moment it looked to me distinctly as if Tony was goading Zack. They had apparently been talking about "the void," the term for nothingness we all used, and Zack must have spoken of his despair, because Tony was telling him with pure scorn that he didn't feel despair because he didn't feel anything. He was always acting, always a fake, generating histrionics to make himself feel real, feel anything at all. Look, jump, if you want, Tony was saying, Who do you think cares? And you know, he said, you might just have to do it because you've talked yourself into it. It was at that point that Zack said, "I feel it." Hitting his stomach: "I feel it. You know the 'nothing that is not there and the nothing that is'? Well, this is the nothing that fucking is, baby." I thought later that there was something like sexual tension between them, and at that moment I thought that Zack really might jump and that Tony was clearly trying to cut off his avenues of escape, but the truth is I was so besotted with literature at the time that I remember mainly being impressed that someone could quote Wallace Stevens at a moment like that.

As it happened, Zack did not jump. The bride, Agnes, came into the room after Zack had climbed out the window and onto the balcony, and she began talking to him and then suggested we all leave, which we did, and after a while they came downstairs together and danced to her father's orchestra. If I were Nabokov, I could leave them dancing to "Have You Ever Seen a Dream Walking," which I have recently read was one of Wallace Stevens's favorite songs and was the kind of song Agnes's father was apt to play, but I'm not and I have some sense of shame. As for the nothing that is, I was soon enough in graduate school, where the discussion of the poem focused on whether or not it was in favor of the pathetic fallacy, which was another matter; and not long after that I had begun to read around in Buddhism and to see that there were other ways of thinking about the void and that what I loved in the cleanness of the writing of that poem might be connected to those other ways. And sometime in that period I came to see that "the nothing that was" was connected to the way the adjectives in "Sea Surface Full of Clouds" played over the nouns, the way that it seemed the quality of things, the accidents (as someone might say who had been dipped in Aristotle) but not their essence, could be known. And I suppose I must have connected that floating thought to the comedy of "The Emperor of Ice Cream," though I don't exactly remember doing so.

• • •

When I was an undergraduate, poetry was much more for me a matter of poems than of poets. But in graduate school I began to acquire some sense of Wallace Stevens. I was never very interested in the Keatsian side of his writing, the wedding cake baroque of "The Comedian as the Letter C." What I loved in him was the clarity. I wasn't against the other so much as I just didn't take it in, and I certainly didn't understand the issues implicit in the two sides of his style. I knew a few poems, and almost as soon as I began to acquire an attitude toward Stevens, various things intervened to qualify my first hypnotic attraction to him. A couple of things that can stand for this change are the civil rights movement and my discovery in my senior year of the essays of James Baldwin, and through him the essays of Albert Camus, which began to awaken a different political and moral sense in me. And also the assassination of John Kennedy in 1963 and the ensuing escalation of the war in Vietnam. I was in a lecture course on poetry given by Yvor Winters when I heard the news of Kennedy's assassination; it was the fall of my first year of graduate study. By then I had some idea of who Stevens was and I had read Winters's essay which, though it's clear Winters thought Stevens was a great poet, nevertheless indicts him for a kind of trivial hedonism at the core of his thought. I was disposed to argue with every word Winters spoke, and I thought he was wrong about Stevens, but not entirely wrong. For different reasons from Winters's, of course. The country we were growing up into—its racism, the violence it was unleashing in Asia, what seemed in those early years the absolute acquiescence of our elders in that violence—changed the tenor of my thinking about literature, and made Wallace Stevens seem much less attractive as a model.

Arguments about him raged in my group of friends. We knew by then that Stevens had been an executive of the Hartford Insurance Company, that he was making good money during the Depression, and lived well. One of my closest friends among the graduate students was Jiri Wyatt, and he was particularly skeptical of Stevens. Jiri had spent his early childhood hidden with his Jewish parents from the Nazis in the attic of a Slovakian farmhouse. He was much more politically sophisticated than the rest of us, and he was very funny and very bright. I remember specifically arguing with him. I was inclined to take Stevens's side. Jiri had gone to school in Boston. He could be scathing on the subject of what he called Harvard aestheticism, a new category to me, and enraged by the idea of a whole generation of English professors and graduate students fawning over the novels of Virginia Woolf and Henry James and the poems of T. S. Eliot as a cover for indulging their fantasies of belonging to a social class that answered to their aesthetic refinement. "They're cripples," he'd say. "Laughable. I mean, my God, look at this century." At Tressider Union under the oak trees in the spring sun. The war was escalating rapidly. We were all listening to Bob Dylan and the Beatles. "But Stevens's subject," I'd argue, "is epistemology." And Jiri, I think it was Jiri, impatiently: "Oh, come on. At some point epistemology is a bourgeois defense against actually knowing anything."

We did know or had heard that Stevens had written a letter to a friend who was buying tea for him in Ceylon, in which he said that he didn't care what kind of tea he was sent, as long as it couldn't be had in the United States; and I took that story to be, classically, an emblem of our relation to South Asia, and thought that its attitude was connected to what I had learned from Winters and Jiri to think of as Stevens's Harvard aesthete 1910 dandyism—not morally repellent, especially because it was so unconscious and so much of its time, but unsatisfactory, not useful. I also knew (it was widely quoted among us) Stevens's reaction to Mussolini's invasion of Ethiopia: that, if the coons had taken it from the monkeys, the Italians might as well take it from the coons. That too seemed provincial blindness, but less forgivable. I also knew—or sensed, it hadn't quite happened yet—that Stevens was in the process of becoming what I think he was not then thought to be, one of the central modern poets.

It was in this context that I began to replay in my mind the lines from "The Emperor of Ice Cream." The first thing that struck me was its lordliness. Part of our pleasure in chanting it several years before had been its imperiousness. Call the roller of big cigars, no doubt a Cuban or a Puerto Rican, and set him to work in the kitchen, where, in some fantasy out of Henry James or Charles Laughton's *Henry VIII*, "wenches" were employed. In 1963 (my students now don't quite believe this), white men of the older generation in the United States still commonly called the black men who worked in airports handling luggage, "Boy." I listened again to the line that commanded "boys to bring flowers in last month's newspapers." And while I was at it, I noticed that "last month's newspapers" was a figure for history, one I feel the sweetness of now. Who cares about history? Let the boys use it to wrap flowers in when they come courting. But at the time—or was it at that age? I was twenty-two; Stevens was forty-three, twice my age, when he wrote the poem—taking history seriously seemed a central task of poetry.

When I tried myself to write poems about history and politics, I had in mind writing a poem about the California landscape and the United States seizure of California after the Mexican-American War, and about the Dow Chemical plant in the southern part of San Francisco Bay that was manufacturing napalm for the Asian War. And I thought vaguely that I would focus that poem on the person of a woman, the daughter of the first harbormaster of Yerba Buena, as San Francisco was then called. Her fiancé had been murdered by Kit Carson in the skirmishes that occurred when the old Californian families resisted the United States expeditionary force. It was a way of writing about the violence in American history; and when I sat down to the poem— which is published in my first book, *Field Guide*, and is called "Palo Alto: The Marshes"—the first line I wrote was, "She dreamed along the beaches of this coast." It was a couple of days before it occurred to me that I had lifted and transposed the first line of "The Idea of Order at Key West," and when I did, I remembered that the name of the fiancé whom Kit Carson killed was Ramon, and it gave me a place for writing the poem. My consciousness of Stevens's poem fell away as I worked, but its starting point is an instance of how polemical my relation to him felt to me in those years. He felt to me as if he needed to be resisted, as if he were a luxury, like ice cream, that I couldn't indulge.

♦ ♦ ♦

Years later, though, when I looked at "The Emperor of Ice Cream" again, I felt much more forgiving of the tone of the poem. I said to myself, this isn't Babbitt fantasizing himself a houseful of servants in Hartford, it is Prospero speaking, as I had read, to his daughter, and speaking in the subjunctive at that. But saying it, one also had to say that in Shakespeare, and throughout English literature, royalty expressed as power over others is a central figure for the power of imagination. And somewhere in those years it occurred to me that the poem is about death, which I thought made it a more wonderful and darker joke than I had understood. And at some still later stage—I think it must have been after reading Helen Vendler on the use of the subjunctive in Stevens, but also after I had had enough experience of failure and disappointment in my own life to get it—I felt the pathos of the wishing in the poem and of the grammar that expresses it, so that by the time I was the age of Stevens when he wrote the poem, the three words "let be be..." struck me as a brilliant and sad figure for the fundamental human wish that seems so often impossible for us, and that Stevens had taken for one of his central themes. And on another occasion—I can remember the shower in which the thought occurred to me, aquamarine tile, the house of a lover—thinking about what I then conceived to be the sadness of the poem, I was wondering about its fundamental gaiety and how it was achieved, and I thought about that delicious phrase that transforms itself from assonance into alliteration, "and bid him whip in kitchen cups concupiscent curds," and lets you know that, at least in language, magic can happen. It struck me suddenly that "bid him whip in kit/chen cups" contained the longest sequence (five in a row) of consecutively assonantal syllables I could think of in a poem. Toweling off, I must have been mumbling the lines to myself. "What are you thinking about," she said. She was wearing a pale, sea-green towel. "I was thinking: Bid him whip in kitchen cups concupiscent curds." "Concupiscent what?" she asked. "Curds," I said, looking her in the eye, trying out an imitation of W. C. Fields, "concupiscent curds."

As I was rereading the poem in the last few weeks, thinking about this essay, I made another discovery. I decided that the crucial thing about it in the end is the rhythm of the first six lines of the second stanza, that stanza I had neglected to take in twenty-five years ago when I was not very interested in hearing about death:

> Take from the dresser of deal
> Lacking the three glass knobs, that sheet
> On which she embroidered fantails once
> And spread it so as to cover her face.
> If her horny feet protrude, they come
> To show how cold she is, and dumb.

This is as pitiless as any verse in Stevens, I think. That enjambment at the end of the fifth line and the stutter of a stop in the sixth deliver the last two syllables as baldly as anyone could contrive, and the rhyme—bum, bum—could not be more hollow. It is writing that returns the word "mordant" to its etymological root. And though I still think it is funny, it seems to me now to be, and to be intended to be, point-blank and very dark. And there are other things to notice. I think my disgust with the class-ridden drollery of the first stanza was not altogether misplaced, but it is certainly undercut by that shabby or melancholy or funny, in any case accurate, domestic touch—the glass knobs missing from the deal dresser. And there is a kind of *memento mori* in the peacock tail that had been—"once," he writes, to suggest the pathos of all our efforts at decor—embroidered on the sheet. And there is also something plain-dealing and very like Robert Frost in the diction: "So as to cover"; and if her horny feet protrude, "they come to show ... " Every detail of the writing is meant to make this death as homely and actual as, what?, not Guatemala certainly. As any death in Emily Dickinson. The second-to-last line of the poem—"Let the lamp affix its beam"—was for a while the only line in the poem that I thought was pure padding. He needed a rhyme for "cream" and a final flourish, hence a spotlight, hence "beam" and the otherwise meaningless lamp. But once you sense how dark, mordant, sardonic, pitiless a reading this poem can sustain, the lamp becomes an interesting figure for the focus of consciousness. It would seem that the beam is affixed on the stage where the final, now supremely ambiguous refrain is going to occur: "The only emperor ... " One paraphrase might be: turn your attention to living, seize the day. If it says that, it also says: by all means turn your attention away from those horny toes. A sort of *memento non mori*. Or, to borrow a phrase from Eliot, humankind cannot bear very much reality. It is also possible to read it to mean the opposite: that one should affix the beam on the horny toes, so that one understands from a clear look at the reality of death that there can be no emperor but ice cream, no real alternative to death but dessert while you can get it. Which is, I suppose, nearer to my first reading of the poem and to what Winters meant by Stevens's hedonism. I think the issue may be undecidable, finally, since both readings are grammatically permissible and both in their way in character.

And perhaps the point lies in the poem's seeming poised on the knife edge between these two attitudes. But however one reads these penultimate lines, they carry their darkness into that last line. Which makes for a very different poem from the one those college boys thought they were chanting thirty years ago as they waded through wet hillside grass in the early spring, and brings it nearer to the nothingness spoken of by Zack, whom I see now and then on late night TV playing a psychotic killer or a gaunt, hunted drug dealer in reruns of *Cagney and Lacey* or *Hill Street Blues*.

It may not be completely accidental that while I was puzzling over the ending of "The Emperor of Ice Cream," a photograph appeared in the newspaper of a pair of stolid Dutch workmen removing a statue of Mikhail Gorbachev (who was briefly and quite literally an emperor) from its stand and carrying it, rigidly horizontal, immobilized in a gesture of seigneurial self-assurance, from Madame Tussaud's Wax Museum in Amsterdam. It made me think also that the poem, if it has anything to say about political power, does so by talking about politics and pleasure and death. And it may not be wrong, in its merciless way, about where power usually resides in the world.

I imagine I am not through thinking about this poem, or about "Sunday Morning" or "The Snow Man" or "Thirteen Ways of Looking at a Blackbird" or "The Idea of Order at Key West" or "Of Mere Being" or "The World as Meditation," which are other poems I have been brooding over and arguing with myself about for much of my adult life. But I heard it early and I've lived with it for some time, and I thought that it would serve for one image of the way poems happen in your life when they are lived with, rather than systematically studied. Which I understand is how Stevens, though he was certainly not against the systematic study of anything, thought poetry mainly lived.

Gertrude Stein

by Elizabeth Hardwick

GERTRUDE STEIN—IN THE MIDST of her unflagging cheerfulness and confidence, she can be a pitiless companion for the reader. Insomniac rhythms and melodious drummings. She likes to tell you what you know and to tell it again and sometimes to let up for a bit only to tell you once more: "To know all the kinds of ways then to make men and women one must know all the ways some are like others of them, are different from others of them, so then there come to be kinds of them."

Her writing, T. S. Eliot once said, "has a kinship with the saxophone." That might be one of her own throwaways, but she would not have used a word like saxophone. The saxophone is an object with a history and she didn't care much for nouns with such a unique signification.

What can Eliot mean? The saxophone was invented in 1846 by a Mr. Adolphe Sax; to this day it has little standing in the hereditary precincts of the classical orchestra. So, it must be that Gertrude Stein is a barbaric and illicit intrusion. Preceding the curiosity of the saxophone, Eliot said about her work: "It is not improving, it is not amusing, it is not interesting, it is not good for one's mind." No doubt, Eliot wasn't aware of the improvisations of the great American masters of the saxophone; it is not quite—O O O O that Shakespeherian Rag—his own jazz.

In any case, Gertrude Stein was born in 1874, thirty years after the birth of the saxophone. Her family and its situation must have been the womb of her outlandish confidence, confidence of a degree amazing. She was, after all, determined to be, even if *in absentia*, or because of that exile, our country's historian.

But there is nothing hothouse in this peculiar American princess. For one thing she is as sturdy as a turnip—the last resort of the starving, and native to the Old World, as the dictionary has it. A tough root of some sort; and yet she is mesmerized and isolated, castle-bound too, under the enchantment of her own devisings.

Confidence is highly regarded by both citizen and nation; it is altogether warm and loving. Without confidence, fidelity to death, as it were, the work Gertrude Stein actually produced cannot easily be imagined. Other writings, perhaps, since possibility was everywhere in her; but not what we have, not what she did. In her life, confidence, and its not-too-gradual ascent into egotism, combined with a certain laziness and insolence. It was her genius to make the two work together like a machine, a wondrous contraption, something futuristic, and patented for her use.

She wrote her Cambridge lecture at the height of her fame, while waiting for her car to be fixed. She sat down on the fender of another car and, waiting around, wrote "Composition as Explanation." Several hours it took her: "Everything is the same except composition and as the composition is different and always going to be different everything is not the same." So it was. And: "Now if we write, we write; and these things we know flow down our arm and come out on the page." Yes. So she told Thornton Wilder.

Many wires and pieces of string went into the contraption, the tinkering, and the one result was that she wrote at great length and used a vocabulary very, very small. It was her original idea to make this vocabulary sufficient for immensities of conception, America, Americans, being perhaps her favorite challenge.

Or, when not tinkering, we can see her like a peasant assaulting the chicken for Sunday dinner. She would wring the neck of the words. And wring the neck of the sentences, also.

She was born in 1874 and lived until 1946, through two world wars and much else. Perhaps she never seemed young, and everyone would certainly have wished her to live on and on, since there is a Methuselah prodigiousness about her. Everything we know about her life contributes to her being.

When was she not a prodigy—and even without exerting herself to represent the exceptional in action? She went to Harvard and studied with William James. Anecdotes appeared on her doorstep, anecdotes quite enduring. No, she didn't want to take an examination because the day was too fine. William James understood and gave her the highest mark in the course, if we can trust the *Autobiography of Alice B. Toklas,* which we can and we cannot.

Premedical studies at Johns Hopkins; that is part of her *aura.* Perhaps she's a scientist, so look, when the pages confuse, for the rigors of the laboratory. She abandoned the medical studies and we must say that too added something to the whole. The willful simplification she practiced can make her, to some, appear to be a philosopher in the most difficult mode of our own period.

It will be said William James taught her everything must be considered, nothing rejected. Simple enough, and not quite a discovery. What you can say is that while she was not learning, taking the action of not learning, other young women were going to finishing schools, primping, dancing, and having babies, and she was becoming Gertrude Stein. Every refusal was *interesting,* a word she liked very much.

Both of her parents were German Jews. Whether she thought of herself as Jewish is hard to say. Perhaps she didn't, or not quite. She didn't like to be defined and that helped her to stay on in Occupied France. Her brother Leo thought of himself as Jewish, even at Harvard—or (why not?) certainly at Harvard.

Her parents were, in terms appropriate for American history, early settlers. That she knew and took in seriously. They arrived in 1841. If, as one can read, the definition of Old New York, of New York aristocracy, is to have made your money before the Civil War, the Steins were aristocrats. The Stein brothers, one of whom was her father, arrived in 1841; her mother's family had settled in Baltimore previously.

A Stein Brothers clothing store was set up in Baltimore with success, but Gertrude's father and the brother moved on to Allegheny, Pennsylvania, where she was born. Then quite soon the characteristic behavior of the family began to assert itself. They showed a desire to take off, for Europe. They are inclined to be Americans abroad.

The family finances are not easy to make out, at the beginning or at the end. But even when the Allegheny store was not quite flourishing, Amelia Stein took herself and the children off to Vienna. There they lived with governesses and tutors, the lessons and practices of the upper class. The Steins early on must have realized that one could be almost rich in Europe at that time without being rich enough at home. And they liked to buy things, to go shopping. The mother and children went on to Paris to buy clothes and trinkets and to have a good time. In a later period, while Gertrude and Leo remained abroad, the older brother, Michael, and his wife, Sarah, came back to stun California with their collection of modern paintings.

From Pennsylvania, the family settled in Oakland, California, and the father, Daniel Stein, went into the streetcar business—a good career move, it would be called nowadays, even if Daniel was not quite the master of it. The father died when Gertrude Stein was seventeen and she wrote about his disappearance: "Then our life without a father began a very pleasant one." But more of that later, about the pleasantness of not having family members and the strain when you have them.

The older brother, Michael, took over the family business, made good investments, for the fine purpose of not having to work. He was able to set up Gertrude and Leo abroad: a princely situation. Michael and his wife, Sarah, were connoisseurs of the new, not of the refectory table from an old monastery or the great decorated urns to put in the hall and fill with dead reeds. For a time they lived just outside Paris in a house designed by Le Corbusier.

In this family you are not concerned with provincials; never at any point in their history. Not one of them seemed afflicted with puritanical, thrifty scruples, with denial or failure of nerve. Works of art were, in the end, their most daring and prudent investment. The paintings, and the great international celebrity of the creative one, Gertrude, and even the fading claims of Leo, make of the Steins one of the truly glittering American tribes. They stand in history, along with the Adams and James families, along with if not quite commensurate. They were immensely important in the history of American taste, by way of their promotion of modern painting in their collections and in their influence in this matter on the many painters, writers, and intellectuals who came to the *salon* on the rue de Fleurus.

The Cone sisters of Baltimore, contemporaries of the Steins, were to merit a kind of immortality when they used their cotton-mill fortune to buy Manets, Renoirs, Cézannes, and Matisses for the later glory of the Baltimore Museum. Acquisition has need of special conviction and taste, but neither of the Cone women could claim for themselves an art to rank with that of the befriended canvasses of Cézanne and Picasso—a claim that gave Gertrude Stein no hesitation.

Picasso, bewildered by the Stein entourage, coming and going in Paris, said: "They are not women. They are not men. They are Americans."

The Stein family was to be *The Making of Americans*. "It has always seemed to me a rare privilege, this of being an American, a real American, one whose tradition it has taken scarcely sixty years to create." There is no doubt Gertrude knows how to look at it, this subject of being American—the sixty years names it just right. An amused chauvinism—that is her tone. And elsewhere she notes that America is the oldest country in the world because it's been in the twentieth century the longest, something like that.

Still, it must be said Gertrude Stein feels more sentiment for America than she does for her fellow Steins, except as a subject. The mother, the Baltimore bride, faded into illness and at last died when Gertrude was fourteen: "...we had already had the habit of doing without her." Simon, older (Gertrude was the youngest), ate a lot and was slow. Bertha, well, she never cared for Bertha: "It is natural not to care for a sister, certainly not when she is four years older and grinds her teeth at night."

The alliance between Gertrude and Leo ended in bitter contempt on both sides. It was said that Gertrude gave Etta Cone Picasso's portrait of Leo in order to get it off the wall. When Gertrude died she and Leo were so greatly estranged he knew of her death only by reading about it in the press. His comment was: "I can't say it touched me. I had lost not only all regard, but all respect for her." They were an odd lot, except for Michael, but then, as she put it herself: "It takes time to make queer people, and to have others who can know it, time and a certainty of means."

•••

Three Lives was finished in 1906, published in 1909—in every way a work of resonating originality, even if no aspect of the striking manner will be carried to the eccentric shape of the works that follow. The stories are composed in the manner of a tale. The characters are sketched by a trait or two and they pace through their lives, as the pattern has ordained; and then each one dies.

Sometimes there is a certain echo of realistic fiction, the setting of a scene, the filling in of detail, but we are given almost everything by assertion and thus there is an archaic quality to the tone. But, of course, the tone is new, partly because of the archaic picturing. No other writer would have composed these moving portraits as Gertrude Stein composed them, and one, "Melanctha," is of a higher order than the other two, "The Good Anna" and "The Gentle Lena."

Nothing is sentimental. We are not asked to experience more emotion than the scene can render; the stories do not manipulate in excess of their own terms. A distance is maintained, a distance—perhaps it is objectivity—that provides a fresh, bare surface for the sketching of the life of the two German women of what used to be called "the serving class," and the extraordinary daring of the picture of Negro life and character in the town she calls Bridgepoint.

"Melanctha" is the most challenging as a composition, and the character is the most challenging because she has an interior life. The presentation is for the most part in dialogue of a radical brilliance, dialogue that lies on the page with a calm defiance. It is as stunning today as when it was first written.

Whether this dialogue is the actual rhythm of Negro speech is not altogether to the point. Such a rhythm if discovered for transcription cannot be copyrighted; no author can own it for a certain number of pages. On the other hand, it is clear that the language of "Melanctha" is some kind of speech rhythm not written down before, some catching of accent and flow the reader recognizes without being able to name. Of course, it is a literary language, constructed of repetition, repeated emphasis, all with great musicality. There is a stilted openness to it; that is, it is both declamatory, unnatural and yet somehow lifelike. It is a courteous dialogue and not condescending because it does not proceed from models, from a spurious idea, from the shelf of a secondhand store.

Inauthenticity is so often remarked when authors need to find a speech for those not from their own class or experience. Stephen Crane's powerful but badly written "Maggie, a Girl of the Streets" is an example of prefab ethnic or class speech. "Hully gee!" said he, "does mugs can't phase me. Dey knows I kin wipe up d'street wid any tree of dem." Hell's Kitchen.

Gertrude Stein's way in "Melanctha" is so simple and arresting that her ear, in an offhand passage, does have a ghostly attuning. Note the distribution of the *yous* in a plain bit of dialogue spoken by Melanctha's father: "Why don't you see to that girl better you, you're her mother." Pure ear, quite different from the formal cadences of Dr. Jeff Campbell, the mellifluent suitor with his high-pitched arias to the "wandering" Melanctha: "...it certainly does sound a little like I don't know very well what I do mean, when you put it like that to me, Miss Melanctha, but that's just because you don't understand enough about what I meant, by what I was just saying to you."

Hemingway learned from Gertrude Stein how to become Ernest Hemingway. Perhaps one could say that. He decided most of all to strip down his sentences. (It is curious to learn condensation from Stein, who stripped, reduced, and simplified only to add up without mercy, making her prose an intimidating heap of bare bones—that among other things.) One can see it in Hemingway's earliest story, written in 1921—before they had met, but not before he would have read *Three Lives*. Perhaps he learned more from the *yous* than from the more insistent rhythms in "Melanctha."

From "Up in Michigan": "Liz liked Jim very much. She liked it the way he walked over from the shop and often went to the kitchen door to watch for him to start down the road. She liked it about his mustache. She liked it very much that he didn't look like a blacksmith. She liked it how much D. J. Smith and Mrs. Smith liked Jim. One day she found that she liked it the way the hair was black on his arms and how white they were above the tanned line when he washed up in the washbasin outside the house." And then he ends the paragraph: "Liking that made her feel funny." Gertrude Stein would not have written the last line. It is too girlish for her, and is a repudiation of the tone and rhythm that goes before.

Soon after *Three Lives, The Making of Americans* was taken up, or resumed, since it had been started earlier. It was taken up—if that is not a contradiction of what it is, a dive into the deep waters of the Stein Sea. Down she went between 1906 and 1908, and the book was not actually published until 1925, for reasons not a mystery. It is very long. It swims about and about and farther and farther out with the murmurous monotony of untroubled, undramatic waters.

The enormous ambition of the book is shown in the roundness of the title. It may be a sort of chronicle, imaginative history, of the Stein family, but that's the least of it. It is the making of Americans just as she says. That is the intention.

In his introduction, Bernard Fay writes, and not without a leaning in the direction of her own style: "She likes too much the present; she is too fond of words; she has too strongly the love of life; she is too far from death, to be satisfied with anything but the whole of America."

Consider her idea of the bottom nature of human beings and it appears to be just that and no more: "A man in his living has many things inside him, he has in him his way of beginning; this can come too from a mixture in him, from the bottom nature of him...." So we live and so we die. "Any one has come to be a dead one. Any one has not come to be such a one to be a dead one. Many who were living have come to be a dead one."

The cold, black suet-pudding of her style: Wyndham Lewis.

◆ ◆ ◆

"The continuous present" is another of her rhetorical discoveries, and it seems to be just a circling round and round, a not going back or forward.

Four in America: not clear how much she knows about her four Americans, how much she wished to know about Grant, James, the Wright Brothers, and George Washington. Her meditations do not run to facts or dates and her vanity would preclude a quotation or even an appropriation. Instead she asks herself what the four would have done had they been other than what they were. Suppose Grant to be a saint, Henry James a general, the Wright Brothers painters, George Washington a novelist.

What is the difference between Shakespeare's plays and Shakespeare's sonnets? "Shakespeare's plays were written as they were written. Shakespeare's sonnets as they were going to be written." Sometimes an interesting bit comes upon one suddenly, like a handout on the street. "Henry James had no failure and no success." Everything is process. There is no need for revision since the work celebrates and represents process itself. Process like an endless stirring on the stove. One gift never boils away. She is a comedian.

Such was her gift and she created a style to display the comedy by a deft repetition of word and phrase. To display the comedy of what? Of living, of thinking? The comedy of writing words down on the page, perhaps that most of all. Repetition as she finds it in her musings cannot be otherwise than comic. She was not concerned with creating the structure of classical comedy, the examination of folly. What she understands is inadvertence and incongruity.

Imperturbability is her mood and in that she is herself a considerable comic actor, in the line of Buster Keaton.

Remarks are not literature, so she said. But the remark is her triumph. She lives by epigrams and bits of wit, cut out of the stretches of repetition, as if by a knife, and mounted in our memory. Her rival in this mastery is Oscar Wilde, with whom she shared many modes of performance: the bold stare that faced down ridicule, a certain ostentation of type, the love of publicity and the iron to endure it.

I like a view but I like to sit with my back to it.

What is the point of being a little boy if you are going to grow up to be a man?

Before the flowers of friendship faded friendship faded.

I am I because my little dog knows me.

Ezra Pound is a village explainer, excellent if you were a village, but if not, not.

Oscar Wilde was an aesthete. Gertrude Stein thought up something more stylish and impressive. She came forth as an aesthetician. More severe and riddling; yet dandyish in her handsome wools and velvety in her sentences.

"Continuous present." Her most valuable continuous present or presence was the alliance with Alice B. Toklas. It appeared she could achieve herself, become Gertrude Stein, without Leo, and she found him expendable. He combined her vanity with a down-turning contentiousness and tedious pretension, all bereft of her revolutionary accent and her brilliant command of dogmatism, her own dogmatism.

But still she pondered ones and twos and twos not being ones and then had the luck to turn a corner and find this small, neat person from California, one with the intelligence, competence, and devotion to complete the drama of the large, indolent, brooding, ambitious sibyl, herself.

They are a diptych: figures gazing straight ahead, with no hint of Cubist distortion. A museum aspect to their image—wooden, fixed, iconographic in the Byzantine style. They are serene and a bit sly in the direct gaze.

Everything works, above all the division of labor. Carl Van Vechten considered that Gertrude couldn't sew on a button, couldn't cook an egg or place a postage stamp of the correct denomination on an envelope. And who can doubt it? Alice's labors over the manuscripts, the copying and proofreading, with a numbing attention to the mysteries of the commas that are and the commas that are not, make of her a heroine of minute distinctions.

The Autobiography of Alice B. overwhelmed by charm and the richness of the cast and the rosy dawn in Paris at the time. The tone and the wit of the composition stand in an almost perfect balance to the historical vividness of the moment. The book is valiant in self-promotion also, boldly forward in conceit, but that is what spurs the recollection. Otherwise it would not have been worth the effort, Gertrude Stein's effort.

She enjoyed the *Autobiography* a good deal more than some of the great personages on the scene. More than one felt himself and herself to be wrongly presented. Matisse was not amused; he charged she knew nothing about painting. Braque was dismayed by her account of the beginnings of Cubism. Tristan Tzara called her "a clinical case of megalomania."

Testimony Against Gertrude Stein appeared in *Transition*. Eugene Jolas, who edited the pamphlet, wrote: "There is a unanimity of opinion that she had no understanding of what really was happening about her, that the mutation of ideas beneath the surface of the more obvious contacts and dashes of personality during the period escaped her entirely...."

No matter, she was now a bona fide international celebrity and had an American public. Books, poems, lectures, plays appeared—and she appeared in person. She returned to America in 1934 for a lecture tour and everyone knew she had said a rose is a rose is a rose. Newspaper men came to the ship, crowds were waiting at the dock. She and Alice were photogenic, and Gertrude was ready with a reply to every question. It is Oscar Wilde landing in the 1880s with nothing to declare but his genius.

She returned to Paris and then there was World War II and the Occupation—tragic, complex events not suitable to her talent and very disrupting to her comfort. Her removal from large events, the hypnotic immersion in the centrality of her own being, made it possible for this very noticeable couple to stay on in France, move here and there, get food, in a sense to brazen it out and be there when the Americans arrived. And wasn't she first and last an American, a true example of the invulnerability of the New World? To be imperturbable, root-strong, can be a kind of personal V-Day.

Wars I Have Seen, ruminating years in the countryside: it reads as a diary, the recording of events of the day. Perhaps it was dictated to Alice in the evenings. The landscape of the Occupation provided splendid vignettes and an awesome and rich cud of complacency. She did not understand the war and she did not like things to be troublesome and so she is increasingly conservative. Both Petain and Franco pleased her—comfort requires order, that she understood.

But at last she had to mull over the question of Jewishness: "The Jews have never been an economic power as anybody knows who knows and as everybody knows who knows. But the Europeans particularly the countries who like to delude their people do not want to know it, and the Jews do not want anybody to know it, although they know it perfectly well they must know it because it would make themselves to themselves feel less important and as they always as the chosen people have felt themselves to be important they do not want anybody to know it."

If it were not for the fact that the reader supplies his own vision of Gertrude and Alice hanging on with the fortitude of lambs hunting for the sheepfold, the whimsicality of *Wars* would offend. "Oh, dear. It would all be so funny if it were not so terrifying and so sad."

She had lived a long time with her wondrous contraption, the Model-T of her style, and sometimes she could run on things with a turn of phrase, but sometimes not. So, she opines, "Soviet Russia will end in nothing so will the Roosevelt administration end in nothing because it is not stimulating it will end in nothing." From the sheepfold, she took up dangerous challenges and offered a work called "Reflections on the Atomic Bomb." She found that the bomb was not interesting.

Anyway, she, the first American, loved the GIs and they loved her. But she didn't know anything about the young men and *Brewsie and Willie* is the aesthetician's defeat. The dialogue is atrocious. She had forgotten that she must fabricate speech, not believe she has captured it at the train station. By now she is speaking in her own voice, just like any other old person, and confident always, she addresses the nation: "Find out the reason why, look facts in the face, not just what they all say, the leaders, but every darn one of you so that a government by the people for the people shall not perish from the earth, it won't, somebody else will do it if we lie down on the job...." And so on.

Finally a strange figure, competitive and jealous and also unworldly in her self-isolation. She could not understand why *Ulysses,* radical and difficult— or so she had been told for perhaps she hadn't read it—why it should have been selling more than *The Making of Americans.* Joyce is difficult because he had in his head more than we know. Gertrude Stein does not ask of us the recognition of a single fact, or the tonal memory of a single work of literature or art; in all her pages there is no reference beyond itself. Still, she has cour- age, the will to be in the world on her own terms.

And then, she is the soldier of minimalism. Minimalism will always recur in the arts as a possibility. She embodies a curious paradox—the loquacity, the verbosity of minimalism. And this too is always waiting in the wings of culture. If anyone should think otherwise, it would be instructive to listen to the compositions of Philip Glass.

Jane Austen vs. Henry James

by Harold Brodkey

LET US START WITH A JOKE, not mine, but Jane Austen's; not a joke exactly: more an exercise of wit. A not very famous, not very rigorous exercise of wit. It is from *Mansfield Park,* its opening sentence:

> About thirty years ago, Miss Maria Ward of Huntingdon, with only seven thousand pounds, had the good luck to captivate Sir Thomas Bertram, of Mansfield Park, in the county of Northampton, and to be thereby raised to the rank of a baronet's lady, with all the comforts and consequences of an handsome house and large income.

Now a more famous sentence:

> It is a truth universally acknowledged, that a single man in possession of a good fortune, must be in want of a wife.

Because these are merely sentences, it is somewhat easier to keep them in mind than it is to keep entire novels and groups of novels in mind. But these are not merely single sentences but opening sentences, and it is a little like meeting a single Frenchman, say, one chosen as an ambassador and meant to represent and introduce a large number of sentences, a population. That is to say, a sentence in a book is not only itself but is one of the general case: one of the elements of a text that is particularly expansionary (something written has always an explosively expansive element in the mind: it grows to the proportions of a stage or landscape or one's experience of one's own life). One way a novel functions is to generate its own generalities intelligibly; this is part of what makes novels didactic and instructive, willy-nilly. (Modern music of the past age attempted to mimic this.) So that, in a good book, an opening sentence is seen, or read, doubly: as itself, and as the first of a category of sentences, a category with a great deal of variety to it; and that first sentence functions like a Rosetta Stone, translating one's knowledge of speech and of other books into knowledge of the language games and systems here in this book.

Novels are the largest chunks of continuous structured language that we have. Criticism directed toward them tends to stretch toward being book length—toward literary theory—in order to deal with them. I will try not to do that. Both the Austen sentences—the jokes—have, if you want to look at them, historically reminiscent qualities; you can, if you want, hear Gibbon and Congreve, Swift, Pope, and Cowper, the ironic historical, actual epic (of the Roman Empire) and mock epic in various forms; and one can hear Defoe and his notion of prose fact. I would assume the young Miss Austen was as well-read as the young Virginia Stephen, who became Virginia Woolf. In writing of a certain quality, the ambition is often present as a driving force of correction of earlier books; and in Austen there is a good deal of internal evidence that she was both trivially and importantly well-read.

The two opening sentences I quoted are literate and impatient, quite complex in their relation to time: we have the generality, or comment; we have the moment in which we read what is written, the real time involved in the act of reading (which is usually swifter than speech); we have an onward momentum of some moment; and we have, in this act of speech and of listening, the time mentioned or referred to (or, in the second example, present by inference) in the story itself—the characters immersed in their time, their age, and in the passages of their speeches and stories. We have, in the onward plunge of our two sentences, a gathering or accumulating of meaning. The rather pronounced hard and soft stresses give a rocking gait, which functions as tempo and which gives mnemonic and structural (or grammatical) aid, imparting a great deal of regularity to the operations of the wit, which concerns itself with human blundering, our sublunary lunacies and realisms and realities. These are accepted in an oddly broad tone and set within the cantering or galloping speed of the sentences.

The irregularity, then, of human things is offered us in relation to rhythm verging on meter, and with a suggestion of absolutes in the tone of *aperçu,* almost epigram. The generality of the statements—Tolstoy does something similar in the opening sentences of *Anna Karenina*—confers a hint of a conviction of meaning in human affairs. There is something Platonically Luminous about the whole shebang, but which is meant to be Christian rather than Platonist.

The penumbral music of the wit—the sense of greed and of the lives and minds of women as relating to greed—and the rhythms of propriety and impropriety in such outspokenness, in such formality and informality, was new in prose. If you read Voltaire—the most successful writer of his time—and then if you read Goethe, *The Sorrows of Young Werther,* for comparison, or

Tom Jones, you can see or feel what it is she did in not being Goethean or Voltairean or Fieldingesque or like Smollett. There are lines of history for novels of other sorts than her sort; but it is from under her cloak that some of Flaubert and some of Tolstoy emerge, and much else besides.

I would attempt to characterize both sentences I quoted above as citizens of the novels they introduce and as *conquistadores* in literature, in which they proceed to occupy and colonize a large tract; and, new in their time, they remain new and conquering still. They propose a kind of speech requiring a kind of attention which is new, which we can never entirely succeed in giving. In a novel, the world happens syllable by syllable. And the author has had some time with the syllables, time which we can never mimic, since the syllables now do not border on real nonexistence as they did for her. In her sentences, evidence of the world is given in a tone which is meaning; the persistent success and half-success of her wit extends throughout the entire verbal and syntactical regions of the sentence and even into the blank space, the silence, the zone of implication at the end, past the end of the sentence. The roller-coaster ride—or rather, the canter; it is a pre-roller-coaster era—its directness and its kind of focus are English, and pragmatic. We are English and provincial here: this is not urban wit; this is not writing from a capital city. But it is provincial in a new way: we are in no way inferior to folk from the capital; we are not without extreme sophistication and vision and a true knowledge of things—even of complex, complicatedly expressive, and partly formal language. The social class placement, the placement in art as well, the modesty and yet the directness, the local Platonism with a claim to a continental or universal Platonism—the ambition—this is new. The truth of statement and the human dexterity of the music indicate that we are in the presence of a voice at a level of artistry within a proclaimed degree of inventiveness so noticeable that it seems (to me, anyway) to be inflected by the spirit of the industrial age. Chapter by chapter, paragraph by paragraph, sentence by sentence, phrase by phrase, she is one of the most inventive writers—inventive structurally and verbally—in prose history. There is little or no cant phrasing and few clichés of any sort in any of her books. She embodies the spirit, if you like, of the factories of England at the time. It is imperialist, such inventiveness and truth, almost military—imperialist toward art; it colonizes art; it is in an English way revolutionary, this voice, this ability, in what it does to art. It is one of the greatest and most important voices in world literature.

If you compare the tone she has to the somewhat pleading tone of *Tom Jones*—its *please read me*—or to the youthfully intellectual, pre-Rilkean, lachrymose tone of *The Sorrows of Young Werther*—its *let us cry over a sad tale*—those worthwhile tones of other created traditions of subsequent lines of descent in the novel —you may, like me, see something particularly central in the Austen, and not simply the switch to a heroine from a hero or to tales of courtship and marriage from tales of masculine education and picaresque adventure, but to social analysis, an analysis focused and steady and dramatic.

And it is done in a tone, a manner, at once healthy and headlong, even reckless, and yet well-regulated in a sunlit humanness of quite extraordinarily unreconciled coldness and acuity—accuracy—of vision. The bitter, financial, financially romantic truth, the apparent correctness of the politico-sexual, psycho-sexual observations is oddly well-grounded, is so couched as to be unarguable, or positivistically sayable; and yet it is quite broadly applicable—it opens toward quite a wide audience.

Her attitude toward the reader is not that of someone trained as a courtier. Fielding and Goethe were courtiers in life and carried that sophistication over into the novel. The great creators in prose and poetry had for centuries largely been court poets and writers and writers in capital cities, aware of and partly educated in court matters, who were trained in the highest contemporary use of language—i.e., at a court or near it.

Here the remarks summon a daily truth like that of *That day the marquise went out at five*, or like that Wittgenstein has in mind when he asks, *What do we say when we say RED*.

The music of the technique—the words, the rhythm, the enclosing music of the effectiveness—amounts to something in an English form, a semi-Platonic tone of pragmatic antifable, real and practical in an Anglo-Saxon manner, with an ungreat Anglo-Saxon greatness to it, literary greatness in a democratic imperial tone: democratic within its class and immodest in its claim to its rights, and imperial in its snobbery (of a kind), in its mastery and control of subject and motion of narrative—and self-willed in the extreme in its inventiveness.

But, notice, she is not using a private tone. It is not the tone of a letter written from the provinces; it is not the tone of religious reflection; it is not a woman's tone of parlor uses, or a woman's boastfulness, as in Lady Mary Montague and Madame de Sévigné. It is a woman's tone, but oddly and not wholly. It doesn't have a particularly indoor sound, as purposefully the voice does—a grim drawing room voice—in *Wuthering Heights*. This is a public tone, but not of political address or outdoor storytelling; and it is not the tone of the coffee house or of the Houses of Parliament or of the court. One doesn't *talk* like this. It is bookish but it is not the tone of letters or of diaries or of newspapers or of military reports. It is not fanciful; it is very factual.

It is a woman's imagined or invented public speech and it takes place in an imagined public space. It is a little like the imaginary halls and stage-like and theatrical recital spaces where poets combat with their predecessors, but it is more imaginary: it has no sense of a streetcorner or of a recital hall. I consider it one of the greatest inventions of literary space ever. It becomes the space of the art novel. It is the governing space of *Madame Bovary*—which may be taken as a considerable revision of *Pride and Prejudice,* say, and which could be subtitled *Actual Provincial Erotic Pride, Actual Human Cruel Prejudice.* It is the governing space for most of Henry James, for Dickinson, and for Whitman. It is the governing space of much postmodernist work. And it is central to modernism—in painting, too. In a visual form, such an invented, provincial-and-central space is the determining element in Picasso. There are other spaces, other traditions as important. But Austen invented this reactive mental space with its discourse held within limits—the limits of the feminine world, so to speak—and these limits supply something like the Aristotelian unities for a nervous century. The whole thing is arbitrary and yet naturalistic and formal both. A version of it, very pure, is to be found in T. S. Eliot's work, especially in *The Waste Land* as it was edited by Ezra Pound. The social world is dominant. The mental space is constricted—and this is part of the drama—but is acknowledged as where the voice is coming from within a naturalistically perceived world which is limited in range, as a woman's is held to be. The unities of place are inexact: a variety of settings are used within a certain limitation and well inside a frame of sticking to the subject. Nothing widens out into the heroic, or descends to picaresque or into farce, or moves into the *bildungsroman.*

In the nineteenth and twentieth centuries, after Austen, we had more women writers of extreme excellence than is true in any other European language—the two Brontës, George Eliot, Emily Dickinson, Christina Rossetti, Virginia Woolf, Elizabeth Bishop. This may well have been cultural, something peculiarly Anglo-Saxon as well; but it almost certainly had more to do with Austen's invention.

There is the presence in European art, after Austen, of images of women in invented spaces—and of women persecuted by invented spaces in their own mind, by their own inventiveness and brilliance. This is partly because she showed how artfully such things could be done: she established the blueprints, the recipes for such characters. And such characters command more brilliant language of presentation and speak more intensely—and brilliantly—than others; and the limits of space and possibility around them consequently enlarge the importance of the mental possibilities of the narrative. Other factors certainly entered in; but let us remember that change begins at one point, and that change initiates further change at once, for which the original impetus is hardly responsible and yet is entirely responsible.

I think that perhaps Austen broke open the sexual harem, but I am not a scholar, merely a writer having a go at this subject. I think the representations of women changed because of Austen, and that women as subject matter and the subject matter of painting passes from the portraits of Reynolds and David through the battle scenes of Delacroix to the Austen-like worlds of the later nineteenth-century artists, the Impressionists and the post-Impressionists, and on to Picasso and Matisse.

Her invention—her inventions—particularly, her invented public space, the space in which she cast the voice of her novels—is, in my view, the first great democratic use of consciousness, a construction of consciousness local and yet literary, Platonically nearly absolute, and, through the literary descent, worldwide in a sense.

Austen's invention—for all I know, her intense appropriation of how her sister Cassandra saw things, or of what some writer unknown to me but of her acquaintance, perhaps a letter writer, may have invented—allowed for a separation of truth from a notion of language experience as limited by precedent. She invented a proper mode of revolution, of innovation, which is sustained in the great writing of the next two centuries: it may be unfairly summarized as *we go to a party* (or do something social and involving a number of voices) *and then we rethink what meaning is and what literature is.* And we need the limitation of parochialism, and the parochialism of middle-class (or upper-middle-class) individuality, for this. Baudelaire's and Eliot's wit and spleen, and inventiveness and careful brilliance of workmanship, and Austen's wit and spleen, and inventiveness and careful brilliance of workmanship, seem to me to be as related as Flaubert's and Austen's (Flaubert's in *Madame Bovary,* that is).

One way to attempt to define, amateurishly, what she did is to say that she elevates honesty—almost as in a Baconian experiment—above literary precedent and artifice. Dickens is truthful but not honest. Dickens mostly emerges from writers other than Austen. The positivism of the novel—the need for a novel to be *right* (usually, or mostly, or entirely depending on the genre of the novel)—requires that most of the events of the novel be taken as true or right or as unarguable; and that the statements made are as often as possible unarguable, either on the grounds of fancy and of comedy, or on the grounds of being acceptable as description. Very good novelists enclose their statements in qualifications and in dialogue; and they use dramatic contradiction and modifications that come about in plot movements as corrections of knowledge. When this is done well, the skill and power with which it is done does tie the art to a precedent, to a kind of truth one associates with art since the Greeks. But part of Greek dramatic and epic art was fated and folkloric and magical; and much art has remained tied to that precedent. Or prefers that precedent. If you compare Austen to Fielding and Congreve—or to *Les Liaisons Dangereuses* and *The Princess of Cleves* and to *Adolphe*—you can see how greatly she is the inventor of the first great common sense *social* novel and you can see how her invention of imaginary space frees her to invent dramatic forms of great width of reference, so that the movements of the characters relative to each other embody truth in a new way—a way unknown to the others, who, rather consistently, must rely on notions of fate and damnation and redemption, of magical intervention. I do not say you will prefer her to the others: that is a matter of taste. But she is a much greater dramatist, a much greater novelist technically. With Austen, you have a well-founded sense of the good sense of the statements you are reading and a sense of the profound wonderfulness of the responsibility of her observation and invention, responsibility of the sort that occurs in the work of Shakespeare and Aeschylus.

Of course, I may be wrong. And I may be exaggerating in the heat of argument. You will have to investigate on your own to find out.

•••

Now I am going to ask you to consider the similarities of tone and of approach to the drama of an opening sentence, and the similarity of the wit or joke—and by that, I mean the tone of unarguability on a secular level—in this compound opening sentence of *The Golden Bowl:*

> The prince had always liked his London, when it had come to him; he was one of the modern Romans who find by the Thames a more convincing image of the truth of the ancient state than any they have left by the Tiber.

The rhythms, the gait are familiar if weaker. The tone of polite and yet presumptuous truthfulness in the Austen has taken on a shabbier aspect of gossip and personalities, an over-elaboration of tone around an arguable observation —certain truths of the ancient state were still more convincing in Rome. And the Catholic church was there. James was writing, perhaps, in a burst of British patriotism, a bit of propaganda. The idiom or usage of London *when it had come to him* is a reversal of *when he came to London* to suggest that this feeling happened to him when he was popular, *when London came to him,* when the thought came to him—the hint is that he was busy and lazy both; provincial; occasionally social. It is a kind of patois, a social jackasserie elevated to something or other. James is certainly a marvelous writer, but this sentence is simply not as good in either of its clauses or in both together as Jane Austen's two, given above. His is not as good English; it is not as solid a piece of observation; it is not of the same order of workmanship. Nor is the meaning it is invoking central thematically to the book that follows it. That said, one can still find it delicious—it is the work, after all, of a master, in his last and most enormous phase. It is not well-founded as observation, but it is wonderful in a certain sad spite it has, which may be central to human nature, and which is a very great thing to portray; and what James does that is so daring and shows such mastery, such sociability, is that he is not superior to it: in fact, it is his—the spite, I mean. There is no generality and no generosity in it and there is no God—this is partly what T. S. Eliot means when he says James's mind was so fine no idea could violate it.

Everything in the sentence is askew, as in a bombed building. The empire we will be dealing with is Verver's and American, not English, not related to London. London is proposed as the center of power here, and later in the book as the center of amusement, rather than Paris. The prince's notions of Roman or English power are not central to the book. James grants the prince no determinative power in the narrative. It would have been better for James to have begun with Maggie, or with the prince in relation to her rather than to London—better, I mean, for the projection of a dramatic context and for establishing meanings. This is an unusually oblique beginning. James usually grants no substantive existence and no potency to men in his fiction, except in their feminine mode—Osmond in *The Portrait of a Lady* as sophisticated malice or Verver, as Lady Bountiful, in this novel. The prince is an impotent figure. I believe that *all* men are impotent in James. James's self-portraits (in that sense), or his predilections in subject matter, do, in the course of each piece of work, give way, and the fictions take on independent life. But they do not retain it to the end in the mind afterwards. The endings tend to be over-determined and cruel in the reattributions of *real* impotence to the men: the male characters are granted their success, if they are allowed any, by women —often caryatid-like, androgynous women, or an angelic one here and there— and by their own efforts never, except their efforts of understanding the monsters, the sphinxes and angels, that James posits.

Here James is seeing through a princeling; this is different from Austen's sarcasm, which is general and outward and not so personal and so inward. Both halves of the Jamesian compound sentence have weak endings. The sentence as a whole works by reference and the boastfulness of condescending to a prince and the evidence then that we—the Londoners of the book and we present admirers of James—are tigers and the prince is not, but is ahistorical, a luxury, something to be not only bought but *entirely* bought: a rarity, I believe, in the titled husband market.

A dry, dull version of James's sentence such as "The prince needed a world capital and found it in London; Rome, being provincial, would not serve his purposes" would not do for James's purposes. The center of the book is not a fact or clear attitude but is a tone suggesting—as if politely—the prince's impotence. The *tone* of James's sentence and not its substance is central to James's pursuits, and that is what some readers in their subtlety find ravishing. Is this a cruel and worldly love letter to the princeling, this book? Tone governing substance is ravishing; it is an act of will and of fantasy; it is usually considered feminine; and it is also, at times (not always), one of the forms— one of the chief forms—that intellectual and emotional swindles take: to give you tone and no substance, and judgments that are not worth much and which will not get you into any trouble, which will not diminish your flexibility in the world.

James here, as so often, is not quite the real thing as a writer: he talks about it so much, about being the real thing, that we know it is a savage issue with him. He is aware. And tone governing substance to the extent that it does in

James is usually held to be decadent or "poetic." The prince went shopping for a life; Maggie went shopping for him. The struggle between prince and heiress over what and who is to rule their life together is not given us. Such a story has substance apart from its tone. Its implications are of a different order from getting the point of James's tone. When you alter or pass over James's tone, you allow the prince some dignity, and not by rewriting or perverting the actions of the book but by returning to the fact. James, here, does not want the fact. The tone does not permit a physical sense of reality; the lifelikeness here is not part of what might be called a full-blooded characterization, but lies in the truth of making everything personal and biased and insiderish and secretive and spiteful and affectionate. The tone, the tone of gossip, is the center of the action, is the central fact, is the objective world here. The music of spiteful gossip is the background as well as the heart of the book, which is about a triumph over such things. James is writing a book with a happy ending (of a kind), and he is writing in very elaborate narrative patterns. His voice originates less sociably and more socially than Austen's, in a smallish, secretive space, a place for urban gossip—he pretends to want an audience, but his voice is not pitched for an audience as hers is. And the extraordinary condescension, the tricks of presentation that make the prince minor and lazy even while he is meant to be the most attractive character in the book—these tricks, which are also a wisdom of a kind, are not for a wide audience. And, as I have been trying to say, they cause the opening sentence to be not even particularly, or essentially, true.

The prince *is* the one the others want—everyone wants him; and his glamour and the life in him enliven the others' lives. He is sneered at and presented in this way to show us that he is nothing much as a prince in the world: he is not the prince that Verver is. This derogation is at once sentimental and a misstatement on James's part. A prince is a specialized creature, as in Tolstoy's and Proust's representations of princes. I think James would be on solid ground if the prince and Verver were in the same field of endeavor—if the prince were a princely young American, an artist of some kind, and Verver and the author were parallel, were novelists. If the prince is not a prince, but a handsome young artist with a fine manner and no real talent—or real talent, but no real reason to deform himself to mine it—and if Verver is a great artist, and Maggie is the emotionally longing daughter aspect of such an artist self, then the book coheres: tones, notions, scenes, opening, and closing; otherwise, not.

That is, I suspect James of being personal in a particular, encoded way in this sentence and in this book. One wonders, then, if beginning the book with a classical reference is an attempt psychologically and aesthetically to deny the claustrophobic privacy of the Jamesian tone and to claim, not the imaginary public space that Austen invented and which is in use here, but a descent from classical art—a claim of descent that Austen circumvented any need for, but which serves to protect James, in his own mind or in ours, from imputations of portraying himself.

James, a sexless man—he mentions in a letter an *obscure hurt*—may be talking here (I think he is) about love and sex, and masculine marriage on a field of common endeavor, between two artists, both male; and Austen is talking about love and sex and marriage on a field of common social endeavor, common social reality. And James's book is fairly open on its own terms about the masculine marriage between Verver and Amerigo, the prince. The secrecies, the encodedness, are very fine—but are, on the face of it, supererogatory. After all, James was—to use a title of my own—telling a story in an almost classical mode: patient Griselda, or Cinderella. In him the classic story is highly modified Austenian rather than Virgilian or Horatian or Shakespearean or French. And James is not Christian, not Dantesque. This is Eliza Bennet and Darcy, but now Eliza Bennet has the fortune, and Darcy lacks sexual probity and is entangled with Mr. Bennet, who marries an old girlfriend of the prince's.... One of the problems for James is that he cannot do desirable characters except as sinister beings. He refuses to desire them, or he cannot, and so we have trouble doing so, and we lose track, then, of the issues of the tale. To judge him on this is to say, yet again, his story is immured in, anchored in, consists mostly of *tone*. We can ask: is James's *tone* wise and knowing or petty and self-loving? I think it is both, and that this is flirtatious and offers us an alternative to living the story or identifying with it: we can watch him being an artist instead. But we cannot relax and accept his mysterious story—we cannot *watch* it happen.

James's subject matter is always, I think, sexual nonexistence, sexlessness, in a sexual universe but in a social world that he suggests is mostly sexless. He cannot do the reality of people who are not sexless, who desire and are desired. He does sexlessness observing or being victimized or triumphing over sexual people. In James, it is sexlessness judging the world—it is sexlessness at large in a universe which has meaning only for the sexual soul. Some readers find that James cannot be read when their lives are boiling along with feelings and serious event. Do you have to be in a deadish state to appreciate the master? Some say you can't be young and you can't be old: the young need more life and the old require more heat, and more evidence, and are short of sympathy for someone who never threw his life away.

James, in a very particular sense, is the master for those in the middle of their lives who are working hard and who are trapped and perhaps not very alive—he is the careerist's master in an admirable sense. And no matter how invidious I become, he is a very, very great observer of human beings. It is just that that observation is off and on, and is not part of the narrative structures of his novels, his données and his course of events.

◆◆◆

Well, but he is a master. Granted, that in James there is no war of voices, no ventriloquism; granted that his arguments seem solipsistic and dismissible, past their aesthetic dimensions, as mere remarks by an opportunist; granted that the alternations within his repertoire—avuncular tones, hasty tones, orotund tones, exact tones, dramatic tones, comic tones—remain unlike Austen's, within the limits of the one overarching tone of a storytelling (and inspired) gossip. (Here let us point out that Pound—a despicable man, but the greatest judge of talent of his time—said that a novel is gossip that stays interesting; and let us point out that Faulkner is Jamesian, by the by.) Let us still celebrate him as a master, and let us then admit that part of Austen's great invention was in the portrayal and even perhaps the further invention of a kind of sexlessness for the sake of one's well-being, not for a spiritual reason but for the sake of reward—at least, a form of sexlessness, a self-control, perhaps even self-deformation.

Now, by sexless, I don't exactly mean sexless. Words are damned odd and skittery. I mean something comparative, something like unsexed or desexed—the sort of thing Lawrence and Forster (and a number of others) attacked as life-denying. A form of what I mean lies in the *sexual terror* and sexual distaste mapped by Eliot and treated with amazingly simultaneous obscurity and clarity by Hemingway (and treated pictorially by Picasso). A religious—or religious-old—version of it is in Tolstoy's self-castigating diaries. Dostoyevsky has brilliant versions of it often perversely set in his soft-focus portraits of whores. But he and Tolstoy—and Picasso—do not propose sexlessness or sexual defeat and sexual terror in the English fashion.

James's is an invented female voice, extremely intelligent, entirely self-involved in a disguised way. Austen manages to be everyone. Austen's tones are greatly varied, like Tolstoy's—a party tone, a quiet tone, a tone of longing—and other voices constantly intermesh with and interrupt hers, and the intruding voices are genuine. She does not suffer technically in comparison to Tolstoy. That she doesn't, and the fact that she does voices and James does not (and that T. S. Eliot commented in a way on this matter of voices), need not be a ground for final judgment. Let us compare her sexlessness to James's. She posits it as choice, spinsterishly, or as semi-choice, or as morality, or as good sense; and she places it in conflict with, or versus, sexuality openly. Her sexlessness is at war with the immoral universe, and is a (she says or implies) Christian device—that is, she proposes it, not as fate, but as self-control and faith.

I think it is this in Austen that often frightens people. She is a rather great pre-Tolstoyan prophet. She does insist that most of what happens to you is your fault. Hers is a different sexlessness from James's, more like that of a child or an adolescent than like that of a wounded and frighteningly social man who has no sex, who is sexually damaged, who is, perhaps, sexually deranged. Certainly his rhetoric is more androgynous than hers. Austen's novels, truthfully or not, give us a set of self-controlled heroines, damaged by problems in their minds and by social realities; but these women are not sexually cowardly or defensive or, seemingly, sexually inexistent. They are as sexless as they are, she seems to say, because they are so responsive once they start to respond. Independence of mind and fineness and a release from ordinary destiny depend on their sexlessness. We never quite know, but we can suspect that they have feelings other than distaste or rage toward the sexual act.

Austen lived at a time when childbirth was dangerous, and families failed if the women did not manage to live, if there was no maternal continuity or presence. I believe that she is the first to explore the subject of sexlessness as not martyrdom but its opposite. In *Tom Jones* and *Clarissa* everyone is more or less sexual. I also think the subject as Austen presented it to us, and which became so important in English, is not as determinative in other languages as it is and has been in English since Austen. Consider how few of the great women writers in English, in the last century and in this, were married, how few were not lesbian or partly so—and that none of them had children. I, of course, omit living writers from this consideration. Then I ask you to consider the forms this subject takes in Dickinson, Whitman, Lawrence, and Woolf. Baudelaire and Tolstoy assume a sexual existence, as do Flaubert and Chekhov. As does Proust. Thomas Mann, however, treats sexlessness in various forms, more often as innocence and fragility than not. But *Death in Venice* is his, in a way, most English novella, is his most pronounced Austen-James meditation on the subject.

In *Mansfield Park* Austen begins by introducing a character she despises for having never been more than sexual. Is she as rude as James is in his introduction of his princeling? Austen deals with the facts of the matter—a Jamesian phrase—and the contempt she feels toward the woman who was once sexual but had no other worth is balanced against the woman's standing and power now: and the events of the book, and Lady Bertram's voice and actions, bear Jane Austen out about the woman's life and mind. James's characters surprise but they have no inner laws of being—they have tone and perversity instead. In *Mansfield Park,* as in *The Golden Bowl,* some very attractive people are counterset to some less attractive people; but where in Austen the glamorous young are intent on throwing away their lives, in James they are construed only as sources of pain to the sexless. Austen places against her various sexually temperamental characters a serious heroine, Fanny Price, whom few readers like until the end of the book, if then—but she is a heroine and she is rarely wrong: if she were not long-suffering she would not be so right. It really is a quite frightening book. And Miss Price is sexless. Her apotheosis comes through her being morally and politically apt and stubborn and untouchable.

Maggie Verver's triumph comes through the power of love backed by a very large fortune. It would seem Austen is more adroit, more interesting, than James here, at least if James means us to take his story seriously. And he may not. He may be intent on parable or allegory and codification. I said earlier, and I repeat, that James is not artist enough to give us *a* prince—or *the* prince—in dialogue and actions, socially or sexually. Again I say: see the princes and princelings in Tolstoy and Proust for comparison. James's prince is dealt with in terms of gossip about him, which is clever but lifeless and, in the end, irresponsible. The essence of art is that it does not ever consist of a single voice without some evidence beyond that voice: art involves at least one convincing voice plus at least one other genuinely existent thing. Not to be able to create the personal reality of the prince is a suffocating aesthetic flaw. James does not love enough to be able to picture the object of love—and we are not given a monstrous love in Maggie for the decadent prince, as we are given a monstrous affection in Charlus for Morel. Because of the misdrawn figure of the prince, we do not believe in Maggie's love—or in the prince's villainy.

And James is so smart that he does not want us to, except as a transcendent thing, as a matter of social sympathy on our part. Something in him wants this love to be read as a fictional act—an act of an artist, just as Austen wants us to read her books and accept the acts of her women as common-sense acts when actually her women are quite visionary and are nearly martyred in most cases and are artists in their intelligence and obstinacy and readiness and their opinionatedness. I would like to propose, not entirely mischievously, that James's novels *The Ambassadors, The Wings of the Dove,* and *The Golden Bowl* can be read as relating indirectly James's history of sexual romance and attachment at the end of his life. In the first novel, a sexless bystander comes to accept the idea and romance of sexuality—if it has sufficient style. In the second novel, the sexless person is embroiled and is the center of the tale, the self-sacrificial victim of the others, but the ultimate victor in terms of the imagination and of moral eminence—as a writer might be said to be. In the last book, a complete personal and sexual triumph is presented to the sexless over the sexual. Well, why not?

Austen's suspicions of sexuality are better founded than James's. The right of women to live a mental existence is not quite the same as the right of the hard-working and sublimely talented sexless to rule over the sexual. Austen is full of emotional violence—one critic speaks of her "well-regulated hatred"—but she is not a bully and James is. Sexuality is very hard to define—whether it is a bullying thing or isn't, for instance: *if a man does not bully you, he doesn't love you,* is an aphorism in a dozen languages; certainly bullying has something to do with desire. But sexuality has to do with the validity of this world as we find it. One might say that sexuality represents a successful bribe on the part of nature—and so Tolstoy presents it. Flaubert and Proust are excessively bitter about it but they accept it. Certainly the bribe is not successful with all of us to the same extent, or equally from week to week or year to year. It can also be defined as the mode, other than parental or blood-similarity, by which we are attached to each other past the point of being able to perform casual betrayals—although perhaps spiritual or congregational bonds are sufficient for that in some of us.

Both James and Austen in their last books—*The Golden Bowl* and *Persuasion*—are at their warmest, whereas earlier they deal chiefly in notions of betrayal and insult. If we add a quantifying clause to our notion of sexuality, we might say: to the extent that we prefer to die rather than see the other seriously harmed—or some sliding scale related to that value of the other person—we love. The definition of sexlessness might be that it prefers death, its own or that of the beloved. Of course, these feelings might be familial. Austen deals directly with the lines of self-sacrifice and when to deny them. James is utterly melodramatic—and unreal—on the subject. The nonsexual attachment he says is sacrificial I believe is not: he is obviously lying (see *The Wings of the Dove* and see what you think). Austen accepts this sacrificial quality to love, but she argues we can control ourselves and love intelligently—we need not sacrifice ourselves to fools. Flaubert and Tolstoy are considerably harsher, Flaubert harsher than Tolstoy. James finds a great many substitutes for love. He is like someone who substitutes money for everything else, except he substitutes artfulness, cleverness, social genius. It is almost enough. After all, Proust does it successfully. The greatest of all novels so far is loveless and sexless—in a way. There is a general love and a general sexuality.

I think Proust shows the major techniques of the novel to be both relativistic and positivistic in combination—grotesque and subjective and factual and sunlit. James cannot qualify as a master of the major techniques, and Austen can. James cannot establish the positivistic frame or justify the relativistic grotesqueries and fantasies he proposes, but he does not entirely need to: his claims and his sense of others proceed often enough in the realm of fable or of art that he escapes any arraignment of real failure on his part. But it is interesting that only in these last books of his, these last hiddenly romantic books, does he become interestingly inventive syntactically. If you glance through Austen you will see the prototypes for most of the various kinds of Jamesian sentences except for some of the sentences of wonderfully high rhetoric in his last three books. That is, Austen's mental grounding, her notions, did allow her to innovate from the beginning, while James, great as he was, does seem to be limited to stirring the ashes.

Why does newness matter? Newness matters because why not otherwise read only the old books? If you compare Molly Bloom to Elizabeth Bennet and Fanny Price and Anne Elliot you will see that the imaginary space from which Molly's thoughts emerge into speech via Joyce is Austenian, I think,

although it is very sexual. And James cannot adapt in that way; he is an observer of *that,* too, a bystander toward literature as well as to life—and that
is his greatness.

Proust, a voyeur and bystander openly, is, in his socio-moral notions, and
in such devices as the little train, Austenian. And Proust is never successfully
sexual in his book (he is probably, on the evidence of *Contre Saint-Beuve,* too
ashamed). But the wake and traces left by sexuality in the Proustian novel are
accurate or don't matter—that is, sexuality is not central to his claims.
Shame makes him dishonest to his life, but he is honest within the frame of
his novel: honest bystanderhood and honest suffering are central to his claims.
And that is precisely what James, in his disguisedly autobiographical late
fictions—or fables—will not settle for. He claims a romantic knowledge and
a personal power he has no right to. It is self-indulgent of him. It is not James's
doctrines or his life or his tone as an artist or his degree of artfulness that I
object to, but merely the plotting and the working out of his meanings as he
sets them forth in his art. His references to things, his depictions, his altera-
tions of geographical reality, of psychological and social topographies and
sequences, are marred by too many lies for such a yet very good book. Liars
do not make the greatest novelists. They may be the best people and the most
truthful in real life, where truth is so often cruel and a lie is a truth of affection
in the moment; and they may be the best friends—but they are not the best
novelists. Novel writing is a truth-telling proposition with (highly) relative
dimensions: the grotesque realities of people and of mental space *and* a shattering factuality are at the heart of the novel. The novel is an enterprise having
truth as its starting point and with truth as its ending; and in between it is a
truthful journey. It is a study in truth about people, about moments, actions,
feelings, and ideas and ideals.

Now what is it in the tones and music of Austen's narrative procedure and
intelligent comment that is unusually unarguable—so seemingly truthful to
such a degree? Why aren't her wit and certainty merely didacticism—or a
mannerism of the age? Furthermore, how can it be truth in "an imaginary
space" and in an invented voice and in formal structures that have no truthful
or complete origin, only a willful, aesthetic origin? What makes her omissive
omniscience acceptable? We know that she knows what she is talking about;
part of the acceptability in Austen of what is so omissive an omniscience
comes from the consistency of emotional topography that she presents and
the convincing consequences she invents: we suspect reality is there. In a recent novel a character, a woman, was said to be "disadvantaged," to have
never been looked at with love although she had slept with a number of men
and often. But in real life, if that were true, it would mean that here was a
woman who was very unpleasant sexually, who was even sexually appalling
and unable to learn from sexual experience, or who refused sexual existence—
or how could such a statement be true of her? Another novel postulated a

woman who mistook the lifelessness of a dying raccoon for affection, for a desirable friendliness. If the ebbing of vitality in death is what you want as animal friendliness and peaceful regard, then it is not surprising, as in the book, that the man she said she loved avoided her. We do not necessarily reason about these literary "facts" that are offered us as we read, so much as we have a sense of untruth, of special pleading and denial of the truth, somewhat in the Jamesian mode but far more extreme. Or we have a sense of psychological estrangement from art, a sense of the disqualifications of the author, which may please us by releasing us from any need to take her or her art seriously as a conduit of truth.

In Austen we are never, so far as I can recall, given such unacceptable facts and asked to accept them. James does it frequently (although never to the extent of entire disqualification): in *The Golden Bowl,* old Verver is presented to us as a good, kind, self-made billionaire. James is nicely obscure about it but it still won't do. In Austen, Knightley is good to his tenants. Who is Verver good to? Maggie and Verver are presented to us without their egos; and the prince and Charlotte are presented to us without their virtues. It's amusing and it is sophisticated but it is not pure-souled with the truthful corruption of the best stuff, of the best art. It is the stuff of fairy tale, a fable with naturalistic elements. Austen is attached to a kind of novelistic and formal optimism which might be fable-like. Her early death and her last book undercut some of the merit of what she argues in the earlier books. Where James is ambiguous and his narrative power too often rests on a sense of fable—of advertising—Austen is clear and open-ended. By open-ended I mean Austen is shrewd and clear-eyed and always gives us an open-endedness in events. Her tales are not made of events cast in iron as if by folkloric retelling; her stories are not known in advance, and her people and marriages are not fated or destined; everything can blow up in an instant. Everything rests on character and sacrifice but is subject to surprise and accident—and to the operations of will and futurity in what might be said to be, or to seem, a normal way. Will and heroism in James are highly melodramatic and are portrayed as fabulous. His system of representation lies a bit about the unknown thing that rests at one edge of real minutes and which the real minutes spill and upend on us as they proceed, whereas Austen accepts the unknowability and accidental and contingent nature of things in a rather pragmatic way, rather like Tolstoy—who got it from her, perhaps. The degree of the reality of the time sequences, the way the events seem to happen in real time, is interestingly similar in Austen and Tolstoy.

Austen is extremely difficult to write about. She is the first and most direct of the unfated or free will writers of the industrial era; and who wants to argue about free will or the industrial era? She is among the elect, among the writers of surprise and of real-time amatory events. Her lovers make their own fates. They are active and dramatic entities. Tolstoy steals a scene from her, from

Persuasion, to represent realistic and actual love in *Anna Karenina:* the proposal scene between Kitty and Levin is taken in great detail from that of Anne Elliot and Wentworth.

For many years in this century, *Pride and Prejudice* was the best-selling book in England after the Bible. We might expect that Austen's influence would not be much studied, since she is a woman and we are chary of ennobling women in certain ways (while we ridicule them with exaggerated ennobling in other ways); and she is a largely sexless moralist, so that only a moralist would be comfortable studying her; and she is very good, which is very daunting. In the mid–nineteenth century Macaulay said that in terms of the convincing creation of numbers of characters—the honorable and aesthetically effective portrayal of human beings, persons—she was second in English only to Shakespeare. That is likely to be the case still. I take her to be in the line of Homer and Tolstoy, and Shakespeare—considerably more limited, but not to the extent you might expect—a maker of sunlit epics in which people are pictured with a wholeness of effect remarkable for the power of representation. This is a strange, rare talent. Words do not automatically represent things and do not automatically suggest human presence. Firstly, words are not exact quantities of sound or meaning; they are areas of attention which we scan, often racingly, in context, and always only in a context of some sort. And it is very difficult to describe how words function as what they are *not* in order to be slidingly what they are. The difficulty in any boundary of definition is the inherent suggestion of what is not being said: to make a comparison as I have here is also to argue that comparisons are foolish and not useful, for instance. Deconstruction follows on definition. The creation of characters has a highly dramatic element of the loss or dissolution of those creations. Words such as *great* and *greater* mean what they do slidingly, in context. What they purport to represent, what they falsely claim, or do successfully represent, is very odd. Austen's tone of antifable is a claim of reality paradoxically supported by the rigor of her formal classicism, sometimes false, sometimes true. But she is very clearly one of the very great heroes of the novel, one of

Fame's Boys and Girls, who never die
And are too seldom born—

In Defense of *Daniel Deronda*

by Christopher Hitchens

IN THE COURSE OF HER LIFETIME, George Eliot had always to confront those who distrusted or suspected her seriousness. If this seemed an ironic reception for a respectable and educated woman at the height of the Victorian age, how much more so it should seem to us, equipped as we are with all the glib means of decoding the unacknowledged contradictions of that epoch. We are supposed to smile knowingly when we read John Fiske, American disciple of Herbert Spencer, as he writes home to his dear wife, having met the lady authoress just after her fifty-fourth birthday in 1873:

> I never before saw such a clear-headed woman. She thinks just like a man, and can put her thoughts into clear and forcible language at a moment's notice. And her knowledge is quite amazing. I have often heard of learned women, whose learning, I have usually found, is a mighty flimsy affair. But to meet a woman who can meet the ins and outs of the question, and not *putting on any airs*, but talking sincerely of the thing as a subject which has deeply interested her—this is, indeed, quite a new experience.

This little demonstration of the limits of positivism comes down to us—doesn't it?—as an example of period condescension. Yet the tendency to condescend to the wife of Mr. G. H. Lewes outlived the 1870s and in many respects persists to our own time. Virginia Woolf, perhaps thinking that Mrs. Lewes needed more money and at least one room of her own, anxiously wrote that her early life of filiality and connubiality had cut her off from experience and that "the loss for a novelist was serious." Added Mrs. Leonard Woolf, as if sighing for what might have been: "She is no satirist."

Marcel Proust, in his *Contre Saint-Beuve,* achieved magnificences of unbending, awarding George Eliot many points for moral *hauteur,* dwelling upon her affinity for the humble in station and her sense of duty before electing to praise her for "A conservative spirit; not too much book-learning, not too many railways, not too much religious reform." He also approved her "sense of the uses of suffering."

Dr. F. R. Leavis, the incarnation of that collision between English literature and high tasks and values which has left so many shattered bodies by the wayside, took longer to uncurl his neck and made, as ever, tremendous use of the awesome "we" and the inclusive "us." Giving George Eliot a beta alpha for her sympathetic rendering of the mental atmosphere at Cambridge (an atmosphere that she had had, as a woman, to imbibe at secondhand by close questioning of Sir Leslie Stephen), he calls the evocation "characteristic of the innumerable things, by the way, that even in George Eliot's weaker places remind us we are dealing with an extremely vigorous and distinguished mind, and one in no respect disabled by being a woman's." Leavis penned this qualified encomium as part of his very reserved treatment of *Daniel Deronda,* George Eliot's last novel and the one which the critics have been most united in deploring—for its alleged vices of affectation, contrivance, strenuousness, and even piety ("the wastes of biblicality and fervid idealism"—F. R. Leavis). I think that the novel can and should be defended from the faint praise and outright sneering which have been directed at it, and I believe that George Eliot's right to be serious can be upheld without any implication of the tedious or the merely didactic.

In his terrible book *Victorian Novelists,* Lord David Cecil reviews George Eliot without one single mention of *Daniel Deronda* but nonetheless manages to say of her that, "like all Victorian rationalists, she is a Philistine.... Constructed within so confined an area of vision, it is inevitable that her criticism of life is inadequate. Compared to Tolstoy, it seems petty, drab, provincial." The last sentence here is like the clutch of a drowning and floundering man. Compared to *Tolstoy,* after all, even the whinnyings of the endless Cecil family seem provincial. To be *comparable* to Tolstoy, who regarded even Shakespeare as a buffoon, is not the disgrace that Lord David seeks so hastily to imply.

In point of fact, George Eliot was neither a moralist—in the sense intended by Lord David—nor a philistine. She is the instance *par excellence* of a woman who took religion too seriously to take it seriously—of what might now be called a freethinker or agnostic. She found the discovery that religion and morality are ill-connected to be a shattering and disturbing one, and she operated as a sort of register of this well-known contradiction. In *Felix Holt, The Radical,* she deals in the first few chapters with book learning, the coming of the railways, and the essence of religious reform (notice that if Proust doesn't get her, Lord David will); and when Harold Transome comes home from a spell of primitive accumulation in the Middle East (at Smyrna, then still the home of Greeks, Jews, and Armenians) and repudiates the Tory ticket, his stricken mother takes it poorly: "There were rich Radicals, she was aware, as there were rich Jews and Dissenters, but she had never thought of them as country people."

In other words, George Eliot had taken the measure of the moralists and philistines of her day by 1866. It was precisely those who, privileged as they were, yet chose to remain "constructed within so confined an area of vision" who aroused her scorn and impatience. By the time that she undertook *Daniel Deronda* she was equipped for a far more thorough settlement of accounts than had been necessary to see off Mrs. Transome.

I suggest the words "undertaking" and "equipment" with a perfect awareness that these are ponderous terms connoting worthy and weighty purposes. But, although she hoped to accomplish something in the world of thought with *Daniel Deronda*, George Eliot was by no means prepared to sacrifice her art to the bearing of a message. In the figure of Gwendolen Harleth, she has provided a central character of uncommon depth and versatility. One is forever being impressed by the resources of this young woman, as she confronts the inescapable dilemma of all Victorian heroines—her marriageability. See how she varies her strategem and her rhetoric:

> "I am aware of that, uncle," said Gwendolen, rising and shaking her head back, as if to rouse herself out of painful passivity. "I am not foolish. I know that I must be married sometime—before it is too late. And I don't see how I could do better than marry Mr. Grandcourt. I mean to accept him, if possible." She felt as if she were reinforcing herself by speaking with this decisiveness to her uncle.

And then, being both more and less artful with her mother than she had been with the good Rector:

> The cheque was for five hundred pounds, and Gwendolen turned it towards her mother, with the letter. "How very kind and delicate ! " said Mrs. Davilow with much feeling. "But I should really like better not to be dependent on a son-in-law. I and the girls could get along very well."
>
> "Mamma, if you say that again, I will not marry him," said Gwendolen, angrily.
>
> "My dear child, I trust you are not going to marry only for my sake," said Mrs. Davilow deprecatingly.
>
> Gwendolen tossed her head on the pillow away from her mother, and let the ring lie. She was irritated at this attempt to take away a motive.

These moments, in which a young woman has to face her own lack of resources while retaining pride and strength of mind, are imperishable. Gwendolen's consciousness, furthermore, is very much that of a woman who knows what she may be missing—an insight that Virginia Woolf, perhaps, credits too little in the life experience of the author.

The portrayal of Gwendolen is not, of course, objected to by any of *Daniel Deronda's* critics. In fact, Leavis suggests that the novel should be retitled *Gwendolen Harleth,* and all the tiresome Jewish and religious material excised from it. Henry James, in the person of Constantius in his "Daniel Deronda, A Conversation," made a similar plea: "I say it under my breath—I began to feel an occasional temptation to skip. Roughly speaking, all the Jewish burden of the story tended to weary me...." "Roughly speaking" is not a habitual Jamesian mode of address, to put it no higher. But it seems intended here to be the approximation of James's own reaction. Constantius goes on: "All the Jewish part is at bottom cold; that is my only objection." Having professed himself so unmoved and so uninterested, he nevertheless adds, after some fairly wretched verbal fencing with the ladies:

> The universe, forcing itself with a slow, inexorable pressure into a narrow, com-placent and yet after all extremely sensitive mind, and making it ache with the process—that is Gwendolen's story. And it becomes completely characteristic in that her supreme perception of the fact that the world is whirling past her is the disappointment not of a base, but of an exalted passion. The very chance to embrace what the author is so fond of calling a "larger life" seems refused to her. She is punished for being narrow and she is not allowed a chance to expand. Her finding Deronda pre-engaged to go to the East and stir up the race-feeling of the Jews strikes me as a wonderfully happy invention. The irony of the situation, for poor Gwendolen, is almost grotesque, and it makes one wonder whether the whole heavy structure of the Jewish question in the story was not built up by the author for the express purpose of giving its proper force to this particular stroke.

Here James stumbles on the point, but picks himself up as if nothing had happened. It is precisely the Deronda dimension that exposes, not just the confined world of Gwendolen, but the constriction and smugness of English society. Yet, confronted with this new horizon, James wastes himself with a snigger about Deronda's being "pre-engaged"—almost as if his dance card were to be too improvidently filled.

It is essential to realize that Gwendolen means it, and so does her creator, when she thinks of Deronda as an "outer conscience." The choice of words is rather a lovely one, bearing the connotation of "outsider" as well as that of a wider sphere of intellectual and moral action. It may owe something to George Eliot's work in translating German philosophy. If its aim was to make the gentry feel slightly uncomfortable with the trammeled lives that they led and celebrated, and which they ordained for others, it seems to have succeeded. Sir Leslie Stephen took an early opportunity of exercising the classic English veto of heavy sarcasm:

> As we cannot all discover that we belong to the chosen people, and some of us might, even then, doubt the wisdom of the enterprise, one feels that Deronda's mode of solving his problem is not generally applicable. *(George Eliot:* 1902.)

What would be the point of its having general applicability? Sir Leslie adds the second classic English veto—that of saying in effect that something is boring or solemn:

> George Eliot's sympathy for the Jews, her aversion to anti-Semitism, was thoroughly generous, and naturally welcomed by its objects. But taken as the motive of a hero it strikes one as showing a defective sense of humour.

Like Sir Leslie (whose use of the term "objects" above is admirable in its intended charity and revealing in its presumption of exclusiveness), many of George Eliot's critics reveal their weakness and want of sympathy by inventing a mystery where none exists. How can she sketch a character as risible as Herr Klesmer, inquire Messrs. James and Leavis and Stephen, and not see that Daniel Deronda himself is a dry old stick? Before I make the obvious retort to this, let me show, *pace* Virginia Woolf, why Herr Klesmer is a demonstration of the satirical gift as well as the grace of deft humor. Here is Gwendolen at his mercy —or is he at hers?

> "One may understand jokes without liking them," said the terrible Klesmer. "I have had opera books sent me full of jokes; it was just because I understood them that I did not like them. The comic people are ready to challenge a man because he looks grave. 'You don't see the witticism, sir?' 'No, sir, but I see what you meant.' Then I am what we call ticketed as a fellow without *esprit*. But in fact," said Klesmer, suddenly dropping from his quick narrative to a reflective tone, with an impressive frown, "I am very sensible to wit and humour."

After this, Gwendolen teases him skillfully, "which made them quite friendly until she begged to be deposited by the side of her mamma."

Julius Klesmer, in other words, lightens the picture in accordance with the wishes of the critics. What else does he do? We find out when he has a slight confrontation with the MP Mr. Bult, who represents the roast beef of old England, "the general solidity and suffusive pinkness of a healthy Briton on the central table-land of life." Mr. Bult mistakes the timbre of one of Herr Klesmer's after-dinner perorations:

> "You must have been used to public speaking. You speak uncommonly well, though I don't agree with you. From what you said about sentiment, I fancy you are a Panslavist." "No, my name is Elijah. I am the Wandering Jew," said Klesmer, flashing a smile at Miss Arrowpoint, and suddenly making a mysterious wind-like rush backwards and forwards on the piano. Mr. Bult felt this buffoonery rather offensive and Polish, but—Miss Arrowpoint being there—did not like to move away.
>
> "Herr Klesmer has cosmopolitan ideas," said Miss Arrowpoint, trying to make the best of the situation. "He looks forward to a fusion of races."

In this almost hilarious dialogue, George Eliot hints at the central contrast of the book, which is between the pallid certainties and unsmiling rules of the well-to-do English, and the exotic, occluded world of the cosmopolitan, or what was then known, significantly, as the Bohemian. Of Klesmer we learn that he grew up "on the outskirts of Bohemia; and in the figurative Bohemia too he had had large acquaintance with the variety and romance which belong to small incomes." Some have seen in Klesmer the figure of Liszt, who George Eliot met in Weimar in 1854, but Liszt was a Hungarian Catholic and Gordon Haight's biography makes it pretty clear that the real model was Anton Rubinstein, also encountered in Weimar, who kept up his acquaintance with her, and to a performance of whose devotional opera *The Maccabees* George Eliot went late in life.

Klesmer is of course the long-maned, emotional, histrionic type; almost a *Punch* cartoon image of a MittelEuropean. Even George Eliot more than once employs the verb "flash" to describe his smiling. His role, coming as he does from haunts of Jews and gypsies, is one of *épater*. Clearly, then, her other Jewish characters could hardly be stereotypical without being—stereotypical. Her purpose was also to show the melancholy, millennial aspect of Jewish existence. It is perhaps to be regretted that this has never been done by any author in such a way as to make Henry James or Sir Leslie Stephen feel that they have had their money's worth of entertainment.

◆ ◆ ◆

George Eliot did not come by chance to her educated interest in Judaism. It evolved from her deep early commitment to Christianity and the gospels. In 1838, during a week spent in London, she forewent the frivolities of the theater and stayed indoors during the evening immersed in Josephus's *History of the Jews*. The impression this may have created in the short term is uncertain; a little later we find her writing to a fellow evangelical in deprecation of a concert at which Mendelssohn's new oratorio *Paul* had been performed by John Braham. Her objection was partly to the showy use of scriptural text, but she added to Marian Lewis that: "For my part I humbly conceive it to be little less than blasphemy for such words as 'Now then we are ambassadors for Christ' to be taken on the lips of such a man as Braham (a Jew too!)."

But these and other pettinesses appear to have evaporated with her self-emancipation from Anglican orthodoxy, her empirical observation that Dissenters were as moral as the Established churchmen, and her discovery from reading Sir Walter Scott that even Papists might have fine characters. Meanwhile, she had been translating the theological work of D. F. Strauss, which had a distinctly rationalist tone, and studying Hegel. In a suggestive letter which may prefigure Klesmer's exchange with Mr. Bult, she wrote in 1848 of the positive effects of intermarriage and of her rejection of the theory of "pure" race. Interestingly, this "pure race" theory was associated in England with the name of Benjamin Disraeli, who wrote grandly of the "Hebrew-Caucasian" species, as well as staking his claim to Tory leadership and an earldom by writing that:

> The native tendency of the Jewish race is against the doctrine of the equality of man. They have also another characteristic—the faculty of acquisition. Thus it will be seen that all the tendencies of the Jewish race are conservative. Their bias is to religion, property and natural aristocracy, and it should be the interest of statesmen that their energies and creative powers should be enlisted in the cause of existing society.

Disraeli became England's first Jewish Prime Minister in the year—1876— that *Daniel Deronda* was published. Within a few years he had persuaded Queen Victoria to crown herself Empress of India. The writing of the novel took place against a background of expansion and innovation—especially the opening that resulted from the digging of the Suez Canal. That is why its action can for the first time comprehend a world outside England.

George Eliot's evolution on the Jewish question took three forms. It took, first, the form of an intense interest in the Jews as a biblical and scriptural people. It took, second, the form of a commitment against religious, particularly Christian, intolerance. And it took, third, the form of an education—an encounter with the cosmopolitan and with the wider horizons of Europe and the East as these became accessible to a woman of formerly insular temperament. But "religion, property and natural aristocracy"—Disraeli's ministering terms—are not presented as unambiguous goods in *Daniel Deronda*, either insofar as they affect Gwendolen Harleth or Mirah Cohen. The tributary stream in Jewish thought which most influenced George Eliot was that which originated from the writings of Spinoza, writing that she was translating into English at the time of the great European emancipation movement of 1848. (She found the exercise of rendering the *Tractatus Theologico-Politicus* "such a rest to my mind," which makes me foolishly want to recall Bertie Wooster's claim, in *Thank You, Jeeves:* "You'll usually find me curled up with Spinoza's latest.")

During her 1854 tour of Europe with George Henry Lewes, she made a point of visiting the Jewish world. In Frankfurt she was very struck by the *Judengasse,* returning two decades later to refresh her memory of it and to employ it as the setting of Deronda's premonitory meeting with Joseph Kalonymos. Returning to England, she busied herself with the study and translation of Heinrich Heine, another non-Jewish Jew of genius who also plays his part, it seems to me, in rounding the character of Julius Klesmer. In an article on Heine's wit, George Eliot drew a distinction between humor and *esprit,* with some reflection on this distinction as it occurs among Teutons, which plainly recurs in the dialogue with Gwendolen quoted above.

In Prague in 1858, she wrote in her journal that:

> The most interesting things we saw were the Jewish burial ground (the *Alter Friedhof*) and the old Synagogue. We saw a lovely dark-eyed Jewish child here, which we were glad to kiss in all its dirt. Then came the grimy old synagogue with its smoky groins, and lamp forever burning. An intelligent old Jew was our cicerone and read us some Hebrew out of the precious old book of the Law.

This is a slightly painstaking and self-conscious progress toward tolerance, but it is a definite one. And it's of interest that Mirah escapes from her father in Prague in the action of the novel. The old Prague synagogue—the *Altneuschul*—incidentally supplied the title for Theodor Herzl's Zionist novel *Altneuland,* or "Old-New Land," which is the only Utopian fiction ever written by the moral father of an actual state. The novel was published in 1902 and has as one of its central characters a brutal, arrogant misogynist named—Kingscourt. I wonder....

As one looks at George Eliot's later development, everything seems to press toward the realization of *Daniel Deronda.* In the mid-1860s, she and her husband began to broaden their social circle, meeting Mr. and Mrs. Robert Browning and being shown by the latter "her Hebrew bible with notes in her handwriting." At the Monckton-Milnes salon in Upper Brook Street, where Lewes and Eliot were frequent guests, Matthew Arnold observed that one could meet "all the advanced liberals in religion and politics, and a Cingalese in full costume; so that, having lunched with the Rothschilds, I seemed to be passing my day among Jews, Turks, infidels and heretics." In 1864 George Eliot became friendly with Mr. and Mrs. Frederick Lehmann and through them with a set of confident, worldly, "cosmopolitan" painters, musicians, and writers.

This essential detour brings us to a little-known intersection—the writing of *The Spanish Gypsy.* Immediately preceding *Middlemarch*, this verse drama is set in medieval Spain. Let me quote the sarcastic account of its plot given by Sir Leslie Stephen. On the eve of her wedding to a Spanish aristocrat, the heroine is visited by a gypsy who

> explains without loss of time that he is her father; that he is about to be the Moses or Mahomet of a gypsy nation; and orders her to give up her country, her religion, and her lover to join him in this hopeful enterprise.

"Why place the heroine in conditions so hard to imagine?" inquires the suddenly realist Sir Leslie, as if he had never hit upon or roared over a Dickensian or Shakespearean coincidence. In fact, George Eliot gave the answer to this question in her own lifetime:

> Nothing would serve me except that moment in Spanish history when the struggle with the Moors was attaining its climax and when there was the gypsy race present under such conditions as would enable me to get my heroine and the hereditary claim on her among the gypsies. *I required the opposition of race to give the need for renouncing the expectation of marriage.* [Italics mine.]

What could be plainer? The "Jewish" part of Daniel Deronda, which the gentleman-critics want to heave over the side in order to give unobstructed play to the internal wrenchings of Miss Harleth, is the necessary counter-point to these emotions and to the awful scale of their disappointment. And moreover, for George Eliot the Jewish issue had come, after long study and reflection, to stand for an entire range of matters that came under the general heading of "emancipation."

Emancipation never comes cheap—it had cost George Eliot considerable emotional strain herself. And she scored it very deep into Gwendolen Harleth:

> The world seemed getting larger round poor Gwendolen, and she more solitary and helpless in the midst. The thought that he might come back after going to the East, sank before the bewildering vision of these wide-stretching purposes in which she felt herself reduced to a mere speck. There comes a terrible mo-ment to many souls when the great movements of the world, the larger destinies of mankind, which have lain aloof in newspapers and other neglected reading, enter like an earthquake into their own lives—when the slow urgency of grow-ing generations turns into the tread of an invading army or the dire clash of civil war, and grey fathers know nothing to seek for but the corpses of their blooming sons, and girls forget all vanity to make lint and bandages which may serve for the shattered limbs of their betrothed husbands.

Here are the punishments that fall on the inattentive or the careless; those who are content to remain within a small compass of the imagination; those who are not prepared for the worst. Deronda's discontent and restlessness appear by contrast, not as a "pre-engagement," but as something daring and worthwhile even if, as Henry James objects, he does continually signal his seriousness by grasping his lapel and going on a bit.

In the passage above, which combines some of the fiercer passages of the Old Testament with the periods of a Marx or a Luxemburg, Gwendolen's awakening to loss is made more poignant by the fact that Jewish life has always been part of the warp and woof of English society, only she has not been edu-cated to realize it. In George Eliot's essay "The Modern Hep! Hep! Hep!" written at about the same time as *Daniel Deronda* and published in *The Impressions of Theophrastus Such* in 1879, she took the old crusader battle cry as a slogan by which to examine and criticize anti-Semitism in England. She compared it directly to the rationalizations for modern slavery:

> And this is the usual level of thinking in polite society concerning the Jews. Apart from theological purposes, it seems to be held surprising that anybody should take an interest in the history of a people whose literature has furnished all our devotional language; and if any reference is made to their past and future destinies some hearer is sure to state as a relevant fact which may assist our judgement that she, for her part, is not fond of them, having known a Mrs. Jacobson who was very unpleasant, or that he, for his part, thinks meanly of

them as a race, though on inquiry you find that he is so little acquainted with their characteristics that he is astonished to learn how many persons whom he has blindly admired and applauded are Jews to the backbone.

George Eliot's scorn was seldom less than splendid and thoroughgoing. In a letter replying to warm praise for the novel from Harriet Beecher Stowe, she later adumbrated the same point in more detail:

> As to the Jewish element in "Deronda," I expected from first to last in writing it, that it would create much stronger resistance and even repulsion than it has actually met with. But precisely because I felt that the usual attitude of Christians towards Jews is—I hardly know whether to say more impious or more stupid in the light of their professed principles, I therefore felt urged to treat Jews with such sympathy and understanding as my nature and knowledge could attain to. *Moreover, not only towards the Jews, but towards all oriental peoples with whom we English come in contact, a spirit of arrogance and contemptuous dictatorialness is observable which has become a national disgrace to us.* [Italics mine.]

"There is nothing I should care more to do," she continued, "if it were possible, than to rouse the imagination of men and women to a vision of human claims in those races of their fellow men who most differ from them in customs and beliefs." But this was no generalized humanitarian emotion. It had a specific object as well: "Towards the Hebrews we Western people who have been reared in Christianity have a peculiar debt and, whether we acknowledge it or not, a peculiar thoroughness of fellowship in religious and moral sentiment." This comes near to "fiction with a message," but it can also be seen as suiting the internal needs of the novel very well. Gwendolen is beset by stultification; she and we must discover the fallacies of regnant assumptions; for this an exotic (in the Greek sense) character is necessary. The Harleth and the Jewish halves of the story, then, can and must be seen not as opposites or antitheses but as a symmetry and, at their most finely realized, a synthesis.

• • •

I have postponed two final critics to the last, one because of his silliness and one because of his gravity. In his "Literature and Social Theory: George Eliot," which appears in his volume *Representations*, Professor Steven Marcus commits himself to the following proposition:

> Deronda's identity is a mystery to himself and has always been. It is only when he is a grown man, having been to Eton and Cambridge, that he discovers he is a Jew. What this has to mean—given the conventions of medical practice at the time—is that he never looked down. In order for the plot of *Daniel Deronda* to work, Deronda's circumcised penis must be invisible, or nonexistent—which is one more demonstration in detail of why the plot does not in fact work. Yet this

peculiarity of circumstance—which, I think it should be remarked, has never been noticed before—is, I have been arguing, characteristic in several senses of both George Eliot and the culture she was representing.

This requires the razor of Occam, which can accomplish in a simple deft stroke what the *mohel* has failed to do for the author of *Sex and the Victorians*. When Deronda confronts his mother, in chapter 51, and surprises her by saying that he is "glad" to hear her revelation of his Jewishness, she replies, "violently": " 'Why do you say you are glad? You are an English gentleman. I secured you that.' "

As one who has spent more time than most critics in the schools which prepare English gentlemen, and the frigid showers in which these schools abound, I think we may take it that Deronda *mère* knew what she was about when she decided his future in his infancy. Professor Marcus has got no nearer the nub than the schoolmen who debated the hypothesis of an earthly foreskin of the Nazarene, left behind for the reliquaries of the pious.

Professor Edward Said does not complain that *Daniel Deronda* is humorless, or unduly bifurcated, or indifferent to the special sensitivity of those who are averse to fictional coincidence. He focuses, with some insistence, on something that is not present in the novel but is absent from it. With his usual mordant sense of the crux, he notices that neither the humane and generous George Eliot, nor any of her characters, pays the least attention to, or shows the slightest concern for, the native inhabitants of that yet-to-be-redeemed Palestine which they make the internal and external object of their multifarious yearnings.

I suppose that it could be objected that Said is viewing the novel through a retrospective optic. Yet George Eliot herself writes, in the opening section of the novel, that:

> A human life, I think, should be well-rooted in some spot of a native land, where it may get the love of tender kinship for the face of the earth, for the labours men go forth to, for the sounds and accents that haunt it, for whatever will give that earthly home a familiar, unmistakeable difference amidst the future widening of knowledge.

No Palestinian or Zionist, writing of "The Land," has put it much more satisfyingly than that. But Said is on slightly weaker ground when he attributes this to a generalized callousness on the author's part:

> The few references to the East in *Daniel Deronda* [he writes in *The Question of Palestine*] are always to England's Indian colonies, for whose people—as people having wishes, values, aspirations—Eliot expresses the complete indifference of absolute silence.

This is true as far as it goes (George Eliot's statement of sympathy for "all oriental peoples with whom we English come in contact" does not appear in the novel), but does not quite bring off the implication that she could not care less about the colonial subjects of the British crown. She could not write with any direct experience of the Indians, but she could catch out Mr. Bult who, if you remember, "rather neutral in private life, had strong opinions concerning the districts of the Niger, was much at home also in the Brazils, spoke with decision of affairs in the South Seas."

In *Theophrastus Such,* and her defense of the Jews against Christian obtuseness and cruelty, George Eliot expressed herself rather forcefully about the hypocrisies of empire. To select a few of her choicest incisions into the contented hide of the Bults:

> We do not call ourselves a dispersed and a punished people; we are a colonising people and it is we who have punished others.

> Are we to adopt the exclusiveness for which we have punished the Chinese?

> He [Mixtus] continues his early habit of regarding the spread of Christianity as a great result of our commercial intercourse with black, brown and yellow populations; but this is an idea not spoken of in the sort of fashionable society that Scintilla collects around her husband's table, and Mixtus now philosophically reflects that the cause must come before the effect, and that the thing to be striven for is the commercial intercourse, not excluding a little war if that also should prove needful as a pioneer of Christianity.

> ...the Irish, also a servile race, who have rejected Protestantism though it has been repeatedly urged on them by fire and sword and penal laws, and whose place in the moral scale may be judged by our advertisements, where the clause "No Irish need apply" parallels the sentence which for many polite persons sums up the question of Judaism—"I never *did* like the Jews."

This scarcely supports a finding of indifference towards the colonized. Even the speech of the fierce and solipsistic Mordechai, cited by Said, speaks only of a land with "debauched and paupered conquerors" and, when it defames the East, is directed only at that ancient and familiar despot, the unfeeling Turkish *pasha,* common foe of Christendom, Jewry, and the Arabs.

Though this does not automatically contradict Said, who concedes that, "curiously, all of Eliot's descriptions of Jews stress their exotic 'Eastern' aspects," it both qualifies and perhaps intensifies his essential critique. George Eliot, like quite a few writers who have had their fill of a stolid, hypocritical, self-satisfied England, had come to an unusual empathy with the agile, versatile, vociferous, ingenious peoples. There is something almost Byronic, mingled with a little German idealism, in her fellow-feeling for Armenians, Jews, gypsies, Bohemians, and all the others for whom her posterity prepared such a frightful relegation. I think it is certain that she had no prejudice—rather the reverse—against the swarthy and the silken. To the question "Had she no room in her heart for the Palestinian Arab?" the reply must be that she was, like most of her contemporaries, quite unaware that any such people, or "problem," existed. This would be a criticism in itself, whether or not it reflected general ignorance, or the propaganda about "a land without a people for a people without a land."

George Eliot was most influenced by Emanuel Deutsch, a Silesian Jew who had come to London and who worked at the British Museum. Encountered at the Lehmanns, he proved to have an infectious enthusiasm and a store of recondite scriptural knowledge. He made a trip to Palestine in 1869, writing with passion about the Wailing Wall and his "wild yearnings." His presence in the figure of Mordechai is evident, and it seems clear that he embodies the religious Zionist rather than the colonizing, state-building sort. Deutsch's friend and patron Lady Strangford, whose husband is thought to have furnished the model of Disraeli's Coningsby, gave George Eliot information about the Near East (as it was then known), telling her that: "Since 1863 the 'Israelitish Alliance' (chiefly of Paris), shamed by the efforts of Christians to promote colonies and agricultural occupations in Palestine, have endeavored to found a colony at Jaffa." She added that this task was made more difficult by rabbinical teaching that Jews in Palestine should be supported by the faithful elsewhere, holding that "it is irreligious of a Jew in Jerusalem to work, so to say." Lady Strangford also urged that George Eliot make the voyage, which she was never strong enough to do. Who knows? Like some of the characters in S. Y. Agnon's *A Guest for the Night,* she might have discovered at first hand that the word "colony" had double meaning, and that Palestine was not an unpeopled wilderness for spiritual contemplation. She could certainly have found out the falsity of a letter from Haim Guedalla, of the London *Jewish Chronicle,* who wrote thanking her for *Deronda* and mentioning his hectic "vision of Syria again in the hands of the Jews."

In denying herself the usual conventions of the love story—the overcoming of unjust opposition or of difference in station; the whole apparatus of what Barbara Hardy calls "moral rescue"—George Eliot set herself a more rigorous standard than that of showing up, say, the sinister etiolation of a Grandcourt, the deference of a rural Rector, or the complacency of a Mr. Bult. Poor Gwendolen is made to face a challenge to happiness that she is not equipped to understand. This is the indirect realization of a pledge made in one of George Eliot's letters:

> The day will come when there will be a temple of white marble where sweet incense and anthems shall rise to the memory of every man and every woman who has had a deep *ahnung,* a presentiment, a yearning, or a clear vision of the time when this miserable reign of Mammon shall end.

But as she strove, without the prop of orthodox religion, to convey the Greek sense of *entheos*—enthusiasm that is "possession" without ceremony—she never scorned the earthbound and the banal, the plain realization that is contained in the closing passage of her penultimate novel *Middlemarch:* "The growing good of the world is partly dependent on unhistoric acts; and that things are not so ill with you and me as they might have been, is half owing to the number who lived faithfully a hidden life, and rest in unvisited tombs." This counterpoint, between the rising incense and the dying cadence, the triumphant and the modest, the prophetic and the quotidian, is nowhere more boldly confronted than in the chapters of *Daniel Deronda,* which have already easily outlived the distinctly earthbound, confining objections made to them.

Elevated *Shtick:*
S. J. Perelman

by August Kleinzahler

IN 1949 S. J. PERELMAN bought a mynah bird named Tong Cha at a Chinese firecracker shop in Bangkok. Perelman adored him. An acquaintance of Perelman is quoted as saying: "Tong Cha was a lot like Perelman. He made horrible noises and pecked at you constantly until he drew blood." Perelman wrote his favorite girlfriend, Leila Hadley, in June of 1949: "Tong Cha is perfect... When I feed him in the morning half a banana and stroke his breast... His eyes roll backward in his head and he gives forth a series of shuddering little sighs... I'm the only one he allows to handle him."

Perelman, the most celebrated humorist of his time, also adored an MG roadster he bought on the same trip. He was endlessly fond of pretty, smart young women like Ms. Hadley (the great-great-great-granddaughter of James Boswell), and one of his pastimes was shopping for naughty lingerie to observe his young friends in. In fact, one of his favorite books was Zola's *Au Bonheur des Dames,* which concerns the world of department stores where Perelman spent so much of his time. He favored custom-tailored English tweeds and was very involved in finding and keeping expert and reliable drycleaners. He collected art and was especially keen on Buddhist sculpture; Thai and Cambodian bronzes were a favorite. The son of working-class Russian-Jewish immigrants, he became a hopeless Anglophile as an adult, ultimately moving to London late in life for a brief period until the isolation and class distinction got to him. He loved travel, especially to the Orient, and Hong Kong particularly. He valued Joyce's *Ulysses* above all books, and Perelman's fascination with language, its store of rhythmic and phonemic effects, usually for comic results, made *Ulysses* an obvious source for him. He was crazy about Benny Goodman's music, but most of all he liked a good corned-beef sandwich, which was another reason he came back from England. Otherwise, he seems to have been, by and large, a miserable son-of-a-bitch: selfish, grudging, uptight, a rotten father, an unfaithful husband, rather cold and not terribly fun to be around; in other words, not like you or me but like a number of people we probably know.

S. J. Perelman moved in fast company: the New York literary and theatrical worlds and Hollywood. He maintained three addresses, an apartment and office in New York and a country place in Bucks County, near the Pennsylvania–New Jersey border. Nice country. When he first hit New York as a cartoonist and writer in the mid-1920s, he immediately had to support both his parents. He was a social man, often at the theater and art openings, and of course literary get-togethers of all sorts. He wasn't a lush like so many of his set, and he was tight with a buck. He chose not to hang out with the crowd at the Algonquin Hotel, though he would have been welcome. One of Dorothy Parker's biographers, John Keats, characterized the Algonquin scene in its heyday:

> They were small-timers, most insecure people, very self-conscious, and addicted to big-shotism. They were, like Alexander Woollcott, garrulous provincials who invested New York City with bogus glamour and "wanted to be smart." They were also, for the most part, young people on the way up; they would become successful popular entertainers and writers of coy ephemera for the magazines, including *The New Yorker,* and the writers of inconsequential plays.

Perelman both was and wasn't of that world, and he's half-deserving of the rap. A number of the Algonquin and *New Yorker* writers went to Hollywood, like Perelman, to make serious dollars. The Los Angeles that Perelman and his cohorts found when they got off the *Super Chief* in the thirties was fragrant with orange blossoms (at least out by Pasadena). A horseback-riding path divided Sunset Boulevard down the middle. Much of Beverly Hills was a beanfield. The couple of brick buildings which made up UCLA, then only a tiny adjunct of its mother university, Berkeley, were the only significant structures in the area now comprising Westwood, Bel Air, and Brentwood. George Kaufman commented around that time that "Southern California is a great place to live—if you're an orange." Many of the writers who came out from New York lived in a bungalow colony called the Garden of Allah. Arthur Marx, Groucho's son, who moved there for a time with his parents, wrote:

> The Garden of Allah featured an immense swimming pool surrounded by lush tropical planting and a number of posh Spanish bungalows whose tenants were either drunk or in bed with somebody else's wife (or husband) or sitting at typewriters on the patios agonizing over movie scripts. When we moved in, some of the Garden of Allah's most celebrated guests—or should I say "celebrating"— were Bob Benchley, Charles Butterworth, Dorothy Parker, Alan Campbell, John O'Hara, F. Scott Fitzgerald, and Maureen O'Sullivan and Johnny Farrow

[Mia and Tia's folks]. At almost any time of the day or night you were likely to see Bob Benchley lolling beside the pool with a martini shaker in his hand, or hear Johnny Farrow beating up his wife in their bungalow. It looked like a fun place when Father showed us around...

Perelman and his wife Laura West (Nathanael West's kid sister) didn't live at the Garden of Allah, but when they were working in Hollywood they hung around there with Parker and Campbell regularly. The work at the studios themselves was long, hard, and demeaning. The writers were pretty much locked in rooms for eight hours at a time. They were treated miserably and their scripts were wrecked by coarse, avaricious studio bosses whom Perelman liked to describe as having no foreheads except "by dint of electrolysis." Perelman managed to convert an ample share of his revulsion at the shallowness, vulgarity, and greed into material for his *New Yorker* sketches. Many of the letters from the posthumous collection *Don't Tread on Me* are to friends in the East detailing his disgust. But he always came back for the money, time after time.

It's important to know that Perelman began as a cartoonist because in a number of respects his prose pieces for *The New Yorker* are cartoons. As a boy he was crazy about the "chalk talks" at the local vaudeville houses where the artists would create dazzling, funny effects in just a few minutes drawing with chalk on blackboards. His favorite comic strip in high school was "Silk Hat Harry's Divorce Suit" by Ted Dorgan. The two characters were chronic womanizers who were forever scheming to steal each other's girlfriends. The characters were depicted as dogs in human clothing. At Brown University in the early twenties Perelman drew cartoons with funny captions for the *Brown Jug*, the student magazine of which he became editor. In 1925 Perelman was offered a job in New York at the national humor magazine *Judge*. The caption under his first cartoon for *Judge*, which showed two men flying through the clouds, read:

"Don't breathe a word, Casper—but think Lord Percey is horribly fastidious."

"You said it, Dalmatia. He even insists on being measured for his coat of arms."

A coeditor of *Judge* at the time was a young man named Harold Ross, who had been hired to boost the magazine's circulation. He wanted to change the format over from a national monthly to a more sophisticated weekly magazine concentrating on New York City.

There was something about the *Weltansicht* of the twenties that hungered for the jokey and naughty. As college students Perelman and his crowd would have certainly worshipped H. L. Mencken, the great debunker and assailer of the "booboisie." Today much of the humor from that era has a brittle, feverish quality to it. It's not merely unfunny, it's irritating. One senses that a desperate impulse was abroad to have Fun and thumb one's nose...at whom or what?...Babbittry, perhaps. Perhaps the age somehow knew what was to follow.

Perelman eventually turned to prose and began writing for *The New Yorker* in the 1930s. From the beginning his pieces poked fun at the pompous and hypocritical. (He had been raised in a poor household where both parents were educated and socialist.) He loved sending up clichés, and his playfulness with language is irrepressible and finally a little maddening. The prose itself is a wild, concentrated mixture of the orotund, slang, Yiddish epithets, and whatever locutions are dearest to him at a given time. For several years, in his letters especially, two of his favorite words are *kapok* and *paresis*, or *paretic*— pejorative, naturally. The characters are all cartoons, caricatures of dolts, boors, Hollywood producers, bimbos, shills, or himself in a variety of guises that fall under the heading of *schlemiel*. Allusions, often literary, turn up in wild asides and non sequiturs. His free-associational leaps are what many found so scintillating and distinctive in Perelman. It was the relatively ob-scure and learned nature of some of these asides that came to be a major problem between Perelman and Groucho Marx when the former worked on *Animal Crackers, Horse Feathers,* and *Monkey Business.*

Much of Perelman's humor is rooted in Jewish *shtetl* humor, which is so distinctive that a ghetto dweller from eighteenth-century Prague could tell a joke to an old Jewish grandma in Brooklyn in 1988 and the joke would be understood and probably chuckled over with a smile of recognition. The smile would acknowledge kinship and the shared experience of being an out-sider, a Jew in a Christian world, and everything that entails culturally, psy-chologically, and otherwise. The nature of the joke would almost certainly be earthy, wry, and a little bit sad. The manner of telling would be matter-of-fact, world-weary. The teller would shrug his shoulders here and there, and the rise and fall of his voice (in a pattern unmistakably Jewish) would suggest resignation at the rather cruel, capricious nature of fate. The content of the joke might be about the butcher *shtupping* the rabbi's wife or the relativistic nature of a Talmudic disputation. It doesn't matter. It is the humor of disap-pointment and vulnerability. Israelis often find it offensive.

At the heart of much Jewish humor is the *schlemiel,* the poor fellow who is forever being victimized by fortune or his own inherent *schlemiel*-ness. Perelman has been quoted: "Humor is only a point of view...For me its chief merit is the use of the unexpected, the glancing allusion, the deflation of pomposity, the constant repetition of one's helplessness in a majority of situations." He is quoted elsewhere about Yiddish words: he liked them "for their invective content. There are nineteen words in Yiddish that convey gra-dations of disparagement from a mild, fluttery helplessness to a state of downright, irreconcilable brutishness. All of them can be usefully employed to pin-point the kind of individuals I write about." It would not be too much to say that Perelman introduced this kind of humor into mainstream American letters. Just as he himself was obsessively natty in the English style of dress and similarly elegant and restrained in speech and manner, so Perelman dressed up his *shtick* to the nines and made it seem highbrow, like literature. Even T. S. Eliot woofed it down. Perelman called his prose pieces *"feuilletons,"* which means "light, amusing sketches" in French.

But they're *shtick*. He can call them what he likes and dress them in a feathery, beautifully cut weave, but they're *shtick* underneath, sometimes gorgeous, always intelligent and well-carpentered, but *shtick*. Among Leo Rosten's definitions of the word in *The Joys of Yiddish* is: "A studied, contrived or characteristic piece of 'business' employed by an actor or actress; overly used gestures, grimaces or devices to steal attention. 'Watch him use the same *shtik*.' 'The characterization would be better without all those *shtiklech*.' 'Play it straight: no *shtiklech*....' "

When Perelman died he was eulogized as a great American humorous writer in the tradition of Twain and Lardner. Not ten years after his death the work is badly dated; and for this reader, who grew up on Perelman, he's as difficult to get through as a tumbler of Kir Royale, frothy and rich. The stuff is primped, the syntax hopelessly fluffed and devoid of sinew. You catch him time after time going by rote to the fustian. The arteries clog. Plaster gingerbread begins falling about one's head. You want to go off and read a half page of Hemingway on how to shoot some poor animal.

In some respects the work is dated because Perelman is lampooning the social and cultural monstrosities of another time. Not that those monstrosities don't exist all around us at the moment, but they have gone through several filters, and Perelman's grotesques haven't the immediacy they once had. The rococo structures and madcap veerings which wowed people like Eliot and Eudora Welty, and which work so successfully in the Marx Brothers movies, now cloy. Perhaps what sinks the writing in the end is how utterly divorced it is from American speech—that and the very real absence of heart in his work, something we do find in Twain, Lardner, and in the Joyce of *Ulysses*.

The success of the Marx Brothers movies over the years gave Perelman fits. Groucho and Perelman became close friends (o boy, would I like to have been a fly on the wall when those two got together) but had a bad falling out. Both men came to speak very unkindly of each other, and both were quite obviously jealous of one another. Groucho downplayed Perelman's role as a writer for the Brothers. Perelman admirers like to suggest that Groucho's character was inspired by their man. I can only suggest that the next time you watch *Animal Crackers,* you listen very closely to some of the wild and inspired abuse coming out of Captain Spaulding's mouth. No one but Perelman could have put it there; and no one else but Groucho could have sung it so sweetly. Their chemistry was short-lived. Forty years later Perelman would write his British agent:

> I am fucking sick and tired of my endless identification with these clowns. If it is not yet apparent after 5 0 years of writing for publication in the U.S., Britain, and elsewhere that my work is worth reading for its own sake; if illiterates and rock fans (synonymous) can only be led to purchase my work by dangling before them the fact that I once worked for the Marx brothers, then let us find some other publisher.

Perelman has a letter or two to Groucho in *Don't Tread on Me*. But they're jokey and cordial, as are most of his letters. Much of the writing is well-written vitriol. There's a lot of complaining about money. The Perelman of the letters is smart, nasty, and a very keen observer of writers. The letters had to be laundered, but one doesn't really feel he's missing anything except a libelous crack or some dirtytalk to a girlfriend. In fact, you can read the entire corpus plus the letters and learn nothing, and feel next to nothing. In contrast, the introduction by Prudence Crowther, who knew Perelman toward the end of his life and edited the letters, is well worth reading. She gives us a first-rate portrait of a complicated, private man. The style is just right, and the piece is revealing in a tender way.

Paul Theroux, who also knew Perelman near the end of his life, writes in his introduction to the final Perelman collection, *The Last Laugh:* "Humorists are often unhappy men and satirists downright miserable, but S. J. Perelman was a cheery soul." Ah, the keen eye of novelists...True, Perelman was probably already taking lithium for his depression when Theroux knew him, and so was able to function in public. Perelman had already been through shock therapy for his depression on at least two occasions. The condition existed, intermittently, throughout Perelman's adult life and would paralyze him for weeks and months at a time.

If we didn't have *S.J. Perelman: A Life,* the biography written by Dorothy Herrmann, there wouldn't be much left to say of Perelman. He will probably come to be regarded as a period or genre writer, along the lines of a Ronald Firbank, but funny, with a distinctive style that lives among his epigones— like Woody Allen, who in his own stories transforms the befuddlement of Perelman's *schlemiel* into self-loathing and turns Perelman's casual erudition into an excruciating pseudo-intellectualism.

But a biography we do have, and it's a corker. The writing is no joy, and when Ms. Herrmann drifts from her excellent research and the intriguing, sad, or sulfurously funny quotes by Perelman's friends and contemporaries, she can sound like the sort of cluck you wouldn't want to listen to Perelman dismantle at a dinner party. But the book is a real bounty, and in spite of himself here's Sidney Joseph, almost all of him, infinitely more sympathetic and interesting in life than he was ever able to be, or tried to be, in his writing.

I find no pleasure in writing about the career of as gifted and unhappy a man as Perelman, who cannibalized his life, as writers do—and in this case an extraordinary life—only to turn it into fluff. From the beginning Perelman's main interest as a writer was to make money. He wrote for the theater, TV, Hollywood. He even wrote jokes for the harmonica player Larry Adler. Like a lot of people who grow up poor, he was forever in a panic about money.

Perelman once collaborated on a play that looked to have a chance at being a major hit, but a New York newspaper strike killed it dead. In his later years he began writing travel pieces, and he circled the globe on three occasions. He enjoyed writing for *The New Yorker* best of all, and he had a high opinion of many of its staff and of writers like Joseph Mitchell, Cheever, and J.D. Salinger, with whom he was friendly and to whom he dedicated one of his collections. He very much liked his editor at *The New Yorker*, Gus Lobrano. But when Lobrano died he was replaced by Katherine White, whom Perelman couldn't stand. The old *New Yorker* and its crew were fast being displaced by a new crowd. Edmund Wilson, a favorite of Perelman, wrote to Katherine White in 1947:

> The editors are so afraid of anything that is unusual, that is not expected, that they put a premium on insipidity and banality...Every first-rate writer invents and renews the language, and many of the best writers have highly idiosyncratic styles: but almost no idiosyncratic writer ever gets into *The New Yorker*. Who can imagine Henry James or Bernard Shaw—or Dos Passos or Faulkner—in *The New Yorker?* The object here is as far as possible to iron all the writing out so that there will be nothing vivid or startling or original or personal in it. Sid Perelman is almost the sole exception and I have never understood how he got by.

Perelman loved words, individual words. They amazed and transported him perhaps even more than a corned beef sandwich or a pretty twenty-eight-year-old in a black teddy. En route to Florida to stay with friends one time, Laura and Sid were involved in a serious car wreck in South Carolina. Both Perelmans were hurt, Laura quite seriously. Perelman went on alone and arrived in Florida breathless with the news: he had come upon a marvelous new word—*totalled!*

Unbridled Restraint:
J. R. Ackerley

by Arthur Lubow

J. R. ACKERLEY WAS THE ENGLISH PROUST. More modest in ambition, restrained in emotion, conservative in demeanor, yes; but those are national peculiarities. Essentially, the lives are alike. Dreary lives driven by a hunt for requited love, a search as hopeless as it was ceaseless, queered from the start by flaws of character—Proust's histrionic jealousy, Ackerley's affectional insularity (national traits, once again). Each life, unexamined, would seem too trivial to reward examination; but it is the quality of the examination that redeems the life. All of Ackerley's published prose is a reworking of his personal history. How drab that history seems in *Ackerley*, Peter Parker's carefully researched biography! An assessment which Ackerley would have endorsed. Yet, in his own telling, these tattered little anecdotes glisten with humor, and the scattered pieces coalesce into an appealing mosaic.

Born in 1896, the second of three children of a London fruit importer widely known as the "banana king," Joe Randolph Ackerley was blessed with the wit to turn a phrase and the beauty to turn a head. He sank most of his writing talent into a twenty-four-year stint as literary editor of *The Listener,* a magazine published by the BBC. He seems to have been an exceptional editor, attracting distinguished writers despite a paltry fee schedule, and shepherding their articles past the pablum-loving BBC bureaucracy. He invested his charm and good looks in what he described as a quest for the Ideal Friend, but which, to an eye less schooled in Housman and Tennyson, appears more prosaically as a frantic sequence of obsessive, unsatisfying homosexual encounters with young heterosexual working-class men. In middle age, he gave up his tricking to devote himself to his one great love—a beautiful but difficult German shepherd bitch called Queenie.

That a distinguished writer should have led such a mediocre life is hardly remarkable. What is unusual, however, is that Ackerley, instead of creating an imagined world, mined his own gray existence for material. Besides some poems (forgettable, to judge from the sample quoted by Parker) and a play, his published work consists of four slender volumes. Two—a novel, *We Think the World of You*, and a memoir, *My Dog Tulip*—concern his relationship with his dog, Queenie. *Hindoo Holiday* is a journal that recounts a few months he spent in the employ of the maharajah of a minor Indian state. Probably his best known work, *My Father and Myself*, is a dual memoir that contrasts his own secret sex life with that of his father.

My Father and Myself derives much of its impact from a deadpan juxtaposition of the conventional and the bizarre. What could be more correct than an appreciation of a Victorian father written by his son? Right from the start, however, Ackerley jolts his book off that dusty shelf. "I was born in 1896 and my parents were married in 1919," he begins his story. (To those familiar with his previous work, the first shock probably comes with the dedication, "To Tulip.") Although it rambles, as obliquely yet purposefully as a path in an English garden, *My Father and Myself* is more focused than its embracing title would suggest. It is Ackerley's attempt to link his own and his father's sexual natures. At least as outrageous as his soldier-besotted son, the senior Ackerley maintained two women and families in separate households, only a few miles apart. Until Roger died, neither Joe nor his mother suspected a thing. (His mother never did find out.) As if that weren't enough of a surprise, Joe, piecing together the past, came to believe that Roger as a young Guardsman had conducted the sorts of relationships with affluent homosexuals that Joe was now enjoying on the other end.

Despite their shared evasion of Victorian sexual mores (which, it would seem from Victorian memoirs, were obeyed no more then than now), Roger and Joe differed fundamentally. Roger was an Englishman of the "jolly good show" school. Bluff and jocular, he skated cheerily on the surface of what he called this "wonderful old world." Joe was a worrier. He was always examining himself—physically, emotionally, intellectually, every which way. He felt that self-obsession was characteristic of the homosexual. I would call it self-consciousness rather than self-obsession, but I agree with the etiology.

A homosexual boy (since that is the gender under scrutiny, I will limit my generalizations) realizes at first intuitively and then specifically that at bottom he is different from his peers. In his own mind, his figure is separated from the crowd by a wide white margin. In time, as he dwells on his distinctiveness, he colors in that space according to his bent. He may, like Walt Whitman or Oscar Wilde, extrude a flamboyant carapace, a larger-than-life and slightly unreal persona. He may, like Ackerley's mentor, E. M. Forster, or like Proust, become a connoisseur of margins, an analyst of the boundaries that divide and connect people. As he develops a personal style to make visible his sense of being different, he may become an aesthete or a dandy, a Walter Pater or a

Ronald Firbank. Fascinated by who he is and how he got that way, he may, like Ackerley, become a memoirist. And of course, these alternatives do not exclude. Most of these names would fit under many of these categories. But all of them, I think, share an overriding self-consciousness—a quality that is certainly key to Ackerley.

So intense was Ackerley's self-regard that it molded his writing style. At times his sentences pause before their periods to look back at their openings. Describing his going up to Cambridge after World War I, he writes in *My Father and Myself:* "After four years of active service and incarceration and at the age of twenty-three I did not enjoy it much, though why I should begin my sentence like that as if I were providing reasons for discontent I don't know." His literary technique depends on a careful balancing, so that each part of a sentence is terribly aware of its neighbors. Sometimes he uses a flat-footed parallelism as a source of humor. Offered pornographic postcards by his Hindustani language tutor in *Hindoo Holiday,* he writes: "I had seen them before—or pictures very similar—at school, where I was disgusted and returned them quickly to their owner, and later in Paris, or Naples, where I was disgusted and bought them." The showiest way to construct a parallel sentence is to bend it in half so it mirrors itself; and in fact, the inversion—we will not make too much of this—is one of Ackerley's favorite devices. "Unable, it seemed, to reach sex through love, I started upon a long quest in pursuit of love through sex," he writes in a celebrated line of *My Father and Myself.* But just as significant is what follows: "Having put that neat sentence down I stare at it. Is it true?"

Although he was an exceptionally elegant stylist, Ackerley distrusted style. He was always stepping back from his literary edifice to ask, Is it true? Reality being what it is, he could never be sure. Typically, he adopted the most self-deprecating version as the truth—another way in which he was very English. He put the worst possible face on himself in *We Think the World of You,* which, since it is a novel, allowed him to relax his hold on the facts. *We Think the World of You* is the story of the narrator's two love affairs, one ending, the other just starting. As Parker relates, Ackerley conducted a lengthy, sporadic relationship with Freddie Doyle, a handsome, vain young man with a less than handsome career as a Guardsman deserter, part-time prostitute, and petty criminal. Frank, the narrator of *We Think the World of You,* is closely based on Ackerley; and Johnny, the young man he adores, is a ringer for Freddie. Like Ackerley, Frank financially supports his beloved boy, even after Freddie/Johnny marries; when he cuts back on the dole, the boy goes on a burglary spree and lands in jail. The literary ploy at the heart of the novel is the reader's growing realization that Frank, the Ackerley-like narrator, is not as attractive or blameless a character as he at first seems. To achieve this effect, Ackerley edits out the real-life circumstances that might place him in a more flattering light: for instance, that to supply funds for Freddie's family, he sold some of his own prized possessions and took on extra work.

We Think the World of You mirrors the confinement of Johnny, whose hold on Frank is starting to weaken, with the equally cruel imprisonment of Evie, whose beauty and affection capture Frank's heart. The real-life model for Evie (and Tulip) was Freddie Doyle's Alsatian bitch, Queenie. When Freddie went behind bars, he sent Queenie to live with his mother and stepfather. Penned in a tiny backyard, she won Ackerley's pity and then his love. After much bickering, he bought her from Freddie. As a fictionalized protagonist in *We Think the World of You* and *My Dog Tulip,* Queenie is depicted with a precise and loving eye. She is one of the great love objects in modern literature.

It is ironic that this lover of his own sex should proleptically parody the work of later writers (Norman Mailer and Philip Roth come to mind), men who plumb in women the unfathomable mystery, the Other. No woman is as Other as Queenie. An early chapter of *My Dog Tulip,* entitled "Liquids and Solids," is devoted to Tulip's excretory habits. The flavor of this work—the exquisite eye and prose directed at this unlikely, some might even say distasteful, subject—is suggested by this passage:

> She has two kinds of urination, Necessity and Social. Different stances are usually, though not invariably, adopted for each. In necessity she squats squarely and abruptly right down on her shins, her hind legs forming a kind of dam against the stream that gushes out from behind; her tail curves up like a scimitar; her expression is complacent. For social urination, which is mostly preceded by the act of smelling, she seldom squats, but balances herself on one hind leg, the other being withdrawn or cocked up in the air. The reason for this seems obvious; she is watering some special thing and wishes to avoid touching it. It may also be that in this attitude she can more accurately bestow her drops. Often they are merely drops, a single token drop will do, for the social flow is less copious. The expression on her face is business-like, as though she were signing a check.

Most of *My Dog Tulip* recounts Ackerley's attempts to mate Tulip. He had no commercial interest in selling her puppies; he was simply after her sexual satisfaction. It's as if Karenin sought out Vronsky for Anna, or Charles Bovary placed ads in the personals for Emma. Actually, it's even more poignant than that, for Tulip (or Queenie; Ackerley changed the name in the book when advised that the original opened him to ridicule) wholeheartedly adored her master, and would have preferred to look at no other male. Acting as Queenie's agent, Ackerley resumed his compulsive cruising. He was still looking for young studs, only furry ones. The vectors of Ackerley's relationship with Tulip are not much odder than those at work in some of the Bloomsbury marriages. The Bloomsbury memoirs, however, deprive us of the detail in which Ackerley revels: the use of vaseline, for instance, which he applied liberally to Tulip, but to no avail; or the mechanics of canine copulation, which involves an inseparable locking of genitals that can last half an hour or more. Tulip does eventually achieve sexual fulfillment with a small mongrel called Dusty—a bliss that lasts until she tries to rise from their postcoital embrace. The image of her panicked realization that she cannot free herself, and her convulsive effort to do so, is one of the many memorable scenes in *My Dog Tulip*. As always, Ackerley is there, observing, and anticipating what the reader may be thinking.

> With a convulsive movement [Tulip] regained her feet and began to pull Dusty, who was upside down, along the lawn, trying from time to time to rid herself of her incubus by giving it a nip. The unfortunate Dusty, now on his side, his little legs scrabbling wildly about in their efforts to find a foothold, at length managed, by a kind of somersault, to obtain it. This advantage, however, was not won without loss, for his exertion turned him completely round, so that, still attached to Tulip, he was now bottom to bottom with her and was hauled along in this even more uncomfortable and abject posture, his hindquarters off the ground, his head down and his tongue hanging out. Tulip gazed at me in horror and appeal. Heavens! I thought, this is love! These are the pleasures of sex!

No one better than Ackerley could appreciate the ridiculousness of the situation, since the buffoonery of sex was a subject dear to him. Alert to every nuance of his dog's coupling, he didn't overlook his own situation. He never did, not for a moment. After an afternoon of exercising Queenie in the park, constantly on the alert for broken bottles that might injure her, he confided to his diary: "Once upon a time I was a handsome young man, regarded as one of the most promising writers of the day, much sought after by everyone, involved in countless exciting love affairs—and now look at me, gray haired and going deaf, a dog lover and grovelling about after glass in a public park." The self-pity would be deadening were it not leavened by his sense of the comic. If he himself finds it funny, you too are permitted to laugh.

Ackerley is especially droll about his sexual adventures. In Parker's account, his tomcatting does not seem very amusing. "Ackerley had continued to pursue a promiscuous sex-life in London and was still to be found prowling around Bird Cage Walk and Hyde Park Corner in search of 'love,'" the biographer writes. "What he got was a dose of clap, caught from a guardsman whom he had unwisely allowed to bugger him." This might be called a distillation—in the sense that vinegar is distilled from wine—of Ackerley's own rendition of how he had "weathered a dose of anal clap without much fuss (anal, yes; I *assured* the young Grenadier that I was quite impenetrable, but he begged so hard to be allowed at any rate to try)." Elsewhere in *My Father and Myself*, Ackerley elaborates on his difficulties with fellatio. "Some technical skill seems required and a retraction of the teeth which, perhaps because mine are too large or unsuitably arranged, seem always to get in the way," he writes. "Squeamishness with comparative strangers over dirt or even disease disturbs me, and I have noticed that those normal young men who request for themselves this form of amusement never offer it in return." In fairness, how can a biographer compete with that?

Ackerley's chief sexual problem was what he called "sexual incontinence," or premature ejaculation. No doubt it was associated with his unrelaxing self-consciousness. This affliction plagued him until middle age, when it receded, only to be replaced by impotence. "The constant fear of achieving orgasm before one's partner has even achieved erection, the fear no doubt exacerbating the condition, would have been devastating to sexual confidence," Parker speculates. "Ackerley also believed that premature ejaculation caused him to be sexually inconsiderate for, having achieved release himself (albeit unsatisfactorily) he was disinclined to continue love-making. Guilt, disgust and shame were catastrophically anaphrodisiac. His subsequent manoeuvres in order to disengage himself from further sexual activity, manoeuvres which frequently included deception, merely increased the sense of failure."

What could be seedier, more dismal to read about? It is not to disparage Parker that I once again compare Ackerley's own relaying of these facts. The point is, no one else could put the same spin on what is, by any standard, a fairly unattractive situation, and make it, while still sad, also funny.

> [Incontinence] put an end to my own pleasure before it had begun and, with the expiry of my desire, which was never soon renewed, my interest in the situation, even in the person, causing me to behave inconsiderately to him; I have not been above putting an abrupt end to affairs with new and not highly attractive boys in whose first close embrace, and before taking off our clothes, I had already had my own complete, undisclosed satisfaction. Apart from the probability that I did not then want to go further, how could I go further and reveal to someone who had not yet reached a state of erection the mess I had made of myself? Even a little friendly moralising at such moments as a wriggle out: 'Perhaps we oughtn't to be doing this', has not been beyond my capabilities.

Although it is not my purpose to indulge in close textual analysis, I will point out, in passing, that seemingly every sentence in Ackerley has been twirled to the light and scrutinized by its author; and—to consider only the first sentence in this passage just cited—the uncharacteristically muddled and tortured clumsiness of the opening, and the flat, tagged-on, seemingly endless, anticlimactic bit that follows, are not unrelated to the matter at hand. But, as I say, it is the larger point that concerns us, the tonal difference between Parker's and Ackerley's versions. Here, in a couple of paragraphs, we have the edge of the autobiographer over the biographer. When the memoirist is as acute and as sincere as Ackerley, the biographer is at a hopeless disadvantage. There is so little to add, and so much to subtract.

Ackerley's sojourn in Chhatarpur (disguised as Chhokrapur in *Hindoo Holiday*) occupies a fourteen-page chapter in Parker's biography of more than four hundred pages. Since it lasted half a year in a life that took up almost seventy years, this proportion would seem far from niggardly, especially since nothing "important" occurred in India. Yet the stay in India does occupy one of Ackerley's four books, and the longest one at that. In its careful gradation of tones and values, *Hindoo Holiday* is more an artist's sketchbook than a book. India's importance to Ackerley was as a source of material, and all a biographer can do is point out how the "real" landscape and people of Chhatarpur differed from their simulacra in *Hindoo Holiday*. In the same way, a biographer of Matisse can discuss the weather, the costumes, and the models of Morocco, and then gesture in the direction of the paintings. Constrained by chronology, the biographer can't emulate the most dazzling set-piece of *Hindoo Holiday,* in which Ackerley, watching a squad of resourceful ants carry away the disabled but still living body of a fly he has just swatted, thinks suddenly of a repressed incident in the First World War, when he saw his orderly bound over the top of the trenches, kill a wounded German soldier, and return with a wristwatch, field-glasses, and other souvenirs. Meticulously transcribed, the horror of the ants' dismemberment of the twitching fly reverberates, like a small bell in a large cavern.

Ackerley turned the same coldly twinkling eye on all he surveyed. His dog's sex life, his own sex life, his father, his maharajah—he laid it all out on the dissecting table. He intended, he once wrote, to prowl about his own life as if it were "someone else's and I its historian." Unlike most historians, he never took his eyes off his subject, and he never stopped prowling. His life was forgettable, but when told in his voice, the echo lingers.

The Dead Father:
A Remembrance of
Donald Barthelme

by *Phillip Lopate*

DONALD BARTHELME HAD A SQUARISH BEARD which made him look somewhat Amish and patriarchal, an effect enhanced by his clean-shaven upper lip. It took me a while to register that he had a beard but no mustache; and once I did, I could not stop wondering what sort of "statement" he was trying to make. On the one hand it connoted Lincolnesque rectitude and dignity, like the ex–Surgeon General, C. Everett Koop. On the other hand it seemed a double message: bearded and shaven, severe and roguish, having it both ways. Finally I got up the nerve to ask him, in a kidding way, why he shaved his mustache. He told me that he couldn't grow one because he'd had a cancerous growth removed from his lip. This reply made me aware of all I didn't, probably would never, know about the man, and of my inclination to misjudge him.

I loved to watch Donald. In a way, I could never get enough of him (which is something one says about a person who always withholds a part of himself. I know, because it has been said about me). We worked together for the last eight years of his life, and were close colleagues, friends, almost-friends— which was it? I found Barthelme to be an immensely decent, generous, courtly, and yet finally unforthcoming man. He was difficult to approach, partly because I (and I was not alone here) didn't know what to do with his formidable sadness, partly because neither did he. Barthelme would have made a good king: he had the capacity of Shakespearean tragic monarchs to project a large, self-isolating presence.

The combination of his beard, bulk, and steel-rimmed eyeglasses gave him a stern Ahab appearance which he was perfectly happy to let intimidate on occasion—only to soften it with a warm glint in his eye, like a ship's captain putting his trembling crew at ease. Having read Barthelme's whimsical miniatures, I had expected a smaller, more mercurial, puckish man, certainly not this

121

big-shouldered, hard-drinking, John Wayne type. I couldn't get over the discrepancy between his physical solidity and the filigreed drollness of his art. Somewhere locked inside that large cowman's frame must be a mischievous troll; and I kept stealing glances at Donald to see if the little man would put in an appearance. As time went by, however, I learned to read his jeweled sentences in the manly baritone my ear came to identify as intrinsically Barthelmean, and the sense of contradiction all but disappeared. It became natural that our *fin de siècle* exhaustion and cultural despair should be enunciated by a tall Texan with cowboy boots.

◆◆◆

I had been teaching in the University of Houston's creative writing program for a year—the program, started by two poets, Cynthia Macdonald and Stanley Plumly, had recruited me from New York in 1980 as their first fiction writer—when the great news came down that Donald Barthelme would be joining us. Barthelme's arrival caused universal rejoicing: this would really put our program on the map, not only because Barthelme was a "name" writer, but because he was one of the handful who commanded a following among graduate writing students. Indeed, probably no other short story writer was more imitated by MFA students in the seventies and early eighties.

I was initially surprised that a writer of Barthelme's stature would relocate to Houston. True, he had been offered an endowed chair, a hefty salary, and regular paid sabbatical leaves, but that would not normally be enough to pry most established fiction writers from their comfortable lives. The key to the "seduction" (recruitment is the eros of academia) is that Barthelme was coming home. Though by birth a Philadelphian, he had grown up in Houston and was educated at the University of Houston, the same school that would now employ him. Barthelme was still remembered around town for his youthful cultural activities, reporting for the Houston *Post,* launching the UH literary magazine *Forum,* directing the Contemporary Art Museum in the early 1960s. Then he'd gone off to New York with regional upstart energy to make his mark (like Robert Rauschenberg, Andy Warhol, Merce Cunningham: our avantgardists almost always seem to come from the provinces), and a few decades later was returning famous—or as famous as serious writers become in America. It was also a family move: his aging parents, his three brothers, Pete, Frederick, and Steve, and his sister Joan still lived in Houston or near enough by. Marion Knox, Donald's second wife, was pregnant, and they both thought Houston might be an easier place to raise a child than Lower Manhattan.

I had no idea what to expect from Barthelme as a colleague: whether the weight of such a star might throw off-kilter the fragile balance of our program. But Donald proved not to have an ounce of the prima donna in him. On the contrary, he was the ultimate team player, accepting his full share of the petty, annoying bureaucratic tasks, sitting on boring departmental committees, phoning our top applicants to convince them to choose our program, lobbying university bigwigs with his good-ole-boy communication skills. A would-be graphic artist ("the pleasure of cutting up and pasting together pictures, a secret vice," he once wrote), he designed all our posters and letterheads. Donald had one of the most pronounced civic consciences I have ever come across, and was fond of exhorting us with the Allen Ginsberg line: "Come, let us put our queer shoulders to the wheel."

Each Tuesday noon we would have a meeting of the creative writing staff to determine policy. These lunch meetings took place on campus in the Galaxy Room of the School of Hotel Management; eating there was like going to a barber school for a haircut. Donald would be the first to arrive. He would order a large glass of white wine, which he would ask to have refilled several times during lunch. After we had all settled in and ordered (trial and error had convinced me that, despite poignant attempts to retool the menu, only the grilled cheese sandwich was reliable), Cynthia Macdonald, the program's founding mother and an ex–opera singer, would, with her operatic sense of urgency, alert us to the latest crisis: either our graduate students were in danger of losing their teaching stipends, or some English professor was prejudiced against our majors, or the university was hedging on its budget commitments, or a visiting writer had just called to cancel a reading.

Barthelme, who abhorred stinginess, preferred to settle the smaller crises by dipping into the "Don Fund," as the discretionary monies attached to his academic chair came to be called. He thus made it possible to circumvent the bureaucracy, save the students' literary magazine, advertise an impromptu reading, or preserve the program's honor when a visiting literary dignitary like Carlos Fuentes came to town, by taking him out to a fancy restaurant.

Sometimes, however, the problem was stickier, and had to be thrashed out by Cynthia, Donald, Stanley Plumly (who left after a few years, replaced by the poet Edward Hirsch) and myself, and a rotating visiting cast that included Ntozake Shange, Rosellen Brown, Richard Howard, Joy Williams, Jim Robison, Mary Robison, Meg Wolitzer. In the familial dynamic that developed over the years, Cynthia and Donald were Mommy and Daddy, and the rest of us siblings contending for their favor. During heated discussions, Donald would often wait until everyone else had declared a position, and then weigh in with the final word, more like an arbiter than an interested party. He was good at manipulating consensus through democratic discussion to get his way; and we made it easy for him, since everyone wanted his love and approval. At times he would inhibit opposition by indicating that any further discussion on an issue he regarded as settled was extremely dumb and ill-advised. Still, when a vote did go against him, he bowed sportingly to majority will. He often seemed to be holding back from using his full clout; he was like those professional actors who give the impression at social gatherings of saving their energy for the real performance later.

Sometimes in the midst of the meeting I would raise my eyes and find Donald's gaze fixed on me. What did he *see?* I wondered. He would immediately look away, not liking to be spied in the act of exercising curiosity. At other times, I would catch Donald at this funny habit: he would sniff his sleeve a few inches above the wrist, taking a whiff of his arm, either because he liked the smell of his sweat or he needed to ground himself, establish contact with his body when his mind was drifting toward Mars.

Though we usually agreed on specifics, Donald believed more fully in the mission of writing programs than I could. There was much talk about having to maintain our position as one of the top three writing programs in the country. By what standards, aside from wishful thinking, this ranking had been determined I never could ascertain: presumably it had something to do with the faculty's repute, the number of applications we received, and the publishing fortunes of our alumni. In any case, Donald was ever on guard against anything that might "dilute the quality of the program." Sometimes I would recommend bringing visiting writers who might be less well-known but who could give our students a broader perspective stylistically or multiculturally. "But are they any *good?*" Donald would demand, and I knew what he meant: If they were any good, why hadn't he heard of them?

Donald was a man with a great sense of loyalty to family, neighborhood, academic institution, and publisher. *The New Yorker* had published him throughout his career, and he believed in the worth of those who appeared in its pages; ditto, those authors active on the executive board of PEN, the international writers' organization. The other side of the coin was that he showed a massive incuriosity toward writers outside the mainstream or his personal network. If a novelist was recommended to us for a teaching post by his brother Rick—arriving under the familial mantle, as it were—he would display serious interest. But if you mentioned a good living writer he didn't know, his response was a quick veto. There was something of the air of a Mafia Don about Barthelme's protection: he treated his own circle of friends (Grace Paley, Ann Beattie, Roger Angell, Susan Sontag) as family, and he proposed their names for our reading series year after year. His refusal to consider literary figures who were not inside his particular spotlight used to drive me up the wall, partly because it seemed to leave out many worthy/small press/ experimental writers, and partly because I had not escaped the hell of anonymity so long ago or so conclusively as not to identify with these "unknown" wretches. But to Donald I had nothing to worry about; I was good enough to be on the writing faculty team, therefore I was one of the saved.

Ironically, Barthelme was himself an experimental, iconoclastic writer, so that there was a certain contradiction between his antitraditional literary side and his involvement in rank, the Establishment, continuity. (What else is being a teacher but an assertion of belief in continuity?)

There was always a formal side to Barthelme which I associate with the English—a Victorian dryness he used to comic effect. It crops up in his earliest stories, like the "The Big Broadcast of 1938": "Having acquired in exchange for an old house that had been theirs, his and hers, a radio or more properly radio *station,* Bloomsbury could now play 'The Star Spangled Banner,' which he had always admired immoderately, on account of its finality, as often as he liked." This qualifying, donnish quality was accompanied by an equally British terseness in social situations. "I think not," he would say in response to some proposal he considered dubious, and that would be that.

Or he would signal the conversation was at an end for him by taking your arm at the elbow and guiding you off on your rounds. I was at first astonished by this gesture, which seemed like an eruption of regal impatience. At the same time, I found something reassuring in his physical steering of me, like a father picking up his child and placing him out of harm's way.

• • •

Much of Donald Barthelme's fiction consists of witty dialogue. Yet when I think of Donald in real life, I recall few *bon mots;* I remember rather his underlying silence, which has now, in death, prevailed. Silence seemed his natural condition; his speech had very little flow; you never knew when it was going to dry up. Of course Donald talked well, in the sense that he chose his words economically and with care. His listeners would often smile at the sardonic spin he gave to well-worn figures of speech. (Among other writers, I've known only John Ashbery to take as much delight in fingering clichés.) But the pearls of wit or wisdom one might have expected from him were rare; and this was because, I think, fundamentally he did not view speech as the vehicle for expressing his inner thoughts. Rather, he treated speech as a wholly social medium, to which he subscribed, as a solid, dues-paying citizen, dipping into the common fount.

What one looks for in the conversation of writers is a chance to be taken back into the kitchen where they cook up their literary surprises: a sudden flash of truth or metaphor. Around Donald, what you got was not so much the lyrical, imaginative Barthelme as the one who treated social intercourse like a game, a tennis match, with parrying one-liners keeping the interlocutor off-balance. His remarks tended to stop rather than advance conversation.

When you waxed serious around Donald you would expect to have your wings clipped, since he regarded getting worked up about anything in public as inappropriate. "Down, boy," he frequently mocked if I started to expatiate on a subject. These interventions felt more like a fond head-pat than anything malicious. But I never could figure out if he consistently played the referee in order to keep everyone around him at a temperature suitable for his own comfort, or out of some larger sense of group responsibility, which, in his eyes, conflicted with solo flights of enthusiasm.

Barthelme clearly considered it bad form to talk about books or writing process in public. Perhaps he thought it too pedantic a topic to bring before intellectually mixed company. It also appeared that, towards the end of his life, he was bored with literature, much preferring the visual arts.

I had hoped, given the countless intellectual references sprinkled throughout Barthelme's stories, that the author of "Kierkegaard Unfair to Schlegel" and "Eugenie Grandet" would be as eager as I was to discuss our favorite authors. As it turned out, asking Barthelme what he thought was like demanding a trade secret, though I never gave up clumsily trying to pry loose his literary opinions. Once, at a brunch, on learning that the Swiss writer Max Frisch, who interested me, was a friend of Donald's, I immediately asked: "What do you think of Frisch's work?" Either I had put the question too directly, or shown too naked a desire for a glimpse at a higher circle (those writers of international stature, Frisch and Barthelme included) to let my curiosity be indulged, or Donald's feelings toward the Swiss writer were too complex or competitive for him to untangle them in public. Such speculations proliferate in the absence of a definite answer. Donald managed a grudging few syllables, to the effect that he thought Frisch's work "substantial," though "the fellow had a pretty big ego." He seemed much more comfortable discussing the rumor that Frisch might be buying an expensive loft in Soho.

This professional reticence, I should add, was by no means singular to Donald. Part of the larger loneliness of our literary life stems from the fact that writers, especially those who have reached a successful level, tend to shy away from discussing the things one would think mattered to them most—the other authors who continue to inspire them or the unsolved obstacles in their day-to-day composition—preferring instead to chatter about career moves, visiting gigs, grants, word processors, and real estate, which becomes, in effect, the language of power.

Once, when I managed to get Donald off by myself (we were driving to some forlorn suburb in outer Houston to make a fund-raising presentation), he indulged my hunger for candid literary talk. I asked him what he thought of several recent novels by Texas writers of our acquaintance. He didn't mince words, his assessments were extremely pointed and shrewd. It was exhilarating to gain admittance to the inner tabernacle of Barthelme's judgment—not to mention the fact that two writers dissecting the flaws of a third whom they both know can bond them in a deliciously fratricidal way. But, to my regret, the experience was never repeated.

Perhaps because Donald had begun as a newspaperman, he still had a fair amount of the journalist left in him, which included not only a topical alertness to fashions, but a heavy-drinking, hard-boiled, almost anti-intellectual down-playing of his own identity as practitioner of serious literature. I remember his boasting once that he'd dashed off a review on a Superman sequel, a "piece of hackwork for some glossy for a nice piece of change." Yet when the review came out, I saw that Donald had, as usual, given good weight, with an elegantly amusing, well-constructed essay. Barthelme always worked conscientiously to get the least piece of prose right. But, like the "A" student who hates to admit he studied for a test, he preferred the pretense that he was a glorified grub working to pay the bills. I think he would have *liked* to have been a hack, it was a persistent fantasy of escape from his literary conscience. He fit into that debunking, up-from-journalism tradition of American satirists: Twain, Bierce, Ring Lardner. The problem was that his *faux*-hack pose made it difficult for you to take your own writing seriously in front of him, or discuss other literature with any seriousness.

Barthelme also seemed uncomfortable with psychological conversation, which was either too intimate or too tattling for his taste. His writings make it clear that he was quite astute at character analysis; and yet there was a curious antipsychological side to him, or at least a resistance to discussing such things aloud; in this he was both a gentleman of the old school and a postmodernist. One time Donald and I were talking after a meeting about one of our colleagues, who had thrown a fit over some procedural matter. I remarked with a smile that she seemed to take a certain pleasure in releasing her wrath all the way. Donald replied that he'd known people who had had temper tantrums just for the fun of it, but surely not someone as mature as our colleague. This seemed a perfect instance of Donald's loyalty: having decided that someone was a "good guy," he did not like to acknowledge that that person might still be capable of childish or self-indulgent behavior.

◆ ◆ ◆

Once or twice a year, Marion and Don would invite me to their house: either they'd give a dinner party, or ask my girlfriend and me over for a two-couple evening. Sometimes, after a particularly happy night of warm, sparkling talk and wonderful food (both Barthelmes were superb cooks) and plentiful wine, I would think: Donald and I are actually becoming friends. I would fall under the spell of the man's gruff charm, morality, intelligence, it was like having a crush, I couldn't wait to see him again soon and take it further. But there never was any further.

I would run into him at school and say, "I really enjoyed the other evening at your house, Don."

"Well, good, good," he would reply nervously, which was his favorite way of dismissing a topic. Perhaps he was simply being modest about their hospitality; but I also thought his uneasy look expressed concern that I would start to get "mushy" on him, and make demands for a closeness he had no inclination or ability to fulfill. What I wanted was to remove the evening from the category of "dutiful community socializing which had turned out well" and place it under the file of "possible developing friendship." But the story of Barthelme's and my friendship seemed forever stalled in the early chapters; there was no accrual of intimacy from one time to the next.

In trying to account for this stasis, I often wondered if it was a question of age. Twelve years separated us, an awkward span: I was too old and set as a writer to inspire the parental fondness he bestowed on his favorite graduate students, but too young to be accepted as a peer. I was the same age, in fact, as his younger brother Frederick, who was enjoying considerable success; if anything, insurgent writers twelve years younger may have seemed to him enviable pups, breathing down his neck. Then again, the appetite for shared confidences often dwindles after fifty; at that point, some writers begin to husband their secrets for the page. In any case, I sensed that he'd become used to accepting rather passively the persistent courtship by others (which is not my mode). As a woman novelist said to me: "Donald sits there on the couch and expects you to make a pass at him."

I got a deeper glimpse into his own thinking on friendship one night at a dinner party at the Barthelmes' apartment in Houston. After dinner, Donald and I settled into a rare personal conversation. I asked him if he showed his work to anyone before he sent it off for publication. He said he showed Marion; that was about it. I then inquired if he had any close friends who were his peers, with whom he could talk writing. He surprised me by saying he didn't think so. He said he had had two good friends, and they had both died. One was Thomas B. Hess, the other Harold Rosenberg, both well-known art critics. "I started hanging around them in the sixties. They were older than me and they were my mentors, and it was great that we could talk about art and not necessarily about literature. They taught me a whole lot. I haven't learned anything since. I'm still working off that old knowledge.

"It was distressing how they both died around the same time, which left me feeling rather...odd," he said. "What I really want are older men, father-figures who can teach *me* something. I don't want to be people's damn father-figure. I want to be the baby—it's more fun. The problem is that the older you get, the harder it is to find these older role models."

A reluctant patriarch, still looking for the good father. Having been on that same search off and on, I understood some of Donald's loneliness. It doesn't matter how old you get, you still have an ache for that warm understanding. He began talking about his own father, Donald Barthelme Senior, a highly respected architect in Texas. His father, he said, had been "very uptight" with them when they were growing up: "I think he was terrified of children." As an architecture professor, Barthelme Senior always tried to get the better of his students and demonstrate his superior knowledge. "Well of course we know more than our students, that's not the point!" said Donald.

I thought of his novel, *The Dead Father,* and wondered whether that title had irked Barthelme Senior, who was (and is still) very much alive. The book is Barthelme's best novel and one of his finest achievements. In this part-parody, part-serious Arthurian romance, the Dead Father is an active character, boasting, complaining, demanding attention. Like a corpse that will not acknowledge its demise, this patriarch who has been "killed" (or at least, put in the shade) by his more successful son seems to represent the dead weight of guilt in the Oedipal triumph. *The Dead Father* is an obsessive meditation on generational competitiveness, the division between younger and older men, and the fear of time's decaying hand.

Many of Barthelme's short stories revolve around Oedipal tensions implicit in education, mentorship, and the master-flunky tie. Take, for instance, "The King of Jazz," where Hokie Mokie blows away the young Japanese challenger in a jam session, or "Conversations With Goethe," where the narrator-flunky is triumphantly put in his place at the end:

> Critics, Goethe said, are the cracked mirror in the grand ballroom of the creative spirit. No, I said, they were, rather, the extra baggage on the great cabriolet of conceptual progress. "Eckermann," said Goethe, "*shut up.*"

I always winced when I heard Barthelme read that story aloud (as he often did), partly because of the glee he seemed to express at maintaining the upper hand, and partly because of the hint—at least I took it that way—that any friendship with him would have to grow out of an inferior's flattery.

Sometimes it seemed that Donald was not only bored with everyone around him, but that he had ceased to expect otherwise. In Houston, he drew his social circle from mildly awed professionals—doctors, lawyers, etc.— who could produce a soothing harmonious patter, into which he would insert an occasional barb to perk things up. Mostly Donald preferred to stand back, making sure the social machinery was running smoothly.

In his distance from us, he seemed to be monitoring some inner unease. I suppose that was partly his alcoholism. No matter how sociably engaged alcoholics are, one corner of their minds will always be taking stock of the liquor supply and plotting how to get in another drink without being too obvious about it. I never saw Donald falling-down drunk; he held his liquor, put on a good performance of sobriety; but, as he once admitted, "I'm a little drunk all the time." Sometimes, when he drank a lot, his memory blacked out.

Example: During a spring break, Cynthia Macdonald delegated me to phone Donald in New York and find out which students he wanted to recommend for a prestigious fellowship. I called him around eight in the evening, and he gave his recommendations, then asked me a series of questions about departmental matters, raises, courses for next year, etc. A few days later Cynthia called him and mentioned in passing the telephone conversation he had had with me. Donald insisted he had not spoken to me in weeks. Cynthia told me to call him again, this time making sure it was before five o'clock, when the chances for sobriety were greater. The odd part is that when I did call him, we had the identical conversation: he put the same questions in the same order, with the same edgy impatience, quickly voicing one question as soon as I had answered the last. I never let on that he was repeating himself, but it struck me that he must often have been on automatic pilot, fooling the world with rote questions while his mind was clouded by alcohol.

At times he gave the impression, like a burn victim lying uncomfortably in the hospital, that there was something I was neglecting to do or figure out that might have put him at greater ease. Perhaps there is always a disappointment that an alcoholic feels in a nonalcoholic: an awareness that, no matter how sympathetic the nondrinker may seem, he will never really "get" it. That was certainly true for me: I didn't get it. I knew Donald disapproved of my not drinking—or not drinking enough. He once objected to our holding a meeting at my house, saying, "Phillip never has any liquor on hand." Which wasn't true, but interesting that he should think so. The noon meeting took place at my apartment anyhow; Donald arrived with a bottle, just in case.

I also think he disapproved, if that's the word, of my not philandering. When an artist in town began openly having an extramarital affair, and most of the Houston arts community sided with his wife, Donald reassured the man that these things happened, telling him comparable experiences from his past. One of the ways Donald bonded with someone was through a shared carnal appetite—what used to be called a "vice," like drinking or womanizing.

In keeping with his Southwestern upbringing, Donald combined the strong, silent dignity of the Western male with the more polished gallantry of the South. He liked to be around women, particularly younger women, and grew more relaxed in their company. I don't think this was purely a matter of lechery, though lust no doubt played its classical part. The same enchantment showed in his delight with his older daughter, Anna, a vibrant, outgoing girl from an earlier marriage who had been brought up largely by her mother in Scandinavia, and who came to live with the Barthelmes while studying theater at the University of Houston. Given Barthelme's own (to use his phrase) "double-minded" language, hemmed in by the ironies of semantic duplicity, girl-talk must have seemed a big relief. In his novel *Paradise* (1986), the hero, a middle-aged architect named Simon, shares an apartment with three beautiful young women, and seems to enjoy listening in on their conversation about clothes, makeup, and jobs as much as sleeping with them.

In *The Dead Father*, Barthelme shows an awareness of the way a fifty-year-old's interest in young women might look to one's wife:

Fifty-year-old boys...are boys because they don't want to be old farts, said Julie. The old fart is not cherished in this society.... Stumbling from the stage is anathema to them, said Julie, they want to be nuzzling new women when they are ninety.

What is wrong with that? asked the Dead Father. Seems perfectly reasonable to me.

The women object, she said. Violently.

Certainly some of the women in the writing program objected to what they felt was Barthelme's preference for the pretty young females in class. I ended up being a sort of confidant of the middle-aged women students, who had raised families and were finally fulfilling their dreams to become writers; several complained to me that Barthelme would make short shrift of their stories for being too domestic and psychological. Of course these were the very materials I had encouraged them to explore. It's true that Donald once said to me if he had to read another abortion or grandmother story he would pack it in. I understood that what he really objected to was the solemn privileging of certain subjects over linguistic or formal invention; but I was sufficiently competitive with him for the students' love that it pleased me to hear their beefs. They also claimed that his real pets were the talented young men. This is a standard pattern in writing programs, with their hierarchies of benediction and benefaction. I too observed how certain of our top male students would gravitate to Barthelme, and he would not only help edit their books and get them publishers and agents, but would invite them to hang out with him as his friend. Perhaps "jealous" is too strong a word, but I was certainly a little envious of their easy access to Donald.

In the classroom, Donald could be crusty, peremptorily sitting a student down after a few pages of a story that sounded unpromising to him—a practice his favorites endorsed as honest and toughening-up, while those less sure of their abilities took longer to recover. Where his true generosity as a teacher shone, I thought, was in individual conferences, where he would go over the students' manuscripts he had line-edited as meticulously as if they had been his own. Often, as I was leaving, I would see a line waiting outside his office; he put many more hours into student conferences than I did. I sensed that in the last years his main reading was student work—or at least he led me to believe that. When I would ask Don what he'd been reading lately, he replied: "Class stories, theses. Who has time for anything else?"

Donald loved to play talent scout. When one of his graduate students finished a manuscript he thought was publishable, he would call up his agent, Lynn Nesbit, and some New York editors, maybe start a few fires at *The New Yorker*. I was reluctant to take on this role with students: both because I wasn't sure I had the power to pull it off, and because I didn't like the way the writing program's success stories generated a bitter atmosphere among the unanointed.

But Donald acknowledged no such side-effects: to him, each book contract drew more attention to the program and simply made us "hotter." The students, whatever qualms they may have had about the hazards of brat-pack careerism, in the last analysis wanted a Godfather to promote them. They were no dummies; they knew that one word from Barthelme could start a bidding war.

It's embarrassing to admit, but a few times I also tried to get Donald to use his influence in my behalf. That he had a measure of power in the literary world became steadily clearer to me from remarks he would drop at our lunchtime meetings: how he had helped so-and-so receive a lucrative prize, or had worked behind the scenes at the American Academy of Arts and Letters to snare honors for the "good guys." The Prix de Rome, given out by the Academy, went to several of his protégés in the space of a few years. Well, if goodies were being handed out, what the heck, I wanted some too. Once I asked him shamelessly (trying to make it sound like a joke): "Why don't you ever recommend me for a Prix de Rome or one of those prizes? " After a stunned pause, he answered: "I think they're interested in younger men, Phillip."

Flattering as it was to be told I was past the point of needing such support, I suspected more was involved. During the eight years we taught together, three of my books were published; I sent them to Donald for advance quotes, but he always managed to misplace the galleys until long after a blurb would have done any good. By then I'd had enough good quotes; what disappointed me more was that Donald had not responded to my work.

Months after the time had passed for Donald to "blurb" my novel, *The Rug Merchant,* I continued to hope that he would at least read the book and— tell me honestly what he thought. I asked him a few times if he had gotten to it yet, and he said, "Regrettably, no." Finally, I must have made enough of a pest out of myself to have an effect. We were sitting together at a party, and by this point in the evening Barthelme was pretty well in his cups. His speech slurred, he said he had read my novel and "it was a good job." He was sorry the main character, Cyrus, had not gotten round to marrying the girl in the end. "Anyway—a good job," he said again, tapping my knee.

In that neurotic way we have of probing a loose tooth, I brooded that Donald didn't like my writing. More likely, he simply felt indifferent toward it. A few times he did compliment something I'd written, usually after having seen it in a magazine. But I was insatiable, because his approval meant so much to me—a long-awaited sign of love from the emotionally remote father. The irony is that I so longed for approval from a writer whose own work I didn't entirely accept. Our aesthetics were worlds apart: I was interested in first person confessional writing and the tradition of psychological realism, whereas Barthelme seemed to be debunking the presumptions of realist fiction. I suppose the fact that this blessing would have come from someone who was not in my literary camp but who represented the other orthodoxy, formalism, seemed to make it all the more desirable. I imagined—craved—a reconciliation, a pure respect between his and my style in some impossible utopian space of literary exchange.

For a long while I felt secretly guilty toward Donald because I did not love his work enough. I respected it, of course, but in a detached way. When I first began reading Donald Barthelme in the sixties, he struck me as a trickster, playfully adjusting a collection of veils, impossible to pin down. Later, when I got to know Donald, I saw that almost every line of his was a disguised personal confession—if nothing else, then of inner weather and melancholy: he was masterful at casting deep shadows through just the right feints, a sort of toreador courting and dodging meaning, sometimes even letting himself be gored by it for the sake of the story. Recently, the more I read him, the more I've come to the conclusion that he *was* a great writer. Minor, yes, but great at his chosen scale. He could catch sorrow in a sentence. A dozen of his stories are amazing and will last.

The bulk of his best work, to my mind, was done in the sixties: we sometimes forget how energized Barthelme was by the counterculture, the politics and playful liberatory urges of that period. His peak lasted through the early seventies, up to and including *The Dead Father* (1975). After that, his fiction lost much of its emotional openness, devolving on the whole into clever, guarded pastiche. Always the professional, he could still cobble together a dazzling sentence or amusing *aperçu*, but he became increasingly a master of trifles. There is, however, something noble in a great talent adapting itself to diminished capacities. His 1986 novel *Paradise* is a sweet if thin fabrication. Between the lines of its sportive harem plot, one can read an honest admission of burnout. Donald confessed to me that he thought the book "pretty weak," and I hope I had the hypocrisy to hide my agreement. *Paradise* is honest, too, in departing from his earlier intellectual references, and reflecting the creature comforts which engaged him mentally during his last years: food, decor, and sex.

As he got older and was drawn more to comfort, Houston seemed an appropriate choice of residence. It is an easy city to live in—not as stimulating as one might like at times, but pleasant. The Barthelmes lived on the second floor of a brick Tudor house in one of the city's most beautiful areas, the oak-lined South Boulevard. Just across the street was Poe School, an excellent elementary school where his little girl Katharine started to go when she was old enough. Nearby were the tennis courts where Marion played regularly. In Houston the Barthelmes enjoyed more of a black-tie, upper-middle-class life than in New York, going regularly to the opera, the symphony, the ballet; Donald became a city booster, telling outsiders that the Houston performing companies were good and getting better every year. Houston proved an ideal place for him to act out his civic impulse: of the ten established writers in town, each one called upon to do one's community share, Donald was the most famous and most cherished, being a native son. This is what his compatriots in the New York literary world, for whom his resettlement in Texas seemed a perverse self-exile, found so hard to understand.

I remember telling one of Don's Manhattan friends, who was worried that he might be wasting away down there, how packed the literary life was in Houston, how needed he was. Secretly, I asked myself whether living in Houston had indeed dried up some of his creative juices. Having never known Barthelme during his "conquering years," I had no way to compare; but I suspect that Houston was not a factor. His creative crisis had already started in the late seventies, when he was still living in New York; if anything, he may have accepted the move to Texas partly in the hope of being shaken out of stagnation and personal loss.

◆ ◆ ◆

Barthelme's sardonic, Olympian use of brand names in his fiction led me to the mistaken idea that he took a dim view of consumerism, whereas I found him to be more a happy captive of it. He would often talk to me about new types of VCRs or word processors, a sportscar he was fantasizing buying; or the latest vicissitudes with his pickup truck—assuming incorrectly that I knew as much as the typical American male about machines. He was also very interested in food: I would run into him shopping at the supermarket, wicker basket in hand, throwing in a package of tortellini; one time he began talking about the varieties of arugula and radicchio, then added that he could never leave the place without spending a fortune. "They create these needs and you can't resist. They've figured out a way to hook you," he said.

These disquisitions on arugula were not exactly what I had hoped for from Barthelme. I kept waiting for him to give me more of his innermost thoughts. But later I began to think: suppose I had been misinterpreting him all along, because of my own Brooklyn-Jewish expectations of conversation—that mixture of confiding anecdote, analytic "delving," and intellectual disputation—when in fact he was disclosing his inner self with every remark, and I was too dumb or incredulous to perceive it. Maybe he was not trying to frustrate me by holding back the goods of his interior life, but was confiding his preoccupation with things, comforts, sensual pleasures.

And why couldn't I accept that? I seemed to have to view it as a copout, a retreat into banality; I wanted him to stand up and be the staunch intellectual hero-father. Part of me responded with a line from Ernest Becker's *The Denial of Death:* "The depressed person enslaves himself to the trivial." Another part suspected that I, long-time bachelor, was merely envious of his settled domestic family life. It should be clear by now that Donald Barthelme was an enormously evocative figure for me. The difficulty is distinguishing between what was really Donald and what he evoked in me—not necessarily the same thing. If I came to regard Donald as the prisoner of a bourgeois lifestyle dedicated to discreet good taste, down to the popular Zurburan reproduction of fruit above his dining room table, this probably says less about Donald than about my own pathological attraction-repulsion vis-à-vis the Good Life, or what passes in today's world for *joie de vivre.*

No doubt Barthelme *was* often depressed and withdrawn, underneath all that fixation on obtainable pleasures. But he also seemed reasonably contented much of the time, at home with Marion and his two daughters. The younger Barthelme had written scornfully about married life: "The world in the evening seems fraught with the absence of promise, if you are a married man. There is nothing to do but go home and drink your nine drinks and forget about it" ("Critique de la Vie Quotidienne"). The later Barthelme, now remarried, wrote in "Chablis":

> I'm sipping a glass of Gallo Chablis with an ice cube in it, smoking, worrying. I worry that the baby may jam a kitchen knife into an electrical outlet while she's wet. I've put those little plastic plugs into all the electrical outlets but she's learned how to pop them out. I've checked the Crayolas. They've made the Crayolas safe to eat—I called the head office in Pennsylvania. She can eat a whole box of Crayolas and nothing will happen to her. If I don't get the new tires for the car I can buy the dog.

The tires, the baby, the Crayolas, the dog: the tone seems more fondly engaged with domesticity. If the later stories seem to have lost an edge, it's also possible that Donald was simply happier.

His moments of joy seemed most often connected with his child of middle age, Katharine, whom he was smitten by and who was in truth a remarkably adorable, lively, bright little girl. I remember once hailing him as he carried Katharine on his shoulders across the street. "We're just setting off for an ice cream cone," he explained, blushing to his roots as if I had come upon him in a guilty secret. I had indeed caught him at his most unguarded, a doting father/horsie, without his irony or gravity buckled on.

When Donald went back to New York for the summer months, he became slightly more nervous and speedy—or, as Marion put it ruefully, he "reverted to Type A"; but for that very reason, I think, I felt closer to, more in harmony with him there. In New York, also, we were removed from the demands of the writing program, and so I found it easier to pretend that we were not only colleagues but friends. The Barthelmes had retained, after protracted warfare with the landlord, their great floor-through apartment on West 11th Street: the walls were painted Pompeiian red; a large framed Ingres poster greeted the visitor; the radio was usually tuned to jazz; on the coffee table were oversized art books, often with texts by friends, such as Ann Beattie's *Alex Katz*. Barthelme may have been a postmodernist, but his furnishings held to the scrupulous purity of high modernism, the leather and chrome of MOMA's design galleries. As soon as you entered, Donald offered you a drink, and it was bad form to refuse, if only because your not having one undercut his pretext for imbibing. He was an extremely gracious host, perhaps overdoing the liquor refills, but otherwise attentive as a Bedouin to your comfort.

In May of 1987, by a coincidence having nothing to do with Donald, I sublet an apartment in the same brownstone on West 11th Street where the Barthelmes lived. Kirkpatrick and Faith Sale, their writer-editor friends, occupied the garden apartment below them, and I was two flights up in a tiny studio, sublet from an ailing Finn who had gone back to his native country for medical treatment. Though the building had more than its share of literary vibrations and timeworn, rent-stabilized charm, I quickly grew dissatisfied with my bare studio cubicle. It was overlooking the street, and very noisy, especially on weekends when the rowdy packs spilling out of Ray's Pizza on Sixth Avenue clamored up the block.

Donald knocked on my door the day he arrived in New York (I had preceded him by three weeks) and immediately began rearranging my room. "That bed doesn't belong there," he said, pointing to the Finn's futon. "The lamp's in the wrong place, too." The interior decorator side of Donald took over; I became passively content to let him dictate the proper placement of objects. He insisted on loaning me some excess furniture from his apartment, and in no time at all I had an attractive Scandinavian rug, a chair ("You can borrow my Wassily chair—it's a facsimile of the Breuer"), a typewriter table, a trunk that would do as a coffee table, and some art posters for the walls. He kept running up and downstairs, hauling pieces up from the basement storage.

Donald was a true good neighbor, and I could see he was delighted to have hit upon a way to help me. As long as I expected any sort of intimacy from him, it made him uncomfortable, but if I approached him as one generic human being to another, with a problem that needed fixing, he would be there instantly. If I had a flat tire, if my car engine needed a start-up, if I lacked home furnishings, I knew I could come to Donald for help. This neighborliness and common decency struck me as very Texan. Once, when my apartment in Houston had been burglarized and all my appliances stolen, Donald offered to loan me the little black-and-white television he and Marion used to keep in the kitchen for the evening news while they were preparing dinner. The generosity of this sacrifice I only understood when I returned the set three months later, and saw how happy they were to get it back.

In any case, that summer Donald continued to take an active interest in my housing situation; and when I found a charming one-bedroom apartment on Bank Street, three blocks away, and signed a two-year lease, he went with me to have a look. By now I had accepted him as my habitational guru. Through his eyes I suddenly saw it as much smaller than I'd remembered, but he passed over that in silence. "Very nice. Very nice. If I were you, though, I'd have these wall stains removed," he said. "It's simple to do. I can help. Also, if you decide to paint the place, I'm good at paint jobs."

Here was a man who had barely addressed ten sentences to me during the past six months in Houston, and now he was volunteering to paint my house and wash the stains from my walls. I tabled the repainting idea, but I did enlist Donald's help in lugging my belongings the three blocks from West 11th to Bank Street. On the Saturday I moved it was ninety-four degrees, naturally, and several trips were required, and we must have looked a sight, Sancho Panza and the Don with his scraggly beard, pulling boxes roped together on a small dolly. At one point the cart tipped over and spilled half my papers onto the sidewalk. After that, I let Donald carry the lion's share of the weight, he having a broader back and a greater liking (I told myself) for manual labor than I, as well as more steering ability. He was hilarious on the way over, joking about the indignity of being a beast of burden, and I must admit it tickled me to think of using one of America's major contemporary writers as a drayhorse. But why not take advantage when he seemed so proud of his strength, so indestructible, even in his mid-fifties?

When I was set up in my new apartment I invited the Barthelmes over for Sunday brunch. It was both a return for the many dinner parties they had invited me to, and a way of asserting that I was now a responsible adult entertaining on my own. Marion, who had just been in Vermont with Katharine, showed up looking radiant and tanned in a sundress. Donald was ill-at-ease that day, as though having to get through an unpleasant obligation—or else hung over. I remember there was a direct overhead sun out on the terrace that bothered him into changing his seat several times, and made me worry about the food melting. I had overdone the spread, with so much lox, bagels, quiche, focaccia, orange juice, fruit, pie, and coffee as to leave little room for our plates. But I pulled out all the stops to be amusing, and gradually Donald began to unbend, as we sat out on the terrace gabbing about the latest plays and movies and art shows and people we knew. Meanwhile, Katharine had discovered the hammock, and was having a great time bouncing in and out of it and performing "risqué" peekaboo fandangos. As usual, she and I flirted, Donald pretended to look paternally askance, and Marion was ladylike, furthering the conversation with her journalist's bright curiosity while supervising Katharine with a light hand.

◆ ◆ ◆

Whenever, in the face of his opaque silence, I began wondering if I had fallen out of Barthelme's good graces, someone would reassure me: "Oh, but Don's very fond of you. He always asks after you in an interested way." During the spring semester of 1988, however, I kept having the feeling that Donald was becoming cooler toward me. Interactions that used to take up thirty-five seconds were now clipped to twelve. Nor had I been invited to the Barthelme house for their customary dinner. Had I done something to offend him? I raised the question to Ed Hirsch, who was closer to Donald than I was, and Eddie told me that he had detected the same curtness in Barthelme of late—which consoled me, I must admit.

Then on April 15th, we received the awful, sickening news that Donald had had to go to the hospital for throat cancer. His doctor, we learned now, had been treating it with antibiotics, but eventually decided an operation would be necessary, as the tumor turned out to be larger than originally thought. All along Donald had kept his illness secret from us, whether out of privacy or stoicism scarcely matters. I was ashamed that I had been taking his withdrawal personally. We were told he would be in the hospital anywhere from five to fourteen days, but not to visit him there as he didn't want people seeing him in such condition.

About a week after he had come home from the hospital, and we were informed it was all right to pay a brief visit, I dropped by the Barthelme house. Knowing his love for jazz, I had bought him five archival jazz albums as a get-well present. With his newly shaven chin, Donald looked harshly exposed and rubicund. His eyes were dazed. He had a tube running from his nose to his mouth like an elephant's proboscis; its purpose was to feed him liquids, as his throat was still too sore to take in solids.

We sat in his living room, staring across at each other, having nothing to say. When I handed him the stack of jazz records he patted them wordlessly, without bothering to examine what they were. Though I knew he must be extremely weak, I still felt hurt: wouldn't he have at least read the titles if someone he liked more had brought them? I told myself I was being ridiculous, the man was gravely ill—put ego aside for once!—and began cranking up conversation. As usual, Donald was the master of one-liners. "Demerol is great stuff." And: "I'm tired of sounding like Elmer Fudd." The tube pinching his nose did make his speech sound gurgled.

He asked testily about our having moved to offer someone a teaching position for next year while he was in the hospital. Though Donald definitely liked the writer, I sensed an undercurrent of breached protocol. I explained that it was an emergency and we couldn't keep the man waiting any longer. "Well good, good," he said. I apologized for our having acted without his final input. Barthelme nodded. His daughter Katharine ran into the room, naked and wet. "Don't look at me!" she commanded. "I just took a showw-er!" Donald smiled, followed her with his eyes. I excused myself after another minute or two. A painful half-hour.

The next week, though there was really no need for him to do so, Donald came to our Tuesday lunch meeting. He said he was bored hanging around the house. He also seemed to be telling us with this visit: I may be sick but it doesn't mean I'm giving up my stake in the program. Perhaps because he was up and about, and therefore one expected an improvement, his pasty, florid appearance shocked me more than when I had seen him at home. He looked bad. We wanted him to go home and lie down, not sit through our boring agenda.

I could only agree when someone said afterward: "That just wasn't Donald." Not only had he lost his beard, but his glass of white wine. The doctors had told him from now on he was to give up all alcohol and tobacco; these two habits had probably irritated the throat cancer in the first place.

Over the next few weeks, Donald began to enjoy a remission, and we let ourselves hope that he was out of danger. That summer I moved back to New York, quitting the job at Houston, but I kept tabs on him from mutual friends. They told me he was becoming the old Donald again, except that he seemed miraculously to have given up liquor and smoking—oh, every now and then cadging a cigarette or sneaking a sip of wine at a party when Marion's back was turned.

During the spring of 1989, Barthelme went to Italy, invited by the American Academy of Rome and visiting Ed Hirsch, who was there on a Prix de Rome. From all accounts, Donald was in good spirits in Rome. Passing up sight-seeing, he preferred to spend his days marketing, cooking, and working on his new novel, *The King*. So in July, when I ran into someone who told me Donald was in bad shape, I wanted to argue that that was old news, no longer current. But it was current. I was stunned, yet at the same time not: when you learn that someone in remission from cancer has had a relapse, it is never a total surprise. I prayed that Donald would somehow be strong enough to pull out of it again.

A week later, waiting by the cash register for a breakfast table at the Black Labrador Inn in Martha's Vineyard, I was turning the pages of the *New York Times* and came across Donald Barthelme's obituary. There was that familiar face, staring at me with unruffled calm. It wore the same expression he wrote about in his story, "Critique de la Vie Quotidienne": "you assume a thoughtful look (indeed, the same grave and thoughtful look you have been wearing all day, to confuse your enemies and armor yourself against the indifference of your friends)..."

I suddenly remembered the time I had written an essay on friendship for *Texas Monthly*, and I had described a "distinguished colleague" (transparently Donald), whom I liked but with whom I could never establish a real friendship. To my surprise, since Barthelme generally shunned confrontation of any sort, he confronted me on it. "I saw what you wrote about me in that *Texas Monthly* piece," he said, letting me know by his ensuing silence that if I felt there was anything needing to be cleared up, he was willing to give me the opportunity.

"Did it...distress you ? " I asked.

"I was a bit distressed, yes. But I recognize that that's your style as a personal essayist. You write about people you know; I don't."

"Did you think that what I wrote was...inaccurate?"

"No, no, not necessarily. I grant you it's hard for me to make friends. Ever since my two best friends Tom Hess and Harold Rosenberg died..." and he repeated substantially what he had told me the first time.

After his death, a wise man who knew us both said: "Maybe Donald couldn't be a friend, but I think he had deep feelings for all of us." It was hard for me sometimes to distinguish between the taciturnity of deep feeling and unconcern. On my side, I felt guilty for having been one of those indifferent friends, who didn't take the trouble to call near the end and ask about his condition. I had told myself, Don't bother them, you're not in the inner circle anyway—a poor excuse.

I have been assessing him in these pages through the prism of my needs, hence probably misjudging him. Certainly it is perverse of me to have manufactured a drama of being rejected by Barthelme, when the objective truth is that he was almost always kind to me—distant (such was his character) but benevolent.

It has not been easy to conjure up a man who, for all his commanding presence, had something of the ghost about him even in his lifetime. My relationship to him all along was, in a sense, with a rich, shifting absence. Donald is still hovering on the page, fading, I am starting to lose him. I had hoped to hold onto him by fixing his portrait. And now I hear him knocking, like the statue of the slain Commendatore in *Don Giovanni,* warning me that I will be punished for my sins, my patricidal betrayals of his privacy.

I have one more memory to offer: the night of the first fund-raising ball for the creative writing program. When the ball had ended, I could sense an air of letdown afterwards as Donald and Marion, Cynthia and I drove in the Barthelmes' pickup truck to their house for a nightcap. The event had been pretty successful, but not as large a windfall financially as we had fantasized, after the year's work we had put into it. I tried a few jokes, but I could see the others had invested too much in the evening to jest about it. When we arrived, instead of sitting around having a postmortem, we—began singing songs. Cynthia has a fine trained voice, and Donald had a lovely baritone and a great memory for lyrics: Cole Porter, musical comedy, jazz ballads. It turned into a wonderfully pleasurable evening. Each of us alternated proposing songs, and the others joined in, to the best of our memories. Slowly the tension of organizing and ball arrangements seeped away. Donald seemed particularly at ease. There was no need to articulate his thoughts, except in this indirect, song-choosing fashion. It was another instance of Barthelme expressing himself most willingly through another outlet than his chosen vocation: Donald the would-be graphic artist, the moving man, the decorator, the pop singer.

Looking
and
Listening

Bob Dylan

by Christopher Ricks

I WANT TO TALK* ABOUT ENDINGS. I'm interested in questions of technique, under the aegis of T. S. Eliot's remark that we cannot say at what point technique begins or where it ends. Endings are a very important part of Dylan's art, and I want to talk about endings particularly in relation to rhymes. You'll remember the stroke of genius that makes the line, "Oh, Mama, can this really be the end?" be the antepenultimate line of the song in which it regularly appears. It's a question that you keep asking yourself in the course of that song, what is really going to be the end of this song? And the rhyme in that refrain is beautifully metaphorical, because it's a rhyme of the word "end" with the word "again": "Oh, Mama, can this really be the end / To be stuck inside of Mobile / With the Memphis blues again." "End" and "again" are metaphorically a rhyme because every rhyme is both an endness and an againness. That's what a rhyme is, intrinsically, a form of again, and a form of an ending.

Dylan's always been fascinated with the question of how you end a songbook, how you end a concert, how you end an interview, how you end an album. And therefore fascinated by the unending. There's a moment early in his immensely long film *Renaldo and Clara*, when you hear the man on the radio who is warning drivers about the wet road and saying, "Hydroplaning can seriously impair your stopping ability." And meanwhile something happens to the music in the background. Dylan is interested in "stopping ability." A key thing again and again in his songs, and I think it's one of the reasons his recent songs have not been as good, his having lost this (perhaps he'll

---

*Literally. This, like several of the other pieces in the book, was originally delivered as a talk in a lecture series sponsored by *The Threepenny Review,* and was subsequently published in the magazine. (*Ed.*)

recover it*), is the question how long can you go on doing something? That is, a characteristic Dylan song may be assuring someone: "All I really want to do / Is, baby, be friends with you." Now, how long can you go on saying that? I mean, you can say it a few times, but there's a point at which it wears thin, or sounds demented. How long can you go on urging somebody, "Don't think twice, it's all right"? You can say it more than twice, but can you tell somebody fifty times not to think twice?

There are some words of his which don't get printed in the songbooks or in the book of words, and that's where the women in "New Pony" sing in chorus all the time, "How much longer?" "How much longer?" they keep singing. This is a question partly about how much longer you will be satisfied with your new pony-woman and not have to shoot her to put her out of her misery and get some other new pony. But the words also mean how much longer is the song going to go on? How much longer? This is the question all the time.

Philip Larkin was to record his poems and the publishers sent round a slip asking you to buy it. It had a statement from the poet, encouraging you. Philip Larkin was insisting, with that great lugubrious relish of his, "The proper place for my poems is the printed page," and he warned you how much you would lose if you listened to them. "Think of all the mis-hearings, the *their/there* confusions, the submergence of rhyme, the disappearance of stanza shape, even the comfort of knowing how far you are from the end." When you read a poem, when you see it on the page, you register—whether consciously or not—that this is a poem in three stanzas: I've read one; I'm now reading the second; one to go. This is the feeling as you read it, and it's a terrible collapse when you turn the page and find, "Oh, that was the end. How curious." Larkin's own endings are consummate. And what he knows is that your ear cannot *hear* the end approaching as your eye—the organ which allows you to read—*sees* the end of the poem approaching. This makes the relationship of an artist like Dylan to song and ending quite different from the relation of an artist like Donne or Larkin to ending. The eye sees that it is approaching its ending, as Jane Austen can make jokes about your knowing that you're hastening towards perfect felicity because there are only a few pages left of the novel. The novel physically tells you that it is about to come to an end. *The French Lieutenant's Woman* didn't work, because you knew perfectly well that since it wasn't by Idries Shah there was going to be print on the last hundred pages. So it couldn't be about to end, isn't that right? because this chunk of it was still there, to come.

◆ ◆ ◆

*He has. *Oh Mercy* (September 1989) is alive again to this; such a question haunts, for instance, "Most of the Time."

Think back to early days with endings, and to how Dylan chose to end "Just
Like Tom Thumb's Blues." What makes the end of that feel truly an ending?
The last two lines, remember: "I'm going back to New York City / I do believe I've had enough." End of song. Now this feels like an ending for the perfectly simple stroke that all the lines in that stanza rhyme, which is not true
of any previous stanza in the song. You don't have to be conscious of it, but it
works on your ear to tell you there's something different about this stanza;
all its lines are rhyming. Whether you consciously record this, you register it.
It's this that makes the last stanza feel truly an ending and not just the stopping of the song. And ("going back to New York City") it has an allusive
comic relation to the first song on his first album, "Talking New York," the
end of which, again you'll remember, is "So long, New York. / Howdy, East
Orange." Now, why is that such a wonderful ending? Because of the comic
relationship of an apple to an orange. That is, it depends upon what New
York is known as, apple-wise, and so there's a curious subterranean semantic
rhyming going on. But it depends, too, upon the fact that "orange" famously
is a word that does not have a rhyme in English. Dylan was asked about this
on one occasion in an interview. Somebody kept harassing him in 1968, "Do
you have a rhyme for orange?" And he kept saying, "Ah yeah, rhyme for orange,
fine," you know, "I'll tell you the rhyme in a minute," and so on. It goes on,
and he doesn't produce a rhyme for orange, whereas apple is very easy to
rhyme with. Dylan uses the curious feeling in that particular part of such a
blues song, where the last moment doesn't rhyme—stanzas rhyme, don't
they?—and instead there is this curious sidling movement, "Howdy, East
Orange," which doesn't rhyme. The reason why Marvell's line about the
orange is so beautiful is that the inversion is justified: "He hangs in shades
the orange bright, / Like golden lamps in a green night." The inversion of
"orange bright" is justified by the fact that there isn't a rhyme for orange
anyway, and if he'd said "He hangs in shades the bright orange," he'd have
had to have recourse to a mountain range in Wales called Blorenge. Even the
later, greater rhymester Robert Browning didn't have a satisfactory rhyme
for orange. There's a kind of comedy which wants to use the fact that some
words do and other words don't rhyme.

If you take the other one of Dylan's own songs on the first album, which is
"Song for Woody," it raises the question about how you end a gratitude song.
Dylan has always been a genius in gratitude, a virtue very underrated in human
affairs and extremely difficult to take into art. The song has to cease, ultimately,
but it must not just stop being grateful. Let me remind you how it ends. "I'm
a-leaving tomorrow, but I could leave today, / Somewhere down the road
someday. / The very last thing that I'd want to do / Is to say I've been hittin'
some hard travelin' too." The very last thing I'd want to do, in my respect for
you, is to lay claim to the kind of authority and experience that you've got.

The rhymes in this stanza are completely different from the rhymes in the previous ones, first because it rhymes "day" with "day," and second because it then rhymes "do" with "too," which is the only rhyme in the song which comes back. There's a lovely stroke which simply takes advantage of the idiom, "The very last thing that I'd want to do." Now that's *not* the last line in the song—it is the penultimate line—but it begins the last sentence of the song. It hits hard with very strong internal rhyming: "The very last thing that I'd want *to do* is *to* say...*too.*" There's a conviction in the thoughts being plaited together at the end through the very sounds.

He's always been wonderful with rhymes, and it's quite right for him to give "Byron" as a name to one of his children. People have objected. Ellen Willis: "He relies too much on rhyme." It's like some awful school report: you're allowed to rely on rhyme 78 percent but Master Dylan relies on rhyme 81 percent. Ian Hamilton said of Dylan—grudgingly but well said—about "All I Really Want To Do": "Many of Dylan's love songs are a kind of verbal wife-battering: she will be rhymed into submission." I think it is true that the women are rhymed into submission, but that isn't the same as battering. Ginsberg, you remember, writing to Dylan about "Idiot Wind," "Blowing like a circle round my skull, / From the Grand Coulee Dam to the Capitol"—Ginsberg says, "It is the great disillusioned national rhyme." *Rolling Stone* reported it. "No one else, Dylan writes Ginsberg, had noticed that rhyme, a rhyme which is very dear to Dylan. Ginsberg's tribute to that rhyme is one of the reasons he's here": that is, on the Rolling Thunder Review and then *Renaldo and Clara.* And it's a great rhyme because of the metaphorical relationship of skull to Capitol. (You can see that more clearly on my bald head than you can on every head.) Dylan adapts what is the Capitol there to the White House elsewhere, in this which is from "11 Outlined Epitaphs": "how many votes will it take / for a new set of teeth / in the congress mouths?/ how many hands have t' be raised / before hair will grow back / on the white house head?" Somebody accused Dylan of baldism—my word, but that's what was meant—and he said, "I didn't mean bald heads, I meant bald minds." But he didn't, he meant bald heads, and there's a generational point there. It's a true rhyme because of what the head of the state is, and the body politic, and the relationship of the Capitol to the skull, with which it so felicitously rhymes.

"Woody Guthrie told me once that songs don't have to rhyme, that they don't have to do anything like that, but it's not true." That was in New York, 1964. "The highway is for gamblers, better use your sense. / Take what you have gathered from coincidence." One of the best rhymes, that. All rhymes are coincidences of sense. It is a pure coincidence that "sense" rhymes with "coincidence," and from it you gather something. And it is risky, for gamblers. (*Better,* you see.) Dylan *uses* his sense.

Arthur Hallam, Tennyson's friend for whom he wrote "In Memoriam," referred—with a fine paradox—to rhyme as "the recurrence of termination."

If it's termination, how can it recur? Can this really be the end when there is a rhyme? The great rhymes in Dylan: everybody would have their own. Mine include these. The rhyme of "ouch" with "psychiatric couch." The rhyme of "nonchalant" with "it's your mind that I want" ("Rita May, Rita May, / You got your body in the way. / You're so damn nonchalant / It's your mind that I want.") You don't have to *believe* him, but "nonchalant" and "want" is a delicious rhyme, because nonchalant is so undesiring of her, it's so cold. We don't even know for sure how to say it, it's a word you read again and again but don't much hear. It feels very affected to say *"Nawn-shalawn"* (*n'est-ce pas?*). "Nonchalant" doesn't really feel like an English or an American word. Then there's the rhyme of "Mozambique" with "cheek to cheek": there's always something strange about place names, or person's names, rhyming, because they don't really seem to be words. My favorite is the rhyme of "Utah" with "Me Pa," as if "U-" in Utah were spelled "You-." "Build me a cabin in Utah, / Marry me a wife, catch rainbow trout, / Have a bunch of kids who call me 'Pa,' / That must be what it's all about." That's not a rhyme of "-tah" and "Pa," it's a rhyme of "Utah" and "Me Pa," like "Me Tarzan, You Jane." How comically the rhyme is worked there.

Back to Arthur Hallam. "Rhyme has been said to contain in itself a constant appeal to memory and hope." Rhyme contains this because when you have the first rhyme you hope for the later one, and when you have the later one you remember the previous one. So rhyme is intimately involved with lyric, and there are particularly few good unrhymed lyrics of any kind because of the relationship between lyricism and memory and hope. Dylan therefore loves rhyming on the word "memory." "With your sheet-metal memory of Cannery Row" works because of the memory within the song that takes you back to the "your sheets like metal" earlier, and because of the curious undulation which is in "memory" and "cannery." And, in "Mr. Tambourine Man," rhyming "free" with "memory." What you find is that the word "free" is not really free, because it's got a bonded relationship to another word; and the word "memory" is made real to you because you have to remember, whether consciously or not, the previous element of the rhyme. Or you can rhyme on the word "rhyme." The beginning of "Sad Eyed Lady of the Lowlands" is supreme in what it does with its three rhyme-words: "With your mercury mouth in the missionary times, / And your eyes like smoke and your prayers like rhymes, / And your silver cross, and your voice like chimes, / Oh, who among them do they think could bury you?" "Times," "rhymes," and "chimes" rhyme only because they come several times, and they chime.

◆ ◆ ◆

Dylan understands not only the comedy but the tragedy which can be instinct in rhyming, in sounding. "The Lonesome Death of Hattie Carroll" began for him in the coinciding of a newspaper item with a cadence. William Zanzinger,

Hattie Carroll. The thing about those names—you can say this starts as purely technical—is their endings. What the killer and the killed have in common is that they've got feminine endings, both in their first names and in their surnames. She's Háttiĕ Cárrŏll, where the first syllable is stressed and the second unstressed; and he's Wílliăm Zanzíngĕr. Dylan hears this, and the whole of the song is based on the particular cadence of their names. Hattie Carroll has her persistent enslaved rhyming to "the table...the table...the table." Her name is very powerful—it ends the first line of the song; the second stanza is a William Zanzinger stanza; the third stanza is a Hattie Carroll stanza, which comes back to William Zanzinger at the end, and so on. And then neither of them is named in the last stanza, where he is "the person"—Zanzinger becomes "the person who killed for no reason." She never appears in the last stanza. But she is still there, because when the stanza begins with "In the courtroom of honor the judge pounded his gavel / To show that all's equal and that the courts are on the level," you're not only back to the word "level" from before ("And emptied the ashtrays on a whole other level"), but you're back to everything which sounds as "Carroll," "table," "table," "level"... That's her sound. And it goes with the "gentle": Zanzinger was "doomed and determined to destroy all the gentle."

The challenge known clearly to the song was how to save it from melodrama and from sentimentality. Dylan knows what he does in adopting that particular cadence with the feminine ending. For one thing about the feminine ending is that it is always related either to a dying fall or to some act of courage in the face of death, or of something that falls away. It can be heard in two lines of Wordsworth: "The thought of death sits easy on the man / Who has been born and lived among the mountains." The *moun*tains. And it's imperative that it not be on the man who has been born and lived among the hills, rocks, crags, or any of those words. It's the play of the masculine ending ("man") against the feminine ending ("mountains")—and what the voice has to do is hold out that second syllable like a flag, which is either limp or, as it were, patriotically out. It will fall away, that cadence, *unless* the voice holds it out. You haven't got a direction, you've got—as always—an axis, there in the feminine ending.

That is what Dylan hears from the beginning: "William Zanzinger killed poor Hattie Carroll / With a cane that he twirled around his diamond ring finger / At a Baltimore hotel society gath'rin'. / And the cops were called in and his weapon took from him." And that last is a beautiful one because it brings out that the feminine ending doesn't have to do with how many syllables there are in the word. It's not "took from *him*," it's "took *from* him." So that "him," although it's a monosyllable, is a feminine ending. There is only one moment in the song when this cadence is broken, and it's when he kills her. "Got killed by a blow, lay slain by a cane"—not "killed by a blow, lay slain by a truncheon"—"Got killed by a blow, lay slain by a cane / That sailed through the air and came down through the room"—not "came down through the ballroom," or "came down through the chamber." What happens is there's an amputation there, which is exactly understated yet you register it. Something is cut short at that moment, and this without the song's having to melodramatize it.

It's like what he does later in the song, when he puts in the tiniest pause after the word "a," lengthens the word to "ā" (as in "say"): "Handed out strongly, for penalty and repentance, / William Zanzinger with a...six month sentence." And he doesn't sing: "With a—[pause: for Jesus Christ! Is this adequate?]—six month sentence?!" All he does is just lengthen "a" to "ā," and put in this microsecond pause of indignation. Indignation, a very good servant, and a very bad master. The song understands that indignation must be curbed, all the way through.

It is a matter of this cadence which is there all the time, running through the whole sound of the song. It's there in the internal rhyme, the way in which "Got killed by a blow, lay *slain* by a *cane*," comes back as "He *spoke* through his *cloak*, most deep and distinguished." That's the only other moment where you've got a line which has that kind of internal rhyme, and it's the moment when the judge had better remember that somebody "lay slain by a cane" (there's very strong assonance there as well—lay/slain/cane). Dylan crucially pivots a line ending into an immediate internal rhyme: "That sailed through the air and came down through the room, / Doomed..." It's a penetrating move from the end of that line to the beginning of the next line. Of course you think at first it's Hattie Carroll who's doomed, but it isn't, it's Zanzinger. "...Doomed and determined to destroy all the gentle." In some terrible way, Zanzinger too is doomed, isn't in control of himself either. Yet part of the feeling in the word "determined" is that he wills it. It's Freud's "antithetical sense of primal words." "Determined" means either that you didn't have any choice in the matter (determinism); or, on the contrary, that you've chosen—determined—to destroy all the gentle.

Or there is the turn within the refrain, or the wheel, whatever you're going to call it: that's all masculine endings. Disgrace/fears/face/tears. "Disgrace" is a dissyllable, but it is not *dis*grace, it's dis*grace*. So the stanzas all the way through have feminine line endings, but there's a refrain which does not—a refrain which begins with the effect of a turret turning in accusation. "But you who..." That "you who" reminds me—and I'm not talking about allusion, or anything like that—it reminds me of what Shakespeare does at the beginning of *Richard III,* when Richard has gone through all those vexing things and then says, "Why, I, in this weak piping time of peace..." *Why, I.* Again it's very threatening, like a tank turret turning: "you who," that's the leveled gaze in it.

Staving off sentimentality: for instance, the way "poor" is saved from sentimentality because it's economic fact. "William Zanzinger killed poor Hattie Carroll" is compassion for her, but the reality of it is that she is poor. He is not poor; he has "rich wealthy parents." They're not just rich, and they're not just wealthy; they're "rich wealthy." He has a tobacco farm; she empties the ashtrays. He has parents; she gave birth to ten children. "Gave birth to" is piercing (how many lived?). It just reminds you that if you're poor the infant mortality rate is lethal—and of course if you're black. The song never says she's black, and it's his best civil rights song because it never says she's black. Everybody knows she's black and it has nothing to do with knowing the newspaper. You just know that she must have been black. It's a terrible thing that you know this from the story, and you know it from the light prison sentence, and the song never says so. It's white against black, it's young against old, it's rich against poor, but "poor" is saved from easy pity at the beginning by that hard fact.

There are these precisions all the way through. "Rich wealthy parents who provide and protect him." Now, we think of parents as providing *for* you. No, no: his parents didn't provide for him, they provided him. Some people say, well, that's just because Dylan couldn't get the word "for" in. The fact is, Dylan could get five hundred words into any line, if he wanted to. He has this amazing ability to get in as many words as necessary. Talk about Hopkins's sprung rhythm—this is more than sprung, it's hypersprung. He means they "provide him." It's related to transitive and intransitive verbs. "Stared at the person who killed for no reason." One of the horrible things in that line is that Dylan doesn't say "Who killed Hattie Carroll," it's just "who killed." It's become an intransitive verb, flat, hideous, indifferent.

Or there is the way in which nouns are seen as property. "William Zanzinger killed poor Hattie Carroll / With a cane that he twirled around his diamond ring finger." It's not that he had a finger which had a diamond ring on it; he had a diamond-ring-finger. He probably therefore also had an amethyst-ring-finger, an opal-ring-finger, and a ruby-ring-finger. His diamond ring finger has this extraordinary feeling of affluent agglomeration. "At a Baltimore hotel society gath'rin'." Bank up the nouns like that and you're really propertied. Nouns are items, and you can possess them, you can own them. It's partly the reminder of a newspaper headline, yes, "Baltimore Hotel Society Gathering," but it's also the way in which the nouns bank up so very, very powerfully.

But I want above all to point out the effects of rhyme and the internal rhyming. So I draw your attention to two things that change in the last stanza. One is the extremely sardonic rhyme of "caught 'em" and "bottom." You haven't had anything like that. It's basically an unrhyming song, except in the refrain. But when you get "caught 'em" and "bottom," something is happening, and there is a curious Byronic, sardonic feeling about that rhyme. Then you end the song with the one and only full end-rhyme, "Handed out strongly, for penalty and repentance, / William Zanzinger with a six-month sentence." And "sentence" and "repentance" had better be what this is going to be about. They are an ancient rhyme. As with a prison sentence, there's a point of timing, of punctuation. The old nineteenth-century book *Punctuation Personified* says of a full stop: "Which always ends the perfect sentence / As crime is followed by repentance." Would that this were not just a true rhyme but true. But there's no reason to suppose that Zanzinger was or is in any way repentant. If you follow the Dylan magazines, you can find out how successful Zanzinger currently is in real estate. "Concerned Citizens" for something or other, his real estate firm; he really exists, except he has a "t" in his name as well as a "z."

I always see this as an instance of the difference between writing a political song, and writing a song politically—the way in which Eliot would think of the difference between writing religious poems, and writing poems religiously. It is good to be able to write religious poems, but the great thing is being able to write poems religiously, to have religion not be the subject of the poem, but be the element. And this, I think, is one of Dylan's greatest political songs not because it has a political subject but because everything in it is seen under the aspect of politics.

He cannot reperform the song. He unfortunately still does. There is no other way of singing this song than the way in which he sings on *The Times They Are A-Changin'*. If he sings it any more gently, he sentimentalizes it. If he sings it any more ungently, he allies himself with Zanzinger. The 1988 performance, like the 1974 one, allies him with Zanzinger, because he's sneering— "And swear words and sneering, and his tongue it was snarling." True, Dylan is one of the great tongue snarlers of all times, but above all in this song he must not do that. He must have this extraordinary feeling of being very strong but very gentle all the way through. "In a matter of minutes on bail was out walking." A wonderful turn of the ordinary, walked out on bail. He didn't just walk out on bail: "In a matter of minutes on bail was out walking." That is leisure and freedom and amplitude. And contrast a "matter of minutes" with "a six month sentence"—the whole way in which those numbers are used all the way through. That, and the scale of the stanzas; they build up. The third stanza and the fourth stanza are exactly the same length. You start off with six and then seven lines plus the refrain and you build up and they get gradually longer. But then they stay the same length. That last stanza must be equipollent with the third one. Nothing must trump what happened.

It's very brave not to mention her at the end. It's not indifference but the fact that it's too late, that now is the time for your tears. Or as he sings, "For now's the time..." If I'd had the genius to come up with the song, having sung "Now ain't" all the way through, I would have sung "now is." He never sings "now is," he sings "now's." The contraction at the end, again, quietly takes out anything easily hortatory.

◆ ◆ ◆

"The Lonesome Death of Hattie Carroll" asks, about oppression, "How long, O Lord—." There, "how much longer" is the tragedy of unjust power. Elsewhere in a Dylan song it can be a comedy of command. "Lay, Lady, Lay." The old question is how long you can go on saying something. Here it's how long you can go on asking somebody to lay or lie across your big brass bed. There's a certain point at which she either does lie across your big brass bed, or she does not. You would seem a total turkey if into the small hours you continued to say "Lay, lady, lay." The repetition is there very, very strongly from the beginning, but there's a real problem about how, with dignity, you extricate yourself once you've issued this injunction. So the rhyming becomes a very important part of that, and clearly rhyming is going to be important in any song that begins "Lay, lady, lay." What happens is that "lady" seems to be simply a happily languorous and expansive and open version of "lay." I'll leave aside all the puns on "lay" which there are, and which American English makes plausible. If you say "Lie, lady, lie"—you're John Simon and you must use the language accurately—that would open up the possibility, "Lie, lady, lie...you usually do on these occasions" and so on. You'd be into the other, mendacious sense of the word "lie." But "Lay, lady, lay, lay across my big brass bed": he sings the word "bed" kingsizedly. It's not a monosyllable when he sings it, something happens to it by which it becomes extraordinarily wide. It isn't quite a disyllable. What he does with it is like the way Tennyson says you should register the word "tired," in "The Lotos-Eaters": "Music that gentlier on the spirit lies, / Than tir'd eyelids upon tir'd eyes." Tennyson says that it's neither one syllable nor two, "but a dreamy child of the two." You are to imagine something which isn't quite "tyr'd" and isn't quite "tiy-erd," but is just hovering, undulating, between the contracted and the expanded. That's what Dylan does with the word "bed."

One crucial effect in the song's rhyming is that there are, as you will have noticed whether consciously or not, two lines that don't rhyme. This matters very much in a love song, particularly since the one of those two that matters more is the word "love." He pairs them syntactically so that you'll pick up on them. "Why wait any longer for the world to begin," and "Why wait any longer for the one you love." They're clearly a pair of lines. The first one has some relation, in the sound of "begin," to the rhyme of "clean" and "seen" as Dylan sings it in the previous stanza. Nevertheless, there isn't a word which completes the rhyme begun with the word "begin." That is, "begin" doesn't fully rhyme with anything. And nor does "love." The song intimates—urges— that the rhyme would not be any word or any sound: it would be an action.

That is, the act of love, if she will lie across his big brass bed. That would be the answer to the question, "Why wait any longer for the one you love," which isn't really a question after all (Dylan doesn't sing it or print it with a question-mark), but an invitation. "Love" doesn't rhyme there. Yet it's comic and perfectly happy, because it trusts that the rhyme will be consummated by behavior—by love and acquiescence.

◆◆◆

"Señor" too is very much a "how long" song. You can hear it all through. "How long are we gonna be ridin'? / How long must I keep my eyes glued to the door?" "Can't stand the suspense anymore." "Give me a minute, let me get it together." "I'm ready when you are." The whole song has this feeling of suspense, of an endless waiting for some sort of shoot-out. "Señor (Tales of Yankee Power)." It begins with the end (the war to end wars), in the Byronic sardonic rhyme of "headin'" and "Armageddon." And it ends with an unobtrusive feat of straight rhyming, the *recurrence* of termination: "This place don't make no sense to me, no more. / Can you tell me what we're waiting for, señor?" And that's the only occasion, throughout the song, where what you get is a double rhyme. It's not simply that "señor" rhymes with "more," it's that what you've got is "for" rhyming with "no more," and then "señor" rhyming with them both. If you look back to the previous stanzas, they're "before" / "señor," "anymore" / "señor" and "floor" / "señor." But here it's "This place don't make sense to me no more. / Can you tell me what we're waiting for, señor?" That rhyme is conclusive. It's related to the way in which rhymes exert power (Yankee and other), and especially to the necessarily arbitrary acts of power at the ends of poems and songs. You remember Marvell ending the "Horatian Ode": "The same arts that did gain / A power must it maintain." That's not the rhyme of "gain" against "-tain"; it's the doubled rhyme of "gain" against "main-tain." There isn't another rhyme in the poem that's like that. It's as if there are two turns of the lock at the end there. The rhyme is clamped into place. Although Dylan is talking at the end of his song about disconnecting cables, what you get at the end is a doubling of the cables of rhyming: "This place don't make sense to me no more. / Can you tell me what we're waiting for, señor?"

"Señor" is about God's power and man's, God's empire and the Yankee one. "What Can I Do for You?" is about a Christian's sense of all-but-impotence. I think the Christian songs are wonderful, and that the opposition to them is very unfortunate. It is often extremely bigoted, with a certain kind of liberal bigotry against Christianity; and often a mask for anti-Semitism. "Something is happening, and you don't know what it is, do you, Mr. Jew?" That was offered as a remark about Dylan's having become a Christian, but it seemed to me to be availing itself of a rather ugly streak within some Christianity itself.

"What Can I Do for You?" is a song about reciprocity. The question is a truly Dylanesque one, because the answer is from one point of view nothing, and from another point of view everything. Dylan has always loved questions that have to be answered yes and no. "Are you ready?" You cannot answer it yes, and you cannot answer it no. You can answer it only by saying, as Dylan sings in "Are You Ready?": "I hope I'm ready." And "How does it feel?" is a question that has to be answered by *terrible*, and *wonderful*. It is wonderful to be "on your own, with no direction home, like a rolling stone," but it is also terrible at the same time. "What Can I Do for You?" craves reciprocity with God, which is inconceivable. "You have given everything to me. / What can I do for You?" Now those won't meet; the activities won't meet. All the way through there's an impetuosity that longs for a perfect fit. It's near a fit in the one but last stanza. "You have given all there is to give. / What can I give to You?" (So Dylan sang it on *Saved;* he printed it "do for.") The song moves away here from "What can I *do for* You" to "What can I *give to* You." That's a certain kind of reciprocity, but it's unsatisfactory. It then makes this supreme turn in the whole feeling of the song, into "You have given me life to live. / How can I live for You?" It ceases to be a "what" answer; the answer becomes a "how." It isn't any longer "What can I do," "What can I do," "What can I give"; it's "how." That is, the whole terms of the question have to be changed.

• • •

Before I end, I need to show that I'm not besotted with the man, so let me take a song which actually has something wrong with it: "Love Minus Zero / No Limit." It's simultaneously something that's wrong with the rhyming, and something that's wrong with the whole impulse of the song, though the song is an astonishing one. I think something ugly happens at the end, which is masked by the great beauty of his voice and of the tune. In the first stanza, lines one and two rhyme: "My love she speaks like silence, / Without ideals or violence." "Silence" and "violence" is a deep rhyme, for all kinds of reasons. Rhyming on the word "silence" is always in a way comical, because a rhyme is a sound; there's something odd about the criss-cross of the meaning of the word and the fact that you're using it for a sound effect. Silence / violence: it's not really a violent rhyme, and you can hear that it isn't a perfect rhyme either. So the question of violence is brought up at the very beginning, but it sort of fits. Lines one and two rhyme; and four and eight rhyme—that is, "fire" and "buy her"; and lines six and seven rhyme—"hours" and "flowers." And three and five don't. It's a funny, intricate little stanza. It's set up that way: nothing rhymes with "faithful," and nothing rhymes with "roses." You're therefore asked to bring into relationship not only the lines that do rhyme, but the ones that don't. The point is that her being faithful doesn't have anything to do with roses. People carry roses, but it isn't because people bring roses that she's faithful. It doesn't turn on that. Apart from the meaning that nothing in her wants roses to rhyme, nothing wants faithful to rhyme. An end in itself, in herself.

Now in the last verse what you get is this curious rounding on the woman. She has been described in a way that seems to me completely incompatible with her being like "some raven with a broken wing." Why is she like "some raven with a broken wing?" Because Dylan just hit her with a hammer. It's a terrible thing that happens at the end of the song. It's a song which turns out to be saying that "What I like about her is that she is so wonderfully independent of me, she doesn't really need me, other people do this and that...come to think of it, that isn't what I like about her...and I mean to smash her with a hammer, and convert her into some raven with a broken wing." She's absolutely nothing like that. She's so little like some raven with a broken wing that Michael Gray, writing a book about Dylan, has to have recourse to Blake's tiger. Now that's a pretty desperate move by a man. I mean, she's even less like Blake's tiger than she is like some raven with a broken wing. What is happening here? There's something ugly in "The wind howls like a hammer, / The night blows rainy." It silently invokes raining blows on somebody with a hammer. That's really the thing holding it together. What happens is that when "rain" and "blows" and "hammer" go together, "perfection" meets "hammer," as the unrhymed things in this last stanza. And her perfection is smashed by the hammer of his obduracy. He sings it so sweetly. I'm not saying it's misogynistic—it needn't matter which way round the sexes go, or the genders go. What happens is that you believe that you love somebody for his or her curious independence of your wishes and needs, and then in the end you turn on your love so that she's like "some raven with a broken wing" and needy.

It's in a way an extremely mild brutality, smashing the word "perfection" with the word "hammer." And it is so different from the relation of "faithful" to "roses," or from the unique and delicate unrhymedness of "softly." In the last stanza Dylan has had lots of shots at that line "The night blows rainy." You can hear him sing "The rain blows cold." But then "cold" has no rhyme at all—it has an extraordinarily chilling effect if you do that—you really break the whole sense of the stanza. You can hear him sing "The night blows cold and rainy." When he does that, he separates the word "blows" from the word "rain(y)." If you put in "cold and" (as printed by Dylan), you've opened up some *cordon sanitaire* between "rain" and "blows." In a sense, you've done something to mitigate the violence. But these changes in the words sung don't really deal with this odd, I think undramatized, change of feeling. It feels to me like some Donne poems, in that it is wonderful, but very ugly at the end. Something happens to the spirit of the song, which is disguised by the way he sings it. "Even the pawn must hold a grudge." Even the king. Even Dylan, whom I ungrudgingly admire.

You see what I mean about the problem about how you end. I have that problem too.

As News Spreads:
Danny Lyon's Photographs

by Daniel Wolff

THE PHOTO IS CAPTIONED: "Dawn on February 7th. As news spreads that Jean-Claude Duvalier is gone, a soldier disarms a Tonton Macoute." It is 1986, and two hours have passed since Baby Doc Duvalier fled Haiti in a plane provided by the United States government. At this moment, for the first time in thirty years, the Duvaliers' private terrorist force, the Tonton Macoute, are without a leader. In the center of the picture, one uniformed man grabs at the rifle of another. Around them is a crowd of men in light tropical clothes: some are clapping, all have serious, concentrated expressions. The crowd is moving from left to right—moving, that is, against the Macoute. One man even has his arm between the two antagonists as if giving specific instructions on how to disarm the enemy. There are some children in the crowd and a few women standing back in the shade of a building. Only the soldier and the Macoute have weapons. The thirty other people in the black-and-white photograph clap their bare hands or stride along: an audience to their own future.

In the next picture—"The soldier is greeted as hero. February 7, Port-au-Prince"—the movement is reversed. The soldier has turned back, triumphant, into the crowd. The Macoute's rifle is under his arm; the Macoute has disappeared. One man pats the grinning soldier on the back. Another spreads his arms wide, upper body leaning back from the hips, hand splayed out against the sky in an ecstatic gesture of congratulations.

For what was, in February 1986, a newsworthy event, these are clearly not news photographs. They don't have the focused intensity—that sense of the story in a nutshell—that we're used to seeing in our daily papers. Nor, for such a critical moment, do they have the composed, artistic sensibility of the Cartier-Bresson school of photography. They appear, instead, to be snapshots: uncropped, messy with detail, and dependent on the accompanying text to tell their story.

The book where these images appear—*Merci Gonaïves,* by Danny Lyon—also includes pictures of more mundane matters. A group of women—white dresses and headbands against the black earth—wait to plant a ploughed field. Two Dominican hookers loll on an unmade bed. But Lyon's ambition remains consistent: to recover the story of the Haitian revolution from the flood of daily news. "Over the long run," he writes in the text, "those things done and recorded best will have far more influence than an event controlled by a president [Reagan, in this case]. Unfortunately," he adds, "life is not lived in the long run but in the short." *Merci Gonaïves* is not simply about what the Haitian revolution meant, but how and why we can't perceive that meaning.

Danny Lyon began his career in 1962 by drifting into the civil rights struggle in the American South, where he eventually became the staff photographer for SNCC (the Student Nonviolent Coordinating Committee). From there, he went on to photograph the children of Southern whites in Chicago's ghettos, motorcycle gangs, the razing of New York's Lower East Side, and the Texas prison system. As he writes in his retrospective collection, *Pictures from the New World,* by the Vietnam era, "America, the America that I believed in anyway, was standing on her head. If I was going to find a subject that had meaning for me, I was going to have to find it at the bottom of society, not at the top."

The result, *Pictures from the New World,* is one of the most moving and impassioned looks at the decades of the sixties and seventies I know. From the Walker Evans tradition of documentary realism, Lyon forged a highly personal approach to the most public and political subjects. Then in the eighties, burned by the apparently unchangeable inequalities all around him, he dropped, if not out, back. "When I was twenty-five," he wrote, "I wanted to know what the subjects had to say. Now, for better or worse, I am becoming more interested in what I have to say." *Merci Gonaïves* signals his return to political subject matter.

The highly personal style remains. Even in the more formal compositions—a woman standing in profile against a column in a Haitian market, her box of fruit diagonal to the bright square of the street beyond—Lyon conjures up a specific place and time rather than any Universal Beauty. What we are presented with is a kind of private history, and one of Lyon's central beliefs is that there is no other kind.

The problem Lyon faces in trying to recover the truth from the news is similar to the one Walker Percy discusses in *The Message in the Bottle.* How do you actually see something—say, the Grand Canyon—in the late twentieth century, when we're all too aware of what it's supposed to mean? We've had the information served to us through the media. There's even a spot marked on an overlook where you can stand to get the exact angle you're familiar with from a thousand postcards. "The sightseer," Percy writes, "measures his satisfaction by *the degree to which the canyon conforms to the preformed complex*" (Percy's italics).

Lyon attacks the difficulty of preformed history by refusing to stand on the mark. Instead, he mingles with the crowd, wanders the back streets of Port-au-Prince, lets his attention be drawn by what he isn't supposed to see: the beauty of a man's splayed-out hand as he prepares to embrace a soldier. In the process, Lyon rejects the lyrical glibness of the photograph. As a reporter, he refuses to sum up an event. As an artist, he radiates distaste for the idea of the single perfect image. Our North American consciousness is, he believes, "blocked by disease," and he uses the accompanying text to question the comfortable aesthetics we employ to semi-digest outside information.

Take the shot of two kids at Mardi Gras in the city of Gonaïves (where the Haitian revolution began). They are aping the hated Macoute by standing at mock attention in patched-together uniforms. Lyon refuses to leave the image alone, using the text to quote the song the kids are singing: "Tonton Macoute, going to eat shit / They never give us a chance, / Here in Gonaïves!" To some degree, the words make the picture redundant and vice versa, but Lyon keeps piling on the detail, trying to force the image out of the realm of art and into our laps.

Merci Gonaïves is fighting a rearguard action. With the aid of the United States government and, Lyon would argue, the media, our perception of Haitian politics has been stabilized. In other words, this great gash in Haitian history has become as known, as expected, as formalized as our image of the Grand Canyon. Lyon has mostly praise for the reporters covering the uprising, whom he quotes extensively. "But seeing the news about Haiti as it reached America," he goes on, "was a very different thing from watching it be created on the spot." He cites the implicit slant in *Time* magazine's choice of photographs, which seemed to reduce the struggle for freedom to a bloody confrontation between out-of-control blacks. "If there actually is something called 'news,'" Lyon concludes, "one wonders what it is."

An article entitled "Return To Normalcy" in the May 1988 *Atlantic* is a case in point. Author Kevin McDermott explains Haiti's unbearable poverty by laying the blame on "an almost uninterrupted procession of megalomaniacs" in power. Why have Haiti's rulers all exhibited this ailment? All McDermott will say is that the Presidency has "turned even reformers—like Papa Doc Duvalier—into corrupt tyrants." As an explanation this explains nothing, but lest we suspect more down-to-earth factors may have influenced Haiti's recent history, McDermott assures us: "It is hard to find evidence that the U.S. government took an active role in maintaining the army in power." Having thus reduced his analysis to something considerably less rational than voodoo, McDermott wonders at the Haitians' lack of a "usable national past."

Though its aim is to set the record straight, *Merci Gonaïves* occasionally falls under the influence of this kind of mumbo-jumbo. At one point, Lyon states that up until and including Duvalier's departure, "our government had more or less done the right thing." Only the restricted time frame of this book can excuse that statement. Between 1915 and 1934, United States Marines occupied Haiti and placed a mulatto elite in power that still forms the basis for the incredibly unfair distribution of wealth (one percent of the population accounts for almost half of the national income). When Papa Doc Duvalier got elected in 1957, he did so with the support of the military, which (according to the Washington Office on Haiti) "was itself frequently used by the U.S. administration to obtain its own objectives." And when Papa Doc formed the Macoute as his personal terrorist force, he continued to receive full United States aid. With his father's death in 1971, Baby Doc took office and worked out tax and tariff breaks with the Nixon administration that placed Haiti's manufacturing sector in the control of American business. In 1979, when Haitians responded to President Carter by organizing the Haitian League for Human Rights, the first meeting was broken up by government security forces who seriously injured many of the participants. The Carter Administration took no action in reprisal. Finally, under Reagan, Duvalier's regime received a five hundred percent increase in funds. From 1981 on, the United States government continuously certified that Haiti had been making progress in human rights—and that includes a certification in August 1987, a month after three hundred members of a farmers' co-op had been massacred and a presidential candidate hacked to death, both reportedly by mobs under the direction of agents of the Duvalier government.

Lyon has constructed a collage he calls "Haiti, 1983–86." In it, a woman tries to sell her few wares in a dusty market; an unpainted shack stands in the stark sunlight; a human skull stares out from a litter of bones strewn in the underbrush. "What will life be like here in the Americas," Lyon asks, "if off our southern shore lies an island of starving people, their bodies falling like fruit to the ground?" The answer is that life will be a lot like it is right now. Today, Haiti is the poorest country in the Western Hemisphere, with ten times the infant mortality rate of the United States. The minimum wage is three dollars *a day;* average income in rural areas is fifty dollars a year. Eighty percent of the population is illiterate. And the entire nation exists as a vassal to the United States, where sixty percent of Haiti's exports go and from which this tropical island has become a net *importer* of sugar at prices set by the American government.

Writing of his trip to Colombia in 1967, Lyon says: "Naively, I had stepped onto a continent being torn apart by its own contradictions." If Lyon now recognizes that those contradictions aren't all self-produced, *Merci Gonaïves* still exhibits some naiveté—as if Lyon only believes what he himself has seen and thinks that history begins with his camera. Still, this book comes as a blessed relief to mainstream reporting of the Haitian revolution, and a kick-in-the-tail to the sort of North American passivity which has added a sharp pathos to many of these photos.

Yes, the soldier, urged on by the crowd, disarmed the Macoute in the first few hours after Duvalier fled. But a year later, in a mockery of free election, that same army placed Leslie Manigat in power as a figurehead president. Four months later, they had him removed. The crowds seen in Lyon's photographs clapping with delight are still empty-handed, still observers, as powerless as they were under the Macoute.

Lyon compares his experiences in Haiti with those he had as a civil rights worker in the American South. "In both cases," he writes, "real leadership was anonymous, coming directly from ordinary people from the street. The truth is that in the South almost all the organizations that had recognizable leadership, including SNCC, spent most of their time catching up to events that were being created and led by high school students, most of whom are still nameless in America."

Lyon has spent some twenty-five years trying to give the anonymous names. "The power of the camera," he writes in *Merci Gonaïves*, "undermines the power of the State." But that is, as he says, only "in the long run." Art doesn't make history; it can only rewrite it. And then, only when it's given the chance. Toward the end of his text, Lyon describes his attempts to get this book into print. Turned down by, among others, Aperture, which brought out *Pictures from the New World*, *Merci Gonaïves* was eventually self-published. Which leads Lyon to ask not only about the recent United States role in squelching Haiti's fight for freedom, but about the brand of American freedom we pride ourselves on back home. "Free to do what? Free to make pictures that no one will ever see? Free to write reports on events that no one will print? Are we being honored for our collective ineffectiveness?"

It's hard to believe that Lyon's book was rejected because of its politics (which could be a lot harsher). More likely, publishers had trouble with what it implies. It's one thing to champion the snapshot, a stylistic approach that's been fashionable in photography for some time now. It's quite another to link the aesthetics of the single perfect image with the politics of the State and tie our ideal of the great artist making timeless masterpieces with the whitewashing of history, where only the deeds of great men count.

The last image in *Merci Gonaïves* is of a young Haitian girl. She's standing in a patch of shade in the left forefront of the picture, her hat pressed to her chest. Behind her is the glare of the beach at Cap Haitien, where a bunch of boys run in the sand. She is a somber, beautiful individual in a striped dress. She isn't looking at the camera.

On Modern Art & Artists

by W. S. Di Piero

MY MOST FREQUENT CHILDHOOD DREAM was of blocky masses of spongy graywhite vapors. They were terrifying because they could possess me, absorb me into their mass, though that also seemed inviting, even desirable, a return to pure undifferentiated beginnings, flight from the pains of unlikeness. When I first got to know some of Rothko's painting in the 1970s, I was moved in ways I could not understand or articulate. Something in them exercised what Lawrence calls "the insidious mastery of song." Their claim had to do with that old dream, and also with the paintings' nonanecdotal quality, whereby the very abandonment of narrative, of figural and scenic suggestiveness, became a dense presence, a sumptuous forfeiture. I think of his sacred decorations for the Houston chapel. The place turns you back into yourself. The images, their paint films eroded and cracked by lighting and humidity problems over the years, are yet meditative objects. They don't return us to nature, to the massiveness of material reality; they restore us to our means of spiritual preparedness, to disciplines of awareness. Rothko said he wanted high moral themes. He wanted to make tragic painting. We generally experience tragedy not as themes but as dramatic situation, character, anecdote, momentous event and consequence. But tragic feeling may be an inchoate stirring or condition not attached to a specific experience, and it's that feeling— of loss in the fullness of knowledge, of the force of destiny, of a yearning to find in ourselves sacred knowledge and to suffer the consequences of the discovery— which Rothko tried to cast in those forms. (Can they be "huge cloudy symbols of a high romance?") It's more a dream feeling than a waking one. No less intensely lived but not consciously so. It is not lived in time. We experience it out of time, or in the Great Time, the Beginning Time that we are so much closer to when we're children. I can't follow the critics who see in his paintings figures or recapitulations or "traces" of the figurative art of previous centuries, especially when they make the case that he is essentially a religious artist recapitulating or transfiguring traditional religious motifs. If anything made him an artist of the sacred, it was his mission to paint the facelessness of transcendence. He pursued (and illustrated) the post-Romantic consequences of Shelley's statement in *Prometheus Unbound* that "the deep truth is imageless."

◆ ◆ ◆

A useful definition of "imaginative," in Bergson's *The Two Sources of Morality and Religion:* "any concrete representation which is neither perception nor memory." I think that means categorically neither one nor the other. An amalgam, but infused (I would add) with the instinct for form.

◆ ◆ ◆

Over the years Frank Stella has achieved a programmatic novelty, surprises so strategic that they feel more like methodically worked out theories than actual physical events. His is the kind of abstraction that lives entirely for others (and for the systematic advance of art history). Years ago he said, "For a painting to be successful, it has to deal with problems that are always given to painting, meaning the problems of what it takes to make a really good or convincing painting." An artist naturally folds into his expressive work an historical awareness of predecessors and an awareness of formal problems. But the superior artist will not be so concerned with correctness or aptness or timeliness of his response to those pressures. And yet Stella's career is taken as exemplary by many younger artists, even nonabstractionists, in so far as they are more preoccupied with making art that explains or justifies its own existence than with art that is essentially emotive, appetitive, expressive.

◆ ◆ ◆

Museum Going. In Philadelphia, in the Cézanne room with its great centerpiece of the 1906 *Bathers,* a father bustles through the far doorway, two children tugging his hands, bubbling about something. The father, trying to get above their voices, nearly shouts, "But in those days, Jimmy, they didn't have things like VCRs," while they pick up speed and hurry across the room out the far door. In New York at the Degas exhibition the dense weekday crowd, funereal in its attentiveness, paced in silent procession from one image to the next. Rippling the surface of that quiet was the chittering of headsets. More explanations. When we go to a big show, we can acquire more prepackaged information about the artist's work—its social and biographical setting, its art-historical "place," etc.—than ever before. Because of the educational mission of our museums, I suppose this sort of instructive processing of art is inevitable, though I think it must somehow impede the natural streaming of beautiful images into our emotional and spiritual lives. How close are we, though, to believing finally that, in our cultural lives, information is edification? Access sufficient data, compile an adequate body of fact, contrive a theoretical apparatus that will elucidate patterns that connect systems and networks, and the Golem stirs.

◆◆◆

In his chapter on da Vinci in *The Renaissance,* Pater writes: "The way to perfection is through a series of disgusts." For moderns, the way matters more than the perfection, and the disgusts themselves are exemplary.

◆◆◆

Why are the jets and emulsive tracks of paint in Pollock's *Lavender Mist: Number 1, 1950* so compelling? It's not only because he was creating a greater plasticity of space and laying out dozens of contested fields of formal activity where disintegrating patterns pitch against imminent, struggling stabilities. There's something one can't reduce satisfactorily to formal terms. In 1964 Eliade, who was a great admirer of his countryman Brancusi, spoke of "nonfigurative painters who abolish representational forms and surfaces, penetrate to the inside of matter, and try to reveal *the ultimate structures of substance.*" In order to talk about Pollock, and Rothko for that matter, in other than purely formalist vocabularies (and to avoid the useless argument that both were representationalists masquerading as abstractionists), we may have to pick up where Pierre Schneider left off in his discussion of Matisse and talk about the sacred and the mundane. Eliade also says that nonrepresentational art corresponds to the "demythologization" in religion advocated by Rudolph Bultmann. As Christianity may dissolve the images and symbols of its traditional narratives in order to confront once again the freshness of religious experience in our secular, materialist time, certain artists give up the making of representational images so that they can see *through* traditional iconography *to* the world as it could have been seen only on the first day of creation. Moreover, he says, today's artist "sees only the freshness of the first day of the world—he does not yet see its 'face.' The time of the epiphany has not yet arrived, or does the world *truly have no face?*" I think Pollock and Rothko worked to paint that facelessness. For Rothko it was toned with a magisterial, voluminous solemnity. For Pollock the tone was one of self-devouring conflict.

◆◆◆

Why the erotic pinch of photographs? Eros, the divided egg, the desire, the likeness separated forever from its matching, complementary half. Maybe because the whole shape of the ghost of the flesh is already there—and yet is not there, I mean not *here,* not actual (the image tells us that too), its likeness so like what we imagine our own likeness to be. We see ourselves remembered, already posthumous, sometimes smiling. I have an old studio portrait of my grandmother as a young woman in Abruzzo. I see the dignified stillness, the compassionate self-containment that men found so attractive. In a snapshot of my father, taken in South Philadelphia when he was in his early twenties, I see the familiar shadow structure and stress lines of my own face. A third image, of both grandparents, not long after she joined him in South Philadelphia: my young grandfather, who would die a few months later, has the alert, triangulated, almost wolfish features my father bears in that other picture. My grandmother is wearing a dark, simple dress and highlaced boots. Both are dressed in familiar, too-frequently brushed and washed and ironed grays and whites. They have in their faces the strained look of what Henry James called "the launched populations." But now, in my life, my memory, there are other presences that sharpen the pinch even more. Lewis Hine, Walker Evans, Paul Strand, Russell Lee—they are there, too.

◆ ◆ ◆

Realism into Camp. The representation as sitting duck: see Jasper Johns's *Decoy*. The title identifies the image as an easy target, but also a deceptive one meant to draw our attention away from something else, away from the really real likeness. Deception depends on coy verisimilitude. Johns is the realist as sign painter. Each form, even abstract patterns like the famous hatchmarks of the 1970s and 1980s, is a sign meant to stand for something else. So what does a decoy painting mock? The painted image is a stand-in for the original, it's not the duck. So where's the duck? Nowhere present but everywhere signified? Johns's enterprise since the late 1960s seems to be the making of images that are purposive stand-ins for a reality too fragile, intimate, or vulnerable to expose. And what might that reality be? Maybe it's the mind in which correspondences and connections between signs and emblems—flags, numbers, Savarin cans, bathtub fixtures, posters, letters—hold their coherence, generate some system of meaning. Or does an image refer to some originating prototype, the really real, that has fled? Is he mourning the loss of some untold but felt Golden Age of image representation? (Does this become soon numbed by its ritual funereal repetitions?) Or is he so devious or impish or callow as to have devised an art which is essentially a model of the monkey mind? *Decoy* recapitulates familiar motifs in somber indigo and pale blues: framed in the center is a Ballantine can, positioned as an exhibit or lure. Color words (RED ORANGE etc.) form column and buttress patterns. That field is mounted on a lower border illustrating silk-screen images of Johns's earlier works: the Savarin can, a light bulb, a flashlight. *Decoy* and many other pieces of the 1970s and 1980s are essentially design concepts so overdetermined in their impassivity that the felt life has been drained from them. The blandness of purity.

◆◆◆

Baudelaire says in the *Salon of 1846* that the great criterion of art is memory. "Art is a kind of mnemotechny of beauty; and slavish imitation interferes with memory. There is a class of atrocious painters for whom the smallest wart is a great piece of luck; not only would they not dream of leaving it out, but they must needs make it four times life-size." But there is also reality's command to artists (they feel it as a command) who, though practiced in Baudelaire's mnemotechny, cannot ignore the high shine of the world's objects, the allure of the given. Usually, however, such artists would never think of enlarging a wart. The exaggeration and intensification of the given comes from their transformative way of seeing the world. Memory may turn what's before our eyes into a fever dream, and *that* becomes the object the artist copies.

◆◆◆

For Lucian Freud the flesh is a garment worn by an exhausted spirit. His figures seem to bear too much weight of the past, and the burden bores them. They look like ideal sitters because it would be more difficult for them to move than to sit still for long periods. It's the skin, with its vestiges of conscience, that distinguishes the humans from the plants that Freud sometimes paints into their scenes.

◆◆◆

The way Pollock skeined paint onto the canvas would seem the supreme manipulation of accident—decisive accident. He used the brush like a stick, pointing the paint into emergent arcs and spindles on the blank ground of the canvas. He used the action of gravity on a painter's material as a crucial form-making action. He was no more a shaman wielding a medicine stick, as one critic melodramatically described him, than was Courbet or Cèzanne buttering the canvas with heavy loads of paint from the palette knife. Better say Pollock was no *less* the shaman than they. As for accident, in a 1951 interview he said that the drip paintings were products of a controlled application of paint, that he did not use the accident, he *denied* it. Those forms were, in other words, exclusionary. The snarled implosive space the apparent galactic chaos of pigment created came from a discipline of denial. The application of paint by the Wild Man from Cody was a stay against the derangements of form that accident creates.

◆◆◆

The Cibachrome process so saturates the photographic image with color that the tones look hallucinated, engorged with dream-dyes, but at the same time cool, shellacked, almost decorative. I saw somewhere a show of images of sports events. The colors were so ripe and swollen that the tension of physical action—

a soccer player falling, a motorcyclist turning a curve (his knee about an inch off the ground), a gang of racing cars at the starting line—was loosened, drained of energy, because the drawing, I mean the composition of stress lines and tension points, was slack. Intensification of color can't compensate for wobbly structure. Or if it does, it usually makes for visual bombast. But I also think of Richard Misrach's Ektacolor images in his 1983–84 "Desert Fires" series, where the conflagrations of light seem a visionary part of the natural life cycle of the landscape. The paper itself looks as if it has caught fire, ignited by likeness. A color process, used in this way, can set the image in an adversarial or strained relation to its own support.

◆ ◆ ◆

To write or make images in response to Nietzsche's challenge (from the notebook he kept while writing *Thus Spoke Zarathustra*): "He who no longer finds what is great in God will find it nowhere—he must either deny it or create it."

◆ ◆ ◆

Rothko's art is the kind that cultivates the imminence of oblivion, cultivates it with such disciplined passion that possibility comes to seem desirability. How then does one make an art of defiant resolutions out of the knowledge of despair, the tantalus of complete forgetfulness? That's the poet's question, too. One sustaining answer (Rothko's): a feeling tone blending vexed joy and pained (never blissful) forgetfulness.

◆ ◆ ◆

Artists who take their Americanness too literally as a subject are likely to become mere processors of American facts, though in the bargain they may also become well known, maybe rich, producers of such facts as commodities.

◆ ◆ ◆

In much Pop Art the crucial aesthetic decisions seem to have been made before the image comes into existence, so that the action of the materials can't respond in a challenging way to the artist's exertions. In a way it liberates the artist: the image is "nonnegotiable"—but it liberates also into a numbed and numbing exclusivity, and a new academicism waving the banner of cultural criticism. The pleasures it offers are those of good-humored, cautious, and fairly predictable artisanry. One Pop trap was that some of its artists wanted everything, in moral terms. They wanted images having critical adversarial energy—all those votive objects of a market economy: movie stars, comic strip heroes, cars, refrigerators, TVs, canned foods, and hot dogs—but they wanted them also to be celebratory. The critical energy was mostly coopted immediately by the sheer political commodity value of the images. How can an image-maker criticize that which he or she also exalts? Does ironic presentation redeem one from that dilemma? What if Pop irony itself carries a high market value? Is it necessary to do as Warhol did and confuse the public into market delirium by becoming a vendor of your own masterful affectlessness?

◆◆◆

Richard Diebenkorn may have proved by now to be the most masterly of the painters associated with Bay Area figurative art in the 1950s, but during that period David Park was the most exciting because his painting was so anxious. Diebenkorn's pursuit of colorist geometries in the figurative work, then later in the abstraction of the 1960s and 1970s (culminating, I suppose, in the processional varieties of the *Ocean Park* series), shows a tenacity of purpose and investigatory deliberation he learned from Matisse, though Diebenkorn has never really been driven by passion for the figure or by fauvist enthusiasm. By contrast with the serene buoyancies of Diebenkorn's 1950s work, Park's figure paintings from the same time are massive and not yet fully evolved cult objects. In Park the instrumentation of the brush is more a part of the drama of subject, and the color is madder, more incensed and driven, though (in the things of the early 1950s especially) there's an anxious devouring of space by color volumes that seems one moment a terrible violence, another moment a diffident impatience. The flesh in *Standing Male Nude in the Shower* from 1957 glows a bar-neon red, tacky-infernal, painted from the inside out. In the 1954 *Nudes by a River,* built up in broad banded color masses, the flesh, shown in a state of repose, still struggles to define itself against the erosions of space. The 1957 *Bather with Knee Up,* like Park's work generally after 1955, is solidly constructed, but the planks of ochre, brown, and gray look nailed into place. The colorist disruptions of the earlier work—and the instinctual surprise: in portraits like *Head of Lydia* (1953) and *Profile and Lamp* (1952) we're pitched into the intimacy of the subject as we are in genre pictures like *Sophomore Society* (1953) and *Cocktail Lounge* (1952)—are overresolved in frontal, increasingly monumental poses. If there's anxiety in these later pieces, it may lie in the disparity between the often grimly isolated individuals in the figure groups and their representation in loaded, erotically charged masses of paint.

◆◆◆

Baudelaire's praise for the imagination comes from his hatred or dread of nature, of the fallen world of the visible. It's a Catholic's version: "How mysterious is imagination, that Queen of the Faculties! It touches all the others; it rouses them and sends them into combat.... Those men who are not quickened by it are easily recognizable by some strange curse which withers their

productions like the fig-tree in the Gospel. It is both analysis and synthesis....
It is Imagination that first taught man the moral meaning of color, of con-
tour, of sound and of scent." The Imagination thus dissolves and recreates
the world, it redeems nature from itself, saves it from its chaotic beginnings.
Baudelaire's Romanticism—the Imagination as moral adjudicator and melio-
rator of all in nature—cannot accommodate a Cézanne, a Giacometti, a
Matisse. Although they certainly exercised Imagination more or less as Baudelaire understood it, they did so in order to represent nature as they saw it. They
practiced the same degree of moral attentiveness to nature as did Ingres, whom
Baudelaire so disliked, and Manet, who he felt was gifted but misguided. It's
not the fallenness of nature that determined how certain modern artists have
gone about their work, but the fallen condition of the Imagination itself,
which knows it wants to make an image of nature but knows it has lost for
good the innocence of realist representation. (In light of the impossibilities
modern artists faced, splenetic Baudelaire sounds almost cheery.) Maybe one
ambition of Abstract Expressionism was to vaporize the very terms of the question, to take the god out of technique, to replace Eros with erotics, to demythol-
ogize and dismantle all moral analog left over from representationalism.

◆ ◆ ◆

The question of transcendence in painting since 1945 is not God stuff, at least
not exclusively. It has a social meaning, if we accept Erich Fromm's view that
transcendence means overcoming the limits of selfhood, the prison of the
self, of solipsism and alienation, and opening ourselves to others, to relatedness to the world. Jasper Johns may be the exemplary painter of the cell of
selfhood—the game of form being both play activity and ramparts of the
garrisoned self—with no sense of relatedness to anything outside the circuit
of familiar forms, and with very narrow, repetitious relations among those
forms. But he is not bound alone in that nutshell.

◆ ◆ ◆

Is it worth the effort to perfect a rhetoric of coy but conquering persuasion
which mocks its own intentions? Is it worth the effort to make oneself—
painter or poet—a genius of affected affectlessness? *That* is the most discon-
certing sentimentality of our time. We've come so far from Bergson, who less
than a century ago could say that the universe is a machine for the making of
gods! Our time needs an artist who, without the insulating mockeries of
Camp, will be brilliantly and fearlessly antisacred.

◆ ◆ ◆

In the work of some moderns it's impossible to distinguish between the pursuit
of transcendent reality, of the old sacred, and the desacralized commitment

to formal realization. Modernism's necessary blasphemy was to keep alive the idea of the sacred by saying that it inheres in the pursuit of forms. This is what Matisse meant when he said he believed in God only when he was working. It's not historical vestiges or residues of the sacred that exist in their work, it is in fact spiritual essence, the assumption that the drivenness of the form-making imagination is authored by and answerable to some force or energy or historical contingency greater than itself, even if that greater power is a fiction of the eternal, the infinite. In the work of certain first-generation Abstract Expressionists, of Pollock and Rothko and Clyfford Still, I always feel the presence of the sacred in the forms. The boundary has been crossed; nature and likeness disintegrate and recohere as an *otherness* of formal mystery. And their formalism is more infused with a naturalistic, fearful, primitive religiosity than the work of Matisse and Giacometti. In a good deal of Pop and Neo-Expressionist art, figures of sacred power and the sense of the transcendent are taken mainly as materialist cultural residue, or as elements of Camp nostalgia. We've been living through another passage in the expanding and contracting relation between the mortal order and that which it conceives as transcending it. It's a story of estrangements.

◆ ◆ ◆

Greenberg says somewhere that watercolor is a more intimate medium than oil and that American artists consequently feel more comfortable, because they can be more direct and immediate and private, when using watercolor. This is certainly true of Charles Demuth. He seems to feel less obligated to be emblematic, representative, formally constructive and self-conscious in watercolors. Especially the still lifes and the erotic scenes among men. The flowers in his 1923 *Gladiolus* are nature retold as infinitely veiled vacancies—the petals are serial disclosures. An image like the sensuous *Green Pears* is celebratory and analytical, yet these qualities exist as an intimacy rare in his oil paintings. And his images of men are humorous, robust, unapologetic, immediate, and carry the gleeful boldness of hidden pleasures treated as privileged loves. By contrast, an artist like Robert Mapplethorpe, self-consciously postmodern and consequently moodily affectless, makes images which propose intimacies as intellectual commodities. His flowers, with their cool overdetermined effects, have such a pristine aura of lasciviousness that as erotic emblems they are finally quite harmless. Demuth's 1930 watercolor *Two Sailors Urinating*, with its frontal view of unbuttoned sailors holding big penises, is an image of appetite, dangerous fun, anonymity, and obsessiveness. One sailor looks drunk, a cigarette hanging tough-guy fashion from twisted lips; the other, standing behind him, is pretty and stares at him with obvious desire. The black penis hanging from the open zipper in Mapplethorpe's *Man in Polyester Suit* is an aesthetically hermetic (not emotionally intimate or private) event. The image is defined—that is, its emotional effects are defined—entirely by self-consciousness of effect, and that is abstract and intellectualized. There is another image by Mapplethorpe, of a male back, curved, the skin texture almost gritty, pipped, fretted by shadows created (I presume) by studio lighting, which is a dazzling image of flesh as object of desire—purely object. In the watercolors Demuth is not as knowing and formally self-conscious as in his paintings—he's freed from having to seem notable. Mapplethorpe may never have freed himself from that self-awareness. His images may unsettle us, but usually they aren't intimate enough to be truly disturbing. He certainly made images, as if to order, that suit the pristine arguments of postmodernist intellectuals, because he purged chance and uncertainty from his work as if they were a contagion.

• • •

Questions of Anselm Kiefer. In both versions of the 1982 *To the Unknown Painter* the palette is planted in the center of its scene; it doesn't have wings, as in other paintings, it's atop a rickety pole, like a flag or gravemarker, and in both versions it's surrounded by the massive "heroic" architectural motifs of Albert Speer. Is it therefore an image of spindly weakling art holding its place in the bombastic vacancies of the officially heroic? Is Kiefer mocking the worshipful heroizing of art and artists? Is the palette-on-a-pole an image of hermetic isolation, of the artist as Simon Exemplar? Does it mark a gravesite in a cavernous mausoleum? Does the image, so simple in its elements, cohere? ❖ Why isn't the pictorial conceit of *Icarus-March Sand* (1981) ludicrous? A flying palette. Winged aspiration. The painter scorched by ambition and foolhardiness, trusting too much to technology. A hackneyed contrivance? But the presentation is utterly graceless, mineralized, the palette's grossly feathered wing a scorched gluey black. The textures are decayed, clotted, pounded. Icarus, with his kidney-shaped head and fat wings, is a turkey vulture, a carrion feeder out of nightmare, fallen, still falling. ❖ Why is the second great influence on Kiefer after his mentor Joseph Beuys, by his own admission, Andy Warhol? Kiefer often begins with a photograph implanted on the canvas. Then, he says, "I cover up the pure reality of the photograph with my thoughts and feelings, since I paint in layers." (Warhol wanted that pure reality, too, but he wanted it stained, exposed, tinted, combed not covered, and his process was one of refining *out* thoughts and feelings.) Kiefer's layers are visible in the finished work: "I work according to a kind of 'inverted archeological' principle." He constructs a painting not as a digging or unearthing, but as a seeding of the site. A painting thus becomes evidence-trove of its own history. Why Warhol? Does his image-making represent to Kiefer a purity unavailable to him, a historical innocence or indifference so bland, uninflected, and impersonal that to a mythopoetic painter like Kiefer it must seem a perverse ideal? Is Warhol's influence some kind of vaccine? ❖ To know the devil, swallow his spit. Kiefer, as visionary image-maker, exposes, criticizes, grieves over, the imperious myth-making self-exaltations of modern Germany. His scorched, blood-margined images (in his landscapes blood-streaks often root trees and humans) sometimes seem the immediate register of tormented conscience. Yet he practices the gargantuan, emblematic, myth-encoding ceremonialism that is the major style of that Germany, that Wagnerism. Leon Golub, in his flayed, sagging canvasses of paramilitary terrorists, torturers, and mercenaries, enters into a palpably dangerous sympathy with the tormentors he portrays. His monstrous images, however, release in a very disturbing way the moral devastation not only of the actions depicted but also the devastation of the temptation to sympathy and alliance and silent collaboration. Golub is a much older artist and has a more refined sense of moral complexity (and of politically motivated horror). In Kiefer's *Germany's Spiritual Heroes* a sketchy charcoal figure, barely visible from a distance, occupies the center of the composition. Is he a worshiper at the fire-shrines that line the walls? His figure is partly rubbed into the grain of the wooden floor and beams, rubbed into their substance like a troll, but he's drawn slightly across the grain so that he can be distinguished. Is he the not yet materialized challenger (and future cotenant) of those enshrined heroes? Is the painting a self-portrait with figures?

• • •

In 1983 the San Francisco Museum of Modern Art put on an exemplary small exhibition titled *Rothko 1949*, featuring nine paintings: one from 1947, another from 1955, and the rest from the decisive year. In the adjacent room were several large works by Clyfford Still. You could see, with the kind of clarity too few exhibitions allow, not only the influence on Rothko of Still, who by 1949 had already begun to intensify and explore the form-language of ripped seams in the planar colorist unities of his paintings, but also the gradual resolution of Rothko's early modeling of forms into the brooding, morally volatile masses of his mature style. The 1945 *Tentacles of Memory* has some of Klee's menacing whimsy in its floating weedy lines of ink drawn on thick bands of watercolor. *#17* from 1947 shows some of the biomorphic form of other early pieces, but we can see colors being amassed into adjoining mood-fields. The 1949 *Multiform* is a saturated burnt orange field on which, at the bottom, stand two differently sized columnar grays; a faint, broken bluegray outline runs around the large solid upper portion, which in some places breaks down into archipelagoes of color. It looks very much as if those lower columns and the squared upper field will become engorged with their color, filled out into the familiar resolute hieratic forms soon to emerge in Rothko's painting. In his efforts that crucial year, however, there are streaks, nervous or anxious brushwork, runny frontiers of color seeping jaggedly into neighboring fields. Seeing them so close to the Still paintings makes me think that Rothko learned from him most of all how the mediating intellectualism and Jungian conceptualizing of his earlier work could be diffused in expressive need. In 1949 Rothko began to find colorist presence without analytical or illustrational apparatus. But it's not just the color relationships that mattered. Much later he would say: "I'm interested only in expressing basic human emotions—tragedy, ecstasy, doom.... The people who weep before my pictures are having the same religious experience I had when I painted them. And if you... are moved only by their color relationships, then you miss the point!"

The Artist's Model

by Harriet Shapiro

THE LIGHT THE MORNING of Raphael Soyer's death was clear. It sifted through the three tall dirty windows of his empty studio. But he wasn't there. He was at home in a hospital bed, slipping away from us before we had even gotten used to the idea that he was ill. Raphael Soyer, one of the most respected realists of the twentieth century, was eighty-seven years old when he died in November of 1987. Until his final illness he had been working every day at his studio on the Upper West Side. He walked there, a slight man with a limp, from his apartment on Central Park West where he lived with his wife, Rebecca.

I started posing for Soyer more than nine years ago. I was one of the last in a long line of his models—he called us his disheveled girls. We had met late in 1977 when I went to his studio to interview him about a book he had written. I had a feeling then I would become his model but I don't remember if he asked me to sit for him or if I asked him if I could. He told me later that I reminded him of Gitel, one of his first models. She was thin, dark-haired, and brown-eyed like me. Other people commented too that I looked like Gitel, and when I saw paintings Soyer had done of her in the 1930s, I noticed something similar, her face like mine withdrawn into an inner space. But that reflective quality wasn't special to Gitel or me. It drifts across faces in many of his portraits. And in real life I saw that look on Raphael's own. It flickers too across his self-portraits, where he painted himself a melancholy witness at the edge of a crowd.

I sat for Soyer every Sunday morning except during the summer months when he went away on holiday with Rebecca or when I too was out of town. The first years I sat for two hours, from ten to noon. During the last years we began half an hour later. Soyer was always at the studio ahead of me, even a little early, and once or twice, when I was more than ten minutes late, he was out in the hallway waiting.

His fourth-floor studio in a turn-of-the-century building on 74th and Columbus faced north. The lower halves of the windows were covered with cloudy plastic sheets he had tacked up when he moved in more than twenty years ago. On bright days the light was fairly good but on dark days when it rained it was poor. Then he would put on the overhead light and draw. Earlier in his life, he told me, he had had other studios with better exposure in the old Lincoln Arcade building on Broadway and 66th Street and downtown on Third Street and Second Avenue. But I loved this last place; it was old-fashioned. I didn't know but I thought maybe painters Soyer knew like John Sloan, Arshile Gorky, and Edward Hopper might have worked in studios like this one during the thirties.

The furnishings—old wooden chairs, a well-worn table, its surface deeply scratched, two looming easels—were modest. But they were what Soyer required, turning up regularly as background props in his oils. The daybed I rested on during breaks was covered with a worn paisley spread. On it were faint charcoal lines where Soyer had marked out poses for his models. Over the years the hole in the center got bigger and bigger until finally one of his models replaced it with a fresh blue sheet imprinted with butterflies. But I knew he preferred the old spread. In one corner was a space heater to keep the models warm in the winter and nearby a large industrial-size fan to cool us down in the dog days. Old pantyhose, a pair of jeans, and a few ratty sweaters hung over the edge of a folding screen near the door.

I never took my clothes off behind the screen. In the early days I felt shy in front of him but after a while it seemed natural. And Soyer painted many of his models in Degas-like poses, putting on stockings, pulling off slips and petticoats. If it was cold out and I was wrapped up like a Russian doll, he would smile and shake his head as I shed my layers.

It never took long for him to choose a new pose for the next painting, and they were usually simple ones. I sat on a straight hard chair with my hands on my lap or my arms drawn across my chest. But the pose for one of the last paintings he did of me happened to be difficult. I sat at the table with my hands propping up my chin. There was another model, Caroline, who could take more taxing poses. But Soyer was always very solicitous and encouraged me to take lots of breaks. If I wiggled slightly while he was painting, he would say quickly, "Take a rest, take a rest."

The lying down poses on the bed were my favorites because they were the easiest to hold. He would come over and fix my petticoat, back off to study the effect, and then pick up his pad and begin to draw. Sometimes I fell asleep. There was a certain unspoken understanding between us. It was the implicit etiquette between artist and model. And I never knew if it was just between us or the way Soyer was with all his models. But I knew not to look at a painting when he was just beginning. Once I did and I could feel his dissatisfaction.

And I rarely asked him how the painting was coming. I remember once looking at a drawing he had just done which made me, I felt but didn't say, look squatter than I am. As if he read my thoughts, Soyer told me that Degas agreed with a critic who commented that the artist struggled with proportion. "I struggle with proportion too," Soyer said.

Sometimes he worked standing up at his easel. Other times he was seated. Often he carried a clutch of brushes in his free hand. A passionate realist—his gods were Edgar Degas and Thomas Eakins—the closest Soyer came to abstraction was on his palette. It looked like a wild and colorful sea with swirls of browns, reds, greens, and grays. After a while he cleaned it with Kleenex, which drifted through his fingers to the floor. Once in a while he scratched the canvas with his finger and then swiped it clean on the side of the frame, leaving behind little mysterious traces on the white canvas. Sometimes we talked. Not always. He didn't dwell on getting older. Still, it was there in the air and when his friend Alice Neel died, I knew the landscape around him was thinning out.

I asked him once during a break how he began to paint. Imitating how his father had taught him, he half sang, half spoke in Russian, drawing on a piece of paper, an oval for a face and then filling in eyes, ears, and a nose. Soyer, who was born on Christmas Day 1899 in a small town near Borisogliebsk in Russia, came to the United States in 1912 with his family. He used to walk four miles on Saturday mornings from his parents' house in the South Bronx to the Metropolitan Museum of Art with his twin brother, Moses, and their other brother, Isaac. Later all three became painters.

Sometimes we looked at art books together and I remember that we studied closely a photograph of Renoir as an old man in a wheelchair. We talked about how Renoir, his hands crippled with arthritis, had painted at the end of his life with brushes tied to his fingers. Soyer's hands were supple. They looked like the hands of a much younger man.

He cleaned the studio himself. He paid scant attention to the bathroom, except to buy paper towels and toilet paper from the local supermarket, which he left in shopping bags on the floor. The tub spigot didn't work; it was bound like a mummy's crooked finger in black tape. And the sink was in bad need of a scrub. Resting on it were cakes of Ivory soap worn thin in the center by the motion of the brushes which he cleaned at the end of every session. "Raphael," I would tease him, "that bathroom is a disgrace." "Yes," he said happily, "Rebecca thinks so too." One day I came in and found it transformed, the tiles sparkling, the sink so clean the enamel shone. It turned out that Peter Orlovsky, posing then for a portrait with Allen Ginsberg, had taken it upon himself to clean the bathroom. He spent several hours in there, singing cheerily to himself, swabbing down the tile floors. All was fine until the next visitor flushed the toilet. It overflowed into the studio. It seems that Orlovsky, once the cleaning was done, had blithely stuffed all the rags down the toilet.

Very few people came by while I was there, and when they did, it was always at the end of the session. Once in a very great while I brought friends round. Soyer was unfailingly courteous as he hauled his canvases from the back alcove to show. He would have no one help him. He lined them up like large playing cards, resting them one beside the other in a precarious balancing act on the floor. One time I asked him if I could bring around an artist named Michael Heizer. "Who's he?" Soyer asked. I told him that Heizer had once dragged a thirty-ton boulder with a bulldozer back and forth outside the Detroit Museum of Art to make a sculpture. Soyer shrugged. His shrugs were eloquent. But then he said, "I always like to meet those guys."

Sometimes we went out to eat lunch on Columbus Avenue with Rebecca. As we got ready to leave the studio, I thought of how we would seem outside on the street together. I was suddenly conscious of how small he was and how tall I was. "I'm La Goulue," I said, "and you're Toulouse-Lautrec."

I liked going outside and eating lunch with him, but our real life was in the studio. It was peaceful in there, it seemed the most peaceful place in the world, and I had plenty of time to think about what it meant to be his model. It was simple. He painted. I sat for him. After he finished the painting, we walked over to it and looked at it together, at a certain distance from the easel. I saw myself on the canvas. I also saw that I had somehow become him. He had painted his soul on my face.

Rilke Dancing

by Mindy Aloff

RILKE AND THE DANCE? His themes don't promise a link: "sacred solitude," nostalgia for immutability, longing for inner transcendence, the pressure of the invisible on the sensible world. We must search even to find more than one person in his poems at any moment; at the most, he gives us the poet's voice and an invocation of a second presence. Conversation for him seems to be a matter of someone about to answer a ringing telephone. A more exact theatrical comparison would be early silent film acting, close-up by close-up.

> But is there no place at last where, from each to each
>   there is something that might be language, without speech?

These lines from the *Sonnets to Orpheus* might caption the art of Rilke's contemporary, Eleonora Duse, whose mature technique could encapsulate the character's entire spiritual biography in the refocusing of her gaze. Like the poet, Duse was a genius of the imminent. (We can still see why in her 1916 film *Cenere*.) Relating a meeting with the actress in 1912, Rilke wrote, "You can imagine, we were like two characters coming on in an old mystery....A meaning arose immediately from the whole and at once transcended us."

By the peak of his career, Rilke wasn't composing lines so much as receiving them, and to put himself in the proper state of acceptance he arranged an environment that went beyond the tranquil toward the anchoritic. Closeted with a cat before a standing desk in a castle by the sea, having transposed normal human intimacy from a matter of corporeal meetings to correspondence, the poet awaited his poems, tuning his nerves to the pitch of that "heart-work" brimming his inner ear. Much of what we admire him for would seem to exclude the essence of dancing: its mobility, spontaneity, temperament, directness, evanescence, youthful glamour, and, even among its puritans, sensuous perfume. And yet, by immersing himself in all that dancing is not, Rilke became a catalyst for thinking on what it is. In this essay, I sketch a few steppingstones to that thought, touching on how Rilke's work has influenced the theater, how some dancers not directly influenced by him have demonstrated a remarkable sympathy with his vision, and how Rilke himself used images of the dance to project his poetic impulse.

◆ ◆ ◆

In "Rilke's Lamp," an essay from his 1935 collection, *Portraits-Souvenir, 1900–1914,* former Ballets Russes collaborator Jean Cocteau dramatized the idea of Rilke as a lighthouse:

> Long, long afterwards, I was to learn about the lamp which burned every night behind a corner window. It was the lamp of Auguste Rodin's secretary, Monsieur Rilke. I believed I knew a great many things in those days, and I lived in the filthy ignorance of my pretentious youth. Success put me on the wrong track, and I did not know there exists a kind of success worse than failure, a kind of failure worth all the success in the world. And I did not know that one day the far-off friendship of Rainer Maria Rilke would console me for having seen his lamplight without realizing it was signaling me to come and burn my wings in it.

A ballet fan is led helplessly by this passage to the figure of the Sleepwalker in Balanchine's *Night Shadow* (1946), candle in her hand, the body of the impetuous Poet (who effectively "burned his wings" in that light) in her arms as she glides to her tower room, triumphant prisoner over we aren't sure what. Did Balanchine know this Cocteau tribute?

In any case, retreating to the company of fact, it would be difficult to think of a more theatrical abyss than that between Cocteau, the opium-addicted perpetual child, and Rilke, the ascetic sage who evaded the company of his own daughter. Yet Rilke and Cocteau turn out to have been mutual admirers. Cocteau's 1925 play, *Orphée,* with its famous magic mirror through which Death comes and goes, was written under the influence of Rilke's 1922 Orphic sonnets, which Cocteau revered. (In one sonnet, invoking mirrors, we find, "A few / seem to have passed straight into you.... ") "Tell Jean Cocteau I love him," Rilke wrote to a friend in 1926 (the year of Rilke's death); he had seen a German production of the play. "[Cocteau is] the only one who plunges into the myth which lies open to him and from which he returns tanned as from the seashore."

Three decades later, Cocteau would consult the sonnets again, this time for a poem about a unicorn, stimulated by the unicorn tapestries at Cluny. The project was a ballet, *La Dame à la licorne,* to an arrangement of dance tunes from the Renaissance, with libretto and designs by Cocteau and choreography by Heinz Rosen. Given its world premiere in 1953, *La Dame* entered the repertory of the Ballet Russe de Monte Carlo in 1956. It was the first ballet I ever saw in a theater; my sole memory of it shows the unicorn, a small-framed female figure, pawing the air before her as she bends backward until the jousting, spiraled horn between the eyeholes of her milk-white mask cast a shadow on the stage. The horn had the objectivity of a pointe shoe; it belonged to the world of Romantic ballet, where the expressiveness we seek in the face became displaced to the body. It was a construction as real as an arabesque. Rilke's unicorn seems a little different, however:

> Oh, this is the animal that never was.
> They did not know it and, for all of that,
> they loved his neck and posture, and his gait,
> clean to the great eyes with their tranquil gaze.
>
> Really it *was* not. Of their love they made it,
> this pure creature. And they left a space
> always, till in this clear uncluttered place
> lightly he raised his head and scarcely needed
>
> to be. They did not feed him any corn,
> only the possibility he might
> exist, which gave the beast such strength, he bore
>
> a horn upon the forehead. Just one horn.
> Unto a virgin he appeared, all white,
> and was in the silver mirror and in her.

"In the unicorn, no parallel with Christ was intended," Rilke explained in a 1923 letter. "Rather, all love of the non-proven, the non-graspable, all belief in the value and reality of whatever our heart has through the centuries created and lifted up out of itself: that is what is praised in this creature." The only danced unicorn I know which could match the transparency of this "non-graspable" conception is the one that appears to be embedded in the "Diamonds" pas de deux of Balanchine's 1967 *Jewels*. David Daniel and Arlene Croce have suggested connections between this dance and the Cluny tapestries, which Balanchine visited during the mid-1960s. There is no evidence that he knew the Rilke poem, though with Balanchine one can't be certain about influences; he didn't prefer to divulge them. What one can see is that he and Rilke shared the same symbol: for both, the fabulous creature is present but not real, it's the product of love, it's associated with a "clear, uncluttered place," and its transformation ("in the silver mirror and in her") is evident but inexplicable.

"Diamonds" presents a ballerina and her consort-partner. (The roles were made for Suzanne Farrell and Jacques d'Amboise, and they still carry the faint impression of high-risk feminine initiative and steadying male dynamism.)

As the ballerina advances on pointe, knees parallel, in a refined, equine walk, the partner touches her at the waist, like a trainer guiding a steed. She inclines her face so that she gazes along the ground and lifts her straightened, braided arms ahead of her so that her head is between them (the horn). Then, she releases their tension and, still walking, bends backward, now "blind" in her journey and susceptible to her partner's control. In precisely timed periods the double image of creature and girl opens and closes like a pair of shears. Later in the pas de deux, the ballerina draws her arm back, grazing her temple with the outside of her hand (the archer stalking the prey). The sequence has the character of a sacred mystery without spelling out the story; heroine, hunter, and prey continually form and melt through the action of the dance, all of them alive in the girl but brought to light by the support and guidance of the boy. Like Rilke, Balanchine gives one the sense of an underlying, and unifying, mission, a service to an inexpressible ideal. For Balanchine, it is a chivalric service, for Rilke, monastic. And, in the company of Rilke, it's not as surprising to hear Balanchine speak as a visionary as it is in the context of more skeptical theater life. The interchange below, quoted by Lincoln Kirstein in *A Portrait of Mr. B.*, took place in 1972 in the Soviet Union during the New York City Ballet's tour there. ("Grigorovich" is Yuri Grigorovich, head of the Bolshoi Ballet since 1964; "'Nedelia'" signifies an interviewer from the weekly cultural publication of *Izvestia*.)

> BALANCHINE: I believe in the dance as an independent category, as something that really exists in itself and by itself. However, this may be an unreal or inaccurate metaphysical category, something immaterial, perhaps indefinable.

> 'NEDELIA': But you said yourself [at the start of the interview] that your ballets were not "abstractions," that live people performed them...

> BALANCHINE: Yes. They convey the sense of the dance to the spectator, but the dance also exists without spectators!

> GRIGOROVICH: Pray, in what form?

> BALANCHINE: In the form in which it comes to me; in the form in which I set it out.

Rilke's own documented or possible exposure to dancing is, in terms of his oeuvre, a peripheral concern, but it does cast an unmatched light, however frail, on his late work, especially. During trips to Russia at the turn of the century he met the theater critic Akim Volinsky and Alexandre Benois, who was to become one of Diaghilev's most important artists and early advisors. (Benois would also prove a long-time friend to Rilke through letters.) While stopping in Leningrad and Moscow, could Rilke have escaped attending the ballet? And during his years in Paris, did he never attend the Opera? During 1905–6 he served as Rodin's secretary in the City of Light—Cocteau's lamp dates from this time—where he could well have heard about, or perhaps seen, Isadora Duncan. Rodin first met the dancer in 1903, and she immediately overwhelmed him as both an artist and a being. ("Isadora Duncan is the greatest woman I have ever known," Rodin would say in 1925. "And her art has influenced my work more than any other inspiration that has come to me. Sometimes I think she is the greatest woman the world has ever known.") In his two-part monograph on Rodin, completed in 1907, Rilke identifies an innovative "movement" in Rodin's art,

> ...though not at all in that sense in which movement has so often been mentioned as a reproach; for the movement of the gestures, which has been much observed in this sculpture, takes place within these things, like an inner circulation, never disturbing their calm or the stability of their architecture. Of course, it would have been nothing new to have introduced movement into sculpture. What is new is the kind of movement, movement to which the light is compelled by the particular quality of these surfaces, whose inclines are so variously modulated that it flows slowly here and plunges there, appearing now shallow and now deep, now lustrous and now matt. The light which comes in contact with one of these things is no longer ordinary light; it suffers no further chance alterations. The thing takes possession of it, and uses it as its own property.

This idea of movement as an inner dynamic, revealed by light, runs parallel to Isadora's own studio discoveries, notably her epiphany that human movement begins in the solar plexus, the source of breath, a revelation that came to her, she reports in *My Life*, after she stood alone for hours, her arms crossed over her chest, in what might be termed Rilkean waiting. Meanwhile, in performance, with the help of Gordon Craig, she reduced her theatrical support to a set of curtains, musician(s), and lighting. It's a puzzle to figure out whether Rodin submerged Isadora in his sculpture, or she exposed his sculpture through her dancing.

Movement and light are also linked in the Rilke lyric "Spanish Dancer" from his collection *New Poems* [1907]. Here, Rilke seems actually to have studied how the dance progressed, and in drawing an analogy between the flame of a sulphur match and the dancer's crescendos and diminuendos of energy, he conveys an image both attractive and journalistically persuasive: "her round dance begins to flicker and fan out," he writes; then, in a new, one-line stanza, "And all at once it is entirely flame." The dancer, herself, is the match. "With a single glance she sets her hair ablaze, / and suddenly with daring art whirls / all her dress into this fiery rapture, / ...And then: as though she felt the fire grow tight, / she sweeps it all together and casts it off / disdainfully, and with imperious demeanor / looks on: it lies there raging on the ground / and keeps on flaming and refuses to submit—." At last, "she, with self-assurance and a sweet / exultant smile, looks up triumphantly / and stamps it out with furious little feet." A well-written review (the dancer was, in fact, an entertainer at the house of a painter-friend): one sees the pattern of the dance on the floor, the use of the dancer's eyes, arms, and feet, the way the frenzied legwork causes the long dress a kind of after-shock, the sudden, dramatic stillness so characteristic of flamenco ("casts it off / disdainfully"), even the transition from passionate movements of the whole body to cool, bubbling footwork. And one thing more: the dance makes the figure larger and freer; that is, the surrounding space, part of which the dancer vanquishes, belongs to the full experience. The visible and the invisible interpenetrate in a way that any spectator susceptible to dancing can appreciate. Compare, for example, "The Panther" from the same collection. For this beast, caged in the Jardin des Plantes,

> The supple pace of powerful soft strides,
> turning in the very smallest circle,
> is like a dance of strength around a center
> in which a mighty will stands numbed.

In the spring of 1911, Rilke attended the last night of the Ballets Russes's Paris season, when he saw Nijinsky in *Schéhérazade* and *Le Spectre de la Rose.* There was "dance in his every vein," Rilke wrote excitedly to his wife, Clara, about the star. He felt that he must "make something" for Nijinsky, "a poem which could so to say be swallowed and then expressed in dance," but, as Donald Prater, one of Rilke's biographers, relates, the impulse never got beyond a fragment, unpublished, called "Figurines for a Ballet." One wonders whether the poetic wafer would have expressed itself in Nijinsky as the Spanish dancer or the panther, as the outward or inward orbit to the infinite. The suggestion of a text transubstantiated into dancing itself draws in its train an entire line of poetic figuration about the dance, much of it French. In a now-standard essay called "Poet and Dancer Before Diaghilev," Frank Kermode tracks a fascination with Loie Fuller that begins with Mallarmé scribbling his meditation to her in the theater ("The enchantress makes the ambiance, produces it from herself and retracts it into a silence rustling with crêpe de Chine"), and ends with Yeats, remembering Fuller's whirling silks transformed by underlighting and the two wands she used to guide them. "How can we know the dancer from the dance?" he asks in one poem, and in another commemorates the terrible rounds of "blood-begotten spirits...Dying into a dance, / An agony of trance, / An agony of flame that cannot singe a sleeve."

Among the poets in this line was Paul Valéry, for whom dancing was intrinsic to the analogical thought that fueled his poems and his metaphysics. Valéry, like Yeats, was possessed by the dance throughout his career; unlike Yeats, for whom "dancing" seemed to mean acting and mime as well, Valéry kept his concept undiluted. In a remarkable 1936 precurtain lecture at a performance by the Spanish virtuosa, La Argentina, he explains what he means by "pure dance":

It moves in a self-contained realm of its own and implies no reason, no tendency toward completion. A formula for pure dance should include nothing to suggest that it has an end.... It ceases as a dream ceases that might go on indefinitely: it stops, not because an undertaking has been completed, for there is no undertaking, but because something else, something outside it has been exhausted.... Consider the dance as a kind of *inner life*.... [italics are Valéry's]

The links with Valéry's own idea of poetry (for example, that a poem is never finished but abandoned) seem obvious in hindsight, but as he was working out his thoughts their distinctness probably felt magnetic to those for whom his career was as yet unforeseen. One of those fascinated onlookers was Rilke. In 1921, he translated Valéry's Socratic dialogue, *L'Âme et la Danse,* into German. "To me belongs the consciousness of my obedient muscles," says the character of the dancer in the text. "To you the ideas which the figures made by my body must give, as they change into one another according to some purpose or pattern." On January 1st of 1922, he received news of the slow, glandular disease and death of a young girl, the daughter of an acquaintance, a playmate of his own daughter, Ruth. This dead girl, Wera Knoop, was acclaimed for dancing when she was a small child, but as the disease weighed down her body she abandoned the dance for music, then only for drawing. This news, in conjunction with the reading of some Valéry ("I was alone, I was waiting, all my work was within. One day I read Valéry, and I knew that my waiting was at an end"), precipitated one of the most amazing bursts of creativity in literary history. Within two weeks he had written the entire 55-sonnet sequence called *Sonnets to Orpheus,* and by the end of the month he had completed the *Duino Elegies,* to which the sonnets seem filially related, especially in the theme of transformation. Scholars of Rilke can speak more cogently than I of what "dance" means to him: in the sonnets, for example, it's rarely mentioned, although there are plenty of allusions to energy and motion, intellectual and spiritual; and of course Rilke's Eurydice is always basically the dancer to his Orpheus-poet. But one can also sense in these poems the motivations for both classic ballet and modern dance. When, addressing Wera in Sonnet 28 of Part 11 of the cycle, Rilke writes,

> ... You, almost a child, complete,
> for an instant the dance-figure, that it be
> a pure constellation by which we beat
> the order of stupid nature transiently...

he's focusing on the classic geometries of Mallarmé and Valéry, the metamorphic act, the girl autographing the void with her body—a dance that comes in through the eyes. But when, in the fifth (though actually the last to be written) of the *Duino Elegies*—which directly refers to a Picasso painting of acrobats—he brings in movement, he's recreating a more visceral process:

You, that fall with the thud
only fruits know, unripe,
daily a hundred times from the tree
of mutually built up motion (the tree that, swifter than water,
has spring and summer and autumn in so many minutes),
fall and rebound on the grave:
sometimes, in half-pauses, a tenderness tries
to steal out over your face to your seldomly
tender mother, but scatters over your body,
whose surface quickly absorbs the timidly rippling...

Here, we are in the land of Isadora, Martha Graham, Doris Humphrey, Mary Wigman. We're implicated in an inward heaviness that from its own submission to gravity builds up the dance rhythm, in a tenderness that becomes displaced—not a decoration for an image, but a tremor through struggling flesh.

Perhaps Rilke's connections of classicism and praise, expressionism and lament, are merely coincidence, but they are no less valuable to dancers and dancegoers for that. They are the coincidences of the sort that T. S. Eliot refers to in "The Function of Criticism" when he writes: "Between the true artists of any time there is, I believe, an unconscious community." By coincidence, that essay is dated 1923, within a year of Rilke's sonnets.

A Note on Bunraku

by Susan Sontag

> Art is something which lies in the slender mar-
> gin between the real and the unreal.... it is un-
> real, and yet it is not unreal; it is real, and yet it
> is not real.
>
> CHIKAMATSU MONZAEMON
> (1653–1725)

IN BUNRAKU THE PLAY IS IDENTIFIED, first of all, as a physical object: a text. And the text is sacred—that is, generative. Hence, the grave ceremony that opens each performance: the chief reader holds out the text and bows to it, before setting it down on the low lectern and beginning to read. Bunraku is a theater that transcends the actor, by multiplying and displacing the sources of dramatic pathos.

The play is acted; that is to say, recited; that is, read. The text (declaimed, sung, chanted, wailed) is punctuated or italicized by music produced by a string instrument, the shamisen. It is also, simultaneously, enacted—by piercingly expressive large puppets, half or two-thirds life-size. The enacting of the drama occupies the stage proper, in front of the audience: the wide rectangular space where figures—the puppets and their handlers—move. But the source of the words and the music—the one or more reciters and musicians who sit to the right of the stage on a rostrum—constitutes a parallel performance. The dialogue is not "off," as in a certain kind of narrative film, but off-center—displaced, given its own expressive and corporeal autonomy.

The drama has a double displacement of emotion, a double scale, a double physical and emotional gait. On the stage proper the leading principle is a kind of anti-hysteria. There is the muteness of the protagonists—who, instead of being living actors, are puppets; there is the impassivity and omnipresence of the humans who make them move. To the *joruri* reciter, who is not only off-center (from the audience's point of view) but physically immobile, is given the task of maximal expressiveness. Most of the texts, which consist of narrative and commentary as well as dialogue, are floridly emotional, and the narration may modulate into a lengthy crescendo of sobs and gasps. The figure of the reciter, who acts, as it were, by proxy, on behalf of the puppets, is just one of the devices whereby Bunraku isolates—decomposes, illustrates, transcends, intensifies—what acting is.

The puppet is, in prototype, a supple doll operated by a single person. The invention, in 1734, of a puppet to be operated by three persons brought the puppet's emotional and gestural potency to a point never equaled before or since. The Japanese puppet can roll its eyes, raise its eyebrows, smile, clench its fists; it can languish, dress itself, run, convincingly take its own life. No string puppet or hand puppet can perform such complex and detailed actions; and the Bunraku puppets have an ability to move audiences, move them to tears, unmatched in any other puppet tradition.

But apart from widening the emotional range and expressiveness of the puppet (a gain we may or may not choose to identify with "realism"), the fact of multiplying the operators—and, of necessity, putting them onstage with the puppets—decisively shapes and transforms the emotional register of puppet drama. The puppet is literally outnumbered, beleaguered, surrounded. The presence of three outsized handlers contributes an unending pathos to the puppet's movements and efforts. The puppets seem helpless, childlike, vulnerable. Yet they also seem sovereign, imperious, in their very smallness and precision and elegance.

Bunraku works on two scales of spatial relations. The often elaborate decor is constructed to the puppets' measurements. The operators are giants, interlopers. Alongside each delicate puppet head are the three large heads of the operators. The operators look at the puppet as they manipulate it. The audience watches the operators observing the puppet, primal spectators to the drama they animate. The three operators sum up the essence of what it is to be a god. To be seen, and impassive: one has his face bared. And to be hidden: the other two wear black hoods. The puppet gestures. The operators move together, as one giant body, animating the different parts of the puppet body, in a perfected division of labor. What the audience sees is that to act is to be moved. (And, simultaneously, observed.) What is enacted is the submission to a fate. That one operator's face is bared and two are veiled is another device making Bunraku's characteristic double statement: hyperbole and discretion, presence and absence of the dramatic substance.

This relation between the operators and the puppet is not simply an efficient relation; it is the cruel mystery which is at the center of the Bunraku drama. Handing the puppet a comb, rushing the puppet to its doom—some moments the operators seem like the puppet's servants, at other moments its captors. Sometimes the puppet seems to be reposing solidly on the operators or to be borne placidly aloft by them; other times to be in perpetual, hapless flight. There are constant shifts of scale, to delight the senses and wring the emotions. Sometimes the shadowy manipulators shrink and the puppets swell into a normal scale. Then the operators loom once more and the puppets re-become fragile, persecuted Lilliputians.

The situation we call art characteristically requires us both to look very attentively and to look "beyond" (or "through") what is understood as an impediment, distraction, irrelevance. At an opera performance, we look past or over the orchestra to concentrate on the stage. But in Bunraku we are not supposed to look past the shadowy, black-garbed puppeteers. The presence of the operators is what gives Bunraku its elevated, mythic impersonality and heightened, purified emotionality. In order to make the art of the puppets competitive with the art of living actors, says Chikamatsu, the text must be "charged with feeling." But, he adds, "I take pathos to be entirely a matter of restraint." Compare Balanchine, who brought the naively emotive classical ballet tradition to its apex by developing the sense in which dancers are co-sharers, with ideal puppets, in the sublimity of the impersonal: "Silence, placidity, and immobility are perhaps the most powerful forces. They are as impressive, even more so, than rage, delirium, or ecstasy."

In the most profound Western meditation on puppet theater (and, by extension, on the dance), Kleist wrote that the very inanimateness of the puppet was the precondition for expressing an ideal state of the spirit. Kleist's speculative fantasy—he was writing in 1810, about string puppets—is incarnated and fulfilled in Bunraku.

Home and the World:
Reflections on Satyajit Ray

by Steve Vineberg

IN OCTOBER 1981, the Pacific Film Archive in Berkeley screened the Indian filmmaker Satyajit Ray's entire *Apu Trilogy*—*Pather Panchali, Aparajito,* and *The World of Apu,* each about two hours long—in a single stretch, with an hour's break for supper. I'd seen each of the first two movies separately, years earlier (and years apart), but the effect of watching all three, following the story of Apu from his Bengali village childhood through his Calcutta education and into his marriage and reconciliation with his son after the death of his beloved wife, was emotionally overpowering. I can think of only two comparable experiences I've had at the movies: a back-to-back viewing of *The Godfather* and *The Godfather, Part II* and—again, in a single day—the Swedish director Jan Troell's two-part epic, *The Emigrants* and *The New Land.*

As far as I can tell, Ray is the greatest living filmmaker,* but it's almost impossible for Americans to see more than a handful of his movies. Available on video are the trilogy, made between 1955 and 1959 (though the prints of the first two, *Pather Panchali* in particular, are dreadful, and the subtitles so difficult to read that I had to follow along with the published screenplay); the 1960 *Devi; Two Daughters* from 1961 (in India this anthology film is called *Three Daughters,* but one of the three episodes was cut before its release here); *Distant Thunder* (1973); and *The Home and the World,* the last full-length Ray film seen by American audiences. (It was made in 1984.) Over a period of nearly two decades, I've managed to see a dozen others, mostly at universities or Asian cultural centers. (Several of the ones I was lucky enough to catch in Montreal in the seventies have, I'm told, never been screened in this country.) While researching this article, I tried to find 16mm prints of *The*

---

*No longer, alas—he died in the spring of 1992, about eighteen months after this essay was originally published. *(Ed.)*

Music Room, which I'd never seen, and *Days and Nights in the Forest*, which I longed to see again—and learned that both had been dropped by their distributors. I couldn't locate a print of his latest picture, either, based on Ibsen's *An Enemy of the People* (it's his comeback, after a heart attack forced him to take a four-year break), because—though it was shown at Cannes and on Canadian public television last year—it has no American distributor. Even in his native India, Ray's movies don't get seen much beyond Calcutta, because they're in Bengali, a language spoken by only a small minority of Indians. Mira Nair, the director of *Salaam Bombay!*, reports that she never saw one until she left India to attend university in the United States. Talk about a vanishing legacy! Imagine if you learned that almost all the classical labels had dropped their Mozart recordings, or that Dostoyevsky was no longer available in English translations, or that a private collector had snatched up all the Vermeers in the world and only his friends could take a peek at them. But even these aren't fair analogies, because in each case the world would recognize the enormous cultural loss. Not so in Ray's case: though his appreciators have compared him to Renoir and De Sica (his two major influences)—and to Mozart—most people, even movie lovers, draw a blank when you mention his name.

◆ ◆ ◆

Several of Ray's titles—*Pather Panchali* (which means "Song of the Little Road"), *The World of Apu, Distant Thunder, The Home and the World*—suggest the pull of the faraway. And if I were to choose my favorite of the themes that run through Ray's work, it would be the tension between "home" (which is often synonymous with the domestic, with the countryside, or with old-world Indian values) and "the world" (travel, the quest, the city, politics, the new values of industrialized India). Ray's complex, ambivalent vision takes in all the implications of home and the world; he refuses to validate one to the exclusion of the other. Each seems to bring sadness and fulfillment; each is both a constriction and a ticket to freedom. Sarbojaya, Apu's mother (played by Karuna Banerjee), is limited by her lack of education; home is her whole world, so when she loses her husband and her daughter, Apu is her only lifeline, and when he grows away from her (leaving the village to attend school in the city), she dies. But home is what rescues the adult Apu (Soumitra Chatterjee) in the end, reclaiming him from his aimless wanderings. When Nikhilesh (Victor Banerjee), the liberal prince of *The Home and the World* (set in 1907), gives his wife, Bimala (Swatilekha Chatterjee), a British education and insists on bringing her out of purdah, into society, she falls in love with another man—Nikhilesh's boyhood friend Sandip (Soumitra Chatterjee), who leads the movement calling for a rejection of all things English and an embracing of Indian culture. "You freed her from her moorings; now look where she's drifted," Nikhilesh's sister-in-law (Gopa Aich) censures him;

but she lives in the past, still worshiping at the shrine of her dead husband.

You could say that the tragedy of most of Ray's characters lies in their inability to reconcile home and the world, and that he sees in them the collective tragedy of a nation hauled into the twentieth century (the "world") with all the attendant traditions of a slower, more graceful life ("home") still clinging to their backs. But in Ray's films, politics and its inevitable partner, religion, are primarily a way of looking at the psychology of his characters, whose apparent rejection of their Indian heritage is an emblem of their necessary rebellion against their parents. (His most overtly political movie, the elaborate allegory *The Chess Players,* is clever but not very satisfying; the political events he chronicles in *Distant Thunder* and *The Home and the World* are less interesting, insofar as they're treated in these films, than their effect on the lives of the characters.) That's true of the Calcutta businessman (Barun Chanda) in *Company Limited* (also known as *The Target*), who's embarrassed when his old-world parents intrude on the dinner party he's throwing for his friends, where golf and Rolls Royces are the topics under discussion. And it's true of Umaprasad (Soumitra Chatterjee) in *Devi,* whose devout Hindu father (Chhabi Biswas) disdains his "Christian" ways (the adjective is meant more as a synonym for "modern" than as a specific description of his son's beliefs) and whose desire to move out of the house attains an urgency when the old man decides—on the evidence of a dream—that Umaprasad's wife (Sharmila Tagore) is a reincarnation of the goddess Kali.

I can't think of a more potent or imaginative metaphor for the tug of war between parents and children, the struggle between old and new values, than the conflict in *Devi*. Old Kalikinkar blocks his son's growth by appropriating his wife, first reversing the natural order by allowing her to care for him as a mother would (he calls her "Ma"—"little mother") and then removing her altogether from the sphere of human relations—specifically from the realm of sexuality, where Umaprasad is out of his father's reach—by setting her up as a goddess. When Umaprasad, who has been away from home studying for his exams while this transformation has been taking place, returns to see the devotees of Kali paying homage to his wife, she looks up and smiles at him— the private lover's smile we've seen only within the confines of their bedroom. It's a shocking moment, a subversive moment: the sacred is eroticized, violated. But in Ray's scheme, that kind of violation is an expression of a natural impulse. You can find a variation on this idea in *Aparajito,* in the scene where Apu (Pinaki Sen Gupta, the second of four actors who play the character at different ages), carrying an idol for a religious service, part of his priestly training, sees some boys playing in the distance and is drawn to their shouts. At this moment, Ray lets us know that life in its infinite variety will seduce Apu away from the ascetic future the priests have mapped out for him—just as, in a very different culture, it seduces Stephen Dedalus.

You won't find Ray taking a stand on the side of either traditional or modern values in his country. Profoundly humanistic, he's a social commentator on the order of Chekhov—aware of everything, judgmental of no one. (Ray evokes Chekhov most strongly in his short-story films, especially "The Postmaster" in *Three Daughters* and "The Coward" in *The Coward and the Holy Man*.) Somnath (Pradip Mukherjee), the hero of *The Middleman*, grows away from his father's values, too, but the ones he takes on—the ones he needs to get ahead in business—are corrupt: he finds he's expected to pimp for his clients, and in the movie's haunting final sequence he discovers that the whore he's procured is the sister of a childhood friend. As in *Devi*, the traditional is violated, sacred ties are eroticized, but you have the opposite response—you feel the impulse is unnatural. Nor is there any simple affirmation of independence in *Mahanagar (The Big City)*—a contemporary melodrama that covers some of the same ground as *The Home and the World*—where economic conditions force Arati (Madhabi Mukherjee) to get a job in a department store and the transition from the traditional wife's role to the modern role of a working woman alters her perception of herself and her family's perception of her. ("You wouldn't recognize me if you saw me at work," she tells her husband, played by Anil Chatterjee. "Will I recognize you at home?" is his reply. And in fact, when he spies on her one day in a restaurant, adjusting the makeup she doesn't wear in his presence, having tea with another man, it's as if he were watching a stranger—the moment is Pirandellian.)

Some of Ray's characters can only mature or acquire some kind of happiness and self-fulfillment when they lose "the world"—like the student Amulya, a comic version of the grown-up Apu, in the last episode of *Three Daughters,* who grows to deserve his bride (and she to deserve him), or the smug, ungenerous urban sport Ashim, transformed on a country vacation in *Days and Nights in the Forest.* (The endlessly resourceful Soumitra Chatterjee, who has appeared in thirteen of Ray's movies, plays both these roles—as well as the grown-up Apu. Ray is just as inconceivable without Chatterjee as Griffith would be without Lillian Gish.) Others need to lose "home"—to look beyond the values they've accepted without question and embrace the world outside their doors. That's true of the Brahmin (Mohan Agashe) in *Sadgati (Deliverance)* who treats a lower-caste suppliant (Om Puri) carelessly: the man dies of a heart attack while chopping wood for the Brahmin, who's left to bury his body, literally taking on the burden of a man traditionally outside—below—the boundaries of his vision. And in *Distant Thunder,* India's "man-made" famine of 1943 (brought on by the "distant thunder" of the war: Japan's take-over of Burma has impeded India's importation of Burmese rice) creeps over the divisions between castes. At the beginning, Ananga (Babita) casually asks the devoted village girl Moti (Chitra Banerjee) not to touch her, or she'll have to wash all over again; much later, Moti, dying of starvation right outside Ananga's gates, repeats that line. At the end Ray cuts from a shot of Ananga, her Brahmin husband (Soumitra Chatterjee), and half a dozen others, moving toward the city in search of food, to a long shot, in silhouette, that loses them among hundreds of Indians participating in the same exodus.

In the exquisite "Postmaster," home and the world are brought closer, then split apart. The man of the world, the Calcutta-bred Nandalal (Anil Chatterjee), is sent to a postmaster's position in a remote village, where, invited to musicales by the local elders, he sits, a pained smile on his face, longing for the society of the city. He grows fond of the child, Ratan, who cooks and cleans for him and nurses him through a bout of malaria; he brings a small portion of the world outside the village to her by teaching her to read and write. (Ratan is played by Chandana Banerjee, who has a quicksilver glance and that quality so many of the women you see in Ray's movies share, of being deeply expressive and completely modest at the same time. In a little girl, this distinctly Indian kind of femininity is even more mysterious and formidable.) When he recovers, he applies for a transfer and gets it. It doesn't occur to him that he's taking something away from Ratan by leaving her; he shatters her world without even noticing what he's done. The episode ends in an epiphany: at the last moment, Nandalal goes to find her to say goodbye, but she passes him in the road without looking at him, and, as he hears her addressing his successor as "master," his face falls in recognition of both the pain he's caused her and the worth of the relationship he's thrown away.

Of course, there are many ways of characterizing what happens in "Postmaster" that don't have anything to do with the conflict between home and the world. My point here isn't to reduce Ray's work to a single theme, only to focus on one bright thread in the weave. Nandalal's flash of tragic understanding, with its Chekhovian irony (his discovery of a human bond occurs at the moment it's severed forever), is echoed in other scenes where this theme isn't present—the realization of the protagonist Amitava (Soumitra Chatterjee) in "The Coward" that his fear of reclaiming an old love (Madhabi Mukherjee) has robbed him of the only true romance his life has ever contained; the awful moment in *Days and Nights in the Forest* when the reticent Sanjoy (Subhendu Chatterjee) comprehends that the lonely widow Jaya (Kaberi Bose) is making a pass at him that he can't reciprocate. Nothing is simple to Ray—any exchange between two human beings, any shift of a child's focus from one object to another, any application of energy to a daily task suggests innumerable frames through which we can see and understand it. Pauline Kael once wrote, "No artist has done more than Satyajit Ray to make us reevaluate the commonplace," and in his first-rate analysis of the *Apu Trilogy*, Robin Wood keeps returning to the multiplicity of the characters' motives; he suggests four or five reasons why Apu's mother is so hard on his sister Durga (Uma Das Gupta), why Durga picks quarrels with Apu, why, finding the necklace she was accused of stealing among her things after she dies, he throws it into the river. What makes these movies ultimately mysterious— and, I suppose, unsalable in a market dominated by movies where complexity would just get in the way—is that we can't locate the one *true* motive; even when the "case" of the necklace seems to be closed, at the end of *Pather Panchali,* Apu's action reminds us that the only mystery Ray's solved for us is the most superficial one. That's why he can't simply assign a value to "village life" or "city life," "the family" or "education," or even (as Wood points out) "death," which, when it comes near Apu, always leads past grief to some forward movement in his life. Ray knows that taking the full measure of an experience means we'll always be surprised, not only by our own response to it, but by where it's transported us.

• • •

The cyclical movement of the *Apu Trilogy* is as surprising as life. These three films are, as Terrence Rafferty has written, the movies' great *bildungsroman;* they could be called *The Education of Apu. Pather Panchali* (Ray's first movie), set entirely in a small Bengali village, begins just before Apu's birth and ends shortly after the death of Durga, when the family packs up and moves to Benares. Its subject matter is the effect of the life of this family on the child Apu (Subir Banerjee, who has huge, glowing-coal eyes); another way of putting it would be to say that it's Ray's examination of the wonder and intensity of the domestic, the extraordinary nature of the ordinary. Apu's father, Harihar (Kanu Banerjee), is a rent collector and a priest, and he dabbles in medicine; forced to travel to make the meager money they live on, he's seldom at home. So he has less direct influence on Apu than the three females in the family: Sarbojaya, Durga, and old, decrepit Auntie (Chunibala Devi), who tells the children ghost stories. Harihar's role in the boy's life is to inculcate him with the importance of education; when he's around, he teaches the boy himself, and since Apu's the only male child, Sarbojaya—who feels her husband's gifts are underappreciated in this backwater—sends him to the local schoolmaster, a Dickensian character with a booming temper who's also the grocer (and carries on financial transactions during class time). There's a lovely shot of Sarbojaya and Durga preparing Apu for school that shows us the significance of women in Apu's life (as well as the regal treatment a male child receives in this culture).

But relatively little of Apu's education occurs in the schoolroom; in every situation, every domestic crisis, Ray shows us Apu, his eyes wide, taking it all in. And since Ray's characters always open themselves to us completely— there's an emotional fullness in his movies that seems somehow to have been achieved by the simplest possible means (as in De Sica's films)—the cut from, say, Sarbojaya's face, burning with shame after a rich neighbor has called

Durga out for stealing fruit from her orchard, to Apu's as he looks on in silence, conveys the power of the experience for the young boy. We see Apu discover death (he and Durga stumble across Auntie's body in the forest), poverty (their money runs very low during Harihar's absence, and Sarbojaya's pride makes it difficult for her to accept the help of neighbors), and illness (Durga's, which leads her to death)—as well as the magic of the faraway, which tempts him through Auntie's stories, through a performance of a mythological play he attends in the village, through the images of Delhi and Bombay and Calcutta offered by the traveling "bioscope-wallah," and through the train that soars past the fields where he and Durga squat, chewing on sugar cane.

Apu's strongest emotional ties are to his mother, who is presented to us in all her complexity (Karuna Banerjee's performance is magnificent)—loving and shrewish, proud and apprehensive, restless and prone to melancholy—and his sister, who represents for him the wild spirit of adventure (it's she who leads him into the fields to taste the sugar cane), mysteries he can't fathom (the stolen necklace), and the connection with forces outside of himself (like the train, and the rain—he watches her whirl madly around in a rainstorm, as if she were possessed by a nature spirit). Her departure from his life (from a fever, the legacy of her rain dance), even more than Auntie's, means that something magical has left it; he has to seek outside himself for that force, that spirit, that mystery. For the rest of the trilogy, Apu's struggle will be between what's inside and outside him, the village and the city, the taming hearth and the wandering soul, home and the world.

Aparajito (*The Unvanquished*—one of the most beautiful movie titles I know), released the following year, 1956, centers on the way Apu's longing for the faraway distances him from his mother, after Harihar has died and they've left Benares and made a home for themselves in Apu's great-uncle's village. There he trains to be a priest like his father, but his natural bent takes him away from the sacred to the secular—just as it did in Benares, where he roamed along the shores of the Ganges in the morning, turning from the holy men leading prayers (Harihar made his money in Benares translating scripture for women by the holy river) to other, more fascinating objects (like an athlete working out with a club). He secures his mother's permission to go to school with the other boys. A brilliant student, he's given special attention by the proud schoolmaster, who lends him books and puts him forward for a scholarship to attend university in Calcutta. (By this time Pinaki Sen Gupta, who played the ten-year-old Apu, has been replaced by Smaran Ghosal as the teenage Apu, who has a modest moustache and a social reticence but whose eyes still shine with excitement at what the world has to offer.) In the scene where he tells his mother he's won the award and begs her to let him accept it, he waves a globe in front of her face—he wants to show her where Calcutta is—and it glows. Earlier in the film, just after their relocation to the village, we saw him thrill as a train rushed by (it was the same look of wonder he and Durga had for the train they saw in the fields) and we saw a shadow cross Sarbojaya's face: will he long to travel away from their new home? The luminous globe, like the train, symbolizes the world Apu wants to find—beyond home, beyond her.

Generically, *Aparajito* is a triumph-of-education movie, like *The Corn Is Green* and (perhaps the finest American example) *Sounder,* and maybe that's why it's not as highly regarded as the first and third parts of the trilogy. But it's much more complex than other movies in this genre; Ray keeps us acutely aware of what Sarbojaya loses when Apu gains the world. I can't think of a more trenchant examination in movies of the chasm that grows between a parent and a child as the child reaches toward adulthood. Sarbojaya doesn't accede to Apu's desire right away; she fights with him over it—she wants to know why becoming a priest isn't good enough for him, when it was good enough for his father. She gives in, of course; she's pulled between her selfish need to have him near her and her wish for his happiness (and pride in his scholarly achievements). When she packs him off to Calcutta, she tells him to make sure he comes home for the next festival; as always in this movie, his religious obligations are inseparable from his heritage (who his father was) and thus from his ties to home. But his first holiday is difficult for both of them: he's restless, clearly his heart is in Calcutta, she hasn't been well and she yearns for him to say he'll leave school to take care of her. (The first night, she asks him gently if he'd consider it, then realizes he's fallen asleep. She doesn't ask again.) Ray, with his gift for revealing the multiple layers of meaning in domestic interaction, makes a symphony out of the sequence where Sarbojaya, after much hesitation, wakes Apu for his early-morning train back to the city, and then he decides at the last moment to stay one more day. And he shows us the depth of the loneliness the mother feels during her child's absence. Apu stays away during the next holiday, to work, and when she falls ill, she doesn't write him to tell him; she dies before he can see her again. At the end, he walks away from the priest's vocation his great-uncle expects him to take up—from his legacy—assuring the old man that he'll perform the rites for his mother back in Calcutta. So he departs for university once again, taking his memories of Sarbojaya with him, along with the drive for education he inherited from his father and the restless spirit that was his sister's particular gift.

Ray made *The World of Apu* three years later, after *The Philosopher's Stone* and *The Music Room*, and it may be his most amazing film. (It also contains one of the greatest performances on record—Soumitra Chatterjee's, as the adult Apu.) In form, it suggests a fairy tale (or, as Robin Wood suggests, one of Shakespeare's romances, which are essentially fairy tales). Apu, now a university graduate but without employment or prospects of any, accompanies his friend Pulu (Swapan Mukherjee) to the wedding of a cousin, Aparna. The marriage has been arranged, and the bride has never met the groom; on the day of his arrival, her family discovers he's mad, and in order to mitigate their shame—and allay the bad luck that, according to traditional Hindu thought, will attend Aparna if she doesn't marry on the propitious day assigned to her wedding—Pulu asks Apu to take the groom's place. Upon some hesitation, he agrees, and after the marriage takes Aparna back to Calcutta, to work on his novel and support them by tutoring while she makes a home for him. At first he can scarcely believe what he's done, and she, a girl from a wealthy family, weeps when she sees the apartment house they're going to live in. But, to their mutual astonishment, they fall deeply in love with one another, and their life together is a kind of paradise. She gets pregnant and returns to her parents' home to wait for the child. But labor comes prematurely, and she dies in childbirth, while Apu is still in the city. Devastated, Apu refuses to acknowledge his son, Kajal, whom he blames for Aparna's death; he goes abroad, traveling to the ocean, through the forest, to the mountains. Eventually Pulu tracks him down and begs him to see Kajal, now five years old and living with his grandparents. When Apu sees the boy, he is moved in ways he'd never anticipated; but Kajal, feeling abandoned, refuses to believe he's his father (he throws a rock at him). Apu, defeated, sets off once more. Suddenly he realizes Kajal is following him along the beach, at a tentative distance; he turns and coaxes the boy into his arms.

In *Aparajito*, Apu chose the world over home. In this third film of the trilogy, these values are reversed for him. Alone in his apartment in the opening scenes, Apu pulls the shade in shyness and embarrassment when he sees a young woman, a neighbor, in the hall; Pulu castigates him for trying to write a novel when he's never experienced love. At this point in his life, Apu's scholarship is inadequate to fill his life, and—without being conscious of it—he finds himself drawn to the ancient Indian legacy he felt he left behind in the village ("home"). It's significant that he doesn't just meet a woman, fall in love with her, and marry her; he agrees to fulfill the social and religious demands of his culture by stepping into a wedding when he knows nothing of the bride—even though his initial response to Pulu's request, speaking as a university-educated man, is to protest that his friend's family still lives in the Dark Ages. He can't know how much joy his decision will bring him, how it will enrich his life. Ray stages the wedding night scene with Apu standing behind the bed and Aparna, her face turned away, in front of it and on the other side of the frame; the bridal bed, decked with flowers, is the obvious focus of the scene. A couple of scenes later, after they have been married for a little while, we see her awake in their bed in Calcutta, to find that her sari is tied to his sheet. The bed is the source of Apu's joy, which he feels robbed of when Aparna dies. Not until he reconciles himself to the fruits of that bed, the son she bore him, can he recover it.

Ray deliberately films his hero's travels after Aparna's death as a spiritual quest. Standing on a hilltop, watching the dawn, holding up the pages of his novel—a useless remnant of a former life—to the wind and letting it scatter them, the now bearded Apu looks like a doubt-tormented holy man. (Chatterjee, whose depiction of the agony of grief and loss breaks your heart, conveys spiritual emptiness in this sequence without speaking a word; it's his most brilliant scene.) He returns from his journey without any answers; he has to make his way back to Aparna's parents' home, where they first met, to find them. Kajal is the answer. The scene where the boy rushes to his father's arms, turning the chaos of Apu's life to order, is as sublime an affirmation as movies have ever offered us. The last shot reveals Apu walking along the shore with Kajal on his shoulders. In this close-up, all we see is the two faces, totempoled, Kajal's growing out of his father's. As the trilogy comes full circle with this generational image, the title of the movie acquires its new, complete meaning and Ray resolves the opposing forces of home and the world: for Apu, home has become his world at last.

The Zipper

by Leonard Michaels

A man goes to bed with Rita Hayworth and wakes up with me.

> RITA HAYWORTH
> *(b. Margarita Carmen Cansino, 1918)*

My mistress' eyes are nothing like the sun.

> WILLIAM SHAKESPEARE

RITA HAYWORTH STARS IN *Gilda,* but she isn't seen for the first fifteen minutes while the friendship of two men, played by George Macready and Glenn Ford, is established. Macready saves Ford from being robbed on the docks of Buenos Aires, then hires Ford to manage a gambling casino owned by Macready. They become trusting, affectionate pals in a nightlife society where women are marginal. Then Macready leaves on a business trip to the "interior." When Macready returns, Ford hurries to Macready's mansion and he is surprised to hear about a woman whom Macready just met and married. The woman is heard singing, a muted voice in the interior distance, in a bedroom, in the depths of Macready's mansion. Macready leads Ford toward the singing, into the bedroom, to meet the woman, and—cut—Rita Hayworth lifts her face to look into the camera and see who is there. In this gesture, with all the magic of the word, Rita Hayworth "appears." She is bathed in light, seems even to exude it like a personal quality, like her wavy hair, her voice, and the flow of her body when walking or dancing.

She looks into the camera, into me, my interior, and I see that the friendship of Macready and Ford is in trouble, for this is the beautiful face of betrayal, jealousy, murder, suicide, war. It is the face of love from Homer to Shakespeare to the nineteen-forties.

Like other actresses of her day, Rita Hayworth had mythic power, and could carry a movie without a male star. I thought she carried *Gilda* despite George Macready and Glenn Ford. To my view, they were of slightly repulsive dramatic interest, but I was about thirteen when I saw the movie. I took it as seriously as life. How could Rita Hayworth get involved with guys like that?

Macready, playing a Nazi agent who lives in Argentina, walks rigidly erect, carrying a sword cane. He looks frosty, pockmarked, and desiccated, like the surface of the moon. There is something priestly about him, a lofty, ascetic air. Ford, playing a lowlife hustler who cheats at cards and dice, has a soft, dark, sensuous look, sensitive rather than intelligent. He smiles and wiggles around Macready in a flirty way. Wiggly and Rigid form a love triangle with Rita Hayworth, very degrading to her, since she is way out of their league, but then she is repeatedly humiliated in the movie. She seems to ask for it, even to need it badly; once, she actually crawls at Ford's feet. Humiliation, essential plot matter in Hollywood and novels, is probably basic to fiction generally. Even the cherished story *Alice in Wonderland*, where a girl falls into a hole and is then repeatedly insulted in mind and body, has to do with humiliation. When I saw *Gilda*, I didn't wonder if there was a universal need for such subterranean experience.

Much dramatic tension is created when neither Rita Hayworth nor Ford tells Macready—who is made suspicious by their instantaneous, mutual hostility—that they already know each other and were once lovers. Not telling Macready, they betray him. Ford thinks he is loyal to Macready, protecting his peace of mind etc., and he is angry at the intrusion of Rita Hayworth into his paradisal friendship. He says, in a voice-over after Macready presents him to her, that he wanted to hit her, and he also wanted to hit Macready. Ford is bitterly frustrated and confused. I disliked him, but I suffered his anguish.

Trying not to succumb to Rita Hayworth's charms, Ford becomes increasingly self-righteous and more rigid than Macready. There is an excruciating moment when Macready, concerned not to look like a jealous husband, tells Ford to pull Rita Hayworth away as she dances with another man in Macready's casino. But she will not only dance with other men, she will also go out with them. She doesn't love Macready; she fears him, and yet she makes him jealous of Ford, just as she makes Ford jealous of her and other men. It emerges that her licentious bitchery means only that she loves Ford; he loves her, too. They are trapped in a viciously delicious game of mutual detestation which becomes the main plot. It complicates, in a feminine way, through flamboyant gestures and shows of feeling. The subplot, full of male violence—guns, fistfights, crime, war—is turgid and easy to forget. You might say the movie is sexually structured, the woman (feeling) on top.

Rita Hayworth, with her amazing blonde light in this dark movie (where almost everything happens in rooms, and even the outdoors seem indoors), suggests that dark and light are manichean opposites—dark is evil, light is good. Gray represents confusion of good and evil. I certainly didn't think this when I saw the movie in the Loew's theater, on Canal Street, in the Lower East Side of Manhattan. I didn't think anything. I felt the meaning of things, especially the morally murky weight of the gray-lighted bedroom scene where Rita Hayworth asks Macready to unzip her dress as she lies on a bed. She says more than once that she has trouble with zippers, a helpless girl imprisoned in the dress of a grownup. Zippers, a major erotic trope of forties movies, represented a man's access to a woman's body, despite her invisible, metal teeth.

I didn't want Macready to unzipper Rita Hayworth's dress. I didn't want Macready to touch her, though she is married to him, and she herself invites physical intimacy. Macready has told Ford he is "crazy about her," so his heart is in the right place. Nevertheless, I didn't want him to touch Rita Hayworth. I knew he doesn't really love her; doesn't even feel desire or lust, only a sickening idea of possession, and a mysterious need for betrayal. Why else would he hire Ford, a known cheater, as his most trusted assistant? and why else would Macready marry a woman—even Rita Hayworth—he has known only one day?

Macready flaunts his frightening sword cane, which he calls his "friend," but he moves in a delirium of masochistic self-destruction, and he is finally stabbed in the back by his "friend," literally the cane, metaphorically Ford. Macready gets what he deserves, which is what he wants, including sexual betrayal by Ford. Despite Ford's furious resistance to her, Ford gets Rita Hayworth, which is what she wants. Everything seems to work out, to balance and close, but not for me. I left the movie haunted by images of Rita Hayworth, yearning for her.

She had so much beauty and vitality that I assumed she would recover from what Macready did after unzippering her dress. Whatever it was, it wasn't good, but I supposed it happened a lot in Hollywood, where men go about touching women without feeling love, and—utterly unbearable—there are women who want to be Macreadied. Thus: in the religioso movie darkness, I saw Rita Hayworth request her own humiliation by the ascetic, priestly, frightening Macready. Zip. She is sacrificed and apotheosized. I had to remind myself that *Gilda* is a movie, not real life, and George Macready is a fine actor; also, probably, a nice guy.

No use.

The creep touched her.

I understood that real life is this way.

Nothing would be the same for me again.

I wanted to forget the scene, but it had happened as if to me, and was now fixed in my personal history, more indelibly than World War II. Only an instant of zipper business, yet it colored my love for Rita Hayworth with pity and grief. She lay there, utterly still and vulnerable, and Macready leaned over her the way kids play doctor, an eerily erotic game.

Seeing this was like a criminal privilege, though I was only sitting in a movie theater, doing nothing but looking. But I looked. I didn't shut my eyes. Unspeakable apprehensions—pleasure?—were aroused in me, in my head or heart, that secret, interior, moral theater (as opposed to the public showplace, the Loew's Canal) where movies dreamily transpire, differently for each of us. I disapproved of the sensations, the so-called pleasure, but pleasure and disapproval feed on each other. Rita Hayworth will be all right in the morning, I told myself. It won't matter what Macready did, though it was shameful and sad. What I felt was, perhaps, felt by millions.

Today, these feelings are considered sentimental; quaint. They have lost force and spontaneity. We still have them, maybe, but they no longer have us. Macready did it to Rita Hayworth. So? He didn't rape her. The scene ended. I didn't have to watch Macready actually do anything, not that it would have been possible to film Macready in bed, doing things to Rita Hayworth, without destroying the movie. The remake of *Gilda* will, of course, show Macready doing everything, but it must be remembered that *Gilda* was released when feelings—like clothing styles, popular dances, car designs—were appreciated differently from today. Perhaps feelings as such had a far higher value. Movies didn't have to show naked bodies, fucking, paraphilia, or graphic mutilation and bloody murder. Techniques of suggestion were cultivated—the zipper, for example. Less was more except in regard to words. There were long scenes brilliant with words. We didn't so much use our eyes, like roots digging into visible physical bodies for the nourishment of meanest sensation. The ear, more sensuous than sensual, received the interior life of persons, as opposed to what is sucked up by the salacious eyeball.

Later in the movie, Rita Hayworth asks again for help with her zipper, during a nightclub routine, as she does a striptease dance. Several men hurry to oblige and help her become naked. Ford notices, has a tizzy, stops things from going too far. He slaps her. His hand doesn't wither and rot. Not only is there injustice, there is no justice. I feel so sorry for her, not to mention myself, poor kid, having to grow up, to know such things. Rita Hayworth is never seen disrobed in the movie, though it is threatened more than once. The atmosphere of dark repression and mysterious forces—the mood or feeling of the movie—might be destroyed by the revelation of her body. It scared me as she began her striptease dance in the nightclub. I didn't want everybody to see her body, or even to see that Rita Hayworth had a body. (The length of her beautiful left leg—I nearly died—is fleetingly exposed by a slit in her dress, as she dances.)

Two years later, I had sex for the first time, and I was taken by a weird sorrow riding home alone in the subway, as visceral odors lifted from my hands, reminding me that I'd fallen a few hours ago with my girlfriend—both of us virgins—from Heights of Desire, into bodies. (Religious movements, West and East, have cultivated a practice of dreamily disembodied, extended, nonorgasmic sex, as described in John Donne's poem "The Ecstasy.")

In plain sight of Ford, who is obliged by his job to watch her, Rita Hayworth flirts with other men and says, "If I were a ranch, they'd call me the Bar-Nothing." She thus tortures Ford, showing him—in the desires of other men—the body he can't let himself have. Ford watches. He tries to seem angry, then blurts out that Rita Hayworth can do whatever she pleases. It doesn't matter to him. He says he will personally deliver Rita Hayworth to her other men, then pick her up like "laundry" and return her to Macready. In effect, everything Rita Hayworth does with other men will be determined and controlled by Ford. Impassioned and irrational, Ford doesn't know what he means.

My moral notions, already disturbed, were further disturbed—the hero talks like this? I was being introduced to deep stuff, subterranean forces, years before I understood what was happening to me, or maybe the world in the forties. It had to do with sex—hardly anything doesn't—but I didn't know about sex. I believed something more important was at stake. I saw Bad presenting itself—in the form of pleasure—as entertainment; and I was being made to know that I was susceptible to the pleasure of Bad, if for no other reason than that Bad was in me, like Gog and Magog.

Was the experience indeed pleasure, not merely a strong sensation, like the electrical excitement of an idea, or the effect of a novelty, or a demonic, masturbatory fantasy? If it was a real feeling, could I be violated by it, my own real feeling? Could it happen to anyone? If so, could anyone ever be a good person?

I continued to wonder—without words to analyze or describe it—about the distinction—in real life—between pleasure and its innumerable imitations. Saint Augustine says, "the love of this world is fornication against God," and that's that. For me, the question was: if I felt something I believed was bad, but it felt good, would I want to fornicate against God again and again? and would I then despise other pleasures, assuming other pleasures remained to me? Had Macready unzippered me, too? In Flannery O'Connor's masterpiece, "A Good Man Is Hard to Find," a mystical murderer says, "It's no real pleasure in life." I wondered about real pleasure. What is it?

Ford's antiheroic, homoerotic hysteria, basic to the dramatic effect in *Gilda,* is virtually explicit when Rita Hayworth suggests that a psychiatrist can tell Ford that he likes the idea of Rita Hayworth as "laundry," or dirty—that is, of her doing things with other men. I didn't understand this in feeling or thought. Is sexual infidelity—deserving of death in the colorful Mediterranean community I came from—what Ford likes? I didn't see his angry, tyrannical show of controlling power as a refusal to acknowledge that he is the hapless creature of dark impulses. Rita Hayworth understands what's going on in Ford, but Ford never gains understanding of himself. Instead, he becomes sadistically determined to punish Rita Hayworth for his inadmissible need to see her do what he likes her to do.

Gilda—written by a woman, starring a woman, produced by a woman—suggests that women know better than men what men are looking at when men look at women. They know that such looking—a function of blindness—is not seeing. In effect, Rita Hayworth exists fantastically for Macready and

Ford within the so-called male gaze. She is created by their looking, a form of ideological hypnosis, or blindness, or stupidity, perhaps crucial to the perpetuation of human society as it presently exists. In the movie, the male gaze keeps two men fixated on a woman, rather than each other. Outside the movie, in real life, Rita Hayworth was the fixation of millions of men in the armed services, their favorite "pinup girl." An erotic icon, she kept our boys straight.

In *Gilda*, Rita Hayworth famously sings one song several times. (I later found out her voice is dubbed; also, her hair is dyed, her hairline is fake, her name is Margarita.) The refrain of her song is "Put the blame on Mame, boys." Mame (Freudian pun intended) is responsible for cataclysmic occurrences— the Chicago fire, a terrible snowstorm, etc. (She's hot, the city burns; she's cold, "for seven days they shoveled snow.") The song ironically implies that boys, who are exquisitely tortured by her capricious dominatrixiness, want to imagine that Mame has tremendous, annihilating power. I could see the amusement in Rita Hayworth's eyes as she pretends to sing, and I loved her for that, her peculiar quality of spirit. Not quite playing the role, she is more real, nearly accessible, more heartbreaking.

The audience learns that Ford abandoned her in the "interior" when he ran out of money, before the movie begins. To express the audience's contempt for him, the attendant in the men's room of Macready's gambling casino, a comic philosophical figure, lowly and godlike, twice calls Ford a "peasant." Ford lacks aristocratic sensibility, or class. But Rita Hayworth gives him an opportunity to transcend himself by choosing her over his career as Macready's thing. He doesn't choose her until the end of the movie, when he supposes Macready is dead. Ford thus remains a peasant, or, at best, a grubby careerist who takes his work more seriously than love. The movie ends. Poor Rita Hayworth goes off with Ford. A grim, winter night, streetlights, traffic—the shock of the real—awaited me.

I went down Madison Street, passing under the Manhattan Bridge, then turning left on Market Street, walking toward the East River, until I came to Monroe Street and turned right. These directions, these streets, restored me to my life. I passed the tenements with their Italian grocery stores and candy stores, and I passed my old elementary school, a huge grim soot-dark Victorian building, P. S. 177. From the church of Saint Joseph, at the corner of Catherine and Market Streets, I heard a bell tolling the hour. The church stood opposite our first floor apartment in a building called Knickerbocker Village. Walking down Monroe Street, I approached the wavering light of Friday night prayer candles in our kitchen window. The shadow of my mother, against the window shade, moved from refrigerator to stove. Everything as it should be. Italian ladies with shopping bags and baby carriages. Italian kids sitting on the "stoops" of their tenements. This was real. Too different—like a blonde woman who might bring the solidity and value of this neighborhood into question—wasn't good.

The darkness of the movie, like a darkness inside me, contained nothing real, but there was a faint glow of *Gilda* within it, and I felt tumultuous yearning for Rita Hayworth—the woman, not the actress. I yearned to bring her home, where she would descend, or lovingly condescend, to sweet reconciliation with the ordinariness of my life, even its banality and boredom, which I believed was good. The good. My mother, cooking good dinner in the small but good kitchen of our three-room apartment, would be embarrassed. She would apologize to bad Rita Hayworth for not having prepared a more sumptuous dinner, but I hadn't given any warning. "Do you like borscht? It's good. Do you know, Miss Hayworth, the good doctor who delivered your bad baby is my good cousin from Canada? When he told me that he delivered your bad baby, I almost fainted. Maybe you remember him. Tall. Curly hair."

It was like this for me, in a day when love was praised and much desired, even the terrible anguish it was known to inflict. As for Rita Hayworth—dream of heroes, three husbands, millions of service men—she was love, catastrophic, wild, impossible to domesticate. So much of her life was public, spectacular imagery that it is hard to suppose she also had a real life, or to suppose that her feelings about Rita Hayworth were not the same as ours.

The Last American Dream:
The Manchurian Candidate

by Greil Marcus

IN THE MANCHURIAN CANDIDATE, a Hollywood movie made in 1962, it's about 1954. Major Ben Marco, played by Frank Sinatra, is lying on his bed, fully clothed in his uniform, dreaming the same dream he dreams every night. He's sweating; as his lips twitch, the camera moves in and we enter his dream.

We're in an old hotel in Spring Lake, New Jersey: a meeting of the Ladies Garden Club is in progress. On the platform, one Mrs. Henry Whittaker is speaking; seated on either side of her are all the members of the patrol that Major Marco, then Captain Marco, led in Korea in 1952. The soldiers look bored out of their minds. The talk they're listening to, that we're listening to, is beyond boring: "Our Friend the Hydrangea," more or less. The scene is striking: the ghastliness of Mrs. Whittaker's floral print dress is topped only by her hat.

The camera begins a circular pan around the room: an audience of women dressed just like Mrs. Whittaker, most of them over fifty, a few young, listening attentively, taking notes, whispering politely to each other. It's a long, slow pan: when the camera returns to Mrs. Whittaker's lectern, the scene is completely different. Yen Lo, a fat, entertaining Chinese Communist scientist played by Khigh Dhiegh, is now speaking; the soldiers are seated at his sides, as in the New Jersey hotel room. They're in a small, steep, modern auditorium; the seats are filled with Soviet and Chinese cadres. Behind Yen Lo are huge photos of Mao, Stalin, workers, peasants—an ultramodern, postdada montage of great style and elegance.

Yen Lo explains that the soldiers—betrayed by their interpreter, Chunjin, played by Henry Silva—were set up for an ambush while on maneuvers in Korea, then flown by helicopter to a hospital in Manchuria for what Yen Lo calls "conditioning"—"Brainwashing," he says, laughing, "which I understand is the new American term." The soldiers have been made to believe they are waiting out a storm in a New Jersey hotel. Whatever Yen Lo says, all they hear is flower talk.

Mrs. Whittaker reappears—speaking Yen Lo's words in her own voice—a bit harshly now, with an edge of contempt. Behind her are Stalin and Mao.

Yen Lo appears as himself in the auditorium. He speaks as himself, in the New Jersey hotel. From his point of view, we see his audience, the Ladies Garden Club. Mrs. Whittaker speaks Yen Lo's words in the auditorium. In the hotel, Yen Lo speaks as Yen Lo, with Communist cadres filling the garden club seats.

In the audience, a cadaverous Chinese demands an end to Yen Lo's pedantic explanations of the wonders of mental conditioning—Yen Lo, or Mrs. Whittaker, has lost himself, or herself, in footnotes and bibliographies. The question, the man in the audience says, is Lieutenant Raymond Shaw, an upper-class prig played by Laurence Harvey—who, in the opening minutes of *The Manchurian Candidate,* we've seen returning to the United States from Korea to be awarded the Congressional Medal of Honor, for leading his supposedly lost patrol back to safety. The question is, says the Chinese in the audience, "Has he ever killed anyone?"

Mrs. Whittaker replies in Yen Lo's words, and then addresses Raymond Shaw. Yen Lo continues speaking as himself—in the garden club. A member of the club is cradling a bayonet like a kitten, smiling. Mrs. Whittaker, speaking as Yen Lo, is about to take it, when a Russian officer, in the auditorium, objects: "Not with the knife, with the hands." The officer turns into a member of the garden club, gaily waving a handkerchief.

Yen Lo is present in the auditorium as himself: to prove the efficacy of the experiments he has performed on Shaw and the others, Raymond, who (Yen Lo has explained) has been programmed as an assassin who will have no memory of his deeds, will now have to kill the member of the patrol he most likes. "Captain Marco," Shaw says. "No," says Mrs. Whittaker, with Stalin and Mao at her back, "we need him to get you your medal." So Shaw chooses the soldier he likes next best, and begins to strangle him with a towel. The soldier protests—"No, no, Ed," says Yen Lo in a friendly voice. The soldier is polite—he relaxes—it's just one more moment in "Our Friend the Hydrangea." Throughout the sequence, the soldiers have acted naturally, not at all like zombies, just bored. So now this soldier is, again, bored. Raymond Shaw kills him, and the dead man topples off his chair. No one reacts. It is 1952; back in 1954, Major Marco wakes up screaming.

The sequence is structured around the same principles of postdada New Sobriety montage that shape the photo-montage backdrop Yen Lo and Mrs. Whittaker speak against. It's visually irresistible, as lucid as anything beautiful is lucid, and at the same time it's unacceptable—confusing, at first, then an impossibility, then again perfectly possible. The sequence is set up as a dream, but it doesn't come off the screen as a dream, doesn't come off as a blur, with soft edges, dissolves, milky tones—it's severe, mathematical, a fact, true. It's real. You realize that this actually happened.

◆ ◆ ◆

It's here, in this moment, that *The Manchurian Candidate,* a movie based on a best-selling 1959 trash novel by Richard Condon, takes off. It's here that you realize something is happening on the screen that you haven't seen before, that you're not ready for. Even if you've read the book, you aren't ready. All Condon made up was the setting—the soldiers in the hotel—a setting which in the book lies flat, like his dialogue, so much of it used in the film: alive and frightening on the screen, dead in print. Condon imagined none of the cinematic changes that nail the details of the event into your mind, the cinematic changes that scramble the event, that make those details almost impossible to keep straight—I took notes, and I'm sure I haven't gotten it all just right. Watching, you sense, suddenly, that this movie you're watching, a movie that promised no more than an evening's good time, can go anywhere, in any direction—that there's no way you're going to be able to predict what's going to happen next, how it's going to happen, why it's going to happen.

The Manchurian Candidate may be the most exciting and disturbing American movie from *Citizen Kane* to the *Godfather* pictures precisely because this scene is not a set-piece: it is a promise the movie pays in full. To see Raymond Shaw strangle one soldier—and, later, in another patrol member's matching dream, to see Shaw shoot a teenage soldier through the head, to see a wash of blood and brain matter splatter Stalin's face—is to be shocked, and not to be prepared for the atrocities that follow: much quieter, almost silent atrocities, and all the worse for that. And yet there is no message here, no point being made, not even any felt implication that Communists are bad and Americans are good, nothing like that at all—this is all, somehow, taking place in an atmosphere of moral neutrality, of aesthetic suspension. All we're seeing is people. We're seeing the director, John Frankenheimer; the screenwriter, George Axelrod; plus Frank Sinatra, Laurence Harvey, Henry Silva, Khigh Dhiegh, Angela Lansbury (Raymond Shaw's demonic mother), and dozens more—all of them working over their heads, diving into material they've chosen or been given, in every case outstripping the material, and outstripping themselves.

Before and after *The Manchurian Candidate,* John Frankenheimer was and is a crude director without an interesting idea in his head. Frank Sinatra was a good actor, sometimes much better than good, instinctive and wary, but he never came close to the weight, or the warmth, of his performance here. You could say the same for almost anyone involved in the project. Something—

something in the story, something in the times, in the interplay of various people caught up consciously in the story, and unconsciously or half-consciously in the times—came together. Something in the story, or in the times, that had to have been sensed, felt, but never thought, never shaped into a theory or a belief or even a notion, propelled these people out of themselves, past their limits as technicians or actors or whatever they were, and made them propel their material, Richard Condon's cheap paranoid fantasy, past its limits.

There's a special thrill—a unique response—that comes when you recognize an author working over his head, over her head—and in *The Manchurian Candidate* everyone, from Frankenheimer to Sinatra to the unnamed actor who flies across the stage in the carnage at the end of the film, seems like an author. Bob Dylan was not working over his head when he made "Like a Rolling Stone"—he was realizing a talent, and a vision, that was implicit in his previous work. The same was true with Aretha Franklin, when after years of suppressed, supper-club standards she stunned the world with "I Never Loved a Man (The Way I Love You)." But reading *Uncle Tom's Cabin,* even if you've never read the novels Harriet Beecher Stowe wrote before or after, you can sense an author driving her story and being driven by it—being driven by her times, by the smallest, most subtle details inherent in every crude character she's invented, or borrowed, or stolen: the provenance becomes irrelevant. Here, clichés turn into terrors. The ordinary becomes marvelous. Anything can happen. Even with a screenplay, where the director and the actors are playing out a script, where every moment may be storyboarded, defined, fixed in advance—even here, nothing is fixed in advance. There's no storyboard, no script, no director's intention, no actor's intention, that can call up, that can demand, that can account for, the complexity of Major Marco's smile when he finally proves that his dream was not a dream, but a memory—when he begins, finally, to break the case, when he knows that what he dreamed was real life. His smile is warm; it is sadistic. It's happy; it's determined, against all odds. A whole life is in that smile—and a promise of a happy ending, a happy ending the movie won't provide, the ending that the smile, so all-consuming and complete as it appears on the screen, won't get.

The plot of *The Manchurian Candidate* is simple nonsense, an exploitation of terrors floating in the air in 1959: the terror of McCarthyism, the terror of Communist brainwashing—good hooks from the newspapers of the day. The Russians and the Chinese have made a zombie assassin out of an American soldier—and contrived to have him awarded the Medal of Honor, to place him beyond suspicion, beyond reproach. Their comrade in the United States is Raymond Shaw's mother, the wife of Senator John Iselin, Raymond's stepfather (played by James Gregory), a stand-in for Senator Joe McCarthy. Posing as rabid anticommunists, Senator and Mrs. Iselin are Communist agents. Ultimately, Senator Iselin will win the vice-presidential nomination of his party, Raymond Shaw is to assassinate the presidential nominee as the nominee delivers his acceptance speech, and then Senator Iselin will take his place with a great patriotic address—"Defending America even if it means his own death," Raymond's mother explains to him as she gives him his assignment. And then Senator Iselin, or rather Raymond's mother, will be swept into power, which she will exercise as pure sadism, for its own sake, betraying her one-time comrades, destroying them—and, the implication is, everything else. The United States. The republic. Herself. All for the pure pleasure of the act—for the pleasure of its violence.

There is no point in pausing over this plot as a clue to anything—save for the plot as the clue to a certain state of mind. The plot, in this movie, is an excuse—an excuse for the pleasure of the movie's violence. That is, you're going to get to see everything you ever believed was fixed and given suspended in the air and then dashed to the ground. That's a thrill. You're going to believe the notion that a single person could, by means of a single bullet, change history, transform it utterly. Nonsense—even if it happened, in the years after *The Manchurian Candidate* was made. Historians tell us that it didn't happen: that solitary individuals, even solitary individuals acting out great, historic conspiracies, don't make history. History is made by forces beyond anyone's control—by invisible hands.

As it plays, *The Manchurian Candidate* raises none of these questions. It revels in absurdity, works off of it, takes absurdity as a power principle: the power of entertainment. The movie—and I can't think of another movie that in its smallest details is so naturalistic and in its overarching tone is so crazy—is first of all fun. It's slapstick, as Pauline Kael said, who loved the film; "pure jazz," said Manny Farber, who didn't love it, but he had to have been talking about bebop, Charlie Parker, improvisation, not knowing where you're going to go next—this movie is not Duke Ellington. You can see this spirit, this heedlessness, this narrative irresponsibility, in a scene that didn't have to be anything more than a counter in the plot, that didn't have to be more than a transitional device.

Major Marco's paranoid dreams have led him to a near breakdown; the army has relieved him of his duties and reassigned him as a public relations assistant to the secretary of defense. The secretary is holding a press conference, with Marco at his side.

"Mr. Secretary," says a reporter, "can you explain the cut in budget?" The secretary, bulbous and impatient, with a hint of Lyndon Johnson in his vehemence but with none of Johnson's savvy, explodes. "Since you've asked a simpleminded question," he roars, "I'll give you an equally simpleminded answer." The secretary goes on to explain, in words so straightforward you can't imagine them being spoken today, that because no naval power threatens the United States navy, there is no need to build more ships: thus the cut in budget. We see a room filled up with reporters, cameras, TV monitors—like Major Marco's dream, the scene is at once whole and all cut up. Now we see the secretary himself, then on a TV monitor, then as himself, then from the crowd, then the room from his point of view, everything moving fast.

The secretary is responding rudely, with great humor. You're caught by a violation—the violation of plain speech, of all the rules of bureaucratic propriety. Who is this man? How did he get appointed? This is more lively, more real, than government is supposed to be, but it's just a warm-up. As Major Marco tries to end the press conference, Senator Iselin stands up in the back of the room. Mrs. Iselin, sitting off to the side, is silently mouthing the words Senator Iselin is going to speak, words she's written: the accusation that there are two-hundred-and-some card-carrying Communists in the Defense Department.

In utter chaos, the camera moves from the secretary to Iselin to a TV monitor fixed on the secretary, the monitor then panning—blurring, sliding, ripping—to pick up Iselin. He speaks both from the monitor and in the room—it's a kind of epistemological violence, a set of media contradictions fed into an actual event, or vice versa. In any case, the actual event is dissolving, and all that's left are its representations. The secretary is beside himself. He doesn't answer Iselin's absurd charge; he says, "Throw that lunatic out of here! You claim to be a senator? Senator of what, I want to know! If this man is ever here again I want him thrown out, *bodily*. Never, do you understand me! Not EVER!"

For this moment, you lose any real sense of the development of the plot—you're captured by the weird spectacle of a high government official saying exactly what he means. You forget that, of course, the secretary of defense would know who Senator Iselin is. You revel in the secretary's disbelief and refusal. "Not EVER!"—it's merely terrific. Wouldn't it be wonderful, you think, if our government actually talked like that? That's the pleasure—that's what stays in your mind. You don't care about Senator Iselin, about the strange and hideous conspiracy that's unfolding—you want to see the secretary of defense keep talking, you want to see him take over the story. And he does, in a way. Even though we never see him again, his spirit—breaking all the boundaries of what you've come to expect—is what the movie is about: what it's for.

◆ ◆ ◆

When you look at *The Manchurian Candidate*, this 1962 black-and-white Hollywood movie made out of bits and pieces of Hitchcock and Orson Welles, out of *Psycho* and *Citizen Kane*, out of a lot of clean steals, workmanlike thievery, a second-class director using whatever he can get his hands on—when you look at this movie today, what's so overwhelming is a sense of what the movie does that movies can no longer do. The momentum of the film is so strong you may not get any sense of this until the second time you see it, the third time, the tenth time—but that sense, as an itch, will keep calling you back.

I remember seeing it, alone, when it came out in the fall of 1962, at the Varsity Theater in Palo Alto. The first thing I did when it was over was call my best friend and tell him he had to see it, too. We went the next night; as we left the theater, I asked him what he thought. "Greatest movie I ever saw," he said flatly, as if he didn't want to talk about it, and he didn't. He said it stunned, with bitterness, as if he shouldn't have had to see this thing, as if what it told him was both true and false in a manner he could never untangle, as if it was both incomprehensible and all too clear, as if the whole experience had been, somehow, a gift, the gift of art, and also *unfair;* and that was how I felt, too.

We saw—as anyone can see today—too many rules broken. It's one thing to have Raymond Shaw, the nice, boring prig, made into an assassin—the zombie state he's put into when he has to kill is not, really, so far from his everyday life. When his controllers make him kill his boss—in 1954, two years after his conditioning in Manchuria, to see if the mechanisms are still functioning properly—Shaw doesn't do the killing all that differently than he speaks or gestures to the people he works with. But it's something else to see him enter the house of Senator Iselin's nemesis—the liberal senator who is also, for one day, Raymond Shaw's father-in-law. On orders from his mother, his "American operator," Raymond shoots the liberal senator. It's not horrible—until, after shooting the senator through the heart, from a distance, Raymond approaches the body, bends over it, and puts the necessary, professional second bullet into the dead man's brain. As Raymond does so, his wife, the senator's daughter, comes running down the stairs, into the frame—and then Raymond, who has been instructed not only to kill his target but to kill any witnesses to any killing, coolly, casually, without the slightest human response (though he still, somehow, seems to be himself, a real person), turns and shoots his wife through the forehead.

At the end of the movie, at the party convention, as Raymond perches high in Madison Square Garden, hidden in a spotlight booth, positioned to assassinate the presidential nominee—at the end, when Raymond instead shoots his stepfather, Senator Iselin, there is an instant cut to Raymond's mother, seated next to the senator, as she realizes what's coming. A second bullet goes through her forehead, and her hands jerk to her head, just as President Kennedy's hands went to his neck. But by this time we've come to see Raymond Shaw not only as a prig, but as an individual, a man who for all his demons might possibly have a life to live, who deserves that chance. When he commits the final, necessary, fated, heroic crime, when he kills his mother, in that instant, the movie stops, and you stop, and you realize what's happened: the horror of every death is doubled. His father-in-law, his wife, his stepfather, his mother, then himself—he has to kill them all. It's right—but you can't cheer, not even inwardly, when Raymond Shaw shoots his mother. You think: my God, he's killed his mother. What can he do next? He has to kill himself— but that's not the ending you want. And you can't accept it.

This kind of violation, this kind of extremism—presented, for all of its impossibility and absurdity, in a mode of naturalism—is not all that happens in The Manchurian Candidate that doesn't happen in movies today. There is that sense of people working over their heads, which is finally a sense of play-fulness: "What can we get away with?" That's what's happening with the casting of a black actor to play an army psychiatrist—one of the few truly sympathetic characters in the film, along with Sinatra's Major Marco, and Khigh Dhiegh's Yen Lo—Yen Lo, always a joker, a regular guy, someone you'd love to spend an evening with. Here we are, in 1962, and a black man is play-ing a professional, a thinker, and it's not commented on, it's not framed or contextualized, it's not an issue—but still, it's a shock. The man is just doing his job, and no one pays it any mind. How many other American movies use a black actor to play what audiences expect to be a white character without even bothering to point it out, to clap themselves on the back, to congratulate themselves? There is a way in which the black psychiatrist is as displacing as Raymond Shaw's murder of his mother. And that's people working over their heads: "Let's do it! Let's mix it up! Who cares?"

Finally, though, there is another dimension to The Manchurian Candidate that is part of this displacement—not, one might think, part of the glee with which those who made the movie made it; not part of the glee with which they let it happen, played it out, but a dimension that confronts us now, twenty-seven years later. That is, we are watching a movie made in another world.

There are obvious moments that take us out of our own time, as we watch the movie today, moments that seal the movie as a curiosity, as a relic, that take place on the edges of the action—the glimpse we get of the elevator oper-ator in Raymond Shaw's apartment building, who smokes in the elevator. Far more than the sight of 1962 cars on the screen, or the use of the Korean War as a social fact everyone once understood, or Joe McCarthy as a mon-ster or a hero everyone once reviled or applauded, this is odd: you know ele-vator operators can't do that anymore, that even if we get another Korean War, another Joe McCarthy, we won't get any more elevator operators smoking in elevators. There is a way in which such tiny details, as we see them today, make the movie safe, today—protect us from it. Maybe, subliminally, as the movie plays itself out, one tries to hold onto such details, because the rest of the movie is all too familiar.

The Manchurian Candidate, plunging toward the assassination of a would-be president, closing with the assassination of the man who's going to take his place, was taken out of circulation not long after it was released. Not that quickly, not right after the assassination of President Kennedy—even after that, the film was shown on television. Then it was withdrawn—because it was, somehow, not right. It wasn't that the movie in any way predicted the events that followed it, the finally incomprehensible assassinations that filled the late 1960s and the years after that, all the assassinations and near-assassinations: John F. Kennedy, Malcolm X, Martin Luther King, Robert F. Kennedy, Andy Warhol, George Wallace, Gerald Ford, John Lennon, Ronald Reagan. On the part of those who controlled the film, there must have been a sense—an unexplainable sense—that the film might be part of these incomprehensible events, of this somehow whole, complete, singular event, of this current in our public life: a transformation of what was taken as open, public life into private crime, or hidden conspiracy. There must have been a sense, as the film was withdrawn, as year after year it, too, stayed hidden, that our real history, the history we live out every day, might be a kind of awful secret which we will never understand.

It's not that *The Manchurian Candidate* prefigured, let alone prophesied, the events that followed it. It didn't. It is a fantasy in which Joe McCarthy, as Raymond Shaw's liberal father-in-law says, "could not do more to harm this country if he were a paid Soviet agent"—a cheap irony. What *The Manchurian Candidate* prefigured—what it acted out, what it played out, in advance— was the state of mind that would accompany the assassinations that followed it, those violations of our public life: it prefigured the sense that the events that shape our lives take place in a world we cannot see, to which we have no access, that we cannot understand, that we will never be able to explain. I think we will find out someday, Gore Vidal once wrote of Who-Killed-Kennedy; but I don't believe we ever will, not to the satisfaction of any of us. And that disgusting acceptance, today, is part of what *The Manchurian Candidate* is about.

As the movie ends, in its final scene, Marco, Frank Sinatra, understands the whole story—why it happened, how it happened—and he can't accept it. "Hell," he curses. "Hell." That's the end of the film: misery, regret, fury, the secret he has to hold inside himself. It can't be told, that the Soviet Union and the People's Republic of China conspired with apparent American fascists, who linked themselves with fascist tendencies in American life, in order to destroy the American republic: the repercussions would be too great. Marco will have to take the secret to his grave. The truth of the life and near-death of the republic cannot be told to the people who make up the republic. It will be buried, for our own good.

So you look at the movie, lost in its visual delight, cringing at its violence, wondering what it says, if it says anything—wondering what happens. A lot of what happens is unburdened by any weight at all—the great karate fight between Sinatra, Major Marco, and Henry Silva, Chunjin (Chunjin now working as Raymond Shaw's houseboy). Sinatra rings the doorbell to Raymond

Shaw's apartment, Silva opens it, Sinatra sees Silva, the whole betrayal in Korea comes back to him, as a fact, undeniable, and he slams Silva in the face. After the fight has gone on and on, not a second too long, there is that moment when Sinatra has Silva down on the floor, is kicking him in the ribs, again and again, each movement as precise as it is fierce, asking Silva, the Communist agent who betrayed the patrol in Korea, what happened, what *really happened*—and then the cops arrive, and Sinatra, not thinking, acting in the real world, responds to a grab around his shoulders by elbowing the policeman in the stomach, and the cop falls away, and the scene is cut. It's a purely instinctive act—and it catches so much of what's alive about this movie.

But that's not all. After so many years, or after seeing the movie now, more than once, another element enters. You see that, here, everyone acts politically: the villains, the heroes, the characters that barely register, that simply come and go. Everyone acts as a citizen of a republic, or as an anticitizen. What's at stake is a commonwealth. As the movie closes, in that final scene, Sinatra rewrites the dead Raymond Shaw's medal of honor citation. "Made," he says with a long pause, "to commit acts...too unspeakable to be mentioned here. In the end he freed himself, and saved his country."

The words carry enormous weight—the weight of the idea of "one's country," one's community, one's social identity. Of course this is no less an absurdity, no less a fantasy, than anything else in the movie: the idea that a single person could ruin the commonwealth, or save it. But *The Manchurian Candidate* has, perhaps without intention, played against this idea of the single, all-powerful hero, or all-powerful villain, throughout its length. In this film, everyone, hero and villain, minor character and star, has acted not as a function of the plot, but as someone who acts as if the life of the republic depended on his or her actions, on his or her convictions, beliefs, his or her will, desire, motive.

• • •

This is, today, an odd idea—as odd as the casting of a black actor as a psychiatrist, or the characterization of Major Marco as an intellectual: "You don't want to hear about my mother," Raymond Shaw says to Marco in a drunken moment. "Sure I do," says Marco. "It's like listening to Orestes gripe about Clytemnestra." "Who?" says Raymond. "Greeks," Marco says. "Couple of Greeks in a play." The idea of everyone as a citizen is as odd, once one has been subsumed into the world of the movie, as the speech President Bush made on education last week. "Bush Rallies Businesses to Invest in U.S. Education," read the headline in the *San Francisco Chronicle* four days ago. "The businesses that are involved with local schools, developing the workforce at its source," Bush said, "are making fail-safe investments." The anonymous wire-service reporter finished the story: "Bush mentioned no specific reforms or initiatives to give workers the skills and background that will be demanded by economic changes and technological advances." But this was no criticism. The reporter was accepting the terms of the president's world, of the republic he spoke for: the antirepublic.

Just as, today, the paranoia of *The Manchurian Candidate* is absurd, so, within the world defined by *The Manchurian Candidate,* is this little news story. Here, now, the citizen of the republic is reduced to part of "the workforce," as in the People's Republic of China, today; in the movie, all people are citizens, concerned with a commonwealth greater than themselves; they are acting, in small or great ways, purposefully or thoughtlessly, to save or ruin it. And that is the issue. The idea that any man or woman could be merely part of "the workforce," private, concerned only with his or her personal fortune or lack of it, is in *The Manchurian Candidate* as foreign, as strange, as alien, as the smoking elevator operator is to us today.

In the end, *The Manchurian Candidate* is about patriotism—a commitment to a life where every private act has public consequences. This is no longer the world we live in. This is the shock of the movie, now. This Hollywood movie based on a commercial novel, from long ago, or not so far away, is a fantasy of a life we could be living. A fantasy—not so different, in certain ways, from John Wayne in the last shots of a war movie. But I'll take Frank Sinatra, smiling, as he breaks the case, and then almost dead with sorrow and guilt, as he recites Raymond Shaw's epitaph, and then says "Hell...hell." Thunder crashes, but it's not melodramatic, just the sound he has no words for. He looks down, away from himself, as if he cannot bear to look at himself; and the movie is over.

Remembering

Do He Have Your Number, Mr. Jeffrey?

by Gayle Pemberton

DURING THE FALL OF 1984 I worked for three weekends as a caterer's assistant in Southern California. I had gone to that part of the world to seek my fortune—after eleven years teaching American literature at several colleges and universities—partly because the West Coast is the premier place in the United States for people who, like me, have terminal wanderlust, and partly because L.A. is such a mixture of fact, fantasy, and illusion that, as an Americanist, I felt I had to go.

Like lots of others seeking their fortunes in L.A., I was working by day as a temporary typist in a Hollywood film studio. I was moonlighting with the caterer because, like lots of others, I was going broke on my typist's wages.

Though the job was not particularly enjoyable, the caterer and her husband were congenial, interesting people, who certainly would have become good friends of mine had I stayed in California. I spent my three weekends in basic scullery work—wiping and slicing mushrooms, mixing batters, peeling apples, tomatoes, and cucumbers, drying plates, glasses, and cutlery. Greater responsibilities would have come with more experience, but I had brushed off California dust before I learned any real catering secrets or professional gourmet techniques.

One exhausting dinner party, given by a rich man for his family and friends, turned out to be one of the reasons I brushed off that California dust. This dinner was such a production that our crew of five arrived the day before to start preparing for the dinner. The kitchen in this house was larger than some I've seen in fine French restaurants. Our caterer was one of a new breed of fine gourmet cooks who do all preparation and cooking at the client's home—none of your cold-cut or warming-tray catering. As a result, her clients had a tendency to have loads of money and even more kitchen space.

Usually her staff was not expected to serve the meal, but on this occasion we did. I was directed to wear stockings and black shoes and I was given a blue-patterned apron dress, with frills here and there, to wear. Clearly, my academic lady-banker pumps were out of the question, so I invested in a pair of trendy black sneakers—which cost me five dollars less than what I earned the entire time I worked for the caterer. Buying the sneakers was plainly excessive, but I told myself they were a necessary expense. I was not looking forward to wearing the little French serving-girl uniform, though. Everything about it and me was wrong, but I had signed on and it would have been unseemly and downright hostile to jump ship.

One thing I liked about the caterer was her insistence that her crew not be treated as servants—that is, we worked for her, took orders from her, not from the clients, who might find ordering us around an emboldening and socially one-upping experience. She also preferred to use crystal and china she rented, keeping her employees and herself safe from a client's rage in case a family heirloom should get broken. But on this occasion, her client insisted that we use his Baccarat crystal. We were all made particularly nervous by his tone. It was the same tone I heard from a mucky-muck at my studio typing job: cold, arrogant, a matter-of-fact "you are shit" attitude that is well known to nurses and secretaries.

I had never served a dinner before that one—that is, for strangers, formally. I have mimed serving festive meals for friends, but only in a lighthearted way. And, when I was a child, my family thought it a good exercise in etiquette—not to mention in labor savings—to have me serve at formal dinners. "It's really fun, you know," they would say. I never handled the good china, though.

I didn't mind cutting up mushrooms or stirring sauce in some rich man's kitchen for pennies, but I certainly didn't like the idea of serving at this one's table. I saw our host hold up one of his goblets to a guest, showing off the fine line and texture. There were too many conflicting images for me to be content with the scene. He was working hard on his image for his guests; I was bothered by the way I looked to myself and what I might have looked like to the assembled crew, guests, and host. I couldn't get the idea of black servility to white power out of my mind.

The food was glorious. I recall serving quenelles at one point, followed by a consommé brunoise, a beef Wellington with a carrot-and-herb-based sauce that I stirred for a short eternity, vegetables with lemon butter, and a variety of mouth-watering pastries for dessert. We worked throughout the meal, topping up the wine and coffee, removing plates, bumping into each other. As long as I was doing this absurd thing I decided to make some kind of mental work attend it. I made the entire scene a movie, and as I served I created a silent soundtrack. At one point, after the quenelles and the entrée and before the coffee, the table of eight sat discussing literature—a discussion of the "what'd you think of..." variety. My professorial ears pricked up. I discovered that one member of the party had actually read the book in question, while a few others had skimmed condensed versions in some sort of "condensed literature" magazine. My soundtrack could have vied, I thought, with the shrillest Bolshevik propaganda ever written. "You self-satisfied, rich, feeble-brained, idiotic, priggish filthy maggots! You, you sit here talking literature—why, you don't even know what the word means. This is high intellectual discourse for you, isn't it? High, fine. You are proud to say, 'I thought the theme honest.' What, pray tell, is an honest theme? It might be better to consider the dishonesty of your disgusting lives."

Oh, I did go on. My script was melodramatic, with great soliloquies, flourishes, and, for verisimilitude, an Eastern European accent. My comeuppance came as I dried the last of the Baccarat goblets. The crystal, no doubt having heard the dissonance and intensity of my soundtrack, shattered as I held it in my hand. The rest of the crew said they'd never seen anyone look as sick as I did at that moment. The goblet was worth more than the price of my trendy sneakers and my night's work combined. I decided to go home.

I drove slowly back to my room near Culver City: it was well past midnight. I had the distinct sense that I was the only sober driver on the Santa Monica Freeway that night, but given the weaving pattern of my driving—to avoid the other weavers—I fully expected to be picked up and jailed. Then, some alcohol residue from the broken goblet would have transported itself as magically into my bloodstream to make me DWI as it had reacted to my thoughts and sacrificed itself in the name of privilege, money, and mean-spiritedness. I made it home, feeling woozy as I left my car.

I didn't have to pay for the goblet; the caterer did. She was insured. I worked another party for her—another strange collection of people, but a more festive occasion—and I didn't have to wear the French maid's outfit. I got to stand happily behind a buffet, helping people serve themselves. I think back on my catering experience the way people do who say, once it's over, that they're glad they did something—like lassoing a bull, riding him, and then busting ribs and causing permanent sacroiliac distress. The job was just one of many I've had to take to make me believe I could survive when it was obvious that I was going further and further into a hole. I never had more than $10 in my wallet the entire time I lived in L.A., and not much more than that in the bank. Perhaps there's something about L.A. that makes working unlikely jobs— jobs your parents send you to college to keep you from having to do—all right and reasonable, since very little makes sense there anyway, and surviving means bellying up to the illusion bar and having a taste with everyone else.

L.A. has been like that for a long time. It did not occur to me that night, as I moved from one dinner guest to another dressed in that ludicrous outfit, that I might have created some other kind of scenario—linking what I was doing to what my mother had done nearly fifty years before, probably no farther than ten miles away.

❖ ❖ ❖

It was in the middle thirties, Los Angeles. My mother's employers supplied her with a beige uniform with a frilled bib, short puff sleeves, and a narrow, fitted waist. The skirt of the dress was narrow, stopping just below the knee. She wore seamed stockings and low pumps, black. And her job, as far as she could ascertain, was to just be, nothing else. The couple who employed her— the husband wrote screenplays—had no children, and did not require her services to either cook or clean. I suppose they thought that having a maid was a requirement of their social position. So, Mother got the job. She is fair-skinned, and at that time she wore her dark, wavy hair long, in large curls that gathered just below her neck. I've seen pictures from those days and see her enviable figure, an old-fashioned 10, held up by long legs that, doubtless, were enhanced by the seamed stockings and pumps. Her employers were quite proud of her and thought she looked, they said, "just like a little French girl." When I was very young and filled with important questions, Mother explained to me that she thought it "damned irritating that whites who knew full well who they were hiring and talking to went to such lengths to try to make blacks into something else. If they wanted a little French girl, why didn't they go out and get one?" Ah, the days before *au pairs*. Well, I knew the answer to that one too.

Mother had moved to L.A. with her mother (whom my sister and I called Nana). Nana had decided to leave her husband, tired of his verbal abusiveness and profligacy. There were various cousins in California, and I am sure the appeal of the West and new beginnings at the start of the Depression made the choice an easy one. Both of my parents told me that they didn't feel the Depression all that much; things had never been financially good and little changed for them after Wall Street fell. The timing seemed right to Nana. Her other daughter, my aunt, had recently married. My mother had finished her third year at the university and, I bet, got an attack of wanderlust. She went with Nana to help her—and also to get some new air. The circumstances accommodated themselves.

I remember my shock when I learned that Mother had worked as a maid. I had always known that she had lived in California, but as a child it never occurred to me that she would have had to "do something" there. It was not so much that my middle-class feathers were ruffled by the revelation as that I found it difficult to see her in a role that on screen, at least, was so demeaning and preposterous. Mother simply did not fit the stereotype I had been fed.

And, to make matters worse, Grandma (my father's mother) had taken pains to inform my sister and me when we were little girls that we should avoid—at all costs—rooming with whites in college or working in their homes. Her own stints as a dance-hall matron had convinced her, she said, that whites were the filthiest people on earth. The thought of my mother cleaning up after them made me want to protect her, to undo the necessity for that kind of work by some miraculous feat of time-traveling, to rescue her from the demeaning and the dirty.

Mother's attitude about her past employment was more pragmatic, of course. She explained to me—as if I didn't know—that there were really no avenues for black women apart from "service" (as it was called), prostitution, and, perhaps, schoolteaching. Nana had no higher education and Mother's was incomplete, so service was the only route they could take. Mother also assured me that she had not cleaned unimaginable filth, but rather, with nothing else to do, had sat all day long reading novels, memorably *Anthony Adverse* by Hervey Allen, a big best-seller of 1934. My image of Mother became brighter, but in some ways more curious: there she was, imagined as a French maid by her employers, but really a black coed, lolling around a Los Angeles home in 1934 reading *Anthony Adverse*. That's one far cry from Butterfly McQueen as Prissy in *Gone with the Wind*.

All good things must come to an end, as they say, and Mother's job did one day. She had been dating a man, she says, "who was very handsome, looked Latin, like Cesar Romero, but he was black too." Talk about images. He arrived to pick her up for a date as she got off work. He inquired after her at the front door—oops—and there went the job. Seems the little French maid's Spanish-looking boyfriend should have realized that no matter what black might appear to be, it better not act other than what it was. "So it went," Mother said. After that incident she decided to look for a different kind of work and she began selling stockings for the Real Silk Hosiery Company, door-to-door.

Mother was lucky. I suspect that she and Nana might have had a tougher time if they had been brown-skinned, for contrary to many images from movies, white employers' preference went—if they were going to hire blacks at all—to the lighter-skinned variety of black woman. This was true of professions as diverse as chorus girls, maids, schoolteachers, waitresses, and shop clerks, an implied greater worth as blackness disappears drop by drop into ginger, to mocha, to "high yellow," to white. This scale was intraracially internalized too, making a shambles of black life from the earliest slave days to the present. These gradations also made color-line-crossing a popular black sport, particularly since white America seemed to be at once so secure and satisfied in its whiteness and so ignorant of who's who and who's what.

Blacks existed only as whites saw them, blackness affirming white racial self-consciousness and nothing else. This is what Ralph Ellison's invisibility is all about; it is what we have all lived.

•••

In the evenings and on weekends, Mother and Nana used to go to the movies; they both were hooked and on location for Hollywood's Golden Age. I love movies too. It is on the gene, as I frequently remind myself as I sit watching a vintage B from the forties for the fifth time or so when I ought to be reading a book. A major chunk of my misspent youth involved watching them. When I should have been reading, or studying mathematics, or learning foreign languages—like my more successful academic friends—I was hooked on three-reelers.

During my youth Mother was my partner in all this. When I was in kindergarten and first grade on half-day shifts, I never missed a morning movie. When we watched together I would barrage her with important questions: "Who is that?" "Is he dead?" "Is she dead?" "Who was she married to?" "Is this gonna be sad?" Mother was never wrong, except once. We were watching an early Charles Bickford movie and I asked the standard heady question: "Is he dead?" Mother said, "Oh, Lord, yes. He died years ago." Several years later I came home triumphantly from a drive-in and announced that I'd seen Bickford in *The Big Country* and that he looked just fine and alive to me.

Of course, hopeless romanticism is the disease that can be caught from the kind of movie-going and movie-watching my mother and I have done. There she was, with her mother, frequently a part of the crowd being held behind the barricades at Hollywood premieres, sighing and pointing with agitation as gowned and white-tied stars glided from limousines into rococo moviehouses. Both she and Nana read screen magazines—the forerunners to our evening news programs—that detailed the romantic, hedonistic public and private exploits of Hollywood's royalty. It was a time when my mother, as French maid reading *Anthony Adverse,* had to wait only a few months before the novel burst onto the screen, with glorious illusionary history and Fredric March swashbuckling his way into the hearts of screaming fans. The stars were part of the studio system and could be counted on to appear with frequency, even if the roles appeared to be the same and only the titles, and a few plot twists, changed. (I am convinced, for example, that the 1934 *Imitation of Life* was remade as *Mildred Pierce* in 1945, the major change being that the relatively good daughter of the former becomes the monster of the latter. Louise Beavers and Fredi Washington in the black theme of *Imitation of Life* only slightly alter the major plot.) Mother's was the perfect generation to see Hollywood movies when they were fresh, new, and perhaps more palpable than they are now—when comedies of remarriage, as Stanley Cavell calls them, and historical adventures and melodramas dominated the screen, when westerns and political dramas were self-consciously mythologizing the American past and present, and when young French maids and their mothers, along with the impoverished, the disillusioned, the lost, and even the comfortable and secure, could sit before the silver screen and see projected a different world from the one they lived in. And they could dream. Mother loves to sketch faces and clothing, using an artistic talent inherited from her father. She marveled at the stars and their sculpted (sometimes) faces, and would draw from memory the costume designs that made the likes of Edith Head, Cecil Beaton, and Irene famous.

Hopeless romanticism was the threat, but neither Nana nor Mother—nor I, completely—succumbed to it. They never confused reality with anything they saw on either the big or the small screen. And they taught me what they believed. They both warned me, in different ways and at different times, to be wary of the type of people who wake up to a new world every day (and I've met some)—people with no memory, ingenuous, incapable of seeing either the implications or the connections between one event and another, people who willingly accept what the world makes of them on a Tuesday, forget as night falls, and wake up on Wednesday ready to make the same mistakes. It might have been some of that ingenuousness that produced my feelings of discomfort when I learned that Mother had been a maid, and she understood how I felt.

My mother always deplored the depiction of blacks on screen. She saw their roles as demeaning and designed to evoke either cheap sentimentality, cheap laughter, or cheap feelings of superiority in the white audiences they were aimed at. And, although she says she didn't see many of them, Mother loathed the all-black Bs Hollywood made for the "colored" audience, where the stereotypes were broader and more offensive to her, and where the musical interludes did no justice to real talent, she said, but trivialized it, made it small. She even hated musical interludes featuring black performers in the standard white As and Bs. She was—and still is—cold to arguments that say talented black performers needed to take any work they could get, and that black audiences were encouraged and happy to see black Hollywood stars no matter what they were doing. Mother countered by saying that Hattie McDaniel's acceptance speech, when she won an Oscar for her role as Mammy in *Gone with the Wind,* was written for her by whites—and that McDaniel had been denied the status of eating dinner with her peers that night.

We have talked about all of this many, many times, particularly when I have felt it necessary to sort out my own complex and conflicting reactions to Hollywood movies. Like Mother, I have seen as nothing but illusion the world projected on the screen. But as Michael Wood notes in *America in the Movies,* "All movies mirror reality in some way or other. There are no escapes, even in the most escapist pictures....The business of films is the business of dreams...but then dreams are scrambled messages from waking life, and there is truth in lies, too." Mother may have recoiled from black images on screen because they affirmed a reality she did not like. She could suspend her disbelief at white characters and their predicaments, she could enter the dream worlds of aristocrats and chorus girls living happily ever after, or dying romantic, drawn-out deaths, because there was some measure of inner life given these portrayals. The audience demanded some causal foundation to acts ranging from heroism and self-sacrifice to murder, duplicity, and pure cussedness. But black characters on screen, no matter how polished their roles, were ultimately as invisible as she was in her own role as French maid—a projection only of what the white world wanted to see, robbed of the implication of inner lives, nothing but glorified surfaces that really said everything about whiteness and nothing at all about blackness. It didn't matter to Mother if the characters were maids or butlers, lawyers or doctors, simpletons or singers. I knew there was an inner life, a real person in my mother—passionate and shy, lacking self-confidence but projecting intense intelligence and style—and that she had no business being anybody's French girl. The "truth in lies" was that Hollywood rent from us our human dignity while purportedly giving us work, as it sought to defuse and deflect our real meaning—a potentially dangerous meaning—in American life.

Mother found these invisible blacks painful to watch because they were so effective as images created in white minds. These complex feelings are on the gene too. I find Shirley Temple movies abominable, notwithstanding the dancing genius of Bill "Bojangles" Robinson. In *The Little Colonel* young Shirley has just been given a birthday party; there are hats and horns and all sorts of scrubbed white children celebrating with her. At some moment—I refuse to watch the film again to be precise—she gets up and takes part of her cake to a group of dusty and dusky children who are waiting outside in the back yard of the house. The only reason for their existence is to be grateful for the crumbs and to sing a song. There can be no other motivation, no reason to exist at all, except to show the dear Little Colonel's largesse and liberal-mindedness, befitting someone not quite to the manor born but clearly on her way to the manor-life.

I was watching an Alfred Hitchcock festival not long ago. Hitchcock films are some of my mother's favorites. She likes the illusions and twists of plots, the scrambling of images light and dark. I realized that I hadn't seen *Rear Window* since I was a little girl, and that at the time I hadn't understood much of what had taken place in the movie. I was very interested in it this time around. There was James Stewart, as Jeffries, in the heaviest makeup ever, with his blue eyes almost enhanced out of his face, looking at evil Raymond Burr through binoculars in the apartment across the way. I was letting the film take me where it would; I created an *explication de texte,* how it raises questions about voyeurism and images. Indeed, Stewart, in looking at the world from his temporary infirmity, is only content when he places a narrative line on the lives of the people on the other side of his binoculars. He is, in a sense, reacting to images and attempting to order them—as we all do.

At a crucial moment in the movie, Stewart realizes that he is in danger. The evil wife-murderer and dismemberer, Burr, knows that Stewart has figured out the crime. Stewart hobbles to the telephone, trying to reach his friend, Wendell Corey. Corey isn't in, but Stewart gets the babysitter on the line— who speaks in a vaudevillian black accent. He asks her to have Corey call him when he returns. The babysitter asks, "Do he have your number, Mr. Jeffrey?"

I called my mother to tell her that I had an interesting bit of trivia from *Rear Window.* She became angry, said she was appalled. "He should have been ashamed of himself," she said of Hitchcock. Into the white world of *Rear Window,* with its complicated questions about imagery, it was necessary to place a familiar black image—and this time it didn't even have a face.

◆ ◆ ◆

Mother and Nana left L.A. in 1937. Working in service and selling silk stockings could not provide enough money for them to survive. They went back to the frozen North. Mother married in 1939; Nana stayed with her husband (whom we called Papa) until he died in 1967.

Nana and Papa returned to L.A. in 1950, Papa then a semiretired architect. They had a beautiful home on West 4th Avenue. It was right in the middle of a two-block area that became part of the Santa Monica Freeway. One morning, on my way to a catering job, I drove my car as far as I could, to the chain-link fence above the freeway. I got out and thought long and hard about what had been lost—beyond a house, of course—their lives gone, part of my youth as a little girl visiting in summers, and dreams about what life could be in the semitropical paradise of Southern California where they made dreams that seduced the whole world.

On Waitressing

by Irene Oppenheim

IN SEPTEMBER OF 1985 I needed a job that would give me a regular income for a few months. I hadn't worked as a waitress for more than a decade, and at first didn't consider that a possibility. But as I searched for more demure employment, I found that one after another of my interviewers would glance at my resume, sadly mumble something about "all that writing," and proceed, making as much eye contact as I'd permit, to ask "sincerely" about my intentions, naming anything less than full commitment a form of deceit. Unable to assuage their concern with a convincingly forthright response, I soon found myself applying for work at Canter's, a sprawling twenty-four-hour-a-day Jewish (though nonkosher) bakery, delicatessen, and restaurant which for the past forty-five years has been dishing up kishka and knishes in the Fairfax district of Los Angeles. I knew that neither of my most recent waitress references would check out—Herb of Herb's Hamburgers in San Francisco had thrown down his spatula some years ago and gone to work in a hardware store, while the Sand Dollar Cafe in Stinson Beach had changed owners, so no one there would remember just how deftly I could sling hash. I told all this to Jackie Canter, who, in her early twenties, is among a number of Canter relations working in the family business. She hesitated, but I was hired anyway.

While I don't wish to discredit my powers of persuasion, getting hired at Canter's was hardly a difficult affair. The "Help Wanted" sign in Canter's front window was a faded, permanent fixture. And in the two months I ultimately worked at the restaurant, the volume of employee comings and goings was never less than impressive. There were, however, exceptions to this transitoriness, and some among the large Canter crew had been with the restaurant for ten, twenty, or even thirty years. These were mostly older women who remained through a combination of loyalty, age, narrow skills, and inertia.

The younger people tended to find the work too demanding and the income increasingly unreliable. Canter's heyday had been in the pre-McDonalds, precholesterol days of the 1950s and 1960s. And while the erosion was gradual, it was clear that the combination of fast food and *nouvelle cuisine* was steadily reducing Canter's corned beef/pastrami/chopped liver clientele. Despite trendy additions to the menu, such as an avocado melt sandwich (not bad) and the steamed vegetable plate (not good), there were now many quiet afternoons when the older waitresses, wiping off ketchup bottles and filling napkin holders to pass the time, would tell you about the days when the lines for Canter's stretched right down from the door to the corner of Beverly Boulevard.

Canter's could still get enormously busy—on holidays, for instance, or weekend nights. Sometimes for no reason at all the place would suddenly be mobbed. But it all had become unpredictable. And while this unpredictability made the owners niggardly and anxious, its more immediate toll was on the waiters and waitresses, who were almost totally dependent on customer tips. Canter's is a "union house," which means that for $16 a month the workers are covered by a not-too-respected grievance procedure and a well-loved medical/dental plan. The pay for waiting on tables, however, remains $3.37 per hour (two cents above minimum wage), so at Canter's, as with most restaurants, any real money has to come from tips.

Until a few years ago these tips were untaxed, which made waitressing a tough but reasonably lucrative profession. Now tips have to be regularly declared, and through a complicated process that involves the IRS taking eight percent of a restaurant's gross meal receipts and dividing that amount up among the number of food servers, a per-employee tip figure is arrived at, and any waiter who declares less than that may very well be challenged. In some restaurants the management automatically deducts the estimated amount from the paychecks. At Canter's each individual makes a weekly declaration. But in either case there's great bitterness among the table waiters about the way the tax is estimated. In every restaurant, for instance, some shifts are far more profitable than others, a subtlety the IRS doesn't take into account. There's also a built-in bias toward "class" operations where the bills are high and the tips generally run fifteen to twenty percent, while at Canter's, with its soup and sandwich fare, ten percent or less is the norm. Also, waitresses and waiters volubly and resentfully claim that others in service professions, such as porters, cab drivers, or hairdressers, are left to make simple declarations, without the income of the business being involved.

Where it is possible, most restaurant workers under-declare their tips and simply hope they can get away with it. But a few of them at Canter's had been called in each year, and the more canny of the waitresses told me I should keep a daily tally of all my checks in case the IRS claimed I'd made not just more than I'd declared, but more than I really took in. What all this meant in terms of an actual paycheck was that, after meal deductions, regular taxes, and taxes declared on my tips, my average check for a forty-hour week was $74.93 or, in the first week of the month, when union fees were due, $58.93. Whatever else I took home was in the form of tips, and if business wasn't good these could become an unnervingly scarce commodity.

Still, most waitresses at Canter's made more than they would as bank tellers, store clerks, or nonmanagerial office workers. And even for those whose options were somewhat less grim, waitressing was not without its alluring aspects. The range of tips—which, depending on how many customers of what kind you got on a shift, might be as low as $12 or as high as $80—gave the job a gambling flavor which appealed to some. (Gambling, in fact, was rather a big item at Canter's. More than a few of the waitresses played as much bingo as paying their rent allowed, while the kitchen help would, almost every day, pool their money and purchase long strings of lottery tickets, with any winnings divided among the buyers.) Others among the waitresses worked there because they preferred the restaurant's physical demands to the boredom of paperwork, and several were performers or students who took advantage of the night hours and flexible scheduling. But no one was really happy to be at Canter's. It simply wasn't a very happy place.

◆ ◆ ◆

I've never worked anywhere that had more rules than Canter's. The staff bulletin board was so crammed with admonitions that the overflow had to be taped to the adjacent wall. The topics of these missives varied. One sign, for example, warned that bags and purses might be checked on the way out for purloined food; another that those who didn't turn up for their shifts on holidays such as Christmas (Canter's is open every day of the year except Rosh Hashanah and Yom Kippur) would be automatically dismissed; a third firmly stated that no food substitutions were permitted, which meant that it was against regulations to give a customer who requested it a slice of tomato instead of a pickle. When working on the floor, one encountered even more elaborate rules. All ice cream, juice, or bakery items, for instance, had to be initialed on your check by that shift's hostess, lest you serve something without writing it down. To further complicate matters, orders for deli sandwiches had to be written on a slip of paper along with your waitress number (mine was #35), and these slips were then matched against your checks to make sure, for example, that if you ordered two pastrami sandwiches the customer had paid for two. I was castigated by Jackie one day for—along with the more major infraction of not charging fifty cents extra for a slice of cheese—charging ten cents too little for a cup of potato salad. It seems like a small thing, said Jackie (I concurred), but then she added grimly that little mistakes like mine with the potato salad cost the restaurant many thousands of dollars each year. I was tempted to point out that undoubtedly an equal number of errors were made in the restaurant's favor. But I held my tongue, knowing by then that, in the face of a documented Canter's money loss, anything that could be construed as less than acute remorse would only serve to bring my checks under even closer scrutiny.

The waitresses were generally good to each other, though such camaraderie didn't often run deep and rarely extended to any auxiliary personnel such as the busboys. These were constantly (and mostly unjustly) suspected of stealing tips from the tables and thereby adding to their required tips from the waitresses (I'm not sure exactly what this came to per individual busboy, but every waitress contributed about $20 a week, which was divided up among the busboys). At one time Canter's busboy positions had been filled by strapping immigrant Jewish boys from places such as Bulgaria and Lithuania. But now the busboys were almost all Mexican, as were the cooks, and a troublesome plate of blintzes or latkes would be garnished by a storm of Spanish curses. In the back kitchen, too, where they made the soups and mixed together enormous vats of tuna salad, the workers were mostly Spanish-speaking. Things in the back kitchen were usually less frantic than in the front, and the back kitchen guys would smile and try to make conversation as you negotiated your way over the wooden floor slats to the bathroom or the time clock. From the deli and kitchen men, however, surliness was a virtual constant, with their black moods frequently exacerbated into anger by such things as the restaurant's awkward design and organization. It was required, for example, that a waitress serving a cheddar cheese omelette first write a slip for the cheese, which had to be sliced and picked up at the front deli counter, and then, after writing another slip for the kitchen, hand-carry the cheese back to the grill. When the place got busy, tempers also ran short among the waitresses themselves, who would swear at the always recalcitrant toasters, at the bagels (or lack of them), or at each other, as fast movers stumbled into slower ones. But in the arena of churlishness the waitresses never came close to competing with the hardworking deli men. Brandishing knives and hunks of meat with a rhythmic skill and an admirable—even graceful—economy of movement, they set the tone at Canter's. And I remember a time when, having made a mistake, I said to one of the deli men, by way of apology, that I'd try to improve. "Don't try," he snarled back. "Do."

◆ ◆ ◆

One of the more graphic symbols of Canter's changing times was the uniform closet. The male waiters—a relative novelty at Canter's—were allowed to work in a black-pants/white-shirt combo, with some of them opting to appear in the "I Love Canter's" T-shirt available for $8 (*their* $8) at the front cash register.

The women could get "I Love Canter's" stenciled free on the off-work shirt of their choice, but their on-the-job dress code was more severe. No one's memory reached back to a time when Canter's waitresses had worn anything other than cream-colored outfits with a single brown stripe running down from each shoulder. There were many of these lined up in the uniform closet. In most cases the uniforms were well-worn, with underarms stained an irreparable gray and hems which had been let up or down more than once. But their dominant characteristic was size. Most of the available uniforms could have doubled as small tents. And no matter how many pins or tucks you employed, material would billow out over your tightly pulled apron strings, an irrepressible tribute to the amplitude of your predecessors.

Although there was a locker room at Canter's, it was deemed dangerous for reasons I never explored, and I always arrived with my uniform already on. At first I'd worked various shifts—twelve P.M. to eight P.M., eight P.M. to four A.M.—but finally was assigned to days, primarily because I was considered easygoing and the day shift had a contentious reputation. My first task was to relieve Pauline at the counter. She went on duty at six A.M., and technically I was to relieve her at nine A.M. when my shift began. Though the management preferred you didn't clock it in, the rules at Canter's required you to be on the floor fifteen minutes before your shift time, and I'd generally show up around 8:40, which would give Pauline a chance to finish off her checks and put together her own breakfast—usually a mixture of Frosted Flakes and Wheaties from the little boxes kept on display right near the coffee machine.

There was nothing contentious about Pauline. She was a slow, heavy woman in her early sixties. She was having tooth problems during the time I knew her. But her feet were also troublesome, and she'd made long knife cuts in the front of her white shoes so that, defying the beige of her nylons, the flesh of each foot pushed out rosy-pink between the slits. Pauline had been working at Canter's for twenty-five years, and was the only one of the waitresses left who had her name machine-embroidered onto her uniform. The rest of us were given pins with our first names punched out on a black dymo label. But Pauline's was sewn right in, so you knew she represented a different, less transient era at the restaurant. You could tell by watching her, too, by the deliberate way she moved, that this was a place she was intimately familiar with.

Only one part of the counter was open in the morning. It sat around fourteen people and included, as part of the station, three adjacent two-person booths as well as any takeout coffee orders. Almost everyone hated working the counter because the turnover could be impossibly fast and the tips were always small. On the other hand, the counter didn't involve as much running around as the other stations, and Pauline preferred it. She'd move as though she were doing a little dance, reaching toward the coffee machine, and then the toaster, and then scooping up packets of strawberry jam (strawberry was the only jam flavor Canter's served), with a steady elegance that belied her girth—a factor substantial enough to make it virtually unfeasible for both of us to work behind the counter at once.

Pauline was always glad to see me, for the half-hour's rest I represented would be the longest break she'd have until getting off work at two P.M. I liked Pauline too, and we got along well, but the counter was another matter. Generally two kinds of people showed up at the counter: those who were alone and in a hurry to get somewhere else, and a group of "regulars" for whom time was not a consideration. This latter group was dominated by retired men who met at Canter's punctually each day to have windy discussions which would begin focused on a single topic—such as how people on welfare should be prevented from buying lottery tickets—that would gradually merge into a broader lament about the disintegration of the neighborhood, the city, the nation, and onward. From my standpoint, both these counter groups meant trouble: those who were alone tended to be impatient, while those who came in every day expected special treatment which included remembering details about their preferences (water without ice, or a cherry danish heated with soft butter on the side), and they'd become belligerent if these idiosyncrasies were forgotten or if they felt some mere counter itinerant were getting better service. But there were other regulars too, lonely souls who were not part of the clique. As you stopped for a moment to write out their check, they'd start to tell you about painful cataracts or distant children. I remember one woman who liked her single piece of rye toast burnt almost black. She'd occasionally whisper, so that I had to bend down to hear her, that she was short of cash, and would ask to borrow a dollar from me to pay the bill. I'd always do it. And next day the loan would be stealthily but triumphantly repaid, the dollar slipped into my hand or pocket with a conspiratorial smile as though this act of trust and complicity had secretly bonded us together.

◆ ◆ ◆

My Canter's career was to come to an unfortunately abrupt end. A restaurant as large as Canter's was bound to have "walkouts" who'd leave without paying their checks, and I'd had a few. There was one obese woman who asked me a couple of times if she could pay with a credit card (Canter's didn't accept them) and then left me a tip before managing to get away without paying for her hamburger and coke. Another man had me take his bacon and eggs back to the kitchen twice for repairs; he left me a tip too, but the eggs and bacon went unpaid for. Though there was an element of disgrace in having a walkout, these small incidents were too common for much of a fuss to be made. But one busy Saturday I had a party of seven who each ordered around $10 worth of food and then made a calculated escape while I was in the back adding up their check. Jackie sat me down at the staff table and grimly said that while she didn't blame me for what happened, she did want me to know that it was the largest walkout loss in the history of Canter's. Nothing was mentioned about my leaving, though Jackie did say that from this point on she wanted me immediately to report to her or the hostess any of my customers who seemed suspicious. I worked the rest of my shift, but everyone I served began to look vaguely suspicious. And with my reputation securely if infamously etched into Canter's history, it seemed time to move on.

On Dumpster Diving

by Lars Eighner

LONG BEFORE I BEGAN DUMPSTER diving I was impressed with Dumpsters, enough so that I wrote the Merriam-Webster research service to discover what I could about the word "Dumpster." I learned from them that "Dumpster" is a proprietary word belonging to the Dempster Dumpster company.

Since then I have dutifully capitalized the word although it was lowercased in almost all of the citations Merriam-Webster photocopied for me. Dempster's word is too apt. I have never heard these things called anything but Dumpsters. I do not know anyone who knows the generic name for these objects. From time to time, however, I hear a wino or hobo give some corrupted credit to the original and call them Dipsy Dumpsters.

I began Dumpster diving about a year before I became homeless.

I prefer the term "scavenging," and use the word "scrounging" when I mean to be obscure. I have heard people, evidently meaning to be polite, use the word "foraging," but I prefer to reserve that word for gathering nuts and berries and such, which I do also according to the season and the opportunity. "Dumpster diving" seems to me to be a little too cute and, in my case, inaccurate because I lack the athletic ability to lower myself into the Dumpsters as the true divers do, much to their increased profit.

I like the frankness of the word "scavenging," which I can hardly think of without picturing a big black snail on an aquarium wall. I live from the refuse of others. I am a scavenger. I think it a sound and honorable niche, although if I could I would naturally prefer to live the comfortable consumer life, perhaps—and only perhaps—as a slightly less wasteful consumer owing to what I have learned as a scavenger.

While my dog Lizbeth and I were still living in the house on Avenue B in Austin, as my savings ran out, I put almost all my sporadic income into rent. The necessities of daily life I began to extract from Dumpsters. Yes, we ate from Dumpsters. Except for jeans, all my clothes came from Dumpsters. Boom boxes, candles, bedding, toilet paper, medicine, books, a typewriter, a virgin male love doll, change sometimes amounting to many dollars: I acquired many things from the Dumpsters.

I have learned much as a scavenger. I mean to put some of what I have learned down here, beginning with the practical art of Dumpster diving and proceeding to the abstract.

♦ ♦ ♦

What is safe to eat?

After all, the finding of objects is becoming something of an urban art. Even respectable employed people will sometimes find something tempting sticking out of a Dumpster or standing beside one. Quite a number of people, not all of them of the bohemian type, are willing to brag that they found this or that piece in the trash. But eating from Dumpsters is the thing that separates the dilettanti from the professionals.

Eating safely from the Dumpsters involves three principles: using the senses and common sense to evaluate the condition of the found materials, knowing the Dumpsters of a given area and checking them regularly, and seeking always to answer the question, "Why was this discarded?"

Perhaps everyone who has a kitchen and a regular supply of groceries has, at one time or another, made a sandwich and eaten half of it before discovering mold on the bread or got a mouthful of milk before realizing the milk had turned. Nothing of the sort is likely to happen to a Dumpster diver because he is constantly reminded that most food is discarded for a reason. Yet a lot of perfectly good food can be found in Dumpsters.

Canned goods, for example, turn up fairly often in the Dumpsters I frequent. All except the most phobic people would be willing to eat from a can even if it came from a Dumpster. Canned goods are among the safest of foods to be found in Dumpsters, but are not utterly foolproof.

Although very rare with modern canning methods, botulism is a possibility. Most other forms of food poisoning seldom do lasting harm to a healthy person. But botulism is almost certainly fatal and often the first symptom is death. Except for carbonated beverages, all canned goods should contain a slight vacuum and suck air when first punctured. Bulging, rusty, dented cans and cans that spew when punctured should be avoided, especially when the contents are not very acidic or syrupy.

Heat can break down the botulin, but this requires much more cooking than most people do to canned goods. To the extent that botulism occurs at all, of course, it can occur in cans on pantry shelves as well as in cans from Dumpsters. Need I say that home-canned goods found in Dumpsters are simply too risky to be recommended.

From time to time one of my companions, aware of the source of my provisions, will ask, "Do you think these crackers are really safe to eat?" For some reason it is most often the crackers they ask about.

This question always makes me angry. Of course I would not offer my companion anything I had doubts about. But more than that, I wonder why he cannot evaluate the condition of the crackers for himself. I have no special knowledge and I have been wrong before. Since he knows where the food comes from, it seems to me he ought to assume some of the responsibility for deciding what he will put in his mouth.

For myself, I have few qualms about dry foods such as crackers, cookies, cereal, chips, and pasta if they are free of visible contaminates and still dry and crisp. Most often such things are found in the original packaging, which is not so much a positive sign as it is the absence of a negative one.

Raw fruits and vegetables with intact skins seem perfectly safe to me, excluding of course the obviously rotten. Many are discarded for minor imperfections which can be pared away. Leafy vegetables, grapes, cauliflower, broccoli, and similar things may be contaminated by liquids and may be impractical to wash.

Candy, especially hard candy, is usually safe if it has not drawn ants. Chocolate is often discarded only because it has become discolored as the cocoa butter de-emulsified. Candying, after all, is one method of food preservation because pathogens do not like very sugary substances.

All of these foods might be found in any Dumpster and can be evaluated with some confidence largely on the basis of appearance. Beyond these are foods which cannot be correctly evaluated without additional information.

I began scavenging by pulling pizzas out of the Dumpster behind a pizza delivery shop. In general prepared food requires caution, but in this case I knew when the shop closed and went to the Dumpster as soon as the last of the help left.

Such shops often get prank orders, called "bogus." Because help seldom stays long at these places, pizzas are often made with the wrong topping, refused on delivery for being cold, or baked incorrectly. The products to be discarded are boxed up because inventory is kept by counting boxes: a boxed pizza can be written off; an unboxed pizza does not exist.

I never placed a bogus order to increase the supply of pizzas and I believe no one else was scavenging in this Dumpster. But the people in the shop became suspicious and began to retain their garbage in the shop overnight.

While it lasted I had a steady supply of fresh, sometimes warm pizza. Because I knew the Dumpster I knew the source of the pizza, and because I visited the Dumpster regularly I knew what was fresh and what was yesterday's.

The area I frequent is inhabited by many affluent college students. I am not here by chance; the Dumpsters in this area are very rich. Students throw out many good things, including food. In particular they tend to throw everything out when they move at the end of a semester, before and after breaks, and around midterm when many of them despair of college. So I find it advantageous to keep an eye on the academic calendar.

The students throw food away around the breaks because they do not know whether it has spoiled or will spoil before they return. A typical discard is a half jar of peanut butter. In fact nonorganic peanut butter does not require refrigeration and is unlikely to spoil in any reasonable time. The student does not know that, and since it is Daddy's money, the student decides not to take a chance.

Opened containers require caution and some attention to the question, "Why was this discarded?" But in the case of discards from student apartments, the answer may be that the item was discarded through carelessness, ignorance, or wastefulness. This can sometimes be deduced when the item is found with many others, including some that are obviously perfectly good.

Some students, and others, approach defrosting a freezer by chucking out the whole lot. Not only do the circumstances of such a find tell the story, but also the mass of frozen goods stays cold for a long time and items may be found still frozen or freshly thawed.

Yogurt, cheese, and sour cream are items that are often thrown out while they are still good. Occasionally I find a cheese with a spot of mold, which of course I just pare off, and because it is obvious why such a cheese was discarded, I treat it with less suspicion than an apparently perfect cheese found in similar circumstances. Yogurt is often discarded, still sealed, only because the expiration date on the carton had passed. This is one of my favorite finds because yogurt will keep for several days, even in warm weather.

Students throw out canned goods and staples at the end of semesters and when they give up college at midterm. Drugs, pornography, spirits, and the like are often discarded when parents are expected—Dad's day, for example. And spirits also turn up after big party weekends, presumably discarded by the newly reformed. Wine and spirits, of course, keep perfectly well even once opened. My test for carbonated soft drinks is whether they still fizz vigorously. Many juices or other beverages are too acid or too syrupy to cause much concern provided they are not visibly contaminated. Liquids, however, require some care.

One hot day I found a large jug of Pat O'Brien's Hurricane mix. The jug had been opened, but it was still ice cold. I drank three large glasses before it became apparent to me that someone had added the rum to the mix, and not a little rum. I never tasted the rum and by the time I began to feel the effects I had already ingested a very large quantity of the beverage. Some divers would have considered this is a boon, but being suddenly and thoroughly intoxicated in a public place in the early afternoon is not my idea of a good time.

I have heard of people maliciously contaminating discarded food and even handouts, but mostly I have heard of this from people with vivid imaginations who have had no experience with the Dumpsters themselves. Just before the pizza shop stopped discarding its garbage at night, jalapeños began showing up on most of the discarded pizzas. If indeed this was meant to discourage me it was a wasted effort because I am native Texan.

For myself, I avoid game, poultry, pork, and egg-based foods whether I find them raw or cooked. I seldom have the means to cook what I find, but when I do I avail myself of plentiful supplies of beef which is often in very good condition. I suppose fish becomes disagreeable before it becomes dangerous. The dog is happy to have any such thing that is past its prime and, in fact, does not recognize fish as food until it is quite strong.

Home leftovers, as opposed to surpluses from restaurants, are very often bad. Evidently, especially among students, there is a common type of personality that carefully wraps up even the smallest leftover and shoves it into the back of the refrigerator for six months or so before discarding it. Characteristic of this type are the reused jars and margarine tubs which house the remains.

I avoid ethnic foods I am unfamiliar with. If I do not know what it is supposed to look like when it is good, I cannot be certain I will be able to tell if it is bad.

No matter how careful I am I still get dysentery at least once a month, oftener in warm weather. I do not want to paint too romantic a picture. Dumpster diving has serious drawbacks as a way of life.

◆ ◆ ◆

I learned to scavenge gradually, on my own. Since then I have initiated several companions into the trade. I have learned that there is a predictable series of stages a person goes through in learning to scavenge.

At first the new scavenger is filled with disgust and self-loathing. He is ashamed of being seen and may lurk around, trying to duck behind things, or he may try to dive at night.

(In fact, most people instinctively look away from a scavenger. By skulking around, the novice calls attention to himself and arouses suspicion. Diving at night is ineffective and needlessly messy.)

Every grain of rice seems to be a maggot. Everything seems to stink. He can wipe the egg yolk off the found can, but he cannot erase the stigma of eating garbage out of his mind.

That stage passes with experience. The scavenger finds a pair of running shoes that fit and look and smell brand new. He finds a pocket calculator in perfect working order. He finds pristine ice cream, still frozen, more than he can eat or keep. He begins to understand: people do throw away perfectly good stuff, a lot of perfectly good stuff.

At this stage, Dumpster shyness begins to dissipate. The diver, after all, has the last laugh. He is finding all manner of good things which are his for the taking. Those who disparage his profession are the fools, not he.

He may begin to hang onto some perfectly good things for which he has neither a use nor a market. Then he begins to take note of the things which are not perfectly good but are nearly so. He mates a Walkman with broken earphones and one that is missing a battery cover. He picks up things which he can repair.

At this stage he may become lost and never recover. Dumpsters are full of things of some potential value to someone and also of things which never had much intrinsic value but are interesting. All the Dumpster divers I have known come to the point of trying to acquire everything they touch. Why not take it, they reason, since it is all free?

This is, of course, hopeless. Most divers come to realize that they must restrict themselves to items of relatively immediate utility. But in some cases the diver simply cannot control himself. I have met several of these pack-rat types. Their ideas of the values of various pieces of junk verge on the psychotic. Every bit of glass may be a diamond, they think, and all that glisters, gold.

I tend to gain weight when I am scavenging. Partly this is because I always find far more pizza and doughnuts than water-packed tuna, nonfat yogurt, and fresh vegetables.

Also I have not developed much faith in the reliability of Dumpsters as a food source, although it has been proven to me many times. I tend to eat as if I have no idea where my next meal is coming from. But mostly I just hate to see food go to waste and so I eat much more than I should. Something like this drives the obsession to collect junk.

As for collecting objects, I usually restrict myself to collecting one kind of small object at a time, such as pocket calculators, sunglasses, or campaign buttons. To live on the street I must anticipate my needs to a certain extent: I must pick up and save warm bedding I find in August because it will not be found in Dumpsters in November. But even if I had a home with extensive storage space, I could not save everything that might be valuable in some contingency.

I have proprietary feelings about my Dumpsters. As I have suggested, it is no accident that I scavenge from Dumpsters where good finds are common. But my limited experience with Dumpsters in other areas suggests to me that it is the population of competitors rather than the affluence of the dumpers that most affects the feasibility of survival by scavenging. The large number of competitors is what puts me off the idea of trying to scavenge in places like Los Angeles.

Curiously, I do not mind my direct competition, other scavengers, so much as I hate the can scroungers.

People scrounge cans because they have to have a little cash. I have tried scrounging cans with an able-bodied companion. Afoot, a can scrounger simply cannot make more than a few dollars a day. One can extract the necessities of life from the Dumpsters directly with far less effort than would be required to accumulate the equivalent value in cans.

Can scroungers, then, are people who must have small amounts of cash. These are drug addicts and winos, mostly the latter because the amounts of cash are so small.

Spirits and drugs do, like all other commodities, turn up in Dumpsters, and the scavenger will from time to time have a half bottle of a rather good wine with his dinner. But the wino cannot survive on these occasional finds; he must have his daily dose to stave off the DTs. All the cans he can carry will buy about three bottles of Wild Irish Rose.

I do not begrudge them the cans, but can scroungers tend to tear up the Dumpsters, mixing the contents and littering the area. They become so specialized that they can see only cans. They earn my contempt by passing up change, canned goods, and readily hockable items.

There are precious few courtesies among scavengers. But it is a common practice to set aside surplus items: pairs of shoes, clothing, canned goods, and such. A true scavenger hates to see good stuff go to waste, and what he cannot use he leaves in good condition in plain sight.

Can scroungers lay waste to everything in their path and will stir one of a pair of good shoes to the bottom of a Dumpster, to be lost or ruined in the muck. Can scroungers will even go through individual garbage cans, something I have never seen a scavenger do.

Individual garbage cans are set out on the public easement only on garbage days. On other days going through them requires trespassing close to a dwelling. Going through individual garbage cans without scattering litter is almost impossible. Litter is likely to reduce the public's tolerance of scavenging. Individual garbage cans are simply not as productive as Dumpsters; people in houses and duplexes do not move as often and for some reason do not tend to discard as much useful material. Moreover, the time required to go through one garbage can that serves one household is not much less than the time required to go through a Dumpster that contains the refuse of twenty apartments.

But my strongest reservation about going through individual garbage cans is that this seems to me a very personal kind of invasion to which I would object if I were a householder. Although many things in Dumpsters are obviously meant never to come to light, a Dumpster is somehow less personal.

◆ ◆ ◆

I avoid trying to draw conclusions about the people who dump in the Dumpsters I frequent. I think it would be unethical to do so, although I know many people will find the idea of scavenger ethics too funny for words.

Dumpsters contain bank statements, bills, correspondence, and other documents, just as anyone might expect. But there are also less obvious sources of information. Pill bottles, for example. The labels on pill bottles contain the name of the patient, the name of the doctor, and the name of the drug. AIDS drugs and antipsychotic medicines, to name but two groups, are specific and are seldom prescribed for any other disorders. The plastic compacts for birth control pills usually have complete label information.

Despite all of this sensitive information, I have had only one apartment resident object to my going through the Dumpster. In that case it turned out the resident was a university athlete who was taking bets and who was afraid I would turn up his wager slips.

Occasionally a find tells a story. I once found a small paper bag containing some unused condoms, several partial tubes of flavored sexual lubricant, a partially used compact of birth control pills, and the torn pieces of a picture of a young man. Clearly she was through with him and planning to give up sex altogether.

Dumpster things are often sad—abandoned teddy bears, shredded wedding books, despaired-of sales kits. I find many pets lying in state in Dumpsters. Although I hope to get off the streets so that Lizbeth can have a long and comfortable old age, I know this hope is not very realistic. So I suppose when her time comes she too will go into a Dumpster. I will have no better place for her. And after all, for most of her life her livelihood has come from the Dumpster. When she finds something I think is safe that has been spilled from the Dumpster, I let her have it. She already knows the route around the best Dumpsters. I like to think that if she survives me she will have a chance of evading the dogcatcher and of finding her sustenance on the route.

Silly vanities also come to rest in the Dumpsters. I am a rather accomplished needleworker. I get a lot of materials from the Dumpsters. Evidently sorority girls, hoping to impress someone, perhaps themselves, with their mastery of a womanly art, buy a lot of embroider-by-number kits, work a few stitches horribly, and eventually discard the whole mess. I pull out their stitches, turn the canvas over, and work an original design. Do not think I refrain from chuckling as I make original gifts from these kits.

I find diaries and journals. I have often thought of compiling a book of literary found objects. And perhaps I will one day. But what I find is hopelessly commonplace and bad without being, even unconsciously, camp. College students also discard their papers. I am horrified to discover the kind of paper which now merits an A in an undergraduate course. I am grateful, however, for the number of good books and magazines the students throw out.

In the area I know best I have never discovered vermin in the Dumpsters, but there are two kinds of kitty surprise. One is alley cats which I meet as they leap, claws first, out of Dumpsters. This is especially thrilling when I have

Lizbeth in tow. The other kind of kitty surprise is a plastic garbage bag filled with some ponderous, amorphous mass. This always proves to be used cat litter.

City bees harvest doughnut glaze and this makes the Dumpster at the doughnut shop more interesting. My faith in the instinctive wisdom of animals is always shaken whenever I see Lizbeth attempt to catch a bee in her mouth, which she does whenever bees are present. Evidently some birds find Dumpsters profitable, for birdie surprise is almost as common as kitty surprise of the first kind. In hunting season all kinds of small game turn up in Dumpsters, some of it, sadly, not entirely dead. Curiously, summer and winter, maggots are uncommon.

The worst of the living and near-living hazards of the Dumpsters are the fire ants. The food that they claim is not much of a loss, but they are vicious and aggressive. It is very easy to brush against some surface of the Dumpster and pick up half a dozen or more fire ants, usually in some sensitive area such as the underarm. One advantage of bringing Lizbeth along as I make Dumpster rounds is that, for obvious reasons, she is very alert to ground-based fire ants. When Lizbeth recognizes the signs of fire ant infestation around our feet she does the Dance of the Zillion Fire Ants. I have learned not to ignore this warning from Lizbeth, whether I perceive the tiny ants or not, but to remove ourselves at Lizbeth's first *pas de bourrée*. All the more so because the ants are the worst in the months I wear flip-flops, if I have them.

(Perhaps someone will misunderstand the above. Lizbeth does the Dance of the Zillion Fire Ants when she recognizes more fire ants than she cares to eat, not when she is being bitten. Since I have learned to react promptly, she does not get bitten at all. It is the isolated patrol of fire ants that falls in Lizbeth's range that deserves pity. Lizbeth finds them quite tasty.)

By far the best way to go through a Dumpster is to lower yourself into it. Most of the good stuff tends to settle at the bottom because it is usually weightier than the rubbish. My more athletic companions have often demonstrated to me that they can extract much good material from a Dumpster I have already been over.

To those psychologically or physically unprepared to enter a Dumpster, I recommend a stout stick, preferably with some barb or hook at one end. The hook can be used to grab plastic garbage bags. When I find canned goods or other objects loose at the bottom of a Dumpster I usually can roll them into a small bag that I can then hoist up. Much Dumpster diving is a matter of experience for which nothing will do except practice.

Dumpster diving is outdoor work, often surprisingly pleasant. It is not entirely predictable; things of interest turn up every day, and some days there are finds of great value. I am always very pleased when I can turn up exactly the thing I most wanted to find. Yet in spite of the element of chance, scavenging more than most other pursuits tends to yield returns in some proportion to the effort and intelligence brought to bear. It is very sweet to turn up a few dollars in change from a Dumpster that has just been gone over by a wino.

The land is now covered with cities. The cities are full of Dumpsters. I think of scavenging as a modern form of self-reliance. In any event, after ten years of government service, where everything is geared to the lowest common denominator, I find work that rewards initiative and effort refreshing. Certainly I would be happy to have a sinecure again, but I am not heartbroken not to have one anymore.

I find from the experience of scavenging two rather deep lessons. The first is to take what I can use and let the rest go by. I have come to think that there is no value in the abstract. A thing I cannot use or make useful, perhaps by trading, has no value however fine or rare it may be. I mean useful in a broad sense—so, for example, some art I would think useful and valuable, but other art might be otherwise for me.

I was shocked to realize that some things are not worth acquiring, but now I think it is so. Some material things are white elephants that eat up the possessor's substance.

The second lesson is of the transience of material being. This has not quite converted me to a dualist, but it has made some headway in that direction. I do not suppose that ideas are immortal, but certainly mental things are longer-lived than other material things.

Once I was the sort of person who invests material objects with sentimental value. Now I no longer have those things, but I have the sentiments yet.

Many times in my travels I have lost everything but the clothes I was wearing and Lizbeth. The things I find in Dumpsters, the love letters and ragdolls of so many lives, remind me of this lesson. Now I hardly pick up a thing without envisioning the time I will cast it away. This I think is a healthy state of mind. Almost everything I have now has already been cast out at least once, proving that what I own is valueless to someone.

Anyway, I find my desire to grab for the gaudy bauble has been largely sated. I think this is an attitude I share with the very wealthy—we both know there is plenty more where what we have came from. Between us are the rat-race millions who have confounded their selves with the objects they grasp and who nightly scavenge the cable channels looking for they know not what.

I am sorry for them.

Glorious Reflections
upon the Five of Hearts and
Other Wild Cards in
the National Deck

by Gore Vidal

I.

ALTHOUGH THE NEW YORK FAMILY of Auchincloss is of "recent arrival" (1803), as Sitting Bull used to say, they have managed, through marriage, to become related to everyone in the United States who matters—to everyone in the United States who matters, that is. For idle hypergamy and relentless fecundity there has not been a family like them since those much less attractive Mittel-Europa realtors, the Habsburgs. Although the family has produced neither a great man nor a fortune ("each generation of Auchincloss men either made or married its own money"—Louis Auchincloss in *A Writer's Capital*), there are, aside from the excellent novelist, numerous lawyers, stockbrokers, and doctors whose Cosa Nostra is the Presbyterian (not Episcopalian) Hospital in New York. By the mid–twentieth century, the clan's most notorious member was Hugh D. Auchincloss, Jr. A bulky man who stammered, "Hughdie" (usually known as "Poor Hughdie") was heir to a Standard Oil fortune, thanks to his father's marriage to the daughter of a Rockefeller partner named Jennings. This worldly, I think the adjective is, match sharply separated Hughdie's line from those of the brownstone cousinage (fifty-seven male Auchinclosses in 1957), content with their snail-like upwardly mobile marriages to Old as well as Older New York.

Early in life, at Yale, in fact, Hughdie's originality was revealed; *he was unable to do work of any kind.* Since the American ruling class, then and now, likes to give the impression that it is always hard at work, or at least very busy, Hughdie's sloth was something of a breakthrough. The word "aristocrat" is never used by our rulers, but he acted suspiciously like one; certainly he was inert in a foreign way. Would he move to England? But Hughdie's originality in sloth was equally original in ultimate choice of venue. He moved not to London but to Washington, D.C. Not only had no Auchincloss ever moved to Washington, D.C.; *no one* had ever moved there without first undergoing election or appointment. As if this was not original enough, he started a brokerage firm with a million-dollar gift from his oleaginous Jennings mother, and settled into an Italian palazzo next to the Japanese embassy in Massachusetts Avenue. Since the partners did all the work at the brokerage house, he had a great deal of time to woolgather and to fret whether or not he was happy. In fact, each day would end with a careful analysis of the preceding not-so-crowded hours and whether or not others—specifically, the wife of the moment—had contributed sufficiently to his happiness, a somewhat vagrant bluebird with other errands that took precedence in the nation's capital.

As the city had no life other than the political, Hughdie became a "groupie" even though he had little interest in politics as such. He believed in the virtue of the rich and the vice of the poor and that was as far as introspection ever took him. But Hughdie very much believed in celebrity (one of his most attractive monologues was of the date that he had had in youth with the film star Kay Francis) and of all celebrities the politician most fascinated him, and of all politicians the members of the United States Senate were the most visible and glamorous.

For a long time, before and after Franklin Roosevelt, presidents tended to be nonentities kept hidden in the White House while senators were always center-stage. They were, literally, the conscript patriciate of the nation until they were elected directly in 1913. After that, though hereditary nobles continued to sit in the chamber (today one finds a Rockefeller, a Dupont, a Pell, a Heinz, all in place, as well as such recent hustlers as the Kennedys), outsize tribunes of the people joined them and, along with Byrds, Hales, Frelinghuysens, there were Borahs, LaFollettes, and Longs.

From Lincoln's murder to FDR's first inaugural the Senate was the great stage of the republic. At our own century's quarter time there were ninety-six senators and the whole country observed these paladins with awe if not pleasure. When a powerful senator spoke, the galleries would be full. Everyone understood exactly what Borah meant when he said that he would rather be right than president, or did Senator Clay say it first? For Hughdie, the Senate's Reflected Glory was sun enough for him. But few political magnificos came to his Massachusetts Avenue palace during the time of his Russian-born first wife. There was a grim divorce in which an airplane propeller surreally figured. With Hughdie's second wife, the "beauteous" (*Time* magazine's adjective) daughter of the blind Senator Gore, he hit the jackpot, and she filled Merrywood, his new house—or "home" as the press liked to say even then—across the river, with senators and the Speaker, Sam Rayburn, and the likes of Walter Lippmann and Arthur Krock: my mother had persuaded Hughdie that if one wanted true Reflected Glory, certain Jews would have to be invited to the house if only to set up the reflectors.

In due course, after two children, Nina Gore Vidal Auchincloss left Hughdie for Love, and he was promptly married for his money by one of her ladies-in-waiting, who brought him two very poor but very adorable frizzy-haired step-daughters to take my place in his ample heart. For a long time there was no RG, much less G, to illuminate the sad Merrywood until one of the adorable girls married.... But let Hughdie state his victories in Caesarean plainstyle, written for an Auchincloss family publication: "Hugh D. Auchincloss (golf and chess) has twice been connected with the U.S. Senate through marriage; once as the son-in-law of the late Thomas Gore, senator from Oklahoma, and now as step-father-in-law of John F. Kennedy, junior senator from Massachusetts." That was it. All of it, in fact. At the end, there was to be absolute RG.

A decade later Hughdie was acclaimed "the first gentleman of the United States" by Mr. Stephen Birmingham, a society chronicler who should know. But by then Reflected Glory had so paid off that as he and I stood face to face in the Red Room of the White House, he could ask himself rhetorically, "What am I doing here? I am a Republican and I hate publicity." I have never seen anyone so happy but then, next to limelight, RG is best. At the American empire's zenith, there was poor Hughdie, a dusty mirror at the dead center of The Sacred Way.

Tout ça change, as the French say, but with us, unlike the French, the specifics never remain as they were. The actors are constantly changed at our capital; plays, too. I am put in mind of my native District of Columbia and its turbulent club house, the Senate, by Patricia O'Toole's *The Five of Hearts,* by Joseph Alsop's various published reminiscences, by the two Henrys, Adams and James, neither ever very far from my thoughts. In *The Five of Hearts* O'Toole describes that eponymous coven of Henry and Clover Adams, of John and Clara Hay, of Clarence King, the five who, in 1882, came together in Washington as friends and so remained until the last died in 1918, their lives illuminated—indeed set ablaze—by Reflected Glory to which Hay, as secretary of state, gained some of the real thing; while Adams, by constantly saying that RG hurt his eyes, achieved a degree of True Glory not to mention all sorts of Last Words.

2.

In youth, one does not bother with one's own relatives much less their social and historical connections. Even so, although I was unaware at mid-century of the existence of an Annapolis-bound seventh cousin, who would one day achieve Glory as our thirty-ninth president, I was very much aware that my grandfather with whom I lived was Glory; and that my father, much newsreelized as the Director of Air Commerce and airlines-founder, was also Glory (most glorious, in my eyes and probably everyone else's, as an All-American football player at West Point). I was also aware that when I was transported at ten from the house of the Gores in Rock Creek Park to trans-Potomac

Merrywood, I had left Glory for Reflected Glory, and though Hughdie maintained a lavish, by Washington standards, household with five *white* servants,
it was very clear that Senator Gore and Gene Vidal were the people that everyone read and talked about as opposed to the army of shadowy Auchinclosses
and their equally dim to me (if not to Mr. Birmingham) connections up there
in dirty New York City and dull Newport, Rhode Island. Give me Rehoboth
Beach, Delaware, any day.

Although I, too, was RG, I knew from the start that I was out for Glory. So,
too, was Henry Adams at my age. But as grandson and great grandson of two
presidents, he was positively blinded at birth by RG; later, by settling in a house
opposite the White House, he was incessantly bombarded by RG waves. Unlike Adams, I got out at seventeen, and vowed that if I was not elected to anything, I would not come back to live in the capital when there were so many
other worlds and glories elsewhere. At seventeen, I enlisted in the army and,
Mr. Birmingham to the contrary, I was delighted to get my own life started
and be rid of all the RGs of Merrywood, whom Jack Kennedy, years later,
characterized to me as "the little foxes," a phrase taken from that perennial
favorite, *The Old Testament,* by Lillian Hellman.

In later years, Adams's friend and mine, President Theodore Roosevelt's
daughter, Alice Longworth, congratulated me every time we saw each other:
"You got out. So wise. It's a mistake to end up here, as a fixture. Like me. Like
Joe, " she added once, gazing with benign malice at her cousin, Joe Alsop,
across the room. When I was in my early teens, Joe had been a fat, bibulous
journalist in his twenties who often came to Merrywood, and several times
watched me as I played tennis with a schoolmate. Years later, when Joe was
involved with an Italo-American sailor, Frank Merlo (soon to enter RGdom's
all-time Hall of Fame as the inamorato of Tennessee Williams), he told me,
"Of course I know *all* about *The City and the Pillar.* The Who, and Where,
and the…What?" For the great majority that has since joined us, *The City
and the Pillar* was a "glorious" *roman* of the forties, whose *clef* was much
sought by interested parties.

As I read with some pleasure *The Five of Hearts* I was struck, as always, by
what a small world the American one was—and is. For Henry Adams at the
end of the last century, the country was "a long straggling caravan, stretching
loosely toward the prairies, its few score of leaders far in advance and its millions of immigrants, negroes, and Indians far in the rear, somewhere in archaic
time." Today there are more millions at the rear and a few score more leaders
but the ownership of the country is as highly concentrated as ever, and at the
capital of the country there are still ruling families, connected by politics and
marriage and bed. Like papal Rome, each old Washington family descended
from a president or senator who'd come to town and stayed. The Gores were
an aberration: in the eighteenth century much of that part of Maryland which

is now the District of Columbia had belonged to them before they moved west, buying up sequestered Indian lands. When Thomas Pryor Gore came to the Senate in 1907, he was actually returning to the family's original homestead; also, as a senator he was the Hearts' toga-ed enemy.

Twenty-five years earlier, Henry Adams had published anonymously the novel *Democracy*, whose villain was a powerful, corrupt United States Senator and whose protagonist, Madeleine Lee, was attracted to Glory, rather like the Five, but, unlike them, was horrified by "democracy" up close. In many ways, this novel is still one of the best about capitoline ways. Nevertheless, it was that energetic dilettante genius, Clarence King, who saw the flaw in Adams's rendering: "The real moral is that in a Democracy, *all* good, bad and indifferent is thrown in the circling eddy of political society and the person within the whole field of view who has the least perception, who most sadly flaunts her lack of instinct, her inability to judge of people without the labels of old society" was Adams' heroine. One rather wishes that King had got round to excelling at the popular novel as easily as Hay and Adams had. Certainly he had a better grasp of the whole than either Hay or Adams. Also, the gift of phrase. Of England, King wrote: "a big hopeless hell of common people to whom all doors are shut save the grave and America."

John Hay's problems with the Senate began when he first came to town as assistant to President Lincoln's secretary; later, as assistant secretary of state to President Harrison and, finally, most spectacularly, as secretary of state under William McKinley and Theodore Roosevelt, when he ceased to be entirely lunar and became solar—but a sun outshone by the national sun of that huge spotted star, TR, and bedazzled as well as tormented by the ninety competitive capitoline suns clustered at the wrong end of Pennsylvania Avenue. Unlike Henry Adams, Hay was Glory by the end; but he had had to pay for his distinction in a series of pitched battles with the Senate, specifically with the arrogant senator from Massachusetts, Henry Cabot Lodge (known as "Pinky"), a one-time protégé at Harvard of the then professor Henry Adams. Cabot, with his wife, Nannie, was practically a Heart himself; and this made the duels with Hay all the more bitter.

Hay had proved to be a marvelous manager of his wife's money, while Adams had inherited a fortune from his mother. As a result, they were able to build and share a joint "Neo-Agnostic" Romanesque building in Lafayette Park; here they maintained the most civilized pair of establishments in the city until...I suppose Mr. Birmingham would say Merrywood, which was not as unintellectual in the thirties and forties as it became later when the not-so-merry house in the Virginia woods was loud with girlish shrieks, slammed doors, the thud of great feminine feet on the stairs, and poor Hughdie's sighs. But then, even at its zenith, Merrywood's Reflected Glory was never much more than old limelight; certainly nothing was ever generated on the premises. There was no intelligence at the center, only a Meredithian heroine on temporary loan from the Senate.

The love-hate of Hearts for Senate took a powerful turn when widower Henry Adams became the lover—or "lover"—of the splendid Elizabeth Sherman Cameron, wife of Senator Don Cameron from Pennsylvania, while John Hay became the lover (without quotation marks) of the wife of his senatorial nemesis, Henry Cabot Lodge.

As a young journalist in Washington, Adams wrote, "To be abused by a senator is my highest ambition." With *Democracy,* the anonymous author was much abused by many senators, among them the suspected model for Senator Ratcliffe, James G. Blaine. On the other hand, by his love for Lizzie, Adams probably earned not the abuse but the complaisant admiration of the hard-drinking, sad senator from Pennsylvania. Certainly the triangle was a balanced one and gave Henry James the shivers—of excitement and total interest in the oddity, the sheer *American*-ness of it all.

◆ ◆ ◆

O'Toole strikes a balance between today's mindless prurience and what really matters (which once actually mattered to our mindful Protestant founders), the public life of the republic. Sex lives of the glorious and their reflectors are no more interesting in themselves than are those of the bamboozled masses that now crowd our alabaster cities and cover over with cement our fruited plains. In a society with a hereditary monarch the comings and goings of the night are duly noted for their effect upon Grace and Favor and the conduct of public affairs. But as the American oligarchy selects, at what often looks to be absentminded random, its office managers, the private lives of these public functionaries arouse no particular interest unless there is comedy in it.

On the other hand, the private lives of the actual rulers of the country are as out of bounds to American historians as they are to all of the other paid-for supporters of that oligarchy which controls the sources of information and instruction, that is, the "media" and Academe. What is fascinating *inter alia,* in any story of the Hearts, is that the reader, often quite unprepared, is placed at the heart of the oligarchy that he has been told all his life does not—indeed cannot—exist in a "democracy." Yet the whole point to the enchanting Five is that, by birth or design, they are central to the ruling class. As in England, promising plebes have always been absorbed into the oligarchy. Although a fortune is a necessity somewhere in a patrician family, the visible players on the national stage are either plebes for sale (McKinley, Reagan, or that hypergamous railway lawyer, Lincoln) or they are energetic members of the oligarchy who take to public life in the interests of their class: the Roosevelts, the Tafts, currently Mr. Bush of Kennebunkport, Texas. From time to time, regional oligarchies contribute to the national establishment—members of such old clans as the Byrds and the Gores, not to mention more recent combines like the Kennedys and the Longs. But as the First Gentleman of Entropy, Henry Adams, knew, all the clans wear out, usually more soon than late.

Of the Five, only Clarence King was doomed because he was merely brilliant as a geologist and talker. There was no King fortune. When he decided to make one, almost alone among his generation, he failed. The fact that he had secretly married a black nursemaid by whom he had a number of children was no help. The fact that King could not, like Hay, marry a fortune makes one suspect that for all his potency with dusky women of the lower class or exotic foreign primitives, he could not function sexually with women of his own class. This is a common condition too little explored in our democratic orgasm-for-all-the-folks self-help (often literally) books. It might explain Clover Adams's suicide and Henry's chaste passion for Lizzie Cameron not to mention the Virgin of Chartres.

The Five set up shop in Washington and there they remained, except for the peripatetic King. Pleased but not satisfied with the anonymous Glory of *Democracy*, Henry Adams settled in to write a history which was really autobiography, or at least family chronicle; but as he was subtle, he did not write of the administrations of the two Adams presidents—he wrote instead of their coevals and rivals, Jefferson and Monroe. Then, perversely, when he came to write a memoir, he was more historian than memoirist. In any case, Adams's writing is full of tension. To write of the deeds of others, though an act of a sort, is not *action* in the sense that Glory requires. He was permanently soured not so much by the risible republic or its imperial spin-off in whose ruins we have our dull being, but by his own inability to set foot on the national stage as had such sub-Hearts as the awful Theodore Roosevelt or the far worse "Pinky" Lodge. Even Hay was able to turn his great gift for flattering the glorious into high office.

In 1885 Clover abruptly killed herself; grief over her father's death was the official line. But somewhere in Adams's latest—last—novel, *Esther*, there are clues. The protagonist notes how "everything seems unreal" while, in real life, Clover says to her sister in that last year, "Ellen, I'm not real...Oh, make me real—you are all of you real!" Clover's death killed off Henry Adams. But his ghost continued to haunt Washington, where he never ceased to worship the beauteous Lizzie, nor act as sardonic chorus to the American empire, enjoying, all the while, the respectful love of those young women he liked to have about him, his "nieces," as he called them. Finally, he set himself up as a sort of marriage-broker between Virgin and Dynamo, faith and machine; but that match could not be made. Happily, there were Washington politics to delight in, and the Spanish American War, and an unruly campaign in the Pacific, and the First World War, when so many of his worst prophecies were confirmed. Next to "I win," "I told you so" are the sweetest words.

Meanwhile, Adams and Hay had the best seats to observe the national comedy. In their letters, they were so often to the witty point about the actors that two of the mummers struck back when Hay's letters were published posthumously. Theodore Roosevelt deplored Hay's "close intimacy with Henry James and Henry Adams—charming men but exceedingly undesirable companions for any man not of strong nature—and the tone of satirical cynicism which they admired...impaired his usefulness as a public man." TR then took full credit for everything that Hay had accomplished, while Lodge solemnly blamed Hay's problems with the Senate on Hay's bad-mouthing of that collective body. Meanly, Lodge even denied Hay's brilliance as a conversationalist, so reluctantly attested to by TR. Apparently, O. W. Holmes and J. R. Lowell were better at mealtime autocracy than Hay.

◆◆◆

Twenty years after the death of the last of the Adams Circle I can remember half-hearing their names spoken as if they were still contemporary in a city where office-holders are constantly changed but the oligarchy never. I thought of all this recently when I spoke on alumnus John Hay at Brown University, and saw in the audience John Hay's face, the current possession of a great-grandson who wears it almost as nicely as the original Johnny Hay, who was, according to Mark Twain, "a picture to look at, for beauty of feature, perfection of form, and grace of carriage and movement."

As I described Hay's career, I thought of my own mother's involvement with Hay's grandson, John Hay Whitney, known as Jock, while, simultaneously, my symmetrically inclined father was involved with Jock's wife, another Liz like Cameron. In fact, it was Liz Whitney who taught me how to ride in the Virginia hills during that far too short "long summer" before the Second War when my half-sister was born to grow up to marry Jock's first cousin, while summer's end—apotheosis, too—took place in 1939 when the King and Queen of England arrived in town and all of us Reflected Glory extras took to the streets and cheered them while our parents attended the garden party on the lawn at the British Embassy, presided over by the handsome, tactless Sir Ronald Lindsay, whose wife was Lizzie Cameron's niece, Elizabeth Hoyt, a small dark woman often at Merrywood that summer, where she did her best to influence the gathered magnates to come to England's side in a war that most Americans wanted to stay out of. My grandfather was an "isolationist" and so was I. In fact, I did my part so well as an America-Firster at school that, one night at Merrywood, Alice Longworth left the dinner party to come sit on my bed, and give me ammunition to use in her war against foreign entanglements in general and cousin Eleanor in particular.

Although the oligarchy occasionally splits on the no-turning-back issues, taking their positions to one side or the other of the Jefferson-Hamilton fault line that runs through our history when it is not, indeed, our only history, war has always united the oligarchy and it is then that their house-servants, the teachers and communicators, are set to work redecorating the American interior, removing old furniture like the Bill of Rights to the attic, or romanticizing England and demonizing Germany and Japan in those days, the Arab world in these. The First World War was largely a matter of the Hamiltonian oligarchs feeling their oats while the Jeffersonians fell glumly into line.

The Second War, a continuation of the First, hurtled us into the nuclear age as King—a harvest king as it turns out—of the Castle. But since so simpleminded a game cannot be so bloodily played by a serious people, our domestics have been hard at work trying to disguise what really happened. As a result, the American people now believe that the Second World War was fought by two teams. The bad team wanted to kill all the Jews, for reasons unknown; the good team was antigenocide and pro-Zion. As a veteran of that war and of the debates that led up to it, I can only say that the fate of the Jews had no more to do with American policy in 1941 than the ideals of democracy had to do with the First World War. Hitler's treatment of the Jews was not known to the American public when it was placed at war by the oligarchy in order to stop German expansionism in Europe and Japanese in Asia, a pointless enterprise since they have now superseded us anyway.

Henry Adams was the first to anticipate and articulate the realpolitik behind the wars: Germany, he said, was too small a power "to swing the club," and prevail. He predicted the division of the world between the United States and Russia, and as much as he disliked the English he never ceased to favor an "Atlantic Combine" from "the Rocky Mountains on the West" (could he have, presciently, already surrendered the California littoral to Japan?) "to the Elbe on the East."

3.

The short, superficial biography written to be read not taught is an agreeable English specialty. The practitioners are often ladies whose research is often adequate to their task, which to my mind is a most useful one: to tell people something about the interesting or still relevant dead. After all, no one not institutionalized is expected to read, as opposed to teach or quarry, Dumas Malone's six-volume life of Jefferson, but should anyone still at large actually read it, as I did, every page, he will know profound despair. There is no sign of intelligent life anywhere in an artifact comparable only to Gutzon Borgland's Dakota cliff. True, close readers will delight in the footnotes, the work of often inspired graduate students, but the actual dead lunar text exists not to be read but to be worshiped. So there is room for another kind of book between the charming but light *Five of Hearts* and Dumas Malone. Unfortunately, those few Americans who can make sense of history can't write while those who can write usually know nothing at all. For any sensible oligarch, this is a fine arrangement; and will never be altered as long as one American university stands, endowed.

The fact that Henry Adams was not only a gifted writer but a uniquely placed historian carries no particular weight in today's world, where a field is a field, as a book editor of yesteryear used to say, assigning for review the latest biography of Queen Elizabeth I to her last biographer, with predictable (either way) results. Honorably and gracefully, O'Toole covers her complex subject, but without much sense of what they—Adams, above all—were about. Here one must trust to a biography that is literature as well as good academic scholarship, Ernest Samuels's *Henry Adams*.

At times, one senses that O'Toole has not read with sufficient care or interest Adams's Jefferson-Madison volumes, without which the Adams literary character is not graspable; but she is Gibbonian when compared to her reviewer in the Sunday *New York Times,* an Englishwoman who is also known for writing light, readable books about complex figures. The reviewer's confusion about the United States in general and the Hearts in particular would have given joy to the Five, none of whom took very seriously the English who, even then, were turning into eccentric Norwegians as their once-glorious day waned. Although it is plain that the reviewer had never read or, perhaps, heard of any of the Five before she got the book to review, she pluckily strikes the notes that she thinks an American paper like the *New York Times* would want struck. She deplores but does not demonstrate the male sexism that drove Clover Adams to suicide and Clara Hay to fat; affects astonishment over Henry Adams's "anti-Semitism," as nothing compared to that of jolly *Private Eye,* which doubtless gives her a real giggle; even uses the word *zaftig* to show she knows what's what at the *Times*—rather like her ambitious compatriot, a novelist, who recently told an American interviewer that he might have been a much better writer had he been even slightly Jewish.

Genuflections to dumb Americans completed, she mounts her Norse horse. O'Toole has compared the Hearts to Bloomsbury. This is too much for the reviewer, who writes, for one thing, that the Hearts "had an emotional gaucheness that has no counterpart in the England of the 19th century....Bloomsbury would not have gone in for those enameled Five of Hearts pins, worn as the badge of friendship. Virginia Woolf would not have been caught dead using their heart-embossed paper on which the Five wrote their sentimental missives." None of this is true, of course. There were no pins. The notepaper with the hearts was the joke of a season. There were no sentimental missives. There was a tragedy when Clover killed herself and Adams lost his world; when Hay's son died and he shattered. Otherwise, there were splendid, ironic "missives" full of splendid jokes.

Humor is more definitive of a class than anything else. The English instinctively grade humor on class lines, and the one who fails to get the joke gets a one-way ticket back to where he came from. If nothing else, Bloomsbury knew its place: at the very top of the educated middle class. They aspired no higher, and if they had it would have done no good. (Maynard Keynes was the exception, and much resented by the Woolf-pack.) Certainly, they would never have had access to the Hearts, who were too high above them, except for the Hearts' "cousin," Henry James, who lived close by, and since he treated them sweetly, they called him "Master," and not always with the humorous quotation marks.

The point to the Five is that they were far more civilized than their American, much less English, contemporaries. They cannot be compared, finally, to Bloomsbury because, reflected or true glory, they were ruling class, while the Bloomsburyites were simply educated, powerless, middle-class folk who, like Mrs. Dalloway, came all over queer when a great one drove by, pearl-gray kid-gloved hand visible at a back-seat window. American grandees have always mystified the English with their easy manners. They treat Bloomsburyites or taxi drivers as if they were equals, but it would have to be an uncharacteristically dull Bloomsburyite to remain unguarded, if not uncovered, in such a presence.

True aristos as well as idle artists, the Hearts did not take seriously the busyness of the contemporary arts, particularly as commodities. They preferred works of the past; they trafficked with Berenson. The reviewer displays a true Norse envy when Hay hangs a Botticelli on his wall. She has also found a target. This is a "book about things: the acquisition of the marvelous art objects with which the friends stuffed their houses," and about "dependence on possessions and buildings as a source of inspiration and shame, almost a substitute for spiritual life."

Norwegians like to talk about spiritual life which, in Bloomsbury, meant Friendship, as the Hearts perfectly exemplified. Although they could afford pictures that Virginia and Leonard and Vanessa and Quentin and poor Lytton could not, their interests were not in possessions but in each other and their common, curious nation, whose history they not only recorded but helped direct, in office like Hay; in the study, as historian, like Adams; or in the drawing rooms of Clara and Clover.

O'Toole is perhaps wise to deal as superficially as she does with the intellectual life of her characters because it is hard to dramatize something that does not exist for today's uncommon, alas, reader, or someone like the *Times* reviewer who thinks that the Hearts wrote "sentimental" letters to each other when their letters are mostly sharp and shrewd and engaged in the world in a way quite alien to sentimentalists. She finds a lack of spiritual life (can she be born-again?) in Henry Adams, whose last decades were spent in profound spiritual meditation upon the Virgin. But then she cannot have read *Mont Saint-Michel and Chartres* or even *The Education of Henry Adams.*

The Hearts, she tells us, "lived on a knife edge between taste and tasteless-ness." Proof? Poor Clara Hay tried to wear a too-tight wedding dress at her wedding anniversary. But the English mind (to the extent that one can say such a thing exists, Henry Adams mutters in my ear) needs desperately to believe that its American masters are emotionally gauche yet elitist and snobbish, buyers-up of old culture to stuff houses with. When it comes to getting things wrong, the English are born masters. In fact, I was once so impressed by their inability to sort things out that I used Madame Verdurin as a prototype for today's book-chatterers, only to find myself defeated yet again: they hadn't heard of Madame Verdurin either.

4.

Today literature enjoys a certain prestige in the First World, and much is made of successful writers in the press and in the schools. It is salutary to find that neither Adams nor Hay took writing, as such, very seriously. Hay was one of the most popular light-verse writers of his day, and his life of Lincoln, with John Nicolay, was—well, as monumental as a Dakota mountain. But, pseudo-nymously, inspired by Henry Adams, Hay wrote a novel called *The Bread-winners* which was a huge success with both general public and reactionary critics.

As so many of today's celebrities and journalists seem to be born knowing, it is a very easy thing to write a popular novel if one has an exploitable name. But even today it is hard, if not impossible, to reach a wide audience with no name at all, as anonymous John Hay and Henry Adams did. But then the ease with which these two, and Clarence King, too, wrote so very well makes one suspect that education might actually play a part in a process we are taught to think of as charismatic—*creative* writing as a silver spring that gushes miraculously from the psyche's mud. Perhaps if one has learned to speak well, one can probably think well, too, and if one can then coordinate thought and speech one might be able to write it all down in a way that is agreeable for others to read. But I am sure that this is far too simple; in any case, *high* art, even for them, was elsewhere, and they revered their honorary Heart, Henry James, who had chosen to settle in backward England for reasons which they could never appreciate, though Clover Adams thought he'd be better off running a hog ranch in Wyoming. Hog ranch is bad enough, but what Clover really meant was even worse; that is, better: "hog ranch" was period slang for a whore house.

Henry James was very conscious that he had got out and that the Hearts, particularly Clover, were not entirely approving. Yet with them, as with so many American grandees of the period, Europe was just a pleasanter extension of their usual life; and far less foreign than Wyoming. It has often been noted (and never explained) why so many American writers who could get out of the great republic did so and how even those most deeply identified with the republic and its folkways—Mark Twain, Bret Harte, Stephen Crane—all managed to put in quite a lot of time on the other side of the Atlantic. *Douceur de la vie* was one reason. Also, God was doing well, extremely well, altogether too well in the last great hope on earth, while in Europe He was giving ground, if not to reason's age, to societies more interested in cohesive social form than Final Answers to All Questions. Edith Wharton believed that everything published in the States must first be made acceptable to an imaginary Protestant divine in Mississippi—probably named Gore.

In 1882, Henry James made the mistake of confiding to Clover his feeling for their native land, an emotion which had not much love in it. He was also tactless enough to regard her as America incarnate; to which her sharp response: "Am I then vulgar, dreary and impossible to live with?" But James's eye was never so cold and penetrating as when it was turned upon those he loved, and he did coolly love the Hearts if not the Republic for which they sometimes stood. From his not-yet-Norwegian outpost in the North Sea and its still splendid world metropolis, London, he could generalize of things American—of Adamses, too. "I believe that Washington is the place in the world where money—or the absence of it, matters least," he wrote Sir John Clark. As for the Adamses, "They don't pretend to conceal (as why *should* they?) their preference of America to Europe, and they rather rub it into me, as they think it is a wholesome discipline for my demoralized spirit. One excellent reason for their liking Washington better than London is that they are, vulgarly speaking, 'someone' here, and they are nothing in your complicated kingdom." This was written in the last days of our austere, deliberately unprecedented republic. Then, in 1898, the American empire emerged with eagle-like cries (not least a mournful chirp or two from James), and in that year John Hay was recalled as ambassador from London to take over the State Department as well as such new imperial acquisitions as the Philippines. During this time of glory, Hay was aided and abetted by the English magnates; and subsequent visits to London were state affairs for the Hays, who were, most vulgarly, "someone" in the complicated, declining Kingdom; for Henry Adams, too, if he chose. But he chose not to be someone, even though the raffish Prince of Wales as well as that ultimate someone, Gladstone, had admired *Democracy*.

Adams lived long enough to attend the birth of what he had conceived as "The Atlantic Combine," the bringing together of the United States and England, with the old country as the junior partner. When England ran out of money in 1914, the wooing of America began in earnest. Before, the British had encouraged their "cousins" to acquire a Pacific empire in order to contain the Russians, the Germans, and the Japanese. The Hearts, particularly Hay, played a great part in the making of this new alliance with a series of arrangements and treaties that culminated in the Hay-Pauncefote Treaty. Ironically, an adverb which sometimes does duty in these lives for "inevitably," Hay's principal antagonist in the Senate—England's, too—was Henry Cabot Lodge. Did Lodge know that Hay had so elaborately antlered him? O'Toole thinks not. But I think that he did on the ground that totally self-absorbed men, dedicated to their own glory, notice anything and everything that impinges on them.

Henry Adams records an edgy scene between the two when Lodge told Hay that he wished that he "would not look so exceedingly tired when approached on business at the department." It was Adams's view that the worn-out Hay had been "murdered" by Lodge and his senatorial allies. Certainly, after Hay's death, there was little traffic between Adams and Lodge, much less with the great presidential noise across the park. The comedy was grim, Adams wrote Lizzie Cameron. Of himself and the bereft mistress, Nannie, he observed, "We keep up a sort of mask-play together, each knowing the other to the ground. She kept it up with Hay for years to the end." Then Nannie, too, was dead and Lizzie settled in Paris, besotted by the young American poet Trumbull Stickney (friend of Cabot Lodge's poet son, Bay), whom I dutifully read at school because my favorite teacher was writing a dissertation on his work.

5.

Not long ago, I paid my last visit to Joe Alsop. As always, I telephoned and asked him, yet again, for his address in Georgetown. He gave me, yet again, the numbers and the street, "N Street, 'N' as in Nellie," he thundered. The new house was smaller than the one of his heyday; but, as ever, he was comfortably looked after by friends. I found him rather too small for my taste. The body had begun its terminal telescoping. But the brain was functioning and the large face was a healthy puce, like the brick of a Georgetown house, and the huge clown glasses magnified eyes only slightly dulled by a lifetime's reflection of (more of than on) Glory. Nevertheless, Joe was seriously unraveling and we knew that we were meeting, somewhat self-consciously, for the last time. With loved ones, this can be painful, or so the world likes to pretend, but with a lifelong acquaintance, the *envoi* can be rather fun, particularly if you are dying at a slower rate than the other.

As always, Joe was for war anywhere any time in order to "maintain the balance of power." He had used this phrase so long that no one had any idea what—or whose—power was to be balanced. I was for the minding of our own business. He sounded like his great uncle; I sounded like my grandfather. So much for development in political attitudes or increased wisdom among the subsequent generations. As always, we played roles for each other. I was Henry James, returning to the collapsing empire from wicked, thriving Europe, and Joe was Henry Adams, weary with absolute wisdom. We gossiped: this was Washington, after all, Henry James's "city of conversation."

Joe told me how he had made up with cousin Eleanor Roosevelt, the only presidential widow ever to matter, to those who matter, that is. He had spent several decades attacking her dreadful husband and mocking her nobility of character and Sapphic tendencies; but there had been a sea-change before she died, and he spoke with affection of having seen her. I doubt if the affection had been returned. "I forgive," she once said to me, small gray eyes like hard agate, "but I never forget." Joe had been part of the Alice Longworth circle of TR devotees and FDR disdainers, and their wit was murderous, and Eleanor a preordained victim. But she had her own murderous quality, which Joe caught nicely in the *New York Review of Books*, when he likened her sweet nursery school teacher manner to that of his "Auntie Bye" who "had a tongue that could take the paint off a barn, meanwhile sounding quite unusually syrupy and cooing."

Joe was writing his memoirs and so unusually reflective of the past. I was undergoing the attentions of a biographer and in a most uncharacteristically down-memory-lane mood. He remarked that my father was the handsomest man he ever saw, adding, "A colonel, wasn't he?" I took the trick with: "No, a first lieutenant when he left the army." In Washington the military have no status at all. To old Washington, a "colonel" suggests someone lodged in a boarding house in E Street, with a letter to a senator as yet unacknowledged; while generals and admirals are not invited out anywhere except when they are hypergamous, as Robert McAlmon (in *Village*) notes bitterly of my father's marriage with the wealthy daughter of a United States Congressman, giving "him enough of a start so that he would become quite a figure in the army some day." But my father's wife was not wealthy, and he became quite a figure in civil aviation. Still, he was forever a colonel to Joe, while I always referred to Joe's admiral-grandfather as, "Wasn't he something in the *regular* Navy?"

We spoke of the days of our youth and just before. He was convinced that Franklin Roosevelt could never have had an affair with the Roman Catholic Lucy Mercer *before* she had married someone else. Afterward, when she was no longer virgin, she could then commit adultery with an absolvable conscience. We discussed Henry Adams's special status in the city, which Joe had somewhat taken on. Adams never left his card with anyone, something unheard of in those days. He also never invited anyone to his daily breakfasts. The right people (those who were interesting), somehow, turned up. In later life, he almost never went out to other people's houses, including the white one across the road; *they* came to him. I recalled Eleanor's approving comment that though he would not come *into* her house when he took his drive, he insisted that the children come out and get in his carriage for a roughhouse.

Joe and I stayed pretty much away from the subject of Jack Kennedy, since amongst the chroniclers of our time, Joe was chief mourner, even widow. I did remember the amusement that "the old thing" aroused in Jack's vigorous breast, and I was present when someone said that Joe was getting restive, and it was time to have him over for lunch and "hold his head," an odd expression.

Joe shared with me a liking for the English that one could—how to put it without awakening shrieks of "elitist snob" from both sides of the irradiated Atlantic?—"relate to" combined with no particular liking for the fallen big sister nation. But then as the Hay-Adams generation marked the beginning of our national primacy in the world, our generation marked the actual mastery of the whole works, and our disdain for those who had preceded us was unkind to say the least. Once, at Hyannisport, the thirty-fifth president was brooding on the why and the what of great men; he thought, not originally, that great political figures were more the result of the times in which they lived and not so much of character or "genius." I mentioned Churchill as a possible exception. Jack's response was worthy of Joe, his father: "That old drunk! How could he lose? He always knew we were there to bail him out!"

◆ ◆ ◆

In the fragment of memoir that Alsop has so far published, he did do a bit of a Henry Adams number when he diffidently told us how "the WASP ascendancy," to which he belonged, was at an end, and that he himself spoke now as an irrelevant relic of a quaint past when Washington was, in James's phrase, "a Negro village liberally sprinkled with whites," and one wore so very many clothes and changed them so often in a day. But Joe was putting on an act. He knew that the WASP ascendancy is as powerful as it ever was. How could it not be? They still own the banks. Head for head, they may be nearly outnumbered by Roman Catholics at the polls and by Jews in show biz and the press, but they still own the country, which they now govern through such non-WASP employees as Henry Kissinger, or through insignificant members of the family, like George Bush, who are given untaxing jobs in government.

Joe did manage to take a gentle swipe at cousin Eleanor, reminding us that in the old days "Eleanor Roosevelt was not only anti-Semitic, which she later honorably overcame" (like kleptomania?), "she was also quite obstinately anti-Catholic, which she remained until the end of her days." This is disingenuous, to say the least. Like everyone else, Eleanor was many people, not one. But the most important of her personae was that of politician, and no politician is going to be anti *any* minority if he can help it; unless, of course, his constituency requires that he make war on a minority, as George Wallace, say, used to do on blacks and Ronald Reagan always did on the poor. Neither Jews nor Catholics nor blacks, *as such,* figured in Eleanor's private world, which was exclusive of just about everyone or, as she explained to her husband's political manager, Jim Farley, when he complained that he was never asked to private Roosevelt functions, "Franklin is not at ease with people not of his own class." She was the same as a private person. But as a public one, she was there for everyone; hence, her implacable war with the Roman Catholic hierarchy over federal aid to education, which came to a head when that rosy Urning, Cardinal Spellman, denounced her as an unnatural mother, and she turned him into a pillar of salt in her column.

I fear that our imitations of the two Henrys were not much good at my last meeting with Joe Alsop. For one thing, Henry James could not bear his native land and he had, most famously, given reasons (but not the right ones) why. On his last trip to Washington to see the other Henry, he wrote: "There is NO 'fascination' *whatever* in anything or anyone...." And he was worn out with "the perpetual effort of trying to do justice to what one doesn't like." I, of course, am fascinated by my native land and my only not-so-perpetual effort involves restraining myself from strangling at the dinner table those Washington oligarchs who have allowed the republic to become a "national security state" and then refused to hold their employees to account. "Why didn't you impeach Reagan over Iran-Contras?" I asked a very great personage, indeed, a press lord. "Oh, we couldn't! It would have been too soon. You know, after Nixon."

Joe was an absolute romantic, and differed from Henry Adams in that he thought of himself as a participant on the battlefield as a brave journalist, which he was, and in the high councils of state, where he liked to bustle about backstage to the amusement of the actors. As avatars, Joe and I were not much. But we had had a very good time, I thought, as I left the N Street house for the last time.

Happily, for Henry Adams, and all other Hearts, the problem of Glory did not persist after middle age, when acceptance, if not wisdom, traditionally begins. Of himself and friends, Adams wrote: "We never despised the world or its opinions, we only failed to find out its existence. The world, if it exists, feels in exactly the same way toward us, and cares not one straw whether we exist or not. Philosophy has never got beyond this point. There are but two schools; one turns the world into me; the other turns me into the world; and the result is the same." Finally, not they but their great friend, Henry James, united the reflection of glory with the thing itself in a life that was all art, and it is no accident that he should have worked the proposition through not only in his unconscious but in the imagination, the only world there is, finally, that is graspable, artful.

On James's death-bed, he became Napoleon Bonaparte, and in his last coherent but out-of-self raving spoke in the first person as the emperor who personified for the Hearts' century the ultimate worldly glory.

From James's last dictations:

> ...we hear the march of history, what is remaining to that essence of tragedy, the limp?...
>
> They pluck in their tens of handfuls of plumes from the imperial eagle...

The Bonapartes have a kind of bronze distinction that extends to their fingertips...

across the border
all the pieces
Individual Souls, great of... on which great perfections are If one does...

Later:

Tell them to follow, to be faithful, to take me seriously.

The secretary, Miss Bosanquet, wrote, after the end: "Several people who have seen the dead face are struck with the likeness to Napoleon which is certainly great." Thus, Glory and its Reflection had at last combined—not so much in death, where all things must, but in the precedent art and its true sanity.

Clio among the Old Folks

by Thomas Laqueur

EVERY FRIDAY AFTERNOON FOR THE past year or so I have been working as a volunteer at the Home for Jewish Parents. I have no special competence in geriatrics, nor have I any professional interest in problems of aging. The Home is attractively situated, the staff seems caring and attentive, the food is kosher and quite probably as good as in any institutional setting. I am thus not there as a reformer nor as one looking for the sort of revelations one encounters with such lugubrious regularity in accounts of old age homes. I volunteer primarily to schmooz: I usually give a short presentation on current affairs drawn from the week's issues in the *New York Times* and then I take three or four people on a drive through the Oakland hills, to the gardens of the President's house in Kensington, to Tilden Park—ending up at a restaurant or café for tea.

There is something eerie about meeting and talking with people born into the rich, thickly textured, and, to me, exotic culture of Polish or Russian or Egyptian Jewry, and now living all together in East Oakland. What kind of a world brings Abner Cohen, tailor, son of a tailor, born in a Ukranian village so long ago that he remembers as a teenager his misplaced optimism in the 1905 revolution, to 27th and Fruitvale? I knew, of course, about Jews leaving Russia to escape army service, about restrictions on where Jews could stay and so forth. But it seemed almost preternatural, as we were driving with the convertible top down through eucalyptus groves overlooking San Francisco Bay, to hear from Mr. Cohen how he had left home just after his *bar mitzvah* to go on the tramp, working for six months or so in this or that village or town; how he had been drafted into the army and simply walked away when his unit was transferred to Moscow (he wouldn't stay in a place that was off-limits to civilian Jews). He left Russia at an obscure border crossing in company with fifty other people. I asked about passports and he laughed, explaining that contractors paid border guards a few rubles for each person they didn't see walk past their posts. Then, via Breslau and Hamburg, Mr. Cohen ended up in Albany, New York, where a cousin lived. He worked there in his trade, put two sons through college, and, after brief stays in Tulsa, Los Angeles, and Burlingame, now lives with his wife at the Home for Jewish Parents.

There is an incongruous confluence of people there just off Fruitvale Avenue. On one afternoon I took with me on a drive the daughter of a minor Hungarian aristocrat (she is a convert to Roman Catholicism) and a man who had worked in the Lower East Side rag trade. She had memories of the "Bolshevik swine" who had fomented unrest in Hungary in 1919–1920, of the Princess Elizabeth on state visits to Budapest, and of her brother, who had been an Olympic medalist in fencing. He talked of having been purged from the American Communist Party for his anti-Khrushchev sentiments and of having been invited, through the good offices of the party's Maoist wing, to visit China, where he spent three years.

The third member of the group that day was the mother of one of my colleagues at the university, a woman who was staying in the Home for a few weeks to determine whether she might want to settle there permanently. She bravely resolved to remain to the end of her trial period but was counting the days until she could return to her home in the Midwest and to her car. She was the first of several who spoke of being able to drive as the sign of being a paid-up member of society, and conversely of losing one's license as the secular equivalent of excommunication. The Department of Motor Vehicles seems to guard the gates of old age, and I have been told by several of the loneliness, the loss of control, and finally the realization that they could not live "outside" that came with not being able to drive.

◆ ◆ ◆

Going to a place in which are congregated well over a hundred men and women, the youngest well into their eighth decade, makes one contemplate each week the meanings of old age and dying even if one finds such contemplations distasteful. Occasionally when someone has particular difficulties getting in or out of my car I hear a certain grim joke: "Don't get old," a ninety-three-year-old woman told me. "Oh, how might I avoid it?" "Die young." But I know she only half meant it, since she on other occasions had told me that she had had a good and rich life chicken farming, first around Los Angeles and then in Petaluma, where Yiddish-speaking socialist Jews flourished until around World War II. There have also been moments of the macabre. An obviously senile woman who shuffles around the corridors, inquiring where she is, confronted me one day as I was talking to the social director and asked me whether I would help her look down the hall for a place to die. "Not just now," I said, "I have to speak to Ada." "Bullshit," she quite rightly said, and walked away.

At first I was overwhelmed by the sheer physical presence of old age and bodily decrepitude. As I was shown around by the director of volunteers after my initial screening interview, I thought first of how the great preponderance of women in the Home testified pointedly to the demographic disabilities of my sex. All of these aged people, displayed (in the inimitable fashion of total institutions) around the periphery of a large, rather unattractively painted "solarium," had once been young. The lines from the York Cycle *Lazarus* kept coming to mind: "As I am," says Lazarus rising in his shroud from the grave, "so shall you be too. As you are, so was I once also."

This undifferentiated reaction soon gave way to a more nuanced, if not more profound, sensibility. The first-blush horror, the surprised incomprehension of Youth confronted by Death in Renaissance *danse macabre,* has never entirely left me, in part because death does seem very near when I visit the Home. Perhaps half of the people there are so incapacitated physically or mentally that they require skilled nursing care. Many are strapped in large, comfortable wheeled armchairs, not out of cruelty or neglect, but because they haven't the strength to remain upright alone. Others wander about with very little apparent comprehension of the world around them (though I feel somewhat uncomfortable with this sort of judgment). They seem, so many of them, waiting to die. There is no question that the cheery optimism one finds on posters in a "senior citizen center" (the very name is obscurantist)— claiming that "one is only as old as one thinks one is," that somehow culture can triumph over nature—is false. Nature always wins.

Generally the "residents" (the term by which those who live in the Home are called, one I usually associate with unsolicited laundry soap samples that come through the mail impersonally addressed to me by that title) are not tolerant of weakness in others, and want to keep as far away as possible from the sick or deranged. For a few weeks I took an old and quite senile woman from the nursing section to get ice cream at Fenton's, and I tried to get some of my regular riders to come along. It was an uphill struggle. My regulars were convinced that this woman, Rose, could really talk if she wanted to, and that her constant stutter was somehow willful and not the result of a stroke or other real infirmity. Rose had apparently been dumped at the home by her children, and saw or talked to no one but staff except on such occasions as a volunteer could be found to spend some time with her. She carried around a teddy bear that she treated with great affection, though this reversion to childhood won her no friends among her more fit fellow residents. My people don't want to go through the nursing wing on those occasions when we park at the back of the building; they would rather walk a bit further outside than see several score of their contemporaries in pitiable circumstances.

Being at the Home each week has brought me into more intimate contact with the triumphant power of bodily decay than I had hitherto been or would choose to be. But it has also taught me the great extent to which, within the bounds of biology, one accommodates to old age in ways determined by history—one's own and one's culture's. The Home itself is of course a historically specific response to what has come to be termed the "problem of aging." I have no illusions about the reputedly more humane ways in which other times and other societies have dealt with the old. In so-called traditional European society, old couples, widowers, and the far more common widows frequently lived on the fringes of society, kept alive by an often begrudging charity. Old people living with their families strove desperately to retain control of resources which the young coveted, all caught in a web of power, love, and greed.

Yet the large-scale isolation of the old is new. It seems fitting that the Home is on a hill, on a dead-end street, above a poor area of Oakland, bounded on the north by an elementary school (another relatively recent innovation for defining and isolating a particular age group). My impression is that everyone in the Home feels some sense of being removed from what is familiar and organically social, and being thrust into an alien, artificial community. Even very happy and strong people tell me how difficult it was to adjust.

◆ ◆ ◆

The residents in the ambulatory, self-care section seem to fall into two relatively distinct groups with respect to how they situate the Home in the course of their lives: there are those who view it as a less than ideal but nevertheless perfectly manageable solution to the problem of securing food, shelter, and companionship, and those who consider themselves there through some combination of ill fortune and trickery. I have no way of judging the truth of the stories I am told, but undoubtedly the unhappiest people at the Home are those who think they have somehow been manipulated, usually by their children, into being there—those who feel themselves "dumped."

In a good number of instances these are women who, quite probably, all their lives have felt themselves the passive bearers of someone else's destiny. Illness is usually the first episode of the story; depression follows. Then their children, so I am told, suggest that they might just visit for a while and stay in the Home until they feel better. Somehow the children get control of their property—a very old motif—and then the few weeks' recuperation becomes forever. The condo in Florida is sold, the apartment is dismantled, and without any decision on their parts they have become "residents" of an old age home. There are variations. Two men report that their wives, considerably younger than themselves, urged them to enter the home for recuperation and then would not have them back. In one case the husband's continued frailty gave the wife's claim that she could not care for him some plausibility. However, when a physician was finally found who advised stopping sixteen of the seventeen drugs the man in question was taking, and when this simple step markedly improved his health, her case weakened. My point is not that large numbers of the residents are in the Home as a result of knavery, but only that they regard themselves as being there through the ungenerous agency of others, and that their lives are embittered by these thoughts. Spleen and depression, even more than the weaknesses of the flesh, seem to be the minions of old age.

On the other hand, there are those who—or so it seems to me—have always controlled their lives hithertofore and who continue to control them in the Home. Theirs is an extraordinary vitality. My favorite person of this sort is Vicki. Her father owned tobacco factories in Aden, where she was born, though her family's roots were in Cairo, where she was educated. Vicki is one of the final generation of the great Egyptian Jewish community which nurtured Philo and Maimonides, and of which there are now only some few hundred left. My impression is that she grew up in considerable comfort in a polyglot household. In any case, she spoke Spanish and Arabic at home, learned French at one boarding school, English at another, and Italian by virtue of having an Italian girl as best friend. She subsequently learned Chinese in Shanghai.

Vicki has any number of good stories growing out of her linguistic virtuosity. One is how she avoided being cheated by an Arab taxi driver in Paris; after a long debate in French over the fare, he muttered some Arabic curse under his breath, which Vicki met with the appropriate riposte, also of course in Arabic. That saved her five francs and presumably embarrassed the driver. Another is of how she avoided spending a night alone in an Italian railway *couchet* with a Japanese businessman. It appears that after not very satisfactory discussions, more or less all in English, with the man and with the conductor, aimed at finding her a compartment with other women, she broke into Italian and made a histrionic pitch to the surprised trainman to the effect that he most certainly wouldn't let *his* wife spend a night with a strange man. She got a new compartment, proving once again how easy it is to regard someone who doesn't speak one's language as being outside the bounds of ordinary moral consideration.

But back to Aden. Vicki met and married a baker who supplied the British garrison in Aden. His business took a turn for the worse when Indian troops with their own culinary preferences replaced the Europeans and he was unable to satisfy the new market. For reasons that are not clear to me, he went off to Shanghai, where he got a job in a leather factory through the good offices of a former girlfriend of Vicki's father. There he lived in considerable poverty until Vicki and their two children joined him a year or so later. She was so shocked by the squalor of his existence that she fell ill, lapsed into a deep faint, and woke up in a clean white hospital room facing a doctor who proceeded to tell her that he could find nothing organically wrong with her. The doctor then questioned her for clues that might explain the sudden illness and she confessed that after the comforts of her father's house she did not think she could live in a tiny room, hot and dirty from the fumes of a laundry beneath.

I don't quite understand just how the doctor managed to help get her a job with the Singer sewing machine distributor. But over the course of years, Vicki's skills in embroidery and sewing, her business sense, and her charm led to a successful shop and school in the French Concession, catering primarily to prosperous Chinese ladies. She made enough money to move her family to more genteel surroundings, where they remained until they were interred (not for being Jews, but as British subjects) by the Japanese. German Jewish refugees in Shanghai kept her family's money and sent the food and clothing which got them through the war.

Then they came to San Francisco and Vicki took up with Singer sewing machines again, once more building up a successful business. She retired in her mid-seventies and lived alone until an illness forced her to move in for a time with her daughters. She found the dependency and the guilt at interfering with their lives insupportable, and asked to be admitted to the Home. She is in fact proud that she came of her own accord. She says she cried herself to sleep for months at having to share a room when she had previously had a whole house, live on the schedule of an institution when before her time had been her own. But she finds nothing odd about ending a life which began in Aden at 27th and Fruitvale, and seems expansively cheerful.

Vicki is in fact friends with a group of residents who have in an important way made the institution theirs. The toughest of this group is Gussie, who looks to be in her late seventies and is in fact ninety-four; her father was a clothing contractor for the army garrison in San Francisco's Presidio. She was in her late teens when the 1906 earthquake struck. I found out her age when I asked what her son did for a living and she replied that he was in his seventies and had been retired for almost ten years. Gussie has been in the Home for over six years and is very much in charge of her social space, though it belongs, according to the Home's rules, to the community. A nurse does her hair every day before breakfast because she refuses to come downstairs and eat until she looks presentable. This is not a normal nursing function. She controls very strictly who sits at her table or relaxes in her corner of the solarium. She has no tolerance of the "screwballs," as she terms those residents who have retained neither their mental faculties nor a sufficiently fastidious appearance to make them reasonable company for Gussie. She is intolerant even of her friends, but manages to be in command without being quarrelsome; she is clearly born to be in charge. There are some people I can cajole into doing things my way—usually the issue is whether I will keep the convertible top down—but with Gussie there is no use in trying. I can keep the top where I want but she will only go along if it's up. End of discussion.

◆ ◆ ◆

I like Vicki and Gussie in part because their psychically aggressive, somewhat impatient confrontation with old age is what I have come to expect from the lives of my mother and aunt. My mother, at seventy-eight, believes that if she continues to swim a mile a day, regularly carries forty-pound bags of bark for the dog's compound, and keeps up a frenetic schedule she will somehow, like the character in one of Calvino's Italian folktales, be able to outdistance death forever. My father's sister is in some ways still more to the point because her life, even more than my mother's, was made in struggle with the peculiar vagaries of our century. She died two years ago, in Austin, Texas, a few days before my daughter Hannah's birth, and though she was quite blind and in much pain the last five years of her life, and therefore complained a good deal, she seems to have faced illness and death with the same practical energy she had earlier directed at the other problems of life.

My Tante Elli grew up in Hamburg, very much the assimilated German Jew. She read Schopenhauer with my grandfather and kept the notebooks of their tutorials; she patriotically followed the progress of German troops and ships through the First World War. While her eldest sister went to Holland, and remained there to die as part of Hitler's plan, my aunt resolved just after the Nazis' coming to power that the only possible response was to keep as far from Germans as possible. She had earlier shown that same resolute heedlessness—for which I so admired her during my adolescence—when she left home in her late teens, cut her hair in the flapper style, and lived out of wedlock with her husband-to-be while she studied opera, sang in the cabaret to support herself, and traveled about in Berlin artistic circles.

In any case, Tante Elli left for Italy in 1934 to explore opportunities for life there; she ended up in Dubrovnik (I think through a man she met in Venice). She went back to Germany, collected her family, and proceeded to Yugoslavia, where she set up a restaurant, the site of which I visited when I met her there in 1971. Her adventures in Yugoslavia are a story too long to tell, but when the Germans finally invaded she managed, through the help of a Muslim headman in a small Herzogovenian village, to get her family to Albania, where they stood a better chance of being captured by the Italians than by the Germans. Succeeding in this strategy, she spent the war in an Italian concentration camp where she and other musicians supplemented their families' 900-calorie/day/person diet by staging operas for the guards and camp administrators. She also learned to knit (again in return for food) with an astounding speed, a skill from which I subsequently profited in the form of many ill-fitting but quite distinctive sweaters.

Upon liberation she and her husband worked as interpreters for the British Eighth Army. Then they migrated to the United States, where they set up a boarding house catering to foreign and eccentric students at the University of Texas; the actor Rip Torn was one of her boys. This was clearly not the sort of life one born to an *haute bourgeois* family in Wilhelmine, Germany, had been led to expect.

• • •

One of the strangest and to me most poignant aspects of the Home is that there a history has come to an end. It is a history about which, in my bones, I know almost nothing. My family is German Jewish of the most assimilationist persuasion, a family which would undoubtedly have found the nationalistic, "volkish" qualities of National Socialism appealing, had these not been based on a virulent anti-Semitism. My grandfather was a prominent member of a group called "German Citizens of Jewish Belief," a fervid patriot who apparently continued, during Weimar, to fly the imperial flag on national holidays. He died before Jewish holders of World War I decorations were forced to give them up.

My family believed, and I suspect continues to believe, that secular *bildung* is what makes the man and defines even the Jew's relation to society. My grandmother refused to flee Germany to join my mother and father in Istanbul until December 1939. In part, I am sure, this was because she was a woman of monumental emotional passivity, in part because there was always hope that things would get better. (My Tante Toni, her eldest daughter, refused to believe that the Germans would do to Jews in Holland what they were doing to them in the east until the very end. She died of typhus on the way to Treblinka.) But my grandmother claimed that it was largely her Bechstein that kept her in Hamburg. She neither knew, nor would have appreciated the irony, that Adolph Bechstein, who manufactured those wonderful grand pianos, was, along with Krupp and Thysen, one of the earliest industrial backers of the Nazis.

There are very few German Jews at the Home—only one that I know at all well, and she is unregenerately German. During one drive, when the others were attacking her countrymen for having perpetrated the murder of millions of Jews, she said, "Yes, true, but it wasn't the intellectuals." I pointed out that the SS had carefully preserved, in the midst of Buchenwald, the oak under which Goethe had sat and that, on a more mundane level, intellectuals were over-represented in Nazi electoral support. But these observations had no resonance for her.

The world of the Home is that of the Pale, of the *shtetl,* of Pinsk, of Odessa, and of the villages and cities of what are now Rumania and Hungary. The so-called Holocaust is not the central event of the residents' lives; in fact, the Home had a remembrance day at which I was asked, but declined, to give a brief historical account of how the six million died. I thought it presumptuous at the time to be telling them about these events, but in fact they seem to know relatively little about it. Their world is that of the pogroms of the late nineteenth and early twentieth centuries, of the Russian revolution and its aftermath. It is the world of Yiddish culture and Talmudic learning. Though most speak the national languages of their birthplaces, Yiddish (or Jewish, as they usually call it) is literally their mother tongue. Theirs was a world in which the center of learning was not the Konigsberg of Kant or the Weimar of Goethe, but the rabbinical center of Vilna.

When I ask my friends what their fathers did for a living, a remarkable number answer that their fathers did nothing, that they were scholars. Their mothers either had family money or, more usually, worked in a dry goods or grocery or some other kind of retail store to feed and clothe the children and maintain the man of the house in his studies. In a few cases the father seems to have run what might pass for a school, prepping boys for rabbinical studies or *bar mitzvahs*. But my impression is that most were what are called *yeshiva buchers,* men devoted to Talmudic studies. The grandchildren of these men are prosperous merchants in Burlingame, gynecologists in San Francisco, or the like. Their daughters go for drives with me on Fridays.

I try to resist having an overly romantic view of the world we have lost. In the first place, I of course hear stories of pogroms. One woman's grandfather, as she told me, was stupid enough to run out of his store after a major pogrom and shout a curse at the retreating hordes; he was stabbed to death on the street for his indiscretion. I also hear a great deal about poverty, though many of the people in the Home testify to the prosperity of at least a minority of Eastern European Jews. The father of one woman, a tobacco planter in what is now Rumania, sent her via first class to see America; she never returned. Another father was a timber merchant whose servants brought kosher food from the family house to where he was supervising work.

Though a gentle sadness—born no doubt in part of ill-informed nostalgia—informs my vision of the world now coming to an end in places like the Home for Jewish Parents, I also get a certain voyeuristic pleasure from my encounters with it. Perhaps part of the professional emotional equipment of the historian is a certain yearning for intimacy with the past, a desire usually satisfied only through old books or, better yet, manuscripts not originally intended for public view. I like the idea of having tea with a woman who can still work up her indignation against Samuel Gompers and the snobs of the AFL. Gompers, she tells me, offered precious little help when she went in 1911 to ask for assistance with a garment workers' strike; the miners of western Pennsylvania were far more forthcoming. I find it both poignant and reassuring to drive through Tilden Park with four old people who had all reached their majority before, in August 1914, "the lights went out all over Europe." They discuss amongst each other whether before World War I our civilization seemed more secure than it does today. And I take heart in their having survived more than eight decades of the most difficult of centuries.

Mother Tongue

by Amy Tan

I AM NOT A SCHOLAR OF English or literature. I cannot give you much more than personal opinions on the English language and its variations in this country or others.

I am a writer. And by that definition, I am someone who has always loved language. I am fascinated by language in daily life. I spend a great deal of my time thinking about the power of language—the way it can evoke an emotion, a visual image, a complex idea, or a simple truth. Language is the tool of my trade. And I use them all—all the Englishes I grew up with.

Recently, I was made keenly aware of the different Englishes I do use. I was giving a talk to a large group of people, the same talk I had already given to half a dozen other groups. The nature of the talk was about my writing, my life, and my book, *The Joy Luck Club*. The talk was going along well enough, until I remembered one major difference that made the whole talk sound wrong. My mother was in the room. And it was perhaps the first time she had heard me give a lengthy speech—using the kind of English I have never used with her. I was saying things like, "The intersection of memory upon imagination" and "There is an aspect of my fiction that relates to thus-and-thus"— a speech filled with carefully wrought grammatical phrases, burdened, it suddenly seemed to me, with nominalized forms, past perfect tenses, conditional phrases—all the forms of standard English that I had learned in school and through books, the forms of English I did not use at home with my mother.

Just last week, I was walking down the street with my mother, and I again found myself conscious of the English I was using, the English I do use with her. We were talking about the price of new and used furniture and I heard myself saying this: "Not waste money that way." My husband was with us as well, and he didn't notice any switch in my English. And then I realized why. It's because over the twenty years we've been together I've often used that same kind of English with him, and sometimes he even uses it with me. It has become our language of intimacy, a different sort of English that relates to family talk, the language I grew up with.

So you'll have some idea of what this family talk I heard sounds like, I'll quote what my mother said during a recent conversation which I videotaped and then transcribed. During this conversation, my mother was talking about a political gangster in Shanghai who had the same last name as her family's, Du, and how the gangster in his early years wanted to be adopted by her family, which was rich by comparison. Later, the gangster became more powerful, far richer than my mother's family, and one day showed up at my mother's wedding to pay his respects. Here's what she said in part:

"Du Yusong having business like fruit stand. Like off the street kind. He is Du like Du Zong—but not Tsung-ming Island people. The local people call putong, the river east side, he belong to that side local people. That man want to ask Du Zong father take him in like become own family. Du Zong father wasn't look down on him, but didn't take seriously, until that man big like become a mafia. Now important person, very hard to inviting him. Chinese way, came only to show respect, don't stay for dinner. Respect for making big celebration, he shows up. Mean gives lots of respect. Chinese custom. Chinese social life that way. If too important won't have to stay too long. He come to my wedding. I didn't see, I heard it. I gone to boy's side, they have YMCA dinner. Chinese age I was nineteen."

You should know that my mother's expressive command of English belies how much she actually understands. She reads the *Forbes* report, listens to "Wall Street Week," converses daily with her stockbroker, reads all of Shirley MacLaine's books with ease—all kinds of things I can't begin to understand. Yet some of my friends tell me they understand fifty percent of what my mother says. Some say they understand eighty to ninety percent. Some say they understand none of it, as if she were speaking pure Chinese. But to me, my mother's English is perfectly clear, perfectly natural. It's my mother tongue. Her language, as I hear it, is vivid, direct, full of observation and imagery. That was the language that helped shape the way I saw things, expressed things, made sense of the world.

◆ ◆ ◆

Lately, I've been giving more thought to the kind of English my mother speaks. Like others, I have described it to people as "broken" or "fractured" English. But I wince when I say that. It has always bothered me that I can think of no way to describe it other than "broken," as if it were damaged and needed to be fixed, as if it lacked a certain wholeness and soundness. I've heard other terms used, "limited English," for example. But they seem just as bad, as if everything is limited, including people's perception of the limited English speaker.

I know this for a fact, because when I was growing up, my mother's "limited" English limited *my* perception of her. I was ashamed of her English. I believed that her English reflected the quality of what she had to say. That is, because she expressed them imperfectly her thoughts were imperfect. And I had plenty of empirical evidence to support me: the fact that people in department stores, at banks, and at restaurants did not take her seriously, did not give her good service, pretended not to understand her, or even acted as if they did not hear her.

My mother has long realized the limitations of her English as well. When I was fifteen, she used to have me call people on the phone to pretend I was she. In this guise, I was forced to ask for information or even to complain and yell at people who had been rude to her. One time it was a call to her stockbroker in New York. She had cashed out her small portfolio and it just so happened we were going to go to New York the next week, our very first trip outside California. I had to get on the phone and say in an adolescent voice that was not very convincing, "This is Mrs. Tan."

And my mother was standing in the back whispering loudly, "Why he don't send me check, already two weeks late. So mad he lie to me, losing me money."

And then I said in perfect English, "Yes, I'm getting rather concerned. You had agreed to send the check two weeks ago, but it hasn't arrived."

Then she began to talk more loudly, "What he want, I come to New York tell him front of his boss, you cheating me?" And I was trying to calm her down, make her be quiet, while telling the stockbroker, "I can't tolerate any more excuses. If I don't receive the check immediately, I am going to have to speak to your manager when I'm in New York next week." And sure enough, the following week there we were in front of this astonished stockbroker, and I was sitting there red-faced and quiet, and my mother, the real Mrs. Tan, was shouting at his boss in her impeccable broken English.

We used a similar routine just five days ago, for a situation that was far less humorous. My mother had gone to the hospital for an appointment, to find out about a benign brain tumor a CAT scan had revealed a month ago. She said she had spoken very good English, her best English, no mistakes. Still, she said, the hospital did not apologize when they said they had lost the CAT scan and she had come for nothing. She said they did not seem to have any sympathy when she told them she was anxious to know the exact diagnosis since her husband and son had both died of brain tumors. She said they would not give her any more information until the next time and she would have to make another appointment for that. So she said she would not leave until the doctor called her daughter. She wouldn't budge. And when the doctor finally called her daughter, me, who spoke in perfect English—lo and behold—we had assurances the CAT scan would be found, promises that a conference call on Monday would be held, and apologies for any suffering my mother had gone through for a most regrettable mistake.

I think my mother's English almost had an effect on limiting my possibilities in life as well. Sociologists and linguists probably will tell you that a person's developing language skills are more influenced by peers. But I do think that the language spoken in the family, especially in immigrant families which are more insular, plays a large role in shaping the language of the child. And I believe that it affected my results on achievement tests, IQ tests, and the SAT. While my English skills were never judged as poor, compared to math, English could not be considered my strong suit. In grade school, I did moderately well, getting perhaps Bs, sometimes B+s in English, and scoring perhaps in the sixtieth or seventieth percentile on achievement tests. But those scores were not good enough to override the opinion that my true abilities lay in math and science, because in those areas I achieved As and scored in the ninetieth percentile or higher.

This was understandable. Math is precise; there is only one correct answer. Whereas, for me at least, the answers on English tests were always a judgment call, a matter of opinion and personal experience. Those tests were constructed around items like fill-in-the blank sentence completion, such as "Even though Tom was _____, Mary thought he was _____." And the correct answer always seemed to be the most bland combinations of thoughts, for example, "Even though Tom was shy, Mary thought he was charming," with the grammatical structure "even though" limiting the correct answer to some sort of semantic opposites, so you wouldn't get answers like, "Even though Tom was foolish, Mary thought he was ridiculous." Well, according to my mother, there were very few limitations as to what Tom could have been, and what Mary might have thought of him. So I never did well on tests like that.

The same was true with word analogies, pairs of words, in which you were supposed to find some sort of logical, semantic relationship—for example, "sunset" is to "nightfall" as _____ is to _____. And here, you would be presented with a list of four possible pairs, one of which showed the same kind of relationship: "red" is to "stoplight," "bus" is to "arrival," "chills" is to "fever," "yawn" is to "boring." Well, I could never think that way. I knew what the tests were asking, but I could not block out of my mind the images already created by the first pair, "sunset is to nightfall"—and I would see a burst of colors against a darkening sky, the moon rising, the lowering of a curtain of stars. And all the other pairs of words—red, bus, stoplight, boring— just threw up a mass of confusing images, making it impossible for me to sort out something as logical as saying: "A sunset precedes nightfall" is the same as "A chill precedes a fever." The only way I would have gotten that answer right would have been to imagine an associative situation, for example, my being disobedient and staying out past sunset, catching a chill at night, which turns into feverish pneumonia as punishment, which indeed did happen to me.

♦ ♦ ♦

I have been thinking about all this lately, about my mother's English, about achievement tests. Because lately I've been asked, as a writer, why there are not more Asian-Americans represented in American literature. Why are there few Asian-Americans enrolled in creative writing programs? Why do so many Chinese students go into engineering? Well, these are broad sociological questions I can't begin to answer. But I have noticed in surveys—in fact, just last week—that Asian students, as a whole, always do significantly better on math achievement tests than in English. And this makes me think that there are other Asian-American students whose English spoken in the home might also be described as "broken" or "limited." And perhaps they also have teachers who are steering them away from writing and into math and science, which is what happened to me.

Fortunately, I happen to be rebellious in nature, and enjoy the challenge of disproving assumptions made about me. I became an English major my first year in college after being enrolled as premed. I started writing nonfiction as a freelancer the week after I was told by my former boss that writing was my worst skill and I should hone my talents toward account management.

But it wasn't until 1985 that I finally began to write fiction. And at first I wrote using what I thought to be wittily crafted sentences, sentences that would finally prove I had mastery over the English language. Here's an example from the first draft of a story that later made its way into *The Joy Luck Club,* but without this line: "That was my mental quandary in its nascent state." A terrible line, which I can barely pronounce.

Fortunately, for reasons I won't get into today, I later decided I should envision a reader for the stories I would write. And the reader I decided upon was my mother, because these were stories about mothers. So with this reader in mind—and in fact, she did read my early drafts—I began to write stories using all the Englishes I grew up with: the English I spoke to my mother, which for lack of a better term, might be described as "simple"; the English she used with me, which for lack of a better term might be described as "broken"; my translation of her Chinese, which could certainly be described as "watered down"; and what I imagined to be her translation of her Chinese if she could speak in perfect English, her internal language, and for that I sought to preserve the essence, but not either an English or a Chinese structure. I wanted to capture what language ability tests can never reveal: her intent, her passion, her imagery, the rhythms of her speech and the nature of her thoughts.

Apart from what any critic had to say about my writing, I knew I had succeeded where it counted when my mother finished reading my book, and gave me her verdict: "So easy to read."

Chang

by Sigrid Nunez

THE FIRST TIME I EVER heard my father speak Chinese was at Coney Island. I don't remember how old I was then, but I must have been very young. It was in the early days, when we still went on family outings. We were walking along the boardwalk when we ran into the four Chinese men. My mother told the story often, as if she thought we'd forgotten. "You kids didn't know them and neither did I. They were friends of your father's, from Chinatown. You'd never heard Chinese before. You didn't know what was up. You stood there with your mouths hanging open—I had to laugh. 'Why are they singing? Why is Daddy singing?'"

I remember a little more about that day. One of the men gave each of my sisters and me a dollar bill. I cashed mine into dimes and set out to win a goldfish. A dime bought you three chances to toss a ping-pong ball into one of many small fishbowls, each holding a quivering tangerine-colored fish. Overexcited, I threw recklessly, again and again. When all the dimes were gone I ran back to the grownups in tears. The man who had given me the dollar tried to give me another, but my parents wouldn't allow it. He pressed the bag of peanuts he had been eating into my hands and said I could have them all.

I never saw any of those men again or heard anything about them. They were the only friends of my father's that I would ever meet. I would hear him speak Chinese again, but very seldom. In Chinese restaurants, occasionally on the telephone, once or twice in his sleep, and in the hospital when he was dying.

So it was true, then. He really was Chinese. Up until that day I had not quite believed it.

◆ ◆ ◆

My mother always said that he had sailed to America on a boat. He took a slow boat from China, was what she used to say, laughing. I wasn't sure whether she was serious, and if she was, why coming from China was such a funny thing.

A slow boat from China. In time I learned that he was born not in China but in Panama. No wonder I only half believed he was Chinese. He was only half Chinese.

◆ ◆ ◆

The facts I know about his life are incredibly, unbearably few. Although we shared the same house for eighteen years, we had little else in common. We had no culture in common. It is only a slight exaggeration to say that we had no language in common. By the time I was born my father had lived almost thirty years in America, but to hear him speak you would not have believed this. About his failure to master English there always seemed to me something willful. Except for her accent—as thick as but so different from his— my mother had no such trouble.

"He never would talk about himself much, you know. That was his way. He never really had much to say, in general. Silence was golden. It was a cultural thing, I think." (My mother.)

By the time I was old enough to understand this, my father had pretty much stopped talking.

Taciturnity: they say that is an Oriental trait. But I don't believe my father was always the silent, withdrawn man I knew. Think of that day at Coney Island, when he was talking a Chinese blue streak.

Almost everything I know about him came from my mother, and there was much she herself never knew, much she had forgotten or was unsure of, and much that she would never tell.

◆ ◆ ◆

I am six, seven, eight years old, a schoolgirl with deplorable posture and constantly cracked lips, chafing in the dollish old-world clothes handmade by my mother; a bossy, fretful, sly, cowardly child given to fits of temper and weeping. In school, or in the playground, or perhaps watching television I hear something about the Chinese—something odd, improbable. I will ask my father. He will know whether it is true, say, that the Chinese eat with sticks.

He shrugs. He pretends not to understand. Or he scowls and says, "Chinese just like everybody else."

("He thought you were making fun of him. He always thought everyone was making fun of him. He had a chip on his shoulder. The way he acted, you'd've thought he was colored!")

Actually, he said "evvybody."

Is it true the Chinese write backwards?

Chinese just like evvybody else.

Is it true they eat dog?
Chinese just like evvybody else.
Are they really all Communists?
Chinese just like evvybody else.
What is Chinese water torture? What is footbinding? What is a mandarin?
Chinese just like evvybody else.
He was not like everybody else.

◆ ◆ ◆

The unbearably few facts are these. He was born in Colón, Panama, in 1911. His father came from Shanghai. From what I have been able to gather, Grandfather Chang was a merchant engaged in the trade of tobacco and tea. This business, which he ran with one of his brothers, kept him traveling often between Shanghai and Colón. He had two wives, one in each city, and, as if out of a passion for symmetry, two sons by each wife. Soon after my father, Carlos, was born, his father took him to Shanghai, to be raised by the Chinese wife. Ten years later my father was sent back to Colón. I never understood the reason for this. The way the story was told to me, I got the impression that my father was being sent away from some danger. This was, of course, a time of upheaval in China, the decade following the birth of the Republic, the era of the warlords. If the date is correct, my father would have left Shanghai the year the Chinese Communist Party was founded there. It remains uncertain, though, whether political events had anything at all to do with his leaving China.

One year after my father returned to Colón his mother was dead. I remember hearing as a child that she had died of a stroke. Years later this would seem to me odd, when I figured out that she would have been only twenty-six. Odder still, to think of that reunion between the long-parted mother and son; there's a good chance they did not speak the same language. The other half-Panamanian son, Alfonso, was either sent back with my father or had never left Colón. After their mother's death the two boys came into the care of their father's brother and business partner, Uncle Mee, who apparently lived in Colón and had a large family of his own.

Grandfather Chang, his Chinese wife, and their two sons remained in Shanghai. All were said to have been killed by the Japanese. That must have been during the Sino-Japanese War. My father would have been between his late twenties and early thirties by then, but whether he ever saw any of his Shanghai relations again before they died, I don't know.

At twelve or thirteen my father sailed to America with Uncle Mee. I believe it was just the two of them who came, leaving the rest of the family in Colón. Sometime in the next year or so my father was enrolled in a public school in Brooklyn. I remember coming across a notebook that had belonged to him in those days and being jolted by the name written on the cover: Charles Cipriano Chang. That was neither my father's first nor his last name, as far as I knew, and I'd never heard of the middle name. (Hard to believe that my father spent his boyhood in Shanghai being called Carlos, a name he could not even pronounce with the proper Spanish accent. So he must have had a Chinese name as well. And although our family never knew this name, perhaps among Chinese people he used it.)

Twenty years passed. All I know about this part of my father's life is that it was lived illegally in New York, mostly in Chinatown, where he worked in various restaurants. Then came the Second World War and he was drafted. It was while he was in the Army that he finally became an American citizen. He was no longer calling himself Charles but Carlos again, and now, upon becoming a citizen, he dropped his father's family name and took his mother's. Why a man who thought of himself as Chinese, who had always lived among Chinese, who spoke little Spanish and who had barely known his mother would have made such a decision in the middle of his life is one of many mysteries surrounding my father. My mother had an explanation: "You see, Alfonso was a Panamanian citizen, and *he* had taken his mother's name" (which would, of course, be in keeping with Spanish cultural tradition). "He was the only member of his family your father had left—the others were all dead. Your father wanted to have the same last name as his brother. Also, he thought he'd get along better in this country with a Spanish name." This makes no sense to me. He'd been a Chinatown Chang for twenty years—and now all of a sudden he wanted to pass for Hispanic?

In another version of this story, the idea of getting rid of the Chinese name was attributed to the citizenship official handling my father's papers. This is plausible, given that immigration restrictions for Chinese were still in effect at that time. But I have not ruled out the possibility that the change of names was the result of a misunderstanding between my father and this official. My father was an easily fuddled man, especially when dealing with authority, and he always had trouble understanding and making himself understood in English. And I can imagine him not only befuddled enough to make such a mistake but also too timid afterwards to try to fix it.

Whatever really happened I'm sure I'll never know. I do know that having a Spanish name brought much confusion into my father's life and have always wondered in what way my own life might have been different had he kept the name Chang.

◆ ◆ ◆

From this point on the story becomes somewhat clearer. With the Hundredth Infantry Division my father goes to war, fights in France and Germany and, after V-E Day, is stationed in the small southern German town where he will meet my mother. He is thirty-four and she not quite eighteen. She is soon pregnant.

Here is rich food for speculation: How did they communicate? She had had a little English in school. He learned a bit of German. They must have misunderstood far more than they understood of each other. Perhaps this helps to explain why my eldest sister was already two and my other sister on the way before my parents got married. (My sisters and I did not learn about this until we were in our twenties.)

By the time I was three they would already have had two long separations.

"I should have married Rudolf!" (My mother.)

1948. My father returns to the States with his wife and first daughter. Now everything is drastically changed. A different America this: the America of the citizen, the legal worker, the family man. No more drinking and gambling till all hours in Chinatown. No more drifting from job to job, living hand to mouth, sleeping on the floor of a friend's room or on a shelf in the restaurant kitchen. There are new, undreamed-of expenses: household money, layettes, taxes, insurance, a special bank account for the children's education. He does the best he can. He rents an apartment in the Fort Greene housing project, a short walk from the Cantonese restaurant on Fulton Street where he works as a waiter. Some nights after closing, after all the tables have been cleared and the dishes done, he stays for the gambling. He weaves home to a wide-awake wife who sniffs the whiskey on his breath and doesn't care whether he has lost or won. So little money—to gamble with any of it is a sin. Her English is getting better ("no thanks to him!"), but for what she has to say she needs little vocabulary. She is miserable. She hates America. She dreams incessantly about going home. There is something peculiar about the three-year-old: she rarely smiles; she claws at the pages of magazines, like a cat. The one-year-old is prone to colic. To her horror my mother learns that she is pregnant again. She attempts an abortion, which fails. I am born. About that attempt, was my father consulted? Most likely not. Had he been I think I know what he would have said. He would have said: No, this time it will be a boy. Like most men he would have wanted a son. (All girls—a house full of females—a Chinese man's nightmare!) Perhaps with a son he would have been more open. Perhaps a son he would have taught Chinese.

He gets another job, as a dishwasher in the kitchen of a large public health service hospital. He will work there until he retires, eventually being promoted to kitchen supervisor.

He moves his family to another housing project, outside the city, newly built, cleaner, safer.

He works all the time. On weekends, when he is off from the hospital, he waits on table in one or another Chinese restaurant. He works most holidays and takes no vacations. On his rare day off he outrages my mother by going to the racetrack. But he is not self-indulgent. A little gambling, a quart of

Budweiser with his supper—eaten alone, an hour or so after the rest of us (he always worked late)—now and then a glass of Scotch, cigarettes—these were his only pleasures. While the children are still small there are occasional outings. To Coney Island, Chinatown, the zoo. On Sundays sometimes he takes us to the children's matinee, and once a year to Radio City, for the Christmas or Easter show. But he and my mother never go out alone together, just the two of them—never.

Her English keeps getting better, making his seem worse and worse.

He is hardly home, yet my memory is of constant fighting.

Not much vocabulary needed to wound.

"Stupid woman. Crazy lady. Talk, talk, talk, talk—never say nothing!"

"I should have married Rudolf!"

Once, she spat in his face. Another time, she picked up a bread knife and he had to struggle to get it away from her.

They slept in separate beds.

Every few months she announced to the children that it was over: we were going "home." (And she did go back with us to Germany once, when I was two. We stayed six months. About this episode she was always vague. In years to come, whenever we asked her why we did not stay in Germany, she would say, "You children wanted your father." But I think that is untrue. More likely she realized that there was no life for her back there. She had never got on well with her family. By this time I believe Rudolf had married another.)

Even working the two jobs, my father did not make much money. He would never make enough to buy a house. Yet it seemed the burden of being poor weighed heavier on my mother. Being poor meant you could never relax, meant eternal attention to appearances. Just because you had no money didn't mean you were squalid. Come into the house: see how clean and tidy everything is. Look at the children: spotless. And people did comment to my mother—on the shininess of her floors and how she kept her children—and she was gratified by this. Still, being poor was exhausting.

One day a woman waist-deep in children knocked at the door. When my mother answered, the woman apologized. "I thought—from the name on the mailbox I thought you were Spanish, too. My kids needed to use the toilet." My mother could not hide her displeasure. She was proud of being German, and in those postwar years she was also bitterly defensive. When people called us names—spicks and chinks—she said, "You see how it is in this country. For all they say how bad we Germans are, no one ever calls you names for being German."

She had no patience with my father's quirks. The involuntary twitching of a muscle meant that someone had given him the evil eye. Drinking a glass of boiled water while it was still hot cured the flu. He saved back issues of *Reader's Digest* and silver dollars from certain years, believing that one day they'd be worth lots of money. What sort of backward creature had she married?

His English drove her mad. Whenever he didn't catch something that was said to him (and this happened all the time), instead of saying "what?" he said "who?" "Who? Who?" she screeched back at him. "What are you, an owl?"

Constant bickering and fighting.

We children dreamed of growing up, going to college, getting married, getting away.

◆ ◆ ◆

And what about Alfonso and Uncle Mee? What happened to them?

"I never met either of them, but we heard from Mee all the time those first years—it was awful. By then he was back in Panama. He was a terrible gambler, and so were his sons. They had debts up to here—and who should they turn to but your father. Uncle What-About-Mee, I called him. 'Think of all I've done for you. You owe me.'" (And though she had never heard it she mimicked his voice.) "Well, your father had managed to save a couple of thousand dollars and he sent it all to Mee. I could have died. I never forgave him. I was pregnant then, and I had one maternity dress—*one*. Mee no sooner got that money than he wrote back for more. I told your father if he sent him another dime I was leaving."

Somehow the quarrel extended to include Alfonso, who seems to have sided with Mee. My father broke with them both. Several years after we left Brooklyn, an ad appeared in the Chinatown newspaper. Alfonso and Mee were trying to track my father down. He never answered the ad, my father said. He never spoke to either man again. (Perhaps he lied. Perhaps he was always in touch with them, secretly. I believe much of his life was a secret from us.)

◆ ◆ ◆

I have never seen a photograph of my father that was taken before he was in the Army. I have no idea what he looked like as a child or as a young man. I have never seen any photographs of his parents or his brothers, or of Uncle Mee or of any other relations, or of the houses he lived in in Colón and Shanghai. If my father had any possessions that had belonged to his parents, any family keepsakes or mementos of his youth, I never saw them. About his youth he had nothing to tell. A single anecdote he shared with me. In Shanghai he had a dog. When my father sailed to Panama, the dog was brought along to the dock to see him off. My father boarded the boat and the dog began howling. He never forgot that: the boat pulling away from the dock and the dog howling. "Dog no fool. He know I never be back."

◆ ◆ ◆

In our house there were no Chinese things. No objects made of bamboo or jade. No lacquer boxes. No painted scrolls or fans. No calligraphy. No embroidered silks. No Buddhas. No chopsticks among the silverware, no rice bowls or tea sets. No Chinese tea, no ginseng or soy sauce in the cupboards. My father was the only Chinese thing, sitting like a Buddha himself among the Hummels and cuckoo clocks and pictures of alpine landscapes. My mother thought of the house as hers, spoke of *her* curtains, *her* floors (often in warning: "Don't scuff up my floors!"). The daughters were hers, too. To each of them she gave a Teutonic name, impossible for him to pronounce. ("*What* does your father call you?" That question—an agony to me—rang through my childhood.) It was part of her abiding nostalgia that she wanted to raise the children as Germans. She sewed dirndls for them and even for their dolls. She braided their hair, then wound the braids tightly around their ears, like hair earmuffs, in the German style. They would open their presents on Christmas Eve rather than Christmas morning. They would not celebrate Thanksgiving. Of course they would not celebrate any Chinese holidays. No dragon and firecrackers on Chinese New Year's. For Christmas there was red cabbage and sauerbraten. Imagine my father saying sauerbraten.

Now and then he brought home food from Chinatown: fiery red sausage with specks of fat like teeth embedded in it, dried fish, buns filled with bean paste which he cracked us up by calling Chinese pee-nus butter. My mother would not touch any of it. ("God knows what it really is.") We kids clamored for a taste and when we didn't like it my father got angry. ("You know how he was with that chip on his shoulder. He took it personally. He was insulted.") Whenever we ate at one of the restaurants where he worked, he was always careful to order for us the same Americanized dishes served to most of the white customers.

◆ ◆ ◆

An early memory: I am four, five, six years old, in a silly mood, mugging in my mother's bureau mirror. My father is in the room with me but I forget he is there. I place my forefingers at the corners of my eyes and pull the lids taut. Then I catch him watching me. His is a look of pure hate.

"He thought you were making fun."

A later memory: "Panama is an isthmus." Grade-school geography. My father looks up from his paper, alert, suspicious. "Merry Isthmus!" "Isthmus be the place!" My sisters and I shriek with laughter. My father shakes his head. "Not nice, making fun of place where people born."

"Ach, he had no sense of humor—he never did. You couldn't joke with him. He never got the point of a joke."

It is true that I hardly ever heard him laugh. (Unlike my mother, who, despite her chronic unhappiness, seemed always to be laughing—at him, at us, at the neighbors. A great tease she was, sly, malicious, often witty.)

◆ ◆ ◆

Chinese inscrutability. Chinese sufferance. Chinese reserve. Yes, I recognize my father in the clichés. But what about his Panamanian side? What are Latins said to be? Hot-blooded, mercurial, soulful, macho, convivial, romantic. No, he was none of these.

"He always wanted to go back, he always missed China."

But he was only ten years old when he left.

"Yes, but that's what counts—where you spent those first years, and your first language. That's who you are."

I had a children's book about Sun Yat Sen, *The Man Who Changed China.* There were drawings of Sun as a boy. I tried to picture my father like that, a Chinese boy who wore pajamas outdoors and a coolie hat and a pigtail down his back. (Though of course in those days after Sun's Revolution he isn't likely to have worn a pigtail.) I pictured my father against those landscapes of peaks and pagodas, with a dog like Old Yeller at his heels. What was it like, this boyhood in Shanghai? How did the Chinese wife treat the second wife's son? (My father and Alfonso would not have had the same status as the official wife's sons, I don't think.) How did the Chinese brothers treat him? When he went to school—did he go to school?—was he accepted by the other children as one of them? Is there a Chinese word for half-breed, and was he called that name as we would be? Surely many times in his life he must have wished he were all Chinese. My mother wished that her children were all German. I wanted to be an all-American girl with a name like Sue Brown.

He always wanted to go back.

◆ ◆ ◆

In our house there were not many books. My mother's romances and historical novels, books about Germany (mostly about the Nazi era), a volume of Shakespeare, tales from Andersen and Grimm, the *Nibelungenlied,* Edith Hamilton's *Mythology,* poems of Goethe and Schiller, *Struwwelpeter,* the drawings of Wilhelm Busch. It was my mother who gave me that book about Sun Yat Sen and, when I was a little older, one of her own favorites, *The Good Earth,* a children's story for adults. Pearl Buck was a missionary who lived in China for many years. (Missionaries supposedly converted the Changs to Christianity. From what? Buddhism? Taoism? My father's mother was almost certainly Roman Catholic. He himself belonged to no church.) Pearl Buck wrote eighty-five books, founded a shelter for Asian-American children, and won the Nobel Prize.

The Good Earth. China a land of famine and plagues—endless childbirth among them. The births of daughters seen as evil omens. "It is only a slave this time—not worth mentioning." Little girls sold as a matter of course. Growing up to be concubines with names like Lotus and Cuckoo and Pear Blossom.

Women with feet like little deer hooves. Abject wives, shuffling six paces behind their husbands. All this filled me with anxiety. In our house the man was
the meek and browbeat one.

I never saw my father read, except for the newspaper. He did not read the
*Reader's Digest*s that he saved. He would not have been able to read *The Good
Earth*. I am sure he could not write with fluency in any tongue. The older I
grew the more I thought of him as illiterate. Hard for me to accept the fact that
he did not read books. Say I grew up to be a writer. He would not read what I
wrote.

♦ ♦ ♦

He had his own separate closet, in the front hall. Every night when he came
home from work he undressed as soon as he walked in, out there in the hall.
He took off his suit and put on his bathrobe. He always wore a suit to work,
but at the hospital he changed into whites and at the restaurant into dark
pants, white jacket and black bow tie. In the few photographs of him that exist
he is often wearing a uniform—his soldier's or hospital-worker's or waiter's.

Though not at all vain, he was particular about his appearance. He bought
his suits in a men's fine clothing store on Fifth Avenue, and he took meticulous
care of them. He had a horror of cheap cloth and imitation leather, and an
equal horror of slovenliness. His closet was the picture of order. On the top
shelf, where he kept his hats, was a large assortment—a lifetime's supply, it
seemed to me—of chewing gum, cough drops, and mints. On that shelf he
kept also his cigarettes and cigars. The closet smelled much as he did—of
tobacco and spearmint and the rosewater-glycerin cream he used on his dry
skin. A not unpleasant smell.

He was small. At fourteen I was already as tall as he, and eventually I would
outweigh him. A trim sprig of a man—dainty but not puny, fastidious but not
effeminate. I used to marvel at the cleanliness of his nails, and at his good teeth,
which never needed any fillings. By the time I was born he had lost most of
his top hair, which made his domed forehead look even larger, his moon-face
rounder. It may have been the copper-red cast of his skin that led some people
to take him for an American Indian—people who'd never seen one, probably.

♦ ♦ ♦

He could be cruel. I once saw him blow pepper in the cat's face. He loathed
that cat, a surly, untrainable tom found in the street. But he was very fond of
another creature we took in, an orphaned nestling sparrow. Against expectations, the bird survived and learned how to fly. But, afraid that it would not
be able to fend for itself outdoors, we decided to keep it. My father sometimes
sat by its cage, watching the bird and cooing at it in Chinese. My mother was
amused. "You see: he has more to say to that bird than to us!" The emperor
and his nightingale, she called them. "The Chinese have always loved their

birds." (What none of us knew: at that very moment in China keeping pet birds had been prohibited as a bourgeois affectation, and sparrows were being exterminated as pests.)

◆◆◆

It was true that my father had less and less to say to us. He was drifting further and further out of our lives. These were my teenage years. I did not see clearly what was happening then, and for long afterwards, whenever I tried to look back, a panic would come over me, so that I couldn't see at all.

At sixteen, I had stopped thinking about becoming a writer. I wanted to dance. Every day after school I went into the city for class. I would be home by 8:30, about the same time as my father. And so for this period he and I would eat dinner together. And much later, looking back, I realized that that was when I had—and lost—my chance. Alone with my father every night like that, I could have got to know him. I could have asked him all those questions that I now have to live without answers to. Of course he would have resisted talking about himself. But with patience I might have drawn him out.

Or maybe not. As I recall, the person sitting across the kitchen table from me was like a figure in a glass case. That was not the face of someone thinking, feeling, or even daydreaming. It was the clay face, still waiting to receive the breath of life.

If it ever occurred to me that my father was getting old, that he was exhausted, that his health was failing, I don't remember it.

He was still working seven days a week. Sometimes he missed having dinner with me because the dishwasher broke and he had to stay late at the hospital. For a time, on Saturdays, he worked double shifts at the restaurant and did not come home till we were all asleep.

After dinner, he stayed at the kitchen table, smoking and finishing his beer. Then he went to bed. He never joined the rest of us in the living room in front of the television. He sat alone at the table, staring at the wall. He hardly noticed if someone came into the kitchen for something. His inobservance was the family's biggest joke. My mother would give herself or one of us a new hairdo and say, "Now watch: your father won't even notice," and she was right.

My sisters and I bemoaned his stubborn avoidance of the living room. Once a year he yielded and joined us around the Christmas tree, but only very reluctantly; we had to beg him.

I knew vaguely that he continued to have some sort of social life outside the house, a life centered in Chinatown.

He still played the horses.

By this time family outings had ceased. We never did anything together as a family. But every Sunday my father came home with ice cream for everyone.

He and my mother fought less and less—seldom now in the old vicious way—but this did not mean there was peace. Never any word or gesture of affection between them, not even, "for the sake of the children," pretense of affection.

(Television: the prime-time family shows. During the inevitable scenes when family love and loyalty were affirmed, the discomfort in the living room was palpable. I think we were all ashamed of how far below the ideal our family fell.)

Working and saving to send his children to college, he took no interest in their school life. He did, however, reward good report cards with cash. He did not attend school events to which parents were invited; he always had to work.

He never saw me dance.

He intrigued my friends, who angered me by regarding him as if he were a figure in a glass case. Doesn't he ever come out of the kitchen? Doesn't he ever talk? I was angry at him, too, for what he seemed to me to be doing: *willing* himself into stereotype: inscrutable, self-effacing, funny little chinaman.

And why couldn't he learn to speak English?

He developed the tight wheezing cough that would never leave him. The doctor blamed cigarettes, so my father tried sticking to cigars. The cough was particularly bad at night. It kept my mother up, and so she started sleeping on the living-room couch.

I was the only one who went to college, and I got a scholarship. My father gave the money he had saved to my mother, who bought a brand-new Mercedes, the family's first car.

◆ ◆ ◆

He was not like everybody else. In fact, he was not like anyone I had ever met. But I thought of my father when I first encountered the "little man" of Russian literature. I thought of him a lot when I read the stories of Chekhov and Gogol. Reading "Grief," I remembered my father and the sparrow, and a new possibility presented itself: my father not as one who would not speak but as one to whom no one would listen.

And he was like a character in a story also in the sense that he needed to be invented.

The silver dollars saved in a cigar box. The *Reader's Digest*s going back to before I was born. The uniforms. The tobacco-mint-rosewater smell. I cannot invent a father out of these.

I waited too long. By the time I started gathering material for his story, whatever there had been in the way of private documents or papers (and there must have been some) had disappeared. (It was never clear whether my father himself destroyed them or whether my mother later lost or got rid of them, between moves, or in one of her zealous spring cleanings.)

The Sunday-night ice cream. The Budweiser bottle sweating on the kitchen table. The five-, ten-, or twenty-dollar bill he pulled from his wallet after squinting at your report card. "Who? Who?"

♦ ♦ ♦

We must have seemed as alien to him as he seemed to us. To him we must always have been "others." Females. Demons. No different from other demons, who could not tell one Asian from another, who thought Chinese food meant chop suey and Chinese customs matter for joking. I would have to live a lot longer and he would have to die before the full horror of this would sink in. And then it would sink in deeply, agonizingly, like an arrow that has found its mark.

♦ ♦ ♦

Dusk in the city. Dozens of Chinese men bicycle through the streets, bearing cartons of fried dumplings, Ten Ingredients Lo Mein, and sweet-and-sour pork. I am on my way to the drugstore when one of them hails me. "Miss! Wait, Miss!" Not a man, I see, but a boy, eighteen at most, with a lovely, oval, fresh-skinned face. "You—you Chinese!" It is not the first time in my life this has happened. As shortly as possible I explain. The boy turns out to have arrived just weeks ago, from Hong Kong. His English is incomprehensible. He is flustered when he finds I cannot speak Chinese. He says, "Can I. Your father. Now." It takes me a moment to figure this out. Alas, he is asking to meet my father. Unable to bring myself to tell him my father is dead, I say that he does not live in the city. The boy persists. "But sometime come see. And then I now?" His imploring manner puzzles me. Is it that he wants to meet Chinese people? Doesn't he work in a Chinese restaurant? Doesn't he know about Chinatown? I feel a surge of anxiety. He is so earnest and intent. I am missing something. In another minute I have promised that when my father comes to town he will go to the restaurant where the boy works and seek him out. The boy rides off looking pleased, and I continue on to the store. I am picking out toothpaste when he appears at my side. He hands me a folded piece of paper. Two telephone numbers and a message in Chinese characters. "For father."

♦ ♦ ♦

He was sixty when he retired from the hospital, but his working days were not done. He took a part-time job as a messenger for a bank. That Christmas when I came home from school I found him in bad shape. His smoker's cough was much worse, and he had pains in his legs and in his back, recently diagnosed as arthritis.

But it was not smoker's cough, and it was not arthritis.

A month later, he left work early one day because he was in such pain. He made it to the train station, but when he tried to board the train he could not get up the steps. Two conductors had to carry him aboard. At home he went straight to bed and in the middle of the night he woke up coughing as usual, and this time there was blood.

His decline was so swift that by the time I arrived at the hospital he barely knew me. Over the next week we were able to chart the backward journey on which he was embarked by his occasional murmurings. ("I got to get back to the base—they'll think I'm AWOL!") Though I was not there to hear it, I am told that he cursed my mother and accused her of never having cared about him. By the end of the week, when he spoke it was only in Chinese.

One morning a priest arrived. No one had sent for him. He had doubtless assumed from the name that this patient was Hispanic and Catholic, and had taken it upon himself to administer extreme unction. None of us had the will to stop him, and so we were witness to a final mystery: my father, who as far as we knew had no religion, feebly crossing himself.

The fragments of Chinese stopped. There was only panting then, broken by sharp gasps such as one makes when reminded of some important thing one has forgotten. To the end his hands were restless. He kept repeating the same gesture: cupping his hands together and drawing them to his chest, as though gathering something to him.

◆ ◆ ◆

Now let others speak.

"After the war was a terrible time. We were all scared to death, we didn't know what was going to happen to us. Some of those soldiers were really enjoying it, they wanted nothing better than to see us grovel. The victors! Oh, they were scum, a lot of them. Worse than the Nazis ever were. But Carlos felt sorry for us. He tried to help. And not just our family but the neighbors, too. He gave us money. His wallet was always out. And he was always bringing stuff from the base, like coffee and chocolate—things you could never get. And even after he went back to the States he sent packages. Not just to us but to all the people he got to know here. Frau Meyer. The Schweitzers. They still talk about that." (My grandmother.)

"We know the cancer started in the right lung but by the time we saw him it had spread. It was in both lungs, it was in his liver and in his bones. He was a very sick man and he'd been sick for a long time. I'd say that tumor in the right lung had been growing for at least five years." (The doctor.)

"He drank a lot in those days, and your mother didn't like that. But he was funny. He loved that singer—the cowboy—what was his name? I forget. Anyway, he put on the music and he sang along. Your mother would cover her ears." (My grandmother.)

"I didn't like the way he looked. He wouldn't say anything but I knew he was hurting. I said to myself, this isn't arthritis—no way. I wanted him to see my own doctor but he wouldn't. I was just about to order him to." (My father's boss at the bank.)

"He hated cats, and the cat knew it and she was always jumping in his lap. Every time he sat down the cat jumped in his lap and we laughed. But you could tell it really bothered him. He said cats were bad luck. When the cat jumped in your lap it was a bad omen." (My mother's younger brother, Karl.)

"He couldn't dance at all—or he wouldn't—but he clapped and sang along to the records. He liked to drink and he liked gambling. Your mother was real worried about that." (Frau Meyer.)

"Before the occupation no one in this town had ever seen an Oriental or a Negro." (My grandmother.)

"He never ate much, he didn't want you to cook for him, but he liked German beer. He brought cigarettes for everyone. We gave him schnapps. He played us the cowboy songs." (Frau Schweitzer.)

"Ain't you people dying to know what he's saying?" (The patient in the bed next to my father's.)

"When he wasn't drinking he was very shy. He just sat there next to your mother without speaking. He sat there staring and staring at her." (Frau Meyer.)

"He liked blondes. He loved that blonde hair." (Karl.)

"There was absolutely nothing we could do for him. The amazing thing is that he was working right up till the day he came into the hospital. I don't know how he did that." (The doctor.)

"The singing was a way of talking to us, because he didn't know German at all." (My grandmother.)

"Yes, of course I remember. It was Hank Williams. He played those records over and over. Hillbilly music. I thought I'd go mad." (My mother.)

Here are the names of some Hank Williams songs: Honky Tonkin'. Ramblin' Man. Hey, Good Lookin'. Lovesick Blues. Why Don't You Love Me Like You Used To Do. Your Cheatin' Heart. (I heard that) Lonesome Whistle. Why Don't You Mind Your Own Business. I'm So Lonesome I Could Cry. The Blues Come Around. Cold, Cold Heart. I'll Never Get Out of This World Alive. I Can't Help It If I'm Still in Love with You.

Her Secrets
(for Katya)

by John Berger

FROM THE AGE OF FIVE OR SIX I was worried about the death of my parents. The inevitability of death was one of the first things I learnt about the world on my own. Nobody else spoke of it yet the signs were so clear.

Every time I went to bed—and in this I am sure I was like millions of other children—the fear that one or both my parents might die in the night touched the nape of my neck with its finger. Such a fear has, I believe, little to do with a particular psychological climate and a great deal to do with nightfall. Yet since it was impossible to say: You won't die in the night, will you? (when Grandmother died, I was told she had gone to have a rest, or—this was from my Uncle who was more outspoken—that she had passed over), since I couldn't ask the real question and I sought a reassurance, I invented—like millions before me—the euphemism: See you in the morning! To which either my father or mother who had come to turn out the light in my bedroom, would reply: See you in the morning, John.

After their footsteps had died away, I would try for as long as possible not to lift my head from the pillow so that the last words spoken remained, trapped like fish in a rock-pool at low tide, between my pillow and ear. The implicit promise of the words was also a protection against the dark. The words promised that I would not (yet) be alone.

Now I'm no longer usually frightened by the dark and my father died ten years ago and my mother a month ago at the age of ninety-three. It would be a natural moment to write an autobiography. My version of my life can no longer hurt either of them. And the book, when finished, would be there, a little like a parent. Autobiography begins with a sense of being alone. It is an orphan form. Yet I have no wish to do so. All that interests me about my past life are the common moments. The moments—which if I relate them well enough—will join countless others lived by people I do not personally know.

Six weeks ago my mother asked me to come and see her; it would be the last time, she said. A few days later, on the morning of my birthday, she believed she was dying. Open the curtains, she asked my brother, so I can see the trees. In fact, she died the following week.

On my birthdays as a child, it was my father rather than she who gave me memorable presents. She was too thrifty. Her moments of generosity were at the table, offering what she had bought and prepared and cooked and served to whoever came into the house. Otherwise she was thrifty. Nor did she ever explain. She was secretive, she kept things to herself. Not for her own pleasure, but because the world would not forgive spontaneity, the world was mean. I must make that clearer. She didn't believe life was mean—it was generous—but she had learnt from her own childhood that survival was hard. She was the opposite of quixotic—for she was not born a knight and her father was a warehouse foreman in Lambeth. She pursed her lips together, knitted her brows as she calculated and thought things out and carried on with an un-spoken determination. She never asked favors of anyone. Nothing shocked her. From whatever she saw, she just drew the necessary conclusions so as to survive and to be dependent on nobody. If I were Aesop, I would say that in her prudence and persistence my mother resembled the agouti. (I once wrote about an agouti in the London zoo but I did not then realize why the animal so touched me.) In my adult life, the only occasions on which we shouted at each other were when she estimated I was being quixotic.

When I was in my thirties she told me for the first time that, ever since I was born, she had hoped I would be a writer. The writers she admired when young were Bernard Shaw, J. M. Barrie, Compton Mackenzie, Warwick Deep-ing, E. M. Dell. The only painter she really admired was Turner—perhaps be-cause of her childhood on the banks of the Thames.

Most of my books she didn't read. Either because they dealt with subjects which were alien to her or because—under the protective influence of my father—she believed they might upset her. Why suffer surprise from something which, left unopened, gives you pleasure? My being a writer was unqualified for her by what I wrote. To be a writer was to be able to see to the horizon where, anyway, nothing is ever very distinct and all questions are open. Liter-ature had little to do with the writer's vocation as she saw it. It was only a by-product. A writer was a person familiar with the secrets. Perhaps in the end she didn't read my books so that they should remain more secret.

If her hopes of my becoming a writer—and she said they began on the night after I was delivered—were eventually realized, it was not because there were many books in our house (there were few) but because there was so much that was unsaid, so much that I had to discover the existence of on my own at an early age: death, poverty, pain (in others), sexuality...

These things were there to be discovered within the house or from its windows—until I left for good, more or less prepared for the outside world, at the age of eight. My mother never spoke of these things. She didn't hide the fact that she was aware of them. For her, however, they were wrapped secrets, to be lived with, but never to be mentioned or opened. Superficially this was a question of gentility, but profoundly, of a respect, a secret loyalty to the enigmatic. My rough and ready preparation for the world did not include a single explanation—it simply consisted of the principle that events carried more weight than the self.

Thus, she taught me very little—at least in the usual sense of the term: she a teacher about life, I a learner. By imitating her gestures I learnt how to roast meat in the oven, how to clean celery, how to cook rice, how to choose vegetables in a market. As a young woman she had been a vegetarian. Then she gave it up because she did not want to influence us children. Why were you a vegetarian? I once asked her, eating my Sunday roast, much later when I was first working as a journalist. Because I'm against killing. She would say no more. Either I understood or I didn't. There was nothing more to be said.

In time—and I understand this only now writing these pages—I chose to visit abattoirs in different cities of the world and to become something of an expert concerning the subject. The unspoken, the unfaceable beckoned me. I followed. Into the abattoirs and, differently, into many other places and situations.

The last, the largest and the most personally prepared wrapped secret was her own death. Of course I was not the only witness. Of those close to her, I was maybe the most removed, the most remote. But she knew, I think, with confidence that I would pursue the matter. She knew that if anybody can be at home with what is kept a secret, it was me, because I was her son whom she hoped would become a writer.

The clinical history of her illness is a different story about which she herself was totally uncurious. Sufficient to say that with the help of drugs she was not in pain, and that, thanks to my brother and sister-in-law who arranged everything for her, she was not subjected to all the mechanical ingenuity of aids for the artificial prolongation of life.

Of how many deaths—though never till now of my own mother's—have I written? Truly we writers are the secretaries of death.

She lay in bed, propped up by pillows, her head fallen forward, as if asleep.

I shut my eyes, she said, I like to shut my eyes and think. I don't sleep though. If I slept now, I wouldn't sleep at night.

What do you think about?

She screwed up her eyes which were gimlet sharp and looked at me, twinkling, as if I'd never, not even as a small child, asked such a stupid question.

Are you working hard? What are you writing?

A play, I answered.

The last time I went to the theater I didn't understand a thing, she said. It's not my hearing that's bad though.

Perhaps the play was obscure, I suggested.

She opened her eyes again. The body has closed shop, she announced. Nothing, nothing at all from here down. She placed a hand on her neck. It's a good thing, make no mistake about it, John, it makes the waiting easier.

On her bedside table was a tin of handcream. I started to massage her left hand.

Do you remember a photograph I once took of your hands? Working hands, you said.

No, I don't.

Would you like some more photos on your table? Katya, her granddaughter, asked her.

She smiled at Katya and shook her head, her voice very slightly broken by a laugh. It would be *so* difficult, so difficult, wouldn't it, to choose.

She turned towards me. What exactly are you doing?

I'm massaging your hand. It's meant to be pleasurable.

To tell you the truth, dear, it doesn't make much difference. What plane are you taking back?

I mumbled, took her other hand.

You are all worried, she said, especially when there are several of you. I'm not. Maureen asked me the other day whether I wanted to be cremated or buried. Doesn't make one iota of difference to me. How could it? She shut her eyes to think.

For the first time in her life and in mine, she could openly place the wrapped enigma between us. She didn't watch me watching it, for we had the habits of a lifetime. Openly she knew that at that moment her faith in a secret was bound to be stronger than any faith of mine in facts. With her eyes still shut, she fingered the Arab necklace I'd attached round her neck with a charm against the evil eye. I'd given her the necklace a few hours before. Perhaps for the first time I had offered her a secret and now her hand kept looking for it.

She opened her eyes. What time is it?

Quarter to four.

It's not very interesting talking to me, you know. I don't have any ideas any more. I've had a good life. Why don't you take a walk?

Katya stayed with her.

When you are very old, she told Katya confidentially, there's one thing that's very very difficult—it's very difficult to persuade other people that you're happy.

She let her head go back on to the pillow. As I came back in, she smiled.

In her right hand she held a crumpled paper handkerchief. With it she dabbed from time to time the corner of her mouth when she felt there was the slightest excess of spittle there. The gesture was reminiscent of one with which, many years before, she used to wipe her mouth after drinking Earl Grey tea and eating watercress sandwiches. Meanwhile with her left hand she fingered the necklace, cushioned on her forgotten bosom.

Love, my mother had the habit of saying, is the only thing that counts in this world. Real love, she would add, to avoid any factitious misunderstanding. But apart from that simple adjective, she never added anything more.

Vital Signs

by Natalie Kusz

I. IN HOSPITAL

I WAS ALWAYS WAKING UP, in those days, to the smell of gauze soaked with mucus and needing to be changed. Even when I cannot recall what parts of me were bandaged then, I remember vividly that smell, a sort of fecund, salty, warm one like something shut up and kept alive too long in a dead space. Most of the details I remember from that time are smells, and the chancest whiff from the folds of surgical greens or the faint scent of ether on cold fingers can still drag me, reflexively, back to that life, to flux so familiar as to be a constant in itself. Years after Children's Hospital, when I took my own daughter in for stitches in her forehead, and two men unfolded surgical napkins directly under my nose, I embarrassed us all by growing too weak to stand, and had to sit aside by myself until all the work was over.

It seems odd that these smells have power to bring back such horror, when my memories of that time are not, on the whole, dark ones. Certainly I suffered pain, and I knew early a debilitating fear of surgery itself, but the life I measured as months inside and months outside the walls was a good one, and bred in me understandings that I would not relinquish now.

There was a playroom in the children's wing, a wide room full of light, with colored walls and furniture, and carpets on the floor. A wooden kitchen held the corner alongside our infirmary, and my friends and I passed many hours as families, cooking pudding for our dolls before they were due in therapy. Most of the dolls had amputated arms and legs, or had lost their hair to chemotherapy, and when we put on our doctors' clothes we taught them to walk with prostheses, changing their dressings with sterile gloves.

We had school tables, and many books, and an ant farm by the window so we could care for something alive. And overseeing us all was Janine, a pink woman, young even to seven-year-old eyes, with yellow, cloudy hair that I touched when I could. She kept it long, parted in the middle, or pulled back in a ponytail like mine before the accident. My hair had been blond then, and I felt sensitive now about the coarse brown stubble under my bandages. Once, on a thinking day, I told Janine that if I had hair like hers I would braid it and loop the pigtails around my ears. She wore it like that the next day, and every day after for a month.

Within Janine's playroom, we were some of us handicapped, but none disabled, and in time we were each taught to prove this for ourselves. While I poured the flour for new playdough, Janine asked me about my kindergarten teacher: what she had looked like with an eyepatch, and if she was missing my same eye. What were the hard parts, Janine said, for a teacher like that? Did I think it was sad for her to miss school sometimes, and did she talk about the hospital? What color was her hair, what sort was her eyepatch, and did I remember if she was pretty? What would I be, Janine asked, when I was that age and these surgeries were past? Over the wet salt smell of green dough, I wished to be a doctor with one blue eye, who could talk like this to the sick, who could tell them they were still real. And with her feel for when to stop talking, Janine turned and left me, searching out volunteers to stir up new clay.

She asked a lot of questions, Janine did, and we answered her as we would have answered ourselves, slowly and with purpose. When called to, Janine would even reverse her words, teaching opposite lessons to clear the mist in between; this happened for Thomas and Nick in their wheelchairs, and I grew as much older from watching as they did from being taught. Both boys were eleven, and though I've forgotten their histories, I do remember their natures, the differences which drew them together.

They were roommates, and best friends, and their dispositions reverberated within one another, the self-reliant and the needy. Thomas was the small one, the white one, with blue veins in his forehead, and pale hair falling forward on one side. He sat always leaning on his elbows, both shoulders pressing up around his ears, and he rested his head to the side when he talked. He depended on Nick, who was tight-shouldered and long, to take charge for him, and he asked for help with his eyes half open, breathing out words through his mouth. And Nick reached the far shelves, and brought Thomas books, and proved he could do for them both, never glancing for help at those who stood upright. His skin was darker than Thomas's, and his eyes much lighter, the blue from their centers washing out into the white.

When they played together, those boys, Thomas was the small center of things, the thin planet sunken into his wheelchair, pulling his friend after him. It must not have seemed to Nick that he was being pulled, because he always went immediately to Thomas's aid, never expecting anyone else to notice. Janine, of course, did. When Thomas wanted the television switched, and Nick struggled up to do it, she said: "Nick, would you like me to do that?"

"I can do it," he said.

"But so can I," Janine said, and she strode easily to the television and turned the knob to *Sesame Street*. "Sometimes," she said to Nick, "you have to let your friends be kind; it makes them feel good." She went back to sit beside Thomas, and she handed him the erector set. How would he turn the channel, she said, if no one else were here? What could he do by himself? And as the TV went unnoticed, Thomas imagined a machine with gears and little wheels, and Janine said she thought it could work. After that, Thomas was always building, though he still asked for help, and he still got it. Nick never did ask, as long as I knew him, but in time he managed to accept what was offered, and even, in the end, to say thanks.

◆◆◆

In this way and in others, Janine encouraged us to change. When we had new ideas, they were outstanding ones, and we could count almost always on her blessing. We planned wheelchair races, and she donated the trophy—bubble-gum ice cream all around. When she caught us blowing up surgical gloves we had found in the trash, she swiped a whole case of them, conjuring a helium bottle besides; that afternoon the playroom smelled of synthetic, powdery rubber, and we fought at the tables over colored markers, racing to decorate the brightest balloon. Janine's was the best—a cigar-smoking man with a four-spiked mohawk—and she handed it down the table to someone's father.

She always welcomed our parents in, so long as they never interfered, and they respected the rule, and acted always unsurprised. When Sheldon's mother arrived one day, she found her son—a four-year-old born with no hands—up to his elbows in orange fingerpaints. She stood for a moment, watching, then offered calmly to mix up a new color.

We children enjoyed many moments like these, granted us by adults like Janine and our parents, and these instants of contentment were luxuries we savored, but on which, by necessity, we did not count. I've heard my father, and other immigrant survivors of World War II, speak of behavior peculiar to people under siege, of how they live in terms, not of years, but of moments, and this was certainly true of our lives. That time was fragmentary, allowing me to remember it now only as a series of flashes, with the most lyrical event likely at any moment to be interrupted. We children were each at the hospital for critical reasons, and a game we planned for one day was likely to be miss-ing one or two players the next, because Charlie hemorrhaged in the night, Sarah was in emergency surgery, or Candice's tubes had pulled out. I myself missed many outings on the lawn because my bone grafts rejected or because my eye grew so infected that I had to be quarantined. At these times, I would watch the others out the closed window, waiting for them to come stand beyond the sterile curtain and shout to me a summary of the afternoon.

In the same way that the future seemed, because it might never arrive, generally less important than did the present, so, too, was the past less significant. Although each of us children could have recited his own case history by heart, it was rare that any of us required more than a faint sketch of another child's past; we found it both interesting and difficult enough to keep current daily record of who had been examined, tested, or operated upon, and whether it had hurt, and if so, whether they had cried. This last question was always of interest to us, and tears we looked on as marks, not of cowards, but of heroes, playmates who had endured torture and lived to testify. The older a child was, the greater our reverence when her roommate reported back after an exam; we derived some perverse comfort from the fact that even twelve-year-olds cracked under pressure.

Those of us who did choose to abide vigorously in each instant were able to offer ourselves, during the day, to one another, to uphold that child or parent who began to weaken. If her need was to laugh, we laughed together; if to talk, we listened, and once, I remember, I stood a whole morning by the chair of a fifteen-year-old friend, combing her hair with my fingers, handing her Kleenex and lemon drops, saying nothing. At night, then, we withdrew, became quietly separate, spoke unguardedly with our families. We spent these evening hours regrouping, placing the days into perspective, each of us using our own methods of self-healing. My mother would read to me from the Book of Job, about that faithful and guiltless man who said, "the thing that I so greatly feared has come upon me," and she would grieve, as I learned later, for me, and for us all. Or she would sit with me and write letters to our scattered family—my father at work in Alaska, my younger brother and sister with an aunt in Oregon. Of the letters that still exist from that time, all are full of sustenance, of words like *courage* and *honor*. It should have sounded ludicrous to hear a seven-year-old speaking such words, but I uttered them without embarrassment, and my parents did not laugh.

For most of us, as people of crisis, it became clear that horror can last only a little while, and then it becomes commonplace. When one cannot be sure that there are many days left, each single day becomes as important as a year, and one does not waste an hour in wishing that that hour were longer, but simply fills it, like a smaller cup, as high as it will go without spilling over. Each moment, to the very ill, seems somehow slowed down, and more dense with importance, in the same way that a poem is more compressed than a page of prose, each word carrying more weight than a sentence. And though it is true I learned gentleness, and the spareness of time, this was not the case for everyone there, and in fact there were some who never embraced their mortality.

◆ ◆ ◆

I first saw Darcy by a window, looking down into her lap, fingering glass beads the same leafy yellow as her skin. She was wearing blue, and her dress shifted under her chin as she looked up, asking me was I a boy, and why was my hair so short. Behind us, our mothers started talking, exchanging histories, imagining a future, and Darcy and I listened, both grown accustomed by now to all this talk of ourselves. Darcy was ten, and she was here for her second attempted kidney transplant, this time with her father as donor. The first try had failed through fault, her mother said, of the surgeons, and Washington state's best lawyer would handle the suit if anything went wrong this time. This threat was spoken loudly and often as long as I knew Darcy, and it was many years before I realized that her parents were afraid, and that they displayed their fear in anger, and in those thousand sideways glances at their daughter.

As a playmate, Darcy was pleasant, and she and I made ourselves jewelry from glitter and paste, and dressed up as movie stars, or as rich women in France. We played out the future as children do, as if it were sure to come and as if, when it did, we would be there. It was a game we all played on the ward, even those sure to die, and it was some time before I knew that to Darcy it was not a game, that she believed it all. We were holding school, and Nick was the teacher, and Darcy was answering that when she grew up she would own a plane, and would give us free rides on the weekends.

"What if," Nick said to her, "what if you die before then?"

Darcy breathed in and out once, hard, and then she said, "I'm telling my mother you said that." Then she stood and left the playroom, and did not come back that day. Later, her father complained to Nick's, called him foolish and uncaring, and demanded that such a thing not happen again.

After that, Darcy came to play less often, and when she did, her parents looked on, even on days when Janine took us outside to look at the bay. Darcy grew fretful, and cried a good deal, and took to feeling superior, even saying that my father didn't love me or he wouldn't be in Alaska. When I forgave her, it was too late to say so, because I was gone by then and didn't know how to tell her.

Darcy's absence was a loss, not just to her, but to us other children as well. Just as we had no chance to comfort her, to offer our hands when she was weak, we could not count on her during our worst times, for she and her family suffered in that peculiar way which admits no fellowship. I don't remember, if I ever knew, what became of Darcy, because I came down with chickenpox and was discharged so as not to jeopardize her transplant. I like to think she must have lived, it was so important to her, and as I think this, I hope she did survive, and that one day she grew, as we all did in some way, to be thankful.

◆ ◆ ◆

One of my smallest teachers during this time was a leukemia patient, just three years old, who lived down the hall. Because of his treatments, Samuel had very little hair, and what he did have was too blond to see. There were always, as I remember, deep moons under his eyes, but somehow, even to us other children, he was quite beautiful. His teeth were very tiny in his mouth, and he chuckled rather than laughed out loud; when he cried, he only hummed, drawing air in and out his nose, with his eyes squeezed shut and tears forming in the cracks where there should have been lashes. Most children's wards have a few favorite patients, and Samuel was certainly among ours. Those few afternoons when his parents left the hospital together, they spent twenty minutes, on their return, visiting every room to find who had taken off with their son. More often than not, he was strapped to a lap in a wheelchair, his IV bottle dangling overhead like an antenna, getting motocross rides from an amputee.

Samuel possessed, even for his age, and in spite of the fact that he was so vulnerable, an implicit feeling of security, and it was partly this sense of trust which lent him that dignity I have found in few grown people. His mother, I remember, was usually the one to draw him away from our games when it was time for treatments, and, although he knew what was coming, he never ran from it; when he asked his mother, "Do I have to?" it was not a protest, but a question, and when she replied that, yes, this was necessary, he would accept her hand and leave the play room on his feet.

I have heard debate over whether terminally ill children know they are going to die, and I can't, even after knowing Samuel, answer this question. We all, to some extent, knew what death was, simply because each of us had been friends with someone who was gone, and we realized that at some point many of us were likely to die; this likelihood was enough certainty for us, and made the question of time and date too insignificant to ask. I remember the last day I spent with Samuel, how we all invited him for a picnic on the lawn, though he could not eat much. He had had treatments that morning which made him weak, made his smile very tired, but this was the same vulnerability we had always found charming, and I can't recall anything about that afternoon which seemed unusual. The rest of us could not know that Samuel would die before we woke up next morning, and certainly some things might have been different if we had; but I tend to think we would still have had the picnic, would still have rubbed dandelion petals into our skin, would still have taught Samuel to play Slap-Jack. And, for his part, Samuel would, as he did every day, have bent down to my wrist and traced the moonshaped scar behind my hand.

II. ATTACK

Our nearest neighbors through the trees were the Turners, two cabins of cousins whose sons went to my school. Both families had moved here, as we had, from California, escaping the city and everything frightening that lived there. One of the women, Ginny, had a grown son who was comatose now since he was hit on the freeway, and she had come to Alaska to get well from her own mental breakdown, and to keep herself as far away as she could from automobiles.

Brian and Jeff Turner were my best friends then, and we played with our dogs in the cousins' houses, or in the wide snowy yard in between. On weekends or days off from school, my parents took us sledding and to the gravel pit with our skates. Sometimes, if the day was long enough, Brian and Jeff and I followed rabbit tracks through the woods, mapping all the new trails we could find, and my mother gave me orders about when to be home. Bears, she said, and we laughed, and said didn't she know they were asleep, and we could all climb trees anyway. We were not afraid, either, when Mom warned of dog packs. Dogs got cabin fever, too, she said, especially in the cold. They ran through the woods, whole crowds of them, looking for someone to gang up on.

That's okay, I told her. We carried pepper in our pockets in case of dogs: sprinkle it on their noses, we thought, and the whole pack would run away. In December, the day before my birthday, when the light was dim and the days shorter than we had known before, Dad got a break at the union hall, a job at Prudhoe Bay that would save us just in time, before the stove oil ran out and groceries were gone. Mom convinced us children that he was off on a great adventure, that he would see foxes and icebergs, that we could write letters for Christmas and for New Year's, and afford new coats with feathers inside. In this last, I was not much interested, because I had my favorite already—a red wool coat that reversed to fake leopard—but I would be glad if this meant we could get back from the pawn shop Dad's concertina, and his second violin, and mine, the half-size with a short bow, and the guitar and mandolin and rifles and pistol that had gone that way one by one. Whether I played each instrument or not, it had been good to have them around, smelling still of campfires and of songfests in the summer.

It was cold after Dad left, cold outside and cold in our house. Ice on the trailer windows grew thick and shaggy, and my sister and I melted handprints in it and licked off our palms. There had been no insulation when the add-on went up, so frost crawled the walls there, too, and Mom had us wear long johns and shoes unless we were in our beds. Brian and Jeff came for my birthday, helped me wish over seven candles, gave me a comb and a mirror. They were good kids, my mother said, polite and with good sense, and she told me that if I came in from school and she were not home, I should take Hobo with me and walk to their house. You're a worrywart, Mommy, I said. I'm not a baby, you know.

•••

On January 10th, only Hobo met me at the bus stop. In the glare from the schoolbus headlights, his blue eye shone brighter than his brown, and he watched until I took the last step to the ground before tackling me in the snow. Most days, Hobo hid in the shadow of the spruce until Mom took my book bag, then he erupted from the dark to charge up behind me, run through my legs and on out the front. It was his favorite trick. I usually lost my balance and ended up sitting in the road with my feet thrown wide out front and steaming dog tongue all over my face.

Hobo ran ahead, then back, brushing snow crystals and fur against my leg. I put a hand on my skin to warm it and dragged nylon ski pants over the road behind me. Mom said to have them along in case the bus broke down, but she knew I would not wear them, could not bear the plastic sounds they made between my thighs.

No light was on in our house.

If Mom had been home, squares of yellow would have shown through the spruce and lit the fog of my breath, turning it bright as I passed through. What light there was now came from the whiteness of snow, and from the occasional embers drifting up from our stove pipe. I laid my lunchbox on the top step and pulled at the padlock, slapping a palm on the door and shouting. Hobo jumped away from the noise and ran off, losing himself in darkness and in the faint keening dog sounds going up from over near the Turners' house. I called, "Hobo. Come back here, boy," and took to the path toward Brian's, tossing my ski pants to the storage tent as I passed.

At the property line, Hobo caught up with me and growled, and I fingered his ear, looking where he pointed, seeing nothing ahead there but the high curve and long sides of a quonset hut, the work shed the Turners used also as a fence for one side of their yard. In the fall, Brian and Jeff and I had walked to the back of it, climbing over boxes and tools and parts of old furniture, and we had found in the corner a lemming's nest made from chewed bits of cardboard and paper, packed under the curve of the wall so that shadows hid it from plain sight. We all bent close to hear the scratching, and while Brian held a flashlight I took two sticks and parted the rubbish until we saw the black eyes of a mother lemming and the pink naked bodies of five babies. The mother dashed deeper into the pile and we scooped the nesting back, careful not to touch the sucklings for fear that their mama would eat them if they carried scent from our fingers.

The dogs were loud now beyond the quonset, fierce in their howls and sounding many more than just three. Hobo crowded against my legs, and as I walked he hunched in front of me, making me stumble into a drift that filled my boots with snow. I called him a coward and said to quit it, but I held his neck against my thigh, turning the corner into the boys' yard and stopping on the edge. Brian's house was lit in all its windows, Jeff's was dark, and in the yard between them were dogs, new ones I had not seen before, each with its own house and tether. The dogs and their crying filled the yard, and when they saw me they grew wilder, hurling themselves to the ends of their chains, pulling their lips off their teeth. Hobo cowered and ran and I called him with my mouth, but my eyes did not move from in front of me.

There were seven. I knew they were huskies and meant to pull dogsleds, because earlier that winter Brian's grandfather had put on his glasses and shown us a book full of pictures. He had turned the pages with a wet thumb, speaking of trappers and racing people and the ways they taught these dogs to run. They don't feed them much, he said, or they get slow and lose their drive. This was how men traveled before they invented snowmobiles or gasoline.

There was no way to walk around the dogs to the lighted house. The snow had drifted and been piled around the yard in heaps taller than I was, and whatever aisle was left along the sides was narrow, and pitted with chain marks where the animals had wandered dragging their tethers behind. No, I thought, Jeff's house was closest and out of biting range, and someone could, after all, be sitting home in the dark.

My legs were cold. The snow in my boots had packed itself around my ankles and begun to melt, soaking my socks and the felt liners under my heels. I turned toward Jeff's house, chafing my thighs together hard to warm them, and I called cheerfully at the dogs to shut up. Oscar said that if you met a wild animal, even a bear, you had to remember it was more scared than you were. Don't act afraid, he said, because they can smell fear. Just be loud—stomp your feet, wave your hands—and it will run away without even turning around. I yelled "Shut up" again as I climbed the steps to Jeff's front door, but even I could barely hear myself over the wailing. At the sides of my eyes, the huskies were pieces of smoke tumbling over one another in the dark.

The wood of the door was solid with cold, and even through deerskin mittens it bruised my hands like concrete. I cupped a hand to the window and looked in, but saw only black—black, and the reflection of a lamp in the other cabin behind me. I turned and took the three steps back to the ground; seven more and I was in the aisle between doghouses, stretching my chin far up above the frenzy, thinking hard on other things. This was how we walked in summertime, the boys and I, escaping from bad guys over logs thrown across ditches: step lightly and fast, steady on the hard parts of your soles, arms extended outward, palms down and toward the sound. That ditch, this aisle, was a river, a torrent full of silt that would fill your clothes and pull you down if you missed and fell in. I was halfway across. I pointed my chin toward the house and didn't look down.

On either side, dogs on chains hurled themselves upward, choking themselves to reach me, until their tethers jerked their throats back to earth. I'm not afraid of you, I whispered; this is dumb.

I stepped toward the end of the row and my arms began to drop slowly closer to my body. Inside the mittens, my thumbs were cold, as cold as my thighs, and I curled them in and out again. I was walking past the last dog and I felt brave, and I forgave him and bent to lay my mitten on his head. He surged forward on a chain much longer than I thought, leaping at my face, catching my hair in his mouth, shaking it in his teeth until the skin gave way with a jagged sound. My feet were too slow in my boots, and as I blundered backward they tangled in the chain, burning my legs on metal. I called out at Brian's window, expecting rescue, angry that it did not come, and I beat my arms in front of me, and the dog was back again, pulling me down.

A hole was worn into the snow, and I fit into it, arms and legs drawn up in front of me. The dog snatched and pulled at my mouth, eyes, hair; his breath clouded the air around us, but I did not feel its heat, or smell the blood sinking down between hairs of his muzzle. I watched my mitten come off in his teeth and sail upward, and it seemed unfair then and very sad that one hand should freeze all alone; I lifted the second mitten off and threw it away, then turned my face back again, overtaken suddenly by loneliness. A loud river ran in my ears, dragging me under.

• • •

My mother was singing. Lu-lee, lu-lay, thou little tiny child, the song to the Christ child, the words she had sung, smoothing my hair, all my life before bed. Over a noise like rushing water I called to her and heard her answer back, Don't worry, just sleep, the ambulance is on its way. I drifted back out and couldn't know then what she prayed, that I would sleep on without waking, that I would die before morning.

She had counted her minutes carefully that afternoon, sure that she would get to town and back, hauling water and mail, with ten minutes to spare before my bus came. But she had forgotten to count one leg of the trip, had skidded up the drive fifteen minutes late, pounding a fist on the horn, calling me home. On the steps, my lunchbox had grown cold enough to burn her hands. She got the water, the groceries, and my brother and sisters inside, gave orders that no one touch the wood stove or open the door, and she left down the trail to Brian's, whistling Hobo in from the trees.

I know from her journal that Mom had been edgy all week about the crazed dog sounds next door. Now the new huskies leaped at her and Hobo rumbled warning from his chest. Through her sunglasses, the dogs were just shapes, indistinct in windowlight. She tried the dark cabin first, knocking hard on the windows, then turned and moved down the path between dog houses, feeling her way with her feet, kicking out at open mouths. Dark lenses frosted over from her breath, and she moved toward the house and the lights on inside.

"She's not here." Brian's mother held the door open and air clouded inward in waves. Mom stammered out thoughts of bears, wolves, dogs. Ginny grabbed on her coat. She had heard a noise out back earlier—they should check there and then the woods.

No luck behind the cabin and no signs under the trees. Wearing sunglasses and without any flashlight, Mom barely saw even the snow. She circled back and met Ginny under the windowlight. Mom looked that way and asked about the dogs. "They seem so hungry," she said.

Ginny said, "No. Brian's folks just got them last week, but the boys play with them all the time." All the same, she and Mom scanned their eyes over the kennels, looking through and then over their glasses. Nothing seemed different. "Are you sure she isn't home?" Ginny said. "Maybe she took a different trail."

Maybe. Running back with Ginny behind her, Mom called my name until her lungs frosted inside and every breath was a cough. The three younger children were still the only ones at home, and Mom handed them their treasure chests, telling them to play on the bed until she found Natalie. Don't go outside, she said. I'll be back right soon.

Back at the Turners', Ginny walked one way around the quonset and Mom the other. Mom sucked air through a mitten, warming her lungs. While Ginny climbed over deeper snow, she approached the sled dogs from a new angle. In the shadow of one, a splash of red—the lining of my coat thrown open. "I've found her," she shouted, and thought as she ran, Oh, thank God. Thank, thank God.

The husky stopped its howling as Mom bent to drag me out from the hole. Ginny caught up and seemed to choke. "Is she alive?" she said.

Mom said, "I think so, but I don't know how. " She saw one side of my face gone, one red cavity with nerves hanging out, scraps of dead leaves stuck on to the mess. The other eye might be gone, too; it was hard to tell. Scalp had been torn away from my skull on that side, and the gashes reached to my forehead, my lips, had left my nose ripped wide at the nostrils. She tugged my body around her chest and carried me inside.

III. VITAL SIGNS

I had little knowledge of my mother's experience of the accident until many months afterward, and even then I heard her story only after I had told mine, after I had shown how clearly I remembered the dogs, and their chains, and my own blood on the snow—and had proven how little it bothered me to recall them. When I said I had heard her voice, and named for her the songs she had sung to me then, my mother searched my face, looking into me hard, saying, "I can't believe you remember." She had protected me all along, she said, from her point of view, not thinking that I might have kept my own, and that mine must be harder to bear. But after she knew all this, Mom felt she owed me a history, and she told it to me then, simply and often, in words that I would draw on long after she was gone.

She said that inside the Turner's cabin, she laid me on Ginny's couch, careful not to jar the bleeding parts of me, expecting me to wake in an instant and scream. But when I did become conscious, it was only for moments, and I was not aware then of my wounds, or of the cabin's warmth, or even of pressure from the fingers of Brian's grandfather, who sat up close and stroked the frozen skin of my hands.

Ginny ordered Brian and Jeff to their room, telling them to stay there until she called them, and then she stood at Mom's shoulder, staring down and swaying on her legs.

Mom looked up through her glasses and said, "Is there a phone to call an ambulance?"

Ginny was shaking. "Only in the front house, kid, and it's locked," she said. "Kathy should be home in a minute, but I'll try to break in." She tugged at the door twice before it opened, and then she went out, leaving my mother to sing German lullabies beside my ear. *When morning comes,* the words ran, *if God wills it, you will wake up once more.* My mother sang the words and breathed on me, hoping I would dream again of summertime, all those bright nights when the music played on outside, when she drew the curtains and sang us to sleep in the trailer. Long years after the accident, when she felt healed again and stronger, Mom described her thoughts to me, and when she did she closed her eyes and sat back, saying, "You can't know how it was to keep singing, to watch air bubble up where a nose should have been, and to pray that each of those breaths was the last one." Many times that night she thought of Job, who also had lived in a spacious, golden land, who had prospered in that place, yet had cried in the end, "The thing that I so greatly feared has come upon me." The words became a chant inside her, filling her head and bringing on black time.

The wait for the ambulance was a long one, and my mother filled the time with her voice, sitting on her heels and singing. She fingered my hair and patted my hands and spoke low words when I called out. Brian's grandfather wept and warmed my fingers in his, and Mom wondered where were my mittens, and how were her other children back home.

Ginny came back and collapsed on a chair, and Kathy, her sister-in-law, hurried in through the door. Ginny began to choke, rocking forward over her knees, telling Kathy the story. Her voice stretched into a wail that rose and fell like music. "It's happening again," she said, "No matter where you go, it's always there."

Kathy brought out aspirin, then turned and touched my mother's arm. She said that as soon as Ginny was quiet, she would leave her here and fetch my siblings from the trailer.

"Thank you," Mom told her. "I'll send someone for them as soon as I can." She looked at Ginny then, wishing she had something to give her, some way to make her know that she was not to blame here; but for now Mom felt that Ginny had spoken truth when she said that sorrow followed us everywhere, and there was little else she could add.

The ambulance came, and then everything was movement. I drifted awake for a moment as I was lifted to a stretcher and carried toward the door. I felt myself swaying in air, back and forth and back again. Brian's whisper carried over the other voices in the room, as if blown my way by strong wind. "Natalie's dying," he said; then his words were lost among other sounds, and I faded out again. A month later, when our first-grade class sent me a box full of valentines, Brian's was smaller than the rest, a thick, white heart folded in two. Inside, it read: "I love you, Nataly. Pleas dont die." When I saw him again, his eyes seemed very big, and I don't remember that he ever spoke to me any more.

It was dark inside the ambulance, and seemed even darker to my mother, squinting through fog on her sunglasses. She badgered the medic, begging him to give me a shot for pain. Any minute I would wake up, she said, and I would start to scream. The man kept working, taking my pulse, writing it down, and while he did, he soothed my mother in low tones, explaining to her about physical shock, about the way the mind estranges itself from the body and stands, unblinking and detached, on the outside. "If she does wake up," he said, "she'll feel nothing. She won't even feel afraid." When Mom wrote this in her journal, her voice was filled with wonder, and she asked what greater gift there could be.

•••

At the hospital, there were phone calls to be made, and Mom placed them from outside the emergency room. First she called Dick and Esther Conger, two of the only summertime friends who had stayed here over winter. We had met this family on the way up the Alcan, had been attracted to their made-over school bus with its sign, "Destination: Adventure," and to the Alaskan license plates bolted to each bumper. Sometime during the drive up, or during the summer when we shared the same campfires, the children of our families had become interchangeable; Toni and Barry were in the same age group as we were, and discipline and praise were shared equally among us all. It was never shocking to wake up in the morning and find Toni or Barry in one of our beds; we just assumed that the person who belonged there was over sleeping in their bus. Now, as my mother explained the accident to Dick, our friend began to cry, saying, "Oh, Verna. Oh, no," and Esther's voice in the background asked, "What's happened? Let me talk to her." Mom asked the Congers to drive out for my brother and sisters, to watch them until my father came.

Leaning her head to the wall, Mom telephoned a message to the North Slope. She spoke to Dad's boss there, explaining only that "our daughter has been hurt." Just now, she thought, she couldn't tell the whole story again, and besides, the worst "hurt" my father would imagine could not be this bad. The crew boss said a big snowstorm was coming in, but they would try to fly my father out beforehand; if not, they would get him to the radio phone and have him call down. A nurse walked up then and touched Mom's shoulder, saying, "Your daughter is awake, and she's asking for you." A moment before, Mom had been crying, pressing a fist to her teeth, but now she closed up her eyes like a faucet and walked after the nurse, pulling up her chin and breathing deeply in her chest. She had trembled so that she could hardly wipe her glasses, but when she moved through the door and saw the white lights, and me lying flat on a table, she was suddenly calm, and the skin grew warmer on her face.

Mom positioned herself in front of my one eye, hoping as she stood there that she wasn't shaking visibly, that her face was not obviously tense. She need not have bothered; as I lay staring right to where my eye veered off, the room was smoky grey, and I was conscious only of a vicious thirst that roughened the edges of my tongue, made them stick to my teeth. I was allowed no water, had become fretful, and when my mother spoke to me, I complained that the rag in my mouth had not been damp enough, and that these people meant to cut my favorite coat off of me. I have to think now that my mother acted courageously, keeping her face smooth, listening to me chatter about school, about the message I had brought from my teacher, that they would skip me to the second grade on Monday. Mom's answers were light, almost vague, and before she left the pre-op room, she told me to listen to the nurses, to let them do all they needed to; they were trying to help me, she said. A little later, after I was wheeled into surgery, a nurse handed her the things they had saved: my black boots, and the Alice-in-Wonderland watch Mom had given me for Christmas.

My mother made more phone calls, to churches in town and to ones in California that we'd left behind, telling the story over again, asking these people to pray. Old friends took on her grief, asking did she need money, telling her to call again when she knew more. These people knew, as my mother did, that money was not so much the question now, but it was something they could offer, and so they did. And for months and years after this they would send cards, and letters, and candy and flowers and toys, making themselves as present with us as they could. For now, on this first night, they grieved with my mother, and they said to go lie down if she could, they would take over the phones. And each of these people made another call, and another, until, as my mother walked back to the waiting room, she knew she was lifted up by every friend we had ever made.

The Turners had arrived, and for a little while they all sat along the waiting room walls, stuffing fists into their pockets and closing their eyes. None of them wanted to talk about the accident, or to wonder about the progress in surgery, and when my mother said to Kathy, "I just talked to some people in

California who would never *believe* the way we live here," her words seemed terribly funny, and started the whole room laughing. It wasn't so much, she said later, that they were forgetting why they were there; in fact, they remembered very well—so well, that compared to that fact, everything else was hilarious. And they could not possibly have continued for long as they had been, she said, pressing their backs to the walls and waiting. So for hours after Mom's joke, and far into the night, the adults invented names for our kind— "the outhouse set," "the bush league"—and they contributed stories about life in Alaska that would shock most of the people Outside. They joked about styrofoam outhouse seats—the only kind that did not promote frostbite— about catalogues that no one could afford to buy from, but whose pages served a greater purpose, about the tremendous hardship of washing dishes from melted snow and then tossing the grey water out the door. From time to time, Ginny got up from her seat to walk alone in the hall, but when she came back in she was ready again to laugh.

♦ ♦ ♦

My father arrived about midnight, dressed in a week's growth of beard and in an army surplus parka and flight pants. Mom met him in the hall and stood looking up; Dad dropped his satchel to the floor, panting, and he watched my mother's face, the eyes behind her glasses. He spoke first, said his was the last plane out in a heavy snowstorm. Then: "How did it happen," he said. "Did she fall out the door?"

My mother waited a beat and looked at him. "It wasn't a car accident, Julius," she said. She started telling the story again, and my father looked down then at the blood crusted on her sweater, and he closed his eyes and leaned into the wall. My mother told him, "You can't appreciate how I feel, because you haven't seen her face. But I wish that when you pray you'd ask for her to die soon."

Dad opened his eyes. "That must seem like the best thing to ask," he said. "But we don't make decisions like that on our own. We never have, and we can't start now. "

♦ ♦ ♦

Sometime after two A.M., my three surgeons stepped in. My mother said later that, had they not still worn their surgical greens, she would not have recognized them; during the night, she had forgotten their faces.

The men sagged inside their clothes, three sets of shoulders slumped forward under cloth. I was still alive, they said, but only barely, and probably not for long. I had sustained over one hundred lacerations from the shoulders up, and had lost my left cheekbone along with my eye. They'd saved what tissues they could, filling the bulk of the cavity with packings, and what bone fragments they had found were now wired together on the chance that some of them might live.

My father groped for a positive word. "At least she doesn't have brain damage. I heard she was lucid before surgery."

Dr. Butler brushed the surgical cap from his head and held it, twisting it in his hands. His eyes were red as he looked up, explaining as kindly as it seemed he could. A dog's mouth, he said, was filthy, filthier than sewage, and all of that impurity had passed into my body. They had spent four hours just cleaning out the wounds, pulling out dirt and old berry leaves and dog feces. Even with heavy antibiotics, I would likely have massive infections, and they would probably spread into my brain. His voice turned hoarse and he looked across at Dr. Earp, asking the man to continue.

Dr. Earp rubbed hard at the back of his head and spoke softly, working his neck. For now, Dr. Earp said, they had been able to reconstruct the eyelids; that would make the biggest visible difference.

On my parents' first hourly visit to Intensive Care, Mom stopped at the door and put her hand to my father's chest. "No matter how she looks," she said, "don't react. She'll be able to tell what you're thinking."

The nurse at the desk sat under a shaded lamp, the only real light in the room. She stood and whispered that mine was the first bed to the left. "She wakes up for a minute or so at a time," she said. "She's been asking for you."

"First one on the left," my father said after her, a little too loud for that place, and from somewhere inside a great rushing river I heard him and called out. At my bed, Mom watched him as he stood looking down, and when the lines in his face became deeper, she turned from him, pinching his sleeve with her fingers. She walked closer to me and held the bedrail.

IV. THE FEAR

It had to happen eventually, that I found a mirror and looked in. For the first days after my accident, I had stayed mostly in bed, leaning my bandages back on the pillow and peeling frostbite blisters from my hands. The new skin was pink, and much thinner than the old, as sensitive to touch as the nail beds I uncovered by chewing down to them. I had taken to running two fingers over stitches standing up like razor stubble on my face, then over the cotton that covered the right side and the rest of my head. The whole surgical team came in daily to lift me into a chair and unwind the gauze, releasing into the room a smell like old caves full of bones. And all this time I had never seen myself, never asked what was under there, in the place where my eye belonged.

I had asked my mother once if I would again see out of that eye. It was an hour after my dressings had been changed, and the smell of hot ooze still hovered in my room. Mom stood up and adjusted my bedrail. "Do you want your feet a little higher," she said. "I can crank them up if you like."

I said, "Mommy, my eye. Will I be able to see from it?"

"Hang on," she said. "I need to use the little girls' room." She started to the door and I screamed after her, "Mommy, you're not answering me." But she was gone, and after that I did not ask.

Later, when the light was out, I lay back and looked far right, then left, concentrating hard, trying to feel the bandaged eye move. I thought I could feel it, rolling up and then down, ceiling to floor, matching its moves with my other eye. Even after I was grown, I could swear that I felt it blink when I pressed my two lids together.

•••

Men from down the hall visited me during the day, rolling in on wheelchairs or walking beside their IV racks. They all wore two sets of pajamas, one wrong way forward so their backsides were covered. The hospital floor was old, its tiles starting to bubble, and the wheels on my friends' IV racks made mumbling sounds as they passed over. If a nurse passed by the door and looked in, the men waved her away, saying, "It's all right, dear. I'm visiting my granddaughter." For a kiss they gave me a sucker and a story about bears, or they carried me to a wheelchair and took me around to visit. In this way, I passed from room to room, brushing at the green curtains between beds, pouring water into plastic glasses, gathering hugs and learning to shake hands in the "cool" way. I signed plaster casts in big red letters, and I visited the baby room, pressing my chin to the glass.

On a day when I felt at my smallest and was in my bed still sleeping, one of my favorite men friends checked out, leaving on my nightstand a gift and a note that said he would miss me. The gift was a music box in pink satin, with a ballerina inside who pirouetted on her toes when I wound the key. And behind her inside the lid, a triangular looking-glass not much bigger than she was.

My mother came in behind me as I was staring into the mirror, holding it first from one angle, then from another, and she stood by the bed for a moment, saying nothing. When I turned, she was looking at me with her shoulders forward, and she seemed to be waiting.

"My eye is gone, isn't it?" I said.

She kept looking at me. She said, "Yes it is."

I turned again and lifted the box to my face. "I thought so," I said. "Those dogs were pretty mean."

I didn't understand, or was too small to know, what my mother thought she was protecting me from. It must be something very bad, I thought, for her to avoid every question I asked her. "Mommy," I said once. "I don't *feel* like I'm going to die."

She looked up from her book and the light shone off her glasses. She said, "Oh, no. You're certainly not going to do anything like that."

"Then will I be blind?"

"Well," she said. "You can see now, can't you?" And when I pressed her with more questions, she looked toward the door and said, "Sh-h. Here comes your lunch tray."

It all made me wonder if my wounds were much worse than everyone said— and of course they were, but there were long years of surgery still ahead, and no one wanted me to feel afraid. I was angry, too—as angry as a seven-year-old can be—that Mom patted my cheek with her palm and said she'd be taking my malemute to the pound before I came home. I stared at her then with my head up and sputtered out a peevish tirade, telling her I didn't hate all dogs, or even most dogs, but just the ones who bit me. It didn't occur to me until my own daughter was seven, the same age I was when I was hurt, that Mom might have been sending my dog away for her own sake.

V. SMALL PURCHASE

I have bought a one-eyed fish. Drifting around the tank near my desk, his skin ripples silver like well-pressed silk, and he moves under the light and hovers with his one bronze eye turned toward me, waiting to be fed. His body is smooth and flat, like a silver dollar but twice the size, and his fins are mottled gold. He is relative to the piranha, a meat eater with a bold round mouth, but even when the smaller fish challenge him, swishing their tails at his eye, he leaves them alone and swims off. He has not eaten one of them.

I call him Max, because my sister said I should. She did not remind me, when I brought him home, that I had wanted no pets, nothing with a lifespan shorter than my own, nothing that would die or have to be butchered as soon as I had given it a name. She just looked up with her face very serious as if she knew well how one could become attached to a fish, and she said to me, Max. Yes, that should be his name.

I had told us both, when I bought the aquarium, that fish were low-maintenance animals, without personalities and incapable of friendliness, and if one of them died you just flushed it away and got another. And besides, I said, I needed a fish tank. I had begun to feel stale, inert. I needed the sounds of moving water in my house, and I needed, too, something alive and interesting to stare at when I stopped typing to think of a new sentence.

Last summer, when I was tired and the writing was going badly, I got superstitious about the sea and thought that the lurch and pull of waves would freshen my ears and bring on clean thoughts. So I packed some books and a portable typewriter, drove to Homer on the coast, and rented a cabin near the beach. Something about the place, or its fishy air, or my aloneness in the middle of it, worked somehow, and I breathed bigger there in my chest and wrote more clearly on the page. I had forgotten about tides and about the kelp and dried crabs that came in with them, and every morning I shivered into a sweater, put combs in my hair, and walked out to wade and to fill my pockets with what I found. I liked it best when the wind was blowing and the sky was grey, and the sounds of seagulls and my own breathing were carried out with the water.

Kelp pods washed up around my feet, and I stomped on them with tennis shoes to find what was inside. I collected driftwood, and urchins, and tiny pink clam shells dropped by gulls, thin enough to see through and smaller than a thumbnail. When the tide had gone far out, I climbed the bluff back to my cabin and sat writing in front of the window, eating cheese on bread and drinking orange spritzers or tea. The walls and windows there had space in between, and they let in shreds of wind and the arguing of birds and the metal smell of seaweed drying out on the beach. When the tide started back in, I took pen and notebook and sat on a great barnacled rock, letting water creep up and surround me, then jumping to shore just in time. An hour later, the rock would be covered, three feet or more under the grey, and I would only know where it lay because of the froth and swirl of whirlpools just above it.

When I came home I threw my bags on the bed and unfastened them, and a thousand aromas opened up then into my face, drifting out from the folds of my clothes, the seams in my shoes, the pages of my notebook. I had carried them back with me, the smells of wet sand and fish fins, of eagle feathers floating in surf, of candle wax burned at midnight and filled with the empty bodies of moths. I had grieved on the drive home for that place I was leaving, and for the cold wind of that beach, and I had decided that somehow water should move in my house, should rush and bubble in my ears, should bring in the sound of the sea, and the wind and dark currents that move it.

So I bought an aquarium, and fish to go in it, and a water pump strong enough to tumble the surface as it worked. I bought plants for the tank, and waved their smell into the room, and when I thought I was finished I made one more trip to a pet store, just to see what they had.

The shop was a small one, in an old wooden building with low ceilings, and the fish room in back was dark and smelled submarine—humid and slippery and full of live things. All light in the place came from the fishtanks themselves, and the plants inside them absorbed the glow and turned it green, casting it outward to move in shadowed patterns on my skin. When I closed my eyes, the sound was of rivers, running out to the coast to be carried away mixed with salt. And the fish inside waved their fins and wandered between the rocks, opening and closing their mouths.

I glanced, but didn't look hard at the larger fish, because I had found already that they were always very expensive. I browsed instead through tetras and guppies, gouramis and cichlids, trying to be satisfied with the small ones, because after all it was just the water and its motion that I really wanted. So when I saw the wide silver fish and a sign that said "$10," I assumed it was a mistake but decided to ask about it while I ordered some neons dipped out.

With my neck bent forward, I watched as fifty neons swam fast away from the net that would always catch them anyway. Was that big fish back there really only ten, I said.

The clerk said, "You mean the Matinnis with one eye. He's such a mellow guy."

I swung my head to look at her. One eye?

The woman stared at my face for a moment and opened her mouth. Her cheeks grew pinker, but when she answered me, her voice stayed even. She said, "Yes, his former owners thought he was a piranha and put him in the tank with some. They ate out one eye before anyone could get him back up."

"They go for the eyes so their lunch will quit looking at them," I said. I told the woman I would take the Matinnis. I thought we were a match, I said.

And I was right. As absurd as I felt about my affinity with a one-eyed fish, I found myself watching him for the ways he was like me, and I did find many. Max had already learned, by the time I got him, to hold his body in the water so that whatever he was interested in lay always on the same side of him as his eye. In the same way that I situate myself in movie theaters so that my best friend sits on my right side, Max turns his eye toward the wall of his tank, watching for my arm to move toward the food box. When I drop a worm cube down to him, he shifts his eye up to look at it and then swims at it from the side so he never loses it from vision. If the smaller fish fight, or behave defiantly around him, he turns his dead eye against them and flicks himself away to a further corner of the tank.

I don't know if it is normal to befriend a fish. I think probably not. I do know that as I sit by Max's tank and write, I stop sometimes and look up, and I think then that he looks terribly dashing, swimming around with his bad eye outward, unafraid that something might attack him from his blind side. I buy him special shrimp pellets, and I feed them to him one at a time, careful always to drop them past his good eye. My friends like to feed him, too, and I teach them how, warning them to drop his food where he can see it. Now one of my friends wants to introduce me to his neighbor's one-eyed dog, and another wishes she still had her one-eyed zebra finch so she could give it to me.

That's just what I need, I think—a houseful of blind-sided pets. We could sit around together and play Wink-um, wondering was that a wink or just a lid shut down over a dry eyeball. We could fight about who got to sit on whose good side, or we could make jokes about how it takes two of us to look both ways before crossing the street. I laugh, but still I intend to meet the one-eyed dog, to see if he reminds me of Max—or of me. I wonder if he holds himself differently from other dogs, if when he hears a voice he turns his whole body to look.

And I wonder about myself, about what has changed in the world. At first,

I wanted fish only for the water they lived in, for the movement it would bring to my house, the dust it would sweep from my brain. I thought of fish as "safe" pets, too boring to demand much attention, soulless by nature and indistinguishable from their peers. Maybe this is true for most of them. But I know that when the smaller fish chase after Max, or push him away from the food, I find myself fiercely angry. I take a vicious pleasure in dropping down shrimp pellets too big and too hard for the small ones to eat, and I find pleasure, too, in the way Max gobbles the food, working it to bits in his mouth. When he is finished, he turns a dead eye to the others and swims away, seeking things more interesting to look at.

About the Contributors

Mindy Aloff has, since 1988, reported weekly on dance for *The New Yorker*, where she has also published some four dozen "Talk of the Town" stories. Her longer articles on dance and literature have appeared in many periodicals. She is the recipient of fellowships from the Whiting Foundation and the Guggenheim Foundation.

John Berger, born in London in 1926, is one of Britain's most influential art critics. He is also well known as a screenwriter, novelist, and documentary writer. His books include *Pig Earth, Once in Europa, Ways of Seeing, The Success and Failure of Picasso*, and the award-winning novel *G*, among many others. He now lives and works in a small French peasant community.

Harold Brodkey is the author of two collections of short fiction, *First Love and Other Sorrows* and *Stories in an Almost Classical Mode*, and a novel, *The Runaway Soul*. He lives in New York City and writes for *The New Yorker* and *The New York Observer*.

W. S. Di Piero is the author of five books of poetry; the most recent of these are *The Dog Star* and *The Restorers*. He has also published two volumes of criticism, *Memory and Enthusiasm: Essays 1975–1985* and *Out of Eden: Essays on Modern Art*. His translations of Italian literature include *The Ellipse: Selected Poems of Leonardo Sinisgalli* and Giacomo Leopardi's *Pensieri*. He lives in California.

Lars Eighner is completing his memoir of homelessness, *Travels with Lizbeth*. He is the author of *Bayou Boy and Other Stories, B.M.O.C*, and *Lavender Blue: How to Write and Sell Gay Men's Erotica*. His work was selected for the 1992 Pushcart Prize collection.

Louise Glück is the author of six collections of poetry, most recently *The Wild Iris.* Her awards include the Bobbitt National Prize (shared with Mark Strand), the National Book Critics Circle Award, and an award in literature from the American Academy of Arts and Letters. She teaches at Williams College and lives in Vermont.

Stephen Greenblatt's most recent books are *Learning to Curse* and *Marvelous Possessions.* A professor of English at the University of California, Berkeley, he is coeditor of the journal *Representations* and a member of the American Academy of Arts and Sciences. He is currently working on a study of magic, witchcraft, and art in the age of Shakespeare.

Thom Gunn is an Anglo-American poet who lives in San Francisco. His books include *My Sad Captains, The Passages of Joy, Selected Poems,* and, most recently, *The Man with Night Sweats. Shelf Life* (prose) and *Collected Poems* are forthcoming. He teaches English every spring semester at Berkeley.

Elizabeth Hardwick is the author of *Sleepless Nights,* a novel, and *Seduction and Betrayal,* a collection of essays, along with other novels and works of literary criticism. She is a founder and advisory editor of the *New York Review of Books,* a member of the American Academy of Arts and Letters, and the recipient of numerous awards and honorary degrees.

Robert Hass is the author of three books of poems: *Field Guide, Praise,* and *Human Wishes.* His book of essays, *Twentieth Century Pleasures,* won the National Book Critics Circle Award in 1984. He is the recipient of a MacArthur Fellowship, among many other honors, and he currently teaches in the English Department at the University of California, Berkeley.

Christopher Hitchens is an essayist whose books include *Prepared for the Worst* and *For the Sake of Argument.* He writes the "Cultural Elite" column for *Vanity Fair* and the "Minority Report" for *The Nation.*

Diane Johnson, until recently a professor of English at the University of California, Davis, is a novelist and critic. Her essays appear frequently in the *New York Review of Books* and other periodicals. She is the author of one book of criticism, *Terrorists and Novelists;* two biographies, *Lesser Lives* and *Dashiell Hammett;* seven novels; and a book of travel stories called *Natural Opium.* She also wrote, with Stanley Kubrick, the screenplay for *The Shining.* She has received numerous awards, most notably the five-year Strauss Living Award from the American Academy of Arts and Letters.

August Kleinzahler is the author of three volumes of poetry: *Like Cities, Like Storms; Earthquake Weather;* and *Storm Over Hackensack,* which won the

1985 Bay Area Book Reviewers Award. He is the recipient of a General Electric Award for Younger Writers, a Guggenheim Fellowship, and a Lila Wallace-Reader's Digest Writers' Award.

Natalie Kusz lives in Delta Junction, Alaska, and in St. Paul, Minnesota. She has received the Whiting Writer's Award, the General Electric Younger Writer's Award, the Christopher Award, and a Pushcart Prize, and is the author of *Road Song: A Memoir,* now in paperback. She is currently writing another work of nonfiction prose, under contract to Farrar, Straus & Giroux.

Thomas Laqueur is professor of history and the director of the Doreen B. Townsend Center for the Humanities at the University of California, Berkeley. He is the author, most recently, of *Making Sex: Body and Gender from the Greeks to Freud,* and is now working on the cultural history of death in England and on remembering the dead of the Great War.

Phillip Lopate, age forty-nine, is an essayist, novelist, and poet. His books include *Bachelorhood, Against Joie de Vivre, The Rug Merchant,* and *Being with Children.* He has taught at every level, from kindergarten to graduate school. His awards include a Guggenheim Fellowship and two fellowships from the National Endowment for the Arts. He has also served on the New York Film Festival, Pulitzer Prize, and National Book Award juries.

Arthur Lubow writes for *The New Yorker.* He is the author of *The Reporter Who Would Be King: A Biography of Richard Harding Davis.*

Greil Marcus is the author of *Mystery Train: Images of America in Rock 'n' Roll Music, Lipstick Traces: A Secret History of the 20th Century,* and *Ranters & Crowd Pleasers: Punk in Pop Music, 1977–92.* He is a contributing editor of *Artforum.* He lives in Berkeley, California.

Leonard Michaels, professor of English at the University of California, Berkeley, is the author of *Going Places, I Would Have Saved Them If I Could, Shuffle,* and *Sylvia,* and coeditor of *West of the West: Imagining California* and two volumes of *The State of the Language,* published in 1980 and 1990. A collection of his essays, *To Feel These Things,* and an expanded edition of his novel *The Men's Club* are being published by Mercury House in June of 1993.

Sigrid Nunez has published fiction in a number of journals, including *The Threepenny Review, Iowa Review, Fiction,* and *Salmagundi.* She is the recipient of two Pushcart Prizes and of a General Electric Award for Younger Writers. One of her stories was included in the 1992 Selected Shorts program sponsored by Symphony Space in New York City.

Irene Oppenheim, as a teenager, landed a job walking a deaf Doberman pinscher. Her careers since then have been numerous and varied. In addition to documenting these adventures for various publications and anthologies, she spent ten years as a dance and drama critic in San Francisco. She currently lives, writes, and works (at whatever) in Los Angeles.

Gayle Pemberton is associate director of Afro-American Studies at Princeton University. The author of *The Hottest Water in Chicago: On Family, Race, Time, and American Culture,* she is now at work on a book about black women and film. She holds a B.A. in English from the University of Michigan, Ann Arbor, and M.A. and Ph.D. degrees from Harvard University in English and American literature and language.

Robert Pinsky's books of poetry include *An Explanation of America, History of My Heart,* and *The Want Bone.* His most recent prose book is *Poetry and the World.* He has been poetry editor of *The New Republic.* Formerly at Berkeley, he now teaches creative writing at Boston University. His translation of Dante's *Inferno* will be published by Farrar, Straus & Giroux in 1993.

Christopher Ricks teaches English at Boston University. He is the author of *Milton's Grand Style, Tennyson, Keats and Embarrassment, The Force of Poetry,* and of *The New Oxford Book of Victorian Verse.* With Leonard Michaels, he edited *The State of the Language* (1980 and 1990); and with William L. Vance, *The Faber Book of America.* Forthcoming in 1993 is *Beckett's Dying Words.*

Harriet Shapiro, a former senior writer and foreign correspondent for *People Magazine* in New York and Paris, is currently working in London.

Susan Sontag is the author of three novels, *The Benefactor, Death Kit,* and *The Volcano Lover;* a collection of short stories, *I, etcetera;* and six books of essays, including the prizewinning *On Photography.* She is a recipient of a MacArthur Fellowship and a member of the American Academy and Institute of Arts and Letters.

Amy Tan is the author of *The Joy Luck Club, The Kitchen God's Wife,* and *The Moon Lady,* a children's book. In addition, she is the cowriter and producer of the film *The Joy Luck Club.* She is now at work on a new book, *The Year of No Flood.*

Gore Vidal is well known as a novelist, essayist, screenwriter, and playwright. His books include *Myra Breckenridge, Duluth, Matters of Fact and Fiction, Screening History,* and, most recently, *Live from Golgotha.* The author of a major series of novels about American history and politics, he is a former candidate for the United States Senate from California; he now lives most of the year in Italy.

Steve Vineberg, an associate professor at College of the Holy Cross in Massachusetts, writes regularly on film and theater for *The Threepenny Review* and *The Boston Phoenix*. His book *Method Actors: Three Generations of an American Acting Style* won the Joe A. Calloway Prize for the best book of its year on drama. His latest book is *No Surprises, Please: Movies in the Reagan Decade*.

Daniel Wolff's longer essay on Danny Lyon's work appears in the catalogue for a retrospective exhibition that will tour the United States in 1993–1994. He is not the Daniel Wolff who has a photography gallery, nor the one who founded the *Village Voice;* he is the one with poetry and essays published in numerous magazines and journals.

Permissions

Acknowledgments

Primary thanks are due to the authors of the essays, who, in more than the usual sense, made this book possible—first by writing the essays, and second by giving me permission to reprint them. Lisa Mann, my assistant editor at *The Threepenny Review,* capably and intelligently prepared the manuscript for publication; her help, as always, was invaluable. I owe thanks to Greil Marcus for the title, and to Thom Gunn and Daniel Wolff for their honest, witty, and useful readings of the first draft of the introduction. Tom Christensen at Mercury House had the foresight, or the kindness, to see this as a book, and he and his staff—David Peattie, Po Bronson, Barbara Stevenson, Ellen Towell, and especially Hazel White—worked admirably hard to turn it into a good one. I am grateful to Sharon Smith for the beautiful cover, and to the late Raphael Soyer for the painting that adorns it. Finally, it is fitting that Ann Flanagan and Linda Davis should have done the page design and typesetting, since they typeset the first fifty issues of *The Threepenny Review* with unfailing generosity and unmatched competence.

About the Editor

Wendy Lesser was born in California in 1952. She holds a B.A. from Harvard University, an M.A. from King's College, Cambridge, and a Ph.D. in English from the University of California at Berkeley. She has been awarded a Guggenheim Fellowship, two fellowships from the National Endowment for the Humanities, and a Rockefeller Foundation Bellagio Residency.

In 1980 she founded *The Threepenny Review,* a quarterly magazine that she still edits and publishes. In addition, she is the author of two books—*The Life Below the Ground: A Study of the Subterranean in Literature and History* and *His Other Half: Men Looking at Women through Art.* She frequently reviews books for such publications as the *New York Times Book Review,* the *Washington Post Book World,* and *The New Republic,* and her work has appeared in several anthologies, including *The State of the Language* and *The Faber Book of America.* Wendy Lesser lives in Berkeley, California, with her husband, Richard Rizzo, and her son, Nicholas.